STAR TREK®
MYRIAD UNIVERSES
INFINITY'S PRISM

D0008428

STAR TREK®
MYRIAD UNIVERSES
INFINITY'S PRISM

William Leisner
Christopher L. Bennett
James Swallow

Based upon on *Star Trek*
created by Gene Roddenberry

Star Trek: Deep Space Nine®
created by Rick Berman & Michael Piller

Star Trek: Voyager®
created by Rick Berman & Michael Piller & Jeri Taylor

Star Trek: Enterprise®
created by Rick Berman & Brannon Braga

POCKET BOOKS
New York   London   Toronto   Sydney   Kosnelye

Pocket Books
A Division of Simon & Schuster, Inc.
1230 Avenue of the Americas
New York, NY 10020

This book is a work of fiction. Names, characters, places, and incidents either are products of the authors' imaginations or are used fictitiously. Any resemblance to actual events or locales or persons, living or dead, is entirely coincidental.

™, ® and © 2008 by CBS Studios Inc. All Rights Reserved.
STAR TREK and related marks are trademarks of CBS Studios Inc.

⊙CBS CONSUMER PRODUCTS

CBS, the CBS EYE logo, and related marks are
trademarks of CBS Broadcasting Inc.
™ & © CBS Broadcasting Inc. All Rights Reserved.

This book is published by Pocket Books, a division of Simon & Schuster, Inc., under exclusive license from CBS Studios Inc.

All rights reserved, including the right to reproduce this book or portions thereof in any form whatsoever. For information address Pocket Books Subsidiary Rights Department,
1230 Avenue of the Americas, New York, NY 10020

First Pocket Books trade paperback edition July 2008

POCKET and colophon are registered trademarks of Simon & Schuster, Inc.

For information about special discounts for bulk purchases,
please contact Simon & Schuster Special Sales at
1-800-456-6798 or business@simonandschuster.com.

Cover design by Alan Dingman
Cover art by John Picacio

Manufactured in the United States of America

10 9 8 7 6 5 4 3 2 1

ISBN-13: 978-1-4165-7180-3
ISBN-10:   1-4165-7180-9

A Less Perfect Union

William Leisner

Dedicated to the memory of my father

1

There was definitely something out there, coming their way.

Captain Christopher Pike kept his gaze fixed on the forward viewscreen as it once again rippled and distorted the star field ahead. Around him, his crew checked circuits and consulted readouts, attempting to determine what exactly was throwing the *Enterprise*'s sensor array into such an uproar. A pair of oversized spaceborne rocks flew past them, both easily swept aside by the ship's forward deflectors. "Could be these meteorites," said Lee Kelso at his navigator's post.

"Meteor*oids*," the science officer corrected him in a haughty tone.

"No, it's . . . something else," said Number One, looking from the screen to the data readouts on the helmsman's console. "Something is still out there."

And as if to prove the first officer's claim, the Red Alert signal at the center of the forward console began to flash, and the harsh *whoop* of the alarm filled the bridge. The viewscreen distorted again and again, like a shallow pond being hit by a series of pebbles.

"It's coming at the speed of light," Kelso reported. "Collision course."

Number One turned to face the captain. "Evasive maneuvers, sir?"

Pike kept his eyes on the screen. "Steady as we go."

The first officer gaped slightly at that. "Captain, we have no idea what—"

Pike looked away from the screen then, and directed the full power of his intense blue eyes toward the younger man. "Was my order unclear, Mister Kirk?"

Commander Jim Kirk hesitated a half second, then broke eye contact and turned back in his seat. "Steady as we go, sir."

Pike's glare lingered a moment longer on the back of Kirk's head. He knew he shouldn't have slapped him back quite so hard; he was taking a gamble on whatever it was coming at them, and Kirk had good reason to question the wisdom of flying at it straight on. Kirk was a good man, and the best first officer Pike had had in ten years—and the only one in all that time with whom he'd felt comfortable using the nickname "Number One." But he was young, and more than a little cocky. And then, there was what had happened to the *Galileo* six months earlier . . .

Pike turned his attention back to the screen. It was warping wildly now, wavering almost like a flag in a stiff breeze, while the Red Alert klaxon continued its ear-piercing *whoop-whoop-whoop*. Still, no foreign object or vessels appeared on the distorted viewer, even as every sensor on every console indicated that they were seconds from impact.

And then, as suddenly as it had started, the alert ended, and the bridge fell silent except for the quiet chirps and bleeps of standard operation. Kirk and Kelso exchanged confused looks, while Pike waited for someone from one of the rear stations to officially confirm his suspicions.

It was, unsurprisingly, Alden at communications who figured it out first. "It's a radio wave, sir. We're passing through an old-style distress signal."

Pike nodded slightly. "They were keyed to cause interference and attract attention this way." He noticed Kirk had turned in his seat again, looking from Alden to the captain, looking properly chagrined. *Looks like the old man still has a few tricks up his sleeve, eh,* he thought. He wondered if the Academy even still bothered teaching cadets about subwarp emergency procedures.

"A ship in trouble, making a forced landing," Alden added, repeating the communication now coming through the miniature speaker he held to his right ear. "That's it, no other message."

From the other rear station, science officer Ann Mulhall picked up the report. "I have a fix. It originates from . . . inside Coalition territory."

The entire bridge crew reacted to that. Even Pike let his unflappable demeanor drop for a split second. Earth had been at odds with the Interstellar Coalition for over a hundred years, ever since the Vulcans, Andorians, Tellarites, and Denobulans decided to resume the catastrophically ended Coalition of Planets negotiations on their own, without Earth's participation. *What the hell is a human vessel with an obsolete radio disruption beacon doing on their side of the border?* Pike asked himself.

Mulhall continued, "Their call letters check with a survey expedition: *S.S. Columbia.* Reported missing twenty-nine years ago, in 2235."

Twenty-nine years ago—meaning the radio wave had traveled twenty-nine light-years. "That's pretty deep into Coalition territory," Pike said.

The science officer nodded as she continued to scan her library file. "The ship was registered to the American Continent Institute. The expedition's mission . . ." She turned away from her monitor to face the rest of the bridge and offered them a wry expression. ". . . 'to explore strange new worlds.' "

Inwardly, Pike sighed. He could picture them now: a menagerie of scruffy, gray-haired professors, clinging onto an outdated, romanticized notion of space exploration that had gone out of style with the Xindi attack. They'd no doubt ignored every warning once they left Earth, refusing to keep to the regularly traveled trade routes, wandering aimlessly through regions where no man had gone before—or worse, where men *had* gone before, and had been warned not to go again, at least not without a fully charged phaser bank.

"Sir," Number One interrupted, "our charts show the signal originating near Talos, a star system with eleven planets. Long-range studies indicate the fourth planet could be Earth-type."

Pike hesitated. If the *Columbia* crew had managed to land on a habitable world, it was possible that, even three decades later, there could be survivors. The chances were achingly slim, though, and rescuing them would mean traveling through hostile territory.

The captain turned to meet the younger man's gaze. After their exchange earlier, his first officer hesitated to speak up and suggest the course of action he was contemplating. But even if Jim Kirk were a complete stranger to him, Pike could clearly read the thoughts in his eyes. They said that, if there was the slightest hope those humans were still alive, they couldn't just leave them.

Pike sighed. "Any indication of Coalition patrol ships in the area near Talos?"

Both Kirk and Kelso checked their boards. "Negative, sir," the navigator answered. "The system is well off their normal patrol and trade routes."

Pike set his jaw, then moved back to the center chair. "Address intercraft."

Kelso flipped a toggle switch on his console. "System open."

In his mind, Pike saw the entire crew on every deck pausing as the address system came to life. He lifted his head to address them all: "This is the captain. Our destination is the Interstellar Coalition. Our warp factor, five."

All decks reported back ready, and on his order to engage, they started for enemy territory.

There are, of course, no border lines in space. Nor are there any true natural landmarks, along the lines of rivers and mountain ranges, which can be reliably used to demarcate one region of space from another. The Vega Colony was indisputably one of United Earth's commonwealth worlds. Regulus, some nine light-years distant, was a long-time Vulcan base, and thus recognized as part of the Interstellar Coalition. Everything in between was more or less open to interpretation.

Jim Kirk interpreted the *Enterprise*'s long-range sensor reading and astronavigational data, and tweaked the warp propulsion field's output just so, putting the ship on a course that he determined was as close as they could get to Coalition space without risking an interstellar incident.

Not that he would have been averse to trading a couple shots with the bastards, if it came to that. The *Enterprise* was one of Starfleet's top-of-the-line starships, *Constitution* class, named for the legendary American frigate. He had no doubt it would make small work of any Coalition ship that dared to challenge them.

"Coming up on the Robinson Nebula," Kelso reported.

"On-screen," Pike ordered. For a moment, Kirk wondered if the viewer was malfunctioning again, as the only change, so far as he could tell, was that the image of the starscape ahead of them dimmed, with a small area devoid of stars at the center. But then, the captain said, "Enhance image," and striations of color brought the dark matter mass into relief, highlighting its characteristic radiation patterns and gravitational energies.

"My god, will you look at that?" Ann Mulhall spoke in an awed whisper, looking from the main viewing screen to the image inside her station's hooded display, and then back again. "Captain . . . is there any way we could redirect *one* high-res sensor cluster—"

"All available sensors are directed toward the *Columbia* coordinates," Pike said before she'd even finished asking the question. "That's the only reason we're here." The captain's expression softened just a fraction then. "Sorry, Lieutenant."

Mulhall nodded, accepting the captain's decision, but she was still disappointed. "Jonathan Archer discovered this nebula on his *Enterprise,* back in 2153," she informed the rest of the bridge. "We may be the first Earth ship to visit it since."

"So?" Lee Kelso asked. "It's just another cloud of dust and hydrogen."

"No, it's not," Mulhall said, with more than a hint of exasperation in her tone. "It's a *dark matter* nebula."

"Okay. And?"

"And, dark matter was still only theoretical up until Archer's time. We still know almost nothing about its nature, how it's formed, anything."

"Which brings us back to my original question: So?"

"That's enough," Kirk warned the two before the captain had to speak up himself. He understood that Lee's comments were intended as nothing more than good-natured ribbing, of the kind he and Ann often enjoyed engaging in. But he also understood how Mulhall felt as a career scientist who wasn't always content to simply recite the readouts from her station's displays. The term "science officer" was something of an anachronism, carried over from the old days when the United Earth Space Probe Agency was an exploratory organization as well as a military one. A starship still needed its scientific specialists, of course, and it was certainly helpful, when the crew ran into some new and inexplicable interstellar phenomenon, to have someone aboard who knew more than the basic astrophysics and xenobiology courses taught at the Academy. But most of the time, the ship's science officer was the redheaded stepchild of the bridge crew, just sitting on his or her hands as the ship flew along well-established routes between colonies, or transported security troops to one trouble spot or another. That was why Carol decided she couldn't . . .

The lump started to form at the back of his throat again, and Kirk willed himself to stop and swallow it back down. *Keep it together, mister,* he ordered himself. *You have a mission and a crew to think about; wait until your off-duty time to feel sorry for yourself.*

His advice to himself came just in time. Refocusing his attention on the board in front of him, he caught what looked like a small energy flare inside the nebula. His right hand jumped to the navigation sensors' directional controls, even while the rational part of his brain wondered if such a discharge was usual or not in this kind of nebula, and considered bringing it to Mulhall's attention. But the instinctive, action-oriented part of his mind had taken over, and luckily so, as he caught a second flash. "Captain, we've got company," he shouted as his navigation console identified the signature of those energy flashes. Kirk looked at the readout in surprise. "Orion ships," he said. "At least two of them, hiding inside the nebula."

"Orions?" Pike moved right behind Kirk's chair and looked at the readouts from over his shoulder. "What the hell are they doing all the way out here?"

"Good hiding spot," Kirk said. "Remote. And it's not like the Coalition has ever bothered to do anything about pirates working near their borders."

Pike absorbed that, then turned to Mulhall. "I don't suppose there's any chance they somehow haven't seen us through that soup?"

"As I just said, we have no idea how dark matter might affect sensors, if at all," she answered, trying to keep any kind of bitterness from her tone. "But odds are, if we can see them, they can see us."

"Well, let's not make ourselves any more tempting of a target to them than we have to. Alter course, zero-one-one mark three-five-eight."

"Zero-one-one mark three-five-eight, aye," Kirk repeated. That course would mean taking the long way around the nebula, and effectively ending their search for the *Columbia,* at least until they'd gotten around the dark matter mass. He wondered if now Mulhall might get her chance to scan the Robinson Nebula—although that would almost certainly provoke the Orions as well.

As it turned out, it didn't matter; once the Orions realized the *Enterprise* was moving out of striking range, their impulse engines came to full life. Trails of ignited plasma followed them out of the nebula, giving the impression that the small pirate vessels were in fact demons escaped from hell.

"Yellow Alert," the captain ordered. "Mister Alden, hail them."

The communications officer punched a series of buttons, transmitting the standard hail. "No response, sir," he reported.

"Their weapons are fully charged," Kelso shouted once the superheated plasma burned away and he could get a clear read on the alien ships' status.

"Red Alert. Deflector screens on maximum. Evasive maneuvers."

The klaxons started up again. Kirk took the *Enterprise* into a relative dive, as the two Orion ships tried to flank them. The starboard pirate vessel fired phasers, but only managed a glancing blow off the nacelle shields.

"Mister Kirk, pattern alpha-seven," Pike ordered. Kirk complied, and he felt the deck plates under his boots shudder as the ship executed a sharp hairpin turn on the z-axis. Fortunately the inertial dampers compensated, and he was able to stay upright in his seat as the Orions reappeared on the forward viewscreen, upside down to the *Enterprise*'s position. "Fire!" Pike shouted, and Kirk released powerful beams of phased energy toward the enemy ships.

"Direct hit!" Mulhall called from her station. "The port vessel's shielding is down by seven percent."

Kirk silently cheered at that report. It wasn't Coalition ships he was firing at, but they would do for the moment.

"Now delta-four," Pike ordered. "Fire at will."

Kirk had already anticipated the tactic. "Delta-four, aye," he said, and the ship banked again.

This time, though, the inertial dampers cut out as the *Enterprise* took an Orion shot on the ventral side of the saucer section. "Shield generators down by ten percent," Mulhall called out.

"Ten?!" Pike shouted back. "What in blazes are they firing at us?"

Before he could get an answer, the ship was rocked by another blast. Kirk braced himself against the helm console to keep from being thrown over it, and fired phasers. He saw the beam connect with the other Orion ship, though he wasn't quite as jubilant about scoring a hit this time.

"They're using standard phasers," Mulhall answered Pike's query after running an analysis through her computer systems. "But their weapons emitters are at close to 98 percent efficiency."

Pike muttered an obscenity under his breath, then grabbed at his chairside comm unit as if throttling it by its long gooseneck bracket. "Pike to engineering!"

"Scott here, sir," came the thickly accented voice of the ship's chief engineer.

"We need to redirect all the power we can to the shields."

"Aye, Captain. Diverting from all noncritical systems."

The *Enterprise* took another hit before Scott even had a chance to close the channel. The bridge fell suddenly dark, and the artificial gravity briefly released its hold on Kirk's stomach. "The matter/antimatter generator is down," Kelso reported once the backup power systems kicked in.

Pike hit the switch on his comm unit again. "Mister Scott, status!"

"Antimatter containment systems have been compromised," the engineer reported. Kirk shuddered to think what exactly that meant. Obviously, the containment systems hadn't been completely compromised, given the fact that their atoms hadn't been spread across the sector in a fiery blast. The antimatter pods used numerous redundancies, backups, and fail-safes to prevent such a thing from happening. It was probably best not to wonder how many layers of safety they had lost.

Then the *Enterprise* took another bone-jarring blow from the Orions, and Kirk was reminded that loss of antimatter containment wasn't their only worry.

"Shields down to 59 percent," Kelso said.

"We need those engines back, Mister Scott!"

"Working on it, sir."

Pike jumped from his chair and moved toward the science station. "What about the nebula?" he asked, gripping the steel-gray rail separating the command well from the outer stations. "Can we use it for cover?"

Mulhall shook her head. "Sir, there could be a dozen more Orion ships in there, for all we know."

Then it was the captain's turn to shake his head. "Pirates this far out means rogue operators. Is there any danger from the nebula itself?"

"Like I said before, sir," Mulhall said as she turned away from Pike and pressed her forehead to the hooded viewer, "we don't have much data to go on. But since the Orions seem no worse for wear, I'd say limited expos—"

Mulhall was interrupted by another Orion blast, this one coming from behind them, targeted at the top of the saucer section. The beam struck, overwhelming the shield generators. A surge of unbridled energies ripped through the rear bridge stations, shattering the tough polymer panels like glass and exploding in a hailstorm of shrapnel, sparks, and flame. Phil Alden screamed in pain, rolling on the deck beneath his communications console. Mulhall was thrown backward, cracking her head on the rail before dropping lifelessly to the deck.

Pike froze for just a split second at the sight of the flames. Then he vaulted over the rail, knelt at Mulhall's side. Shards of the viewer hood and display assembly had flown into her eyes, turning the sockets into pools of blood-red pulp. Another splinter of the station had embedded itself in her neck, severing the carotid artery and feeding the growing pool of crimson underneath her head.

Seeing there was nothing left to be done for her, Pike moved to check Alden. He too was bloodied and burned, but alive. "Someone get this man to sickbay!" Stiles, the relief navigator, moved to pull Alden's uninjured arm over his shoulder and guide him to the turbolift, while al-Khaled, the lieutenant manning the bridge engineering station, fired a small chemical extinguisher at the smoldering consoles.

Pike stepped back down into the well of the bridge. "We need to buy ourselves some time," he said. "Number One, take us into the nebula."

Kirk got off one more torpedo shot before altering course and fulfilling his orders. Pike saw it detonate against the lead Orion's shields, and could tell they were definitely weakening. Just not as much as the *Enterprise*'s had.

He swallowed a curse as the Robinson Nebula filled the forward viewscreen. The destruction of the science station meant that the higher resolution readouts were gone and that, to all appearances, they were flying into a perfectly black, perfectly empty void. Mulhall's warning that there could be other ships there lying in wait repeated in the captain's mind. He clenched his teeth, and hoped that they weren't flying blindly into some sort of—

"Incoming!" Kelso shouted, as from out of the shadows of dark matter, another ship appeared directly ahead, heading straight for them. This one, though, wasn't an Orion ship, but of a different design Christopher Pike recognized all too well.

Vulcan.

The characteristic wedge-shaped main hull and ringed warp field generators of the *Soval*-class cruiser quickly filled the forward viewscreen. The trilingual identification markings on its bow were fully legible, though no one left on the bridge could read Vulcan, Andorian, or Tellarite script.

As suddenly as it had appeared, the Coalition ship hurtled past the *Enterprise*. Pike's attention switched from the viewer to the circular tactical display between the helmsman's and navigator's seats. A small red triangle joined the two green ones representing the Orions. "They're firing on the Orions," Kelso observed as bright blue lines lanced out from the red symbol and connected with the other two. "Direct hits on both."

"Number One, bring us about," Pike said, "and ready all weapons. I'll be damned if we'll sit here and play the helpless damsel to the Coalition's white knight."

"Aye aye, sir," Kirk answered, and pulled the *Enterprise* into another hard 180-degree turn. The three other ships reappeared on the screen. The Orions had clearly been caught by surprise by the appearance of the Coalition, but were now going back into an offensive stance, attempting to flank the new ship. Either they had forgotten the Earth vessel or no longer considered it a threat.

Pike meant to make them reconsider.

"Mister Scott," he barked into his comm, "give me every drop of power you can for the weapons."

"*Aye, sir.*"

"Targets reacquired," Kirk reported as the phaser power gauge climbed back upward.

Pike leaned into the back of Kirk's chair, sharp blue eyes glued to the enemies on the screen ahead. "Fire!"

Again, the Orions appeared stunned by the unexpected turn of the battle. After Kirk had landed six or seven good phaser shots, the pirates apparently decided they no longer cared for the odds, and both ships suddenly banked and headed back into the nebula.

There was a small break in the tension on the bridge. But nobody was ready to relax just yet. "Captain, we're being hailed," Kelso reported, looking at the signal light rerouted to his console from the inoperative communications station.

Pike sighed and nodded in acknowledgment. "Number One, stand down from Red Alert . . . keep us at Yellow. Mister Kelso, on-screen."

Pike was surprised to realize that the bridge crew of the Vulcan-designed Coalition ship did not in fact include any Vulcans. Seated at the center of bridge was a portly, white-haired

Tellarite, who considered the *Enterprise* crew with tiny black eyes. At his side stood an Andorian female—or a *zhen,* if Pike remembered his xenobiology lessons correctly—with her arms folded across her chest. The two antennae on top of her head looked like cobras ready to strike right through the viewer. Pike couldn't even identify the species of many of the other crew members: there was a two-meter-tall golden bird . . . a short green lizard with a thin red comb atop its head . . . an orange-skinned creature with an elongated skull and . . . was that a third arm sprouting from its chest?

The Tellarite stood, made a snorting, phlegm-rattling sound, and said, *"This is Captain Glal blasch Cheg, of the* Interstellar Coalition Vessel V'Lar. *Are you in need of any further assistance?"*

The captain lifted his chin and answered, "This is Christopher Pike, commanding the *United Earth Starship Enterprise,* and no, we're just fine, thank you."

Cheg squinted at them from the screen, making his beady eyes disappear entirely. *"You're a long way from Earth, Captain. May I ask what you are doing so far from home?"*

"We were investigating a distress call from another Earth ship. We believe it came from inside Coalition space."

"Indeed?" Cheg paused a moment, staring silently at Pike, almost as if he thought the hesitation would get the human to reveal something more. Then he turned toward the port side of his bridge. *"Lieutenant, are you detecting any such signals emanating from anywhere in local space?"*

The communications officer, a catlike creature with a wireless amplifier in its pointed, upturned ear, replied, *"No, sir. Nothing."*

"It's a specially coded transmission," Pike said. "I can give you the specifications for your transceiver assembly settings."

Again, the Tellarite studied Pike wordlessly. The Andorian moved to his side and whispered something in his ear, but the captain did nothing to acknowledge her. Finally, he said, *"Very well,* Enterprise."

Pike leaned over Kirk's shoulder and quickly pulled the promised information up from the ship's computer databank. The first officer turned and looked back at him, silently expressing concern over the sharing of any Earth encryption codes, even ones that had been obsolete for decades. Pike ignored the look and transmitted the data packet. A second later, the felinoid on the other ship murmured softly, *"Data received."* And just a few seconds after that, the *V'Lar* bridge exploded in bedlam as its sirens began to blare and the image on their linked viewscreens began wavering just as the *Enterprise*'s had earlier.

"A human trick!" shouted the three-armed creature.

"Uh-oh," Kelso muttered. If the crew of the *V'Lar* believed the alarms had signaled an actual attack, they were in a perfect position to wreak severe retaliatory action.

Fortunately, the sirens stopped as quickly as they had started. *"There is a signal,"* announced the alien communications officer, keeping her tone at the level of a gentle purr. *"It's what triggered the alerts. Very cleverly done, too."* She pressed a series of buttons on her console and stared at the screen before her. *"It originates from . . . TNC-89422."*

Pike caught the slight hesitation in the cat-woman's voice as she read off the Vulcan star catalog designation, and briefly wondered what exactly it meant. Captain Cheg, however, simply consulted a screen of his own, and then returned his attention to the *Enterprise* crew. *"Hmph. Very well, Captain Pike. We will bring this to the attention of Space Command, and report back to UESPA via official channels."*

"What?" Pike stepped around the astronavigation console and addressed the Tellarite from directly in front of the screen. "Now, see here, we're talking about human beings who have been lost—"

"—for over twenty years," Cheg interrupted. *"Nearly thirty, in Earth years. Time is not particularly of the essence, is it, Captain?"*

"That's beside the point," Pike shot back. "Those people are human beings. That makes them my responsibility. And I will determine their fates for myself."

Pike thought he saw surprise flicker across the Tellarite's face. Then, the gray-haired alien puffed out his chest and pulled his shoulders back. He seemed to grow ten centimeters before their eyes, and a low rumbling growl started to build from the base of his throat. *"I'd been led to believe that humans did not practice the trading of insults during diplomatic encounters. I see now this is incorrect, since you insult my intelligence and my honor as a fellow starship commander."* Cheg thrust a hooflike hand forward, pointing toward the starboard side of the bridge. *"Tell me, Pike, are you not responsible for that human as well?"*

He turned in the direction the Tellarite was pointing. In all that had happened, no one had yet removed Ann Mulhall's lifeless body from the bridge, or even so much as covered her. Pike kept his face turned away from the screen long enough to regain a composed expression, then turned back. "Yes, I am. I'm fully responsible for all four hundred and thirty crew members aboard."

"And yet you sit here blustering," Cheg sneered, *"while your decks are strewn with corpses, your warp generators are operating at less than half capacity, and your shields are all but gone. Your first responsibility is to your surviving crew. Take your ship back to Earth, before you fall prey to other unfriendly forces."*

"Tell me, Captain Cheg," Pike shouted before they could terminate the signal, "exactly how long were you sitting there in that nebula, watching the Orions have at us, before you decided to come to our rescue?"

"We were under no obligation to come to your defense at all, Pike," Cheg grunted. *"Keep that in mind, should you decide to risk your crew further."* With that, the Tellarite waved a cloven hand, and the transmission ended.

Pike's shoulders slumped as he considered the *V'Lar* hovering in space between the *Enterprise* and the Coalition border. After a long moment during which both ships seemed to be at a standoff, Cheg's ship finally pivoted and disappeared into subspace.

"What now, Captain?" Number One asked, looking at him expectantly.

Pike didn't answer directly, but walked back to his chair and toggled the comm open once again. "Bridge to engineering."

"Scott here, sir."

"Have we got warp power back, Mister Scott?"

"I can give you warp two, sir. Three, if you're really needing it. But I wouldn't push the poor battered beastie any harder until we can put in to a proper repair facility."

As Pike listened, his gaze was pulled past the silver unit at his right hand and to poor Ann Mulhall's body. "Thank you, Mister Scott. Bridge out." He toggled the channel closed, and without turning, ordered, "Mister Kirk . . . let's get the hell out of here."

2

T'Pol could not immediately recall the last time she had used the transporter to travel anywhere, but she did not remember the experience being so unpleasant before.

An involuntary shiver went up her spine as the desert heat of home was suddenly replaced by the comparatively frigid temperature of this climate-controlled municipal transit station. Also, her ears became suddenly plugged—an effect of instantaneously traveling from Death Valley, eighty-six meters below sea level, to this mountainside municipality in northern California. She also could not dismiss the fact that she was no longer the vibrant, youthful woman of sixty-three she had been when she'd regularly beam on and off *Enterprise*. All these factors combined to send her swooning once she materialized on the platform.

A uniformed transit attendant appeared suddenly, before she had fallen too far, catching her and helping her straighten back upright. "Careful, ma'am," he said, keeping a steadying hold on her shoulders as she recovered her balance. "It's all right; this happens a lot with first-time transportees," he said with a friendly smile.

"Thank you," T'Pol said, a bit hoarsely. The stranger's physical contact discomfited her, and she gently disengaged by lifting both hands to the scarf she wore tied over her head—and her ears. He released her, but stayed close, waiting until he was convinced she was walking steadily away before turning his attention to newer arrivals. T'Pol wondered, as she moved down a wide corridor into the main area of the transit station, how friendly he would have been toward her had her head covering fallen free.

The corridor opened up into a wide atrium, and T'Pol faced an overwhelming sea of humanity. She shivered again, though it had nothing to do with the unpleasant temperature. They milled all around her—individual travelers and businesspeople; young men and women with the word BERKELEY stitched onto the front of their shirts; couples and families—all talking, laughing, carrying on hundreds of conversations all at once. T'Pol had never liked crowds, not for as long as she could remember, and certainly not since that terrible, hellishly cold night almost half a lifetime ago . . .

"Aw, stop now. It ain't logical t' be afraid of these people, is it?"

Before T'Pol could argue with that thought, a stranger tapped her on the left shoulder. T'Pol spun, startled, and was relieved to find a familiar face beside her. "Lady T'Pol," the human woman said, smiling broadly. She was what humans would refer to as "middle-aged," of Caucasian lineage, with sharp blue-gray eyes and long salt-and-pepper hair which she wore piled high atop her head. "I hope you haven't been waiting here long," she said. "It's an honor to finally meet you face-to-face."

T'Pol nodded and replied, "Likewise, Doctor Grayson."

"Please, call me Amanda," she insisted, as she had repeatedly during their three-year long-distance acquaintance. Grayson was the chairperson of Berkeley's history department, and had petitioned T'Pol relentlessly over that time to visit her university and share her unique view of twenty-second-century history. "I have one of the university's private aircars waiting for us just outside." She indicated the way toward one of several exits, and T'Pol fell in step beside her.

Once they stepped out of the station, T'Pol relaxed. The late afternoon sun, though nowhere near as hot as it was in the desert, still offered a welcome warmth, and T'Pol lifted her face to its light. A gentle breeze blew from over the nearby bay, ruffling her clothing and filling her nostrils with the distinctive scent of salty seawater. For a moment, she was transported back to the old Vulcan Consulate in Sausalito, a young woman newly arrived on this strange, water-rich planet, ready to start a new phase of her life, with so many new experiences ahead of her . . .

They reached a blue-and-gold–painted aircar, and its gull-wing doors opened on either side for them. Grayson set the car's destination and it lifted off the ground, floating almost noiselessly up the hill toward the university campus.

"Lady T'Pol, I want to tell you again how excited I am about your being here to do this lecture tonight," Grayson said, breaking the silence within the car. "I know how much you value your privacy and solitude, and I want you to know how honored I and the entire university are to be the hosts of this rare visit. I've long been fascinated by the history of the mid-twenty-second century . . . and by you, in particular."

"Indeed?" T'Pol said, lifting one eyebrow as she considered the human woman. "The period was certainly eventful and historically significant. But why would you single me out for special interest?"

"Why? A lone woman living and working among aliens, giving up her own world to live in theirs? Finding a lifemate among them, and having to deal with the consequences of that? Who wouldn't find a life story like that fascinating?"

T'Pol stiffened at Grayson's effusive attempt at flattery. "I did not come here to talk about myself or the personal aspects of my life," she said in a tone that made clear she did not appreciate the professor's impertinent line of inquiry.

"I . . . I'm sorry," Grayson stammered, a mortified look on her face. "I didn't mean to offend you, Lady T'Pol . . ."

"Taking offense would be an emotional reaction," T'Pol said, while not claiming that she hadn't, in fact, been offended.

The rest of the short ride into the city passed in silence. As they climbed the Berkeley Hills, T'Pol stared out the rear window of the small vehicle, back toward the San Francisco Bay, and beyond, the city of San Francisco itself. Much of the city's skyline was still familiar from her time at the Vulcan Consulate. The Transamerica Pyramid and Rincon Hill Towers still stood as they always had, proud survivors of both the Third World War and the 2109 earthquake. But much had changed over the last century as well. The current Golden Gate Bridge, though it strongly evoked the original twentieth-century landmark span, was clearly different from its historic predecessor. Its towers were slightly taller, painted a slightly brighter shade of orange, and of course, the Marin County end of the new span was several hundred meters farther to the west, away from the crater John Frederick Paxton had created with his weaponized verteron beam.

T'Pol closed her eyes, her face turned away from Grayson, and focused all her mental energies on keeping her emotional controls in place. Still, she couldn't hold back the massive surge of memories now returning . . .

They saw the smoke plume before they'd even reached Earth orbit.

T'Pol had reluctantly left her child, Elizabeth, in Phlox's care, pushing aside the illogical idea that her constant presence might keep her daughter from dying. Trip seemed no more willing to leave his daughter, but it was his homeworld that had been attacked, and his human emotionalism compelled him to witness the devastation for himself. Together they went up to the bridge, where the main viewscreen displayed the carnage.

Even though Paxton had been impossibly accurate—managing a direct hit on the center of the Starfleet Command Complex from a distance of over one hundred million kilometers—the damage was nowhere near as limited as he had implied it would be. The verteron beam, with enough energy to pull massive comets out of orbit or to vaporize a starship, hit Earth with the power of a high-yield fusion bomb. A black column of toxic plasma residue, mixed with millions of metric tons of debris, had been thrown into the atmosphere, blotting out both ends of the Golden Gate and spreading east over the bay. Through the black cloud, orange flames could be seen burning across the peninsulas both north and south of the narrow strait.

"Oh, my God," Hoshi Sato whispered from her station, tears streaming down her face. She had been left in command of *Enterprise* while Archer and the rest of the bridge crew took a shuttle-pod to the Martian surface to rescue T'Pol and Trip. It had been Sato's responsibility, if the captain failed to reach Paxton's command center, to take out the facility and stop him from carrying out his threat against Starfleet and the alien delegates gathered for the Coalition of Planets negotiations. Archer had managed to shut down the verteron beam once, but Sato had been caught completely off guard when it was reactivated.

The rest of the crew, as well as Minister Nathan Samuels, simply stared at the screen in stunned silence while Sato continued to repeat, "Oh, my God," over and over. At some point, the screen image switched from the *Enterprise*'s own sensors to news coverage being transmitted from the surface. The northern tower of the Golden Gate Bridge had toppled, and fires raged from Sausalito to the Presidio. "It's like the Xindi all over again," Malcolm Reed croaked from his station—a hyperbolic comparison, T'Pol had thought at the time, considering that the Xindi attack the previous year affected an area nearly three thousand kilometers long and killed seven million.

"No," Minister Samuels disagreed. "It's worse; we did this to ourselves. We're supposed to be beyond this!" he shouted as he waved his hand wildly at the images of destruction before him, and then he sagged. "The demons of our past . . . have won."

"Lady T'Pol?"

T'Pol forced herself back to the present, and turned an impassive face back to her host. "Yes?"

"We're here," Grayson said, just as T'Pol registered the fact that their aircar had stopped and settled to the ground near a tall, decorative green copper gate. Silently chiding herself for getting so lost in her memories, she fell in step beside Grayson as they walked onto the campus.

T'Pol had thought, after so many years among humans, that she could no longer be surprised by any aspect of their world or their culture. But her introduction to the Berkeley campus defied all her expectations. Casually dressed young people milled along the broad paved pathway past her and Grayson; none of them seemed in a particular hurry to be anywhere. Numerous others populated the grassy quadrangles on either side of the walkway, and while some appeared to be reading and studying from padds, the majority were engaged in athletic games and other leisure activities. "Are these students?" T'Pol asked.

"Well, yes, of course," Grayson answered, sounding a bit surprised at T'Pol's query.

T'Pol very slightly shook her head. She herself had attended several different learning academies during her young adulthood on Vulcan, as she pursued her studies in sciences, diplomacy, and military security. And while she hadn't expected the same stolid, highly disciplined atmosphere at a human university, neither had she expected the resemblance to a resort town on Wrigley's Pleasure Planet. "And this is typical of human institutions of higher learning?"

Grayson laughed. "I don't think many people have ever accused Berkeley of being 'typical.' We have a long and proud history of breeding movements that run counter to the social and political status quo, going back three hundred years."

Grayson continued her lecture on Berkeley's history, but T'Pol's attention was caught by the sound of a chanting chorus, so faint that she was sure it hadn't reached Grayson's human ears. It echoed from the old brick buildings and over the shouts and music that otherwise filled the campus air, repeating over and over: *"We don't need no Vulcan lies! Send T'Pol back to the skies!"*

"Who is that?"

Grayson blinked, confused. "Who is who?"

T'Pol pointed. "Those chanters. Over that way, around the far end of this building."

Grayson blanched. "You can hear them?"

"I believe I just indicated that I can."

The professor shook her head sharply. "Please, don't pay them any mind. They're just a vocal minority—the price we pay for living in a free society."

"Students?"

"Yes. And young."

T'Pol nodded, and started to move toward the sound of the protesters. "Lady T'Pol!" Grayson herself protested, moving quickly after her, and putting a hand on the Vulcan's elbow in an attempt to gently guide her back the other way.

But T'Pol jerked her arm away without breaking her slow but determined stride. "You invited me here as part of an educational program. It would be unfortunate if these students were denied the benefit of my experience because of their prejudices."

Understanding that she wasn't going to stop the elder woman, Grayson walked with her until they reached the corner of the building, at which point she then stepped out into the lead, putting herself between T'Pol and the small assemblage opposed to her presence on campus, and on Earth. They numbered ten or so, male and female, mostly unremarkable looking. Some held signs reading "Vulcan Go Home" and "Keep Earth Human." Other signs merely sported a simple graphic design, a representation of the globe inside a triangle.

The emblem of Terra Prime.

Given their enthusiasm, the protesters did not immediately notice the two older women who had joined the small semicircle of curious onlookers. One by one, though, they either noticed the stooped and wrinkled figure, or had her pointed out to them, and their chant gave way to awkward silence.

"You haven't stopped on my account, have you?" A quiet current of laughter rippled through the group of spectators, whose numbers were already growing well beyond what the protesters had attracted on their own.

A petite young woman with Asiatic facial features and sharp green eyes took a step toward her. "What do you want?"

"You seem inordinately upset by my presence here," T'Pol answered. "I am curious as to why."

"Because you don't belong here, that's why."

"I was invited here by the chairperson of your history department."

One of the young men of the group scoffed. "Chairperson Herberta. Us and her, we don't reach."

"Yes, clearly, you are at odds," T'Pol agreed. "However, this does not explain why my presence is so offensive."

"You want to know why, sister?" the green-eyed woman asked, pulling herself up to her full height. "Because your people came here when we were set to soar, and you held us back. For a hundred years all we got was the hard lip from you. And when you couldn't cross us anymore, you wormed in, came on our warp-five ship, and got us knotted up into your bad scenes, like P'Jem. It wasn't until we kicked you aliens out and started making our own way that it started to chime for us humans.

"But now here you are to give us your slant, trying to swing us from the truth. And we say no go!"

The other young protesters picked up this cue. "No go! No go!"

T'Pol raised a hand, and the chant subsided slightly. "My slant, if I understand your use of the word, is what I personally experienced. And it should not surprise you that my perspective on the first warp-five mission is a bit more complex than your simplistic summarization of the last two hundred years."

The young woman frowned and put her hands to her temples as she shook her head. "Complex, complicated, confusing—no more smoke, Herberta! You want to tell us the Frisco Blast wasn't your fault, tell someone else!"

T'Pol's eyes widened. "*My* fault?"

"If you aliens would've left Earth when Paxton told you to," the young woman snarled, "a million humans wouldn't have been killed. My great-grandpop's first wife, his first-born son, his entire family—they were all killed in that scene, because of you—"

"Your ancestor's family," T'Pol interrupted, "were victims of John Frederick Paxton's mindless prejudice and hatred. And you dishonor their memories by perpetuating that hatred today."

At that point, Grayson moved to position herself between the two. "Lady T'Pol . . . Takako, please, let's keep some degree of civility—"

T'Pol spun on Grayson. "Civility? This woman is spreading ignorance and misinformation on your campus, and your only concern is that she's treated civilly?"

"She's got the right to speak, Herberta," one of the other young men holding a Terra Prime sign shouted.

T'Pol caught herself before suggesting that right should be revoked. Still staring down Grayson, she pointed at the woman she'd addressed as Takako and asked, "You know who this person is?"

The professor nodded. "Miss Sulu has made quite a reputation for herself in her years here."

"She is one of your students?" It was all T'Pol could do to tamp down her surprise and outrage. "Does this university have no standards whatsoever? Or is her ignorance about one of the worst incidents of human violence of the twenty-second century due to your incompetence as an educator?"

Grayson took a step toward the older woman. "You're upset. I understand—"

"*I am a Vulcan!* I do not get—"

T'Pol clamped her mouth and her eyes shut tight, and after a moment to re-collect herself, spun on her heel. The crowd of young spectators quickly cleared a path as she stormed off, back the way she had come.

"Lady T'Pol . . ." Amanda Grayson called, quickly catching up with the older woman.

"I should never have agreed to come here," T'Pol said, as much to herself as to Grayson. "I should have known better than to hope—"

Grayson jumped in front of T'Pol, forcing her to stop just before passing back through the gate at the edge of campus. "Please, Lady T'Pol. I apologize. From the bottom of my heart, I am sorry for this altercation."

T'Pol sighed. "I wish I could believe that, Doctor Grayson," she said, as she stepped around her toward the aircars. "And I wish that it mattered."

Chief Engineer Scott piloted the shuttlecraft *dePoix* in slow circles around the *Enterprise,* which sat tethered to the bare-bones drydock facility at Vega Colony. They'd managed to hobble back here from the border at warp two, and as they inspected the ship's exterior, Pike was surprised that they had managed that much. "It looks worse than it really is," Scotty assured the captain as they passed along the underside of the saucer section. What had once been an unblemished, brilliant white hull was now marred, from one edge of the saucer to the other, by what looked like large gray bruises. Pike knew Scotty was right in saying it wasn't as bad as it looked; this was cosmetic damage, caused when the individual shield generators beneath the plating overloaded and burned out. An actual weapon hit on the hull would have left a darker, uglier mark . . .

And then the *dePoix* passed over the edge of the saucer, and Pike was given a clear view of the black scar etched on the rear of the ship's bridge. The captain clenched his jaw tight and forced himself not to look away from the spot. Station engineers in bulky silver EVA suits were removing plasma-burnt panels and replacing them with brand-new ones, creating the impression of a small bandage taped over a deep wound.

Scotty sat silent a moment, then said softly, "Ann Mulhall was a fine lass. Hers is a terrible loss."

Pike simply nodded. *They were all terrible losses,* he thought, but then pushed that thought aside, before he went mad remembering all the terrible losses over all these terrible years. "How much longer until we can be back under way?" the captain asked, changing the topic.

"Shouldn't be more than an hour or so," Scotty answered, then added, with an exaggerated shrug, "We can't get much more done here than basic patchwork repairs."

"Yes, Mister Scott," Pike said wearily. For months, since the incident at Draylax, Scotty had been advocating a return to Earth and Bozeman Station, where the *Enterprise* could get the kind of overhaul it had been in need of, in truth, since long before the current chief engineer signed aboard. Pike silently cursed the bureaucratic geniuses at Starfleet HQ who decided they didn't need fully-equipped bases on the frontier, then said, "Plan to be under way in an hour, then. Bring us in, Mister Scott."

Once they'd returned to the shuttlebay, Pike headed for sickbay. There had been eighteen casualties, in addition to the seven who had been killed. *All terrible losses,* the small voice in the back of the captain's head repeated. He forced it aside again. Christopher Pike realized years ago, not long after the ambush they'd suffered at Rigel VII, that he could not take the weight of every casualty on his shoulders and still continue to function as a starship captain. And so he started to grow emotional calluses, convinced himself that the lives lost were acceptable when weighed against the number of lives saved because of their sacrifice.

Pike found Doctor Phillip Boyce, his chief medical officer and longtime friend, in the intensive care ward. He was standing at the bedside of Lieutenant Alden, who had suffered severe third-degree burns over the right side of his face and upper body. The younger man was propped upright in his bed, and though his neck had been immobilized in a hard plastic brace, his eyes followed the captain as he entered the room. "Good to see you awake, Mister Alden," the captain said, giving him a tight smile. "Doctor Boyce isn't boring you with old war stories, is he?"

Alden stared silently at Pike. On the bedside table, on which the lieutenant's one bare, unscarred hand rested, he tapped his fingers once, then twice.

"No," Boyce said. At Pike's curious look, he explained, "Alden's larynx turned out to be burned pretty badly, too. I've asked engineering to rig him up a speech synthesizer of some sort."

Pike looked from Boyce to Alden. "I'm sorry," he said. What a nasty irony, for a communications officer to be reduced to taps for "yes" and "no." "Well, we should be under way in about an hour; Scotty will be able to take care of that then."

Alden's brown eyes flitted from Pike to Boyce, and the doctor stared back, as if some kind of silent conversation were going on between them. Boyce then broke contact and turned to Pike. "Captain, if I could speak to you in my office?"

"Of course." Boyce stood, urged his patient to get some rest, and then led the captain into his small private refuge. "Will he recover?" he asked as they both sat on either side of the doctor's desk.

"If we can get him back to Earth, then yes," the doctor told him.

Pike sighed and nodded, having anticipated that answer. "Well, seeing as we're not going to be heading there any time soon, I suppose you'll want him transferred to the colony's hospital." From there, Alden could either be put aboard a mercy flight or the next regular shuttle back to the Sol system.

"Well, yes . . . ," he said.

Pike waited. "And?"

"And . . ." Boyce looked down at the edge of his desk. "I'd like to transfer off, too, Chris."

Pike's mouth fell open in surprise. "Phil?" Boyce had served as *Enterprise* CMO since Pike first took command fourteen years earlier, and over the course of those fourteen years, the older man had served as trusted friend, confidant, adviser . . . and of course, bartender. "What brought this on?"

Boyce lifted his head and looked straight at the captain. "You and I have been friends a long time, Chris. Too long for me to give you some canned pap about how I've decided I'm getting too old for this job."

"Especially since you've been saying that for the past ten years," Pike said, trying to lighten the suddenly thick mood of the office.

Boyce cracked a polite smile. "I owe it to you to be completely straight with you." He drew a breath, then said, "I don't like what Starfleet has become . . . and with all respect, Chris, I don't like what it's made you into."

Pike stared back at the doctor blankly for a moment, and then shook his head slightly. "You've lost me."

Boyce stood up and turned to the cabinet behind his desk, from which he withdrew a bottle of Irish whiskey. "I joined up in '43, right after the Klingon attack on Sherman's Planet," he said as he turned back, set down a pair of glasses, and began to pour. "I was assigned to the *Excalibur,* and I was with her during the Battle of Donatu V."

Pike knew this part of Boyce's record, of course. And he knew why the older man was bringing up Donatu V now. But he simply sipped at his drink, not daring to interrupt. "The Donatu system was the key to the Empire's war plan. If they had taken it, then half the quadrant would be speaking Klingonese today—including the Coalition. So when the battle came, we had both Starfleet and Space Command combining forces, and we had human ground troops fighting alongside Andorians and Tellarites and Saurians, all willing to put our stupid old grievances and prejudices aside to beat back the Klingon bastards."

Boyce wore a proud smile as he recalled one of the most historic victories of Earth's warp flight era. But it quickly turned to a scowl as he continued, "But as soon as the war was over, everything went right back to the way it was, to the same resentment and suspicion we humans had clung to since the Vulcans first showed up and told Cochrane they didn't like his taste in music."

Pike waited as Boyce took a long slug of his drink before saying, "Okay, yes, it would be nice if Earth and the Coalition didn't have to be on opposite sides sniping at each other all the time. But like you said, it's been this way, on and off, for two hundred years. Why would you want to leave now?"

Boyce fixed the captain with a hard penetrating look. "Chris, what were the odds that we were going to find any hard evidence of any *Columbia* survivors? The only reason for altering course the way you did, planning to skirt the border with all sensors pointing across, was to antagonize the Interstellar Coalition."

That's not true, Pike wanted to tell him, and if it was anyone other than Boyce, he would have stated his denial out loud. Phil, of course, would see right through such a plain lie.

He was saved from having to say anything by the sound of a boatswain's whistle, and Number One's voice calling, *"Bridge to Captain Pike,"* over the comm.

The captain reached for the monitor on the end of Boyce's desk. "Pike here."

"Incoming message, sir, from Admiral Komack, Starfleet Command."

Pike automatically straightened up in his chair at the mention of his immediate superior. It had been several hours since he'd transmitted his initial report on the incident at the Robinson Nebula, just enough time for it to have reached Earth and to have been read by the admiral. Now Komack was initiating a real-time subspace call. Pike couldn't imagine that it was to tell him how well he'd handled the matter.

He looked over to Boyce, who was already out of his chair. "It's time for my rounds," he said as he moved toward the door. Pike nodded his thanks, even though he didn't want to leave off their conversation at that particular point. Pike sighed as he watched the door slide closed behind the doctor, and then turned his attention back to the monitor. "Pipe it down here, Number One."

Seconds later, the white-haired, stern-faced visage of Admiral Wes Komack appeared on the screen. "Hello, Admiral," the captain said.

"Captain Pike. What is your current status?"

No preliminaries, no beating around the bush. "We're at Vega Colony Station, and our repairs are just about complete. We—"

"Good," Komack interrupted, though he certainly didn't seem pleased. *"As soon as repairs are finished, you're to set course for Earth. I want you here at Headquarters for debriefing at oh-nine-hundred hours, GMT, day after tomorrow."*

Pike gaped slightly. "Sir?"

Komack's frown deepened. *"Do you foresee a problem making that schedule, Captain?"*

"Uh, no, sir," Pike answered. At warp five, the *Enterprise* would be there with half a day to spare. But the admiralty normally didn't like calling their ships of the line back to home port, and usually settled for dressing down their captains via subspace. But for whatever reason, Komack wanted Pike to put in a personal appearance. "Oh-nine-hundred. I'll be there," Pike told the admiral.

Once Komack had signed off, Pike slumped in his chair and wondered just what exactly in hell he had gotten himself into.

At 0840 hours on the appointed day, Pike took the *Enterprise* shuttle *Haise,* requested clearance from Bozeman Station Control, and launched from the shuttlebay, heading east for Starfleet Headquarters. Ten minutes later, he was across the Atlantic and descending toward Antwerp. Pike had fallen in love with the ancient Belgian city from his first day at Starfleet Academy, and as he descended, he couldn't help but admire the sight of the sun rising behind the high spire of the Cathedral of Our Lady and the Boerentoren, illuminating the city below. But, he had to switch his attention to UESPA's modern complex of buildings on the west bank of the Scheldt River.

By 0855 he'd landed, and at 0900 sharp he was escorted by a gray-uniformed security officer to the ninth floor and led to a set of wooden double doors. The guard pulled one of the metal door handles, shaped like the swooping arch from the UESPA seal, and admitted him into an oversized hearing room. Four dozen observers' seats, all currently empty, filled the rear half of the room. The white, gold, and blue flag of United Earth hung on the front wall of the room, directly behind an elevated dais, from which two imposing figures sat watching him.

Admiral Komack considered the captain with the inscrutable stare of a Vulcan as he made his way to the front of the hearing room. Pike only took dim notice, though, as his attention was taken by the man seated next to Komack. "Ah. Captain Pike, I presume?" Admiral Kelvar Garth intoned in a deep voice.

Pike halted and snapped to full attention. "Yes, sir. Reporting as ordered, Admirals."

Both men continued to stare at him from their elevated perch wordlessly. Whereas Komack wore his poker face while regarding Pike, Garth's displeasure was undisguised as he glared at the *Enterprise* commander with his harsh ice-blue eyes. Kelvar Garth, famed hero of the First Battle of Axanar, was the youngest man ever to hold the position of commander in chief of the United Earth Starfleet, and did not rise to that position because of his tolerance of subordinates' screw-ups. Once more, Pike wondered how big a can of worms he had split open that it prompted this kind of high-level interest.

A door slid open off in the corner behind the dais, and a fourth person entered the room. "Forgive my tardiness, gentlemen," the new arrival said, and Pike's eyes widened as he recognized the low resonant voice from the news dispatches of the last several months. The man, a civilian, wearing a bright yellow jacket with a white cravat knotted around his neck, climbed the bench, nodded to the admirals, and then looked down. "And you would be Captain Pike," said Carter Winston, smiling at him from behind his thick, dark handlebar mustache.

Pike nodded. "Yes, Mister Prime Minister." Carter Winston was a man about Pike's own age, a self-made millionaire, philanthropist, and, as of five months ago, the highest elected leader of the United Earth government.

And he was personally sitting in on this debriefing. Clearly, Pike realized, the can he'd opened held not worms, but giant Caldorian eels.

"At ease, Captain," Garth growled, at which point Pike realized just how tense his entire body was. "Take a seat, and let's get this thing started."

"Aye, sir." Pike did as he was told, moving through the gallery to the single seat in the center of the room. Once situated, he took a bracing breath and laid his palm on the biosensor to his right. It did not activate.

"Captain, you're not on trial here," Komack said, coming dangerously close to cracking a grin as Pike tried lifting his hand and repositioning it on the unlit circular panel. "Point of fact, this meeting is going to have to be kept somewhat unofficial, for the time being."

Pike raised one eyebrow at his immediate superior. "Unofficial?" he repeated. He looked pointedly to the head of Starfleet and the head of the government. "Lot of officials here for something unofficial."

Prime Minister Winston laughed out loud at that. "One thing I've learned in recent months, Captain, is that far more happens in government in unofficial meetings than in official ones."

"This meeting is unofficial in that the prime minister and I are not really here," said Garth, still looking quite angry. "As far as anyone outside this room is concerned, this is just a typical debriefing, you and your immediate superior. Anything else that is discussed here is to be treated as classified. Is that understood, Captain?"

"Yes, sir."

"Right." Garth pulled a data slate across the desk and glanced down at its display. "So, Captain, your report in a nutshell: you were attacked by two Orion ships in neutral space. The *I.C.V. V'Lar* came to your aid, and the pirates were driven off. You then shared the suspected location of a lost human ship inside Coalition territory with the *V'Lar,* and their captain offered to investigate as you returned to Earth-controlled space. Is that accurate?"

"That's a pretty small nutshell, sir, but yes, it's accurate."

Garth folded his hands and leaned forward. "Something that you think needs elaboration?"

Pike hesitated, then said, "Well, it's not as if the *V'Lar* offered to go looking for the *Columbia* out of the goodness of their hearts. They were just trying to keep us out of their territory."

"And if the situation were reversed, Captain," Prime Minister Winston interjected, "would you have allowed an I.C. ship into our space, on the pretext of searching for a thirty-year-old Vulcan expedition?"

Before Pike could give the obvious answer, Garth spoke up again. "The Talos system, where they traced the *Columbia* signal, is apparently a long-known navigational hazard, not unlike our own Delta Triangle. The *V'Lar* was reported missing en route there two days ago."

Pike paused as that piece of information sank in. "I'm sorry to hear that," he said, dipping his head slightly.

"Are you really, Captain?"

Pike's head snapped up again at Komack's question. He wasn't sure if he was being doubted or disparaged for expressing human compassion, and Komack's mien gave no hint either way. "Yes, I am," he said, and realized that it was true. "I've no reason to wish ill on Captain Cheg or his crew. And if he did, in fact, sacrifice himself on behalf of an Earth ship's crew, then of course I'd regret the loss of such a man." He wished, at the moment, Phil Boyce had been there to witness this revelation, but the doctor was already packed and gone off to his daughter's.

"I'm glad to hear you say that, Captain," Winston said. "Very glad. Have you read John Gill's new book on Nathan Samuels?"

Pike felt a bit of disorientation at that sudden change of topic. "No, sir, I'm afraid I haven't." Of course, he recognized the name of the man who had been prime minister at the time of the Xindi attack in the last century; the author's name meant nothing to him, though.

"It's a fascinating read," the prime minister said. "Gill was able to go through all of the records that had been sealed in the International Archives until seventy-five years after Samuels's death. Did you know that Samuels had been a member of Terra Prime in his teens?"

"No, I didn't," Pike answered, still confused, but his interest slightly piqued.

Winston nodded. "After the attack on San Francisco in 2155, and John Paxton's arrest, his lieutenants couldn't distance themselves from him fast enough. But at the same time, the alien governments who had lost their ambassadors started publicly quarreling about who would be the first to try Paxton. The surviving leaders of Terra Prima managed to pull off a brilliant piece of political jujitsu: they insisted Paxton be tried, on Earth, for crimes against humanity—and *just* humanity. They argued that the other races, by demanding extradition, were devaluing the human lives lost, and succeeded in strengthening the xenophobia of the era. What should have been the end of Terra Prime instead gave rise to a populist political movement, one Samuels had to support, or else be forced from office."

"Mister Prime Minister," Pike said once he was sure Winston

had finished his story, "I'm afraid I don't understand why you're telling me all this."

"Because in his private papers, Samuels says that he always regretted giving in to the nativists, and that he didn't do more to try and get the Coalition of Planets talks back on track. Like Jonathan Archer, he always believed humanity would eventually reach out to the rest of the galaxy again in friendship, and exorcise the demons that have kept us focused inward all these years."

Then he leaned forward across the dais, Samuels's successor directly facing Archer's. "I believe the time to reach out again, Captain, is now."

3

Sunrise over Death Valley.

At the first hint of light, the nocturnal creatures that gave the lie to this place's name started scurrying for the cool shade of their burrows. The temperature, which had dipped down to almost 20 degrees Celsius overnight, had already started to climb again, heading for an expected 50 degrees.

And T'Pol, who had spent the last half hour staring at the ceiling of her bedroom, lifted the thin sheet off her body and pushed herself slowly up out of bed. She slid her bare feet into an old pair of slippers and shuffled into the kitchen, where she turned on the tap and waited patiently for the ancient pump to draw enough water up from the underground spring to fill her teakettle.

The pump, like the house it was in, was over two hundred years old. The small adobe structure had been built just after World War III by a small group of religious cultists who wished to separate themselves from the rest of their violent race. This locale, one of the most forbidding on the planet, proved ideal to this purpose: no one had discovered any evidence of the group's ritual mass suicide until two years after the fact.

Once she'd coaxed enough water out of the spigot, T'Pol placed the kettle on a small heating unit and then reached for her tin of chamomile tea. She was not quite as cut off from the world as the original inhabitants had been—that would be close to impossible on twenty-third-century Earth. But her nearest neighbors, in the town of Furnace Creek several kilometers away, were very protective of their privacy, and hers by extension. One of them, though, a Mister Timbisha, made regular sojourns into Beatty for supplies and provisions, and occasionally gifted her with small comforts, such as tea or fresh fruits. One time, he had brought a small jar of *plomeek* seeds, obviously smuggled to Earth by black marketers. Each time she went out to gather new leaves from her small shaded garden, she wondered how he had known what they were, and how much they must have cost him to obtain. The one time she had offered to compensate him, he refused, saying, "Some of us still remember how much Earth owes you."

Now that T'Pol thought about it, though, Mister Timbisha had been an elderly man when she first moved to the Southern California desert. Most likely . . . yes, she remembered now: Timbisha had died, like so many humans she'd known over the years. He'd been dead for . . . decades? Could that be right? Hadn't she seen him just . . . No. But if he was dead, who was it who had been bringing her her tea?

And with her thoughts returned to tea, the whistle of the kettle finally penetrated her consciousness, though she had the sense that the water had been boiling for some time.

She squeezed her eyes shut, willing her disorganized thoughts and memories to reorder themselves. The scent of chamomile as it was released and carried by the steaming water helped in that regard. Sighing, she lowered herself into a chair at the kitchen table, both gnarled hands drawing warmth from the ceramic cup.

It had been growing increasingly difficult for her to maintain her mental disciplines as the years went by. She'd struggled with her failing abilities for a long time, particularly since her time in the Expanse, and the damage she'd inflicted on herself through the abuse of trellium-D. But matters had gotten to the point recently that she'd begun to worry that she was developing Bendii Syndrome or some other infirmity. She'd lived on Earth for so long, without the benefit of a Vulcan physician; she could be suffering from any number of undiagnosed conditions . . .

But that was just paranoia. T'Pol still retained enough of her logical faculties to understand her current difficulties had begun just over a month ago, shortly after hearing the news about Elizabeth Cutler: at the age of 147 years, the last surviving human member of Jonathan Archer's *Enterprise* crew had died of natural causes at her home in Tycho City, attended by five generations of her progeny.

And with her passing, T'Pol was alone, in yet one more sense.

T'Pol was startled out of her thoughts by a quiet alarm bleeping throughout the house, indicating that the property's proximity sensors had been tripped. Bighorn sheep occasionally came down from the surrounding mountains in search of greenery to graze, but not as the sun was on its way up. Setting her cup down, T'Pol stood and reached for one of the kitchen drawers, from which she withdrew an outdated but still functional phase pistol.

She then activated a small countertop viewscreen, each of its three panels showing different views from the rooftop visual sensors. A man in denim pants and a plain blue cotton shirt was approaching from the direction of the old National Park Visitors Center, following the faint footpath that led to her front steps. T'Pol moved quickly through the house to the foyer and peered outside through a small optical lens set in the door. The man walked with both hands held away from his body, palms forward and empty. He was purposely presenting himself as harmless as he approached, but that did not mean he in fact was. Once he got within fifty meters of the house, T'Pol pushed the door open and aimed her pistol at his chest. "Do not come any closer," she called to him.

The man did as he was told, at the same time lifting his hands a bit higher. "I mean you no harm, Lady T'Pol," he shouted back.

"Nor do I intend to harm you," T'Pol replied. "However, my intentions are subject to change if you do not leave this property right now."

"Ma'am, my name is Christopher Pike, and I'm—"

"I do not care who you are, or what your reasons are for tracking me to my home. I do not welcome visitors, and I will defend my home and my privacy to the fullest."

The man now closed his hands into fists, and dropped them to his sides as he pulled himself up straight to his full height. "Lower your weapon, Commander," he called out in a voice that came from the inner depths of his being and rang with the characteristic authority of a starship captain. The muzzle of T'Pol's phase pistol actually dipped slightly as her long-dormant yet deeply etched military instincts responded to the man's tone and bearing.

Her lapse was only momentary. "Starfleet stripped me of my commission a long time ago," T'Pol informed him.

The man—Pike—started walking again, now ignoring the weapon aimed at him. "Once a Starfleet officer, always a Starfleet officer, they say."

"If you're here on official Starfleet business, shouldn't you be in uniform?"

He cracked a small grin. "I grew up in the Mojave; I know better," he told her. "If I had come to Death Valley in that heavy velour turtleneck, before long I would be begging you to use that phaser on me."

T'Pol lowered her pistol arm to her side, realizing there was no deterrent factor if Pike was making jokes about it. No doubt he'd faced more frightening foes in his life than a 176-year-old hermit lady. "What is this about, Mister Pike? What could Starfleet possibly want with me more than a century after my discharge?"

"Well, it's not Starfleet, per se. It would perhaps be more comfortable for us both if we were to discuss this inside."

T'Pol tried—and failed—to suppress a sigh of resignation. She took a step back, holding the door open for Pike, and then indicated the small parlor that made up the front of the house. It was sparsely furnished and undecorated, as befitting one who did not entertain. Pike took a seat on a hard wooden mission chair as T'Pol settled onto a threadbare but comfortable sofa. "Lady T'Pol,

I was asked by Prime Minister Winston to come speak with you. He intends to petition the Interstellar Coalition to admit Earth as a member. And he wants your support in that goal."

T'Pol raised one eyebrow. "Indeed? And what makes him believe I'd give it?"

"Because you know from firsthand experience that a partnership between humans and nonhumans can work." Every muscle in T'Pol's body tensed at that, from the base of her neck to the fingers still wrapped around the phase pistol in her lap. Somehow, she managed to control her emotional retort as Pike obliviously continued, "You were right there at Captain Archer's side, from the launch of the NX-01 to his court-martial."

"I fail to see the relevance of these statements," T'Pol told Pike calmly, changing her hold on the pistol to minimize the chance of accidentally discharging it. "Carter Winston is not Jonathan Archer."

"No, but like Archer, the prime minister wants to extend the hand of friendship and cooperation to the other powers of the galaxy."

"Carter Winston is a businessman. He spent a lifetime manipulating commodities markets on dozens of colonies and other Earth-subjugated worlds, amassed several financial fortunes, and then used his wealth and reputation to launch a political career, leading him prematurely to United Earth's most powerful governmental office. Forgive me if I find the comparison inapt."

"Listen, I'm as cynical about politicians as the next person," Pike said, lowering his voice to affect the sense that he was sharing a confidence. "But like you said, the guy is a businessman first, and a damned smart one, too. But if the business of politics is getting votes and keeping yourself in power, then petitioning for Earth's admittance into the Interstellar Coalition is a losing deal for him."

T'Pol cocked her head and narrowed her eyes at the human. "You're going to tell me now that Winston is advocating this union selflessly, for a higher, more noble purpose."

"What if I did?"

"I would tell you that you were correct: it would be a losing deal for him," she said, a small touch of regret coloring her tone. "Are you familiar with the reasons Vulcans renounced emotion, Mister Pike?"

"Because of war," the Starfleet captain answered. "You nearly wiped yourselves out, right?"

"Correct. The emotions of fear and hatred are too powerful and too destructive. Your people have turned those emotions against extraterrestrials, which is perhaps the only reason you have avoided the fate my ancestors suffered. And no matter the best intentions of Prime Minister Winston or yourself, a proposal like this will only serve to rekindle that fear and hatred. I have seen it happen too many times over the past one hundred and nine years, as recently as just this past week."

"So, when I report back to the prime minister, I should tell him, don't even bother?"

"I would advise phrasing the message a bit less bluntly."

Pike slid forward to the edge of his chair and leaned toward her. "Would that be the same advice—less bluntly phrased—you gave Captain Archer when he decided to act as mediator at Weytahn?"

T'Pol narrowed her eyes at Pike. That was, in fact, the essence of what she'd told Jonathan when he'd first proposed negotiating a peaceful settlement between Vulcan and Andoria over the long-disputed planet, which Vulcan called Paan Mokar. But that was irrelevant. "As I have already said, Carter Winston is not Jonathan Archer."

"I understand," Pike said. "But let me ask you: at that point in history, was Jonathan Archer yet 'Jonathan Archer'?"

"He's gotcha there, T'Pol."

When she was first introduced to Jonathan Archer, he was suspicious and headstrong, and highly mistrustful of the Vulcans, whom he blamed for holding his father's warp engine research back for decades. Even after the successful negotiations at Wey-tahn, it would be years before T'Pol developed the kind of un-questioning regard for Jonathan they were now talking about.

"I understand you have misgivings," Pike continued. "More than anyone else on Earth, I'd bet. But I'd also bet that you have more reasons to want to see things change than most humans. Our best chance of effecting those changes is with your support, even if it's just tacit."

T'Pol said nothing for a long time. The last thing she wanted to do, so soon after the disaster of her visit to Berkeley, was to put herself out there again, trusting in supposedly well-intentioned humans. But if there was even the slightest chance that she could help advance Jonathan's last unfinished mission . . . "I will have to meditate on the matter before reaching any decision," she finally told Pike.

"Of course." Pike stood up and started to put his right hand out to her, before he remembered the Vulcan aversion to casual physical contact. "Thank you again for your time and your indul-gence, ma'am."

"Captain Pike . . ." He stopped at the door and turned back. "Why did the prime minister send *you* here to make his case?" she asked.

"Because it's my ship that will be undertaking the diplomatic mission to the Coalition," he told her. "And because he thought you might be more favorably inclined if you were asked by the captain of the current *Starship Enterprise*."

Her heart seemed to skip a few beats at the mention of that piece of information. Still, she kept herself steady and said in a dismissive tone, "Sentimentality is an emotion."

"That's what I thought," Pike said, a corner of his mouth twitching upward. "Good day, ma'am."

"Good day, Captain," she said, and stood staring at the door for several seconds after he'd left, deep in thought.

★ ★ ★

A team of four men and women in EVA suits stood atop the *Enterprise*'s saucer. Over their heads, a small Work Bee slowly maneuvered a new modular bridge toward its place at the apex of the ship. The workers watched as the large starship component was lowered toward them. They waved their arms and hands even though they were out of sight of the pilot and had their suits' audio transceivers open to the Bee's operator. Finally, after a slow descent, the workers reached up and lay their gloved hands on the oversized dome, helping to guide it the last two meters into its large circular socket.

Though sound did not travel through the vacuum between the ship and the observation deck overlooking the Bozeman Station drydock slip, Jim Kirk still imagined the gentle metallic clunk of the module settling in place, followed by the whir of locking clamps. The entire top of the bridge module lit up, indicating that the duotronic circuits had connected and that ship's systems were now integrated with its new command center.

Kirk smiled at the sight of the now perfectly refurbished starship. The scorched hull plating had been replaced, and the rest had been restored to its original pristine white. He put his hand out, until his fingertips were stopped by the transparent aluminum window, and traced the curve of the forward hull and the newly repainted black lettering on the upper hull, spelling out the name *U.E.S.S. Enterprise* NCC-1701.

"Now I know why it's called 'she,'" said a teasing voice beside him.

Kirk dropped his hand and turned away to face his friend. "I'm only appreciating the work your people have done, Gary," he said, betraying only a hint of a sheepish grin.

"Of course you are," Gary Mitchell said, giving him a sly wink. "Just be careful; she belongs to another man, and I hear Pike is the jealous type."

Kirk just laughed. Gary Mitchell was one of Jim Kirk's best friends at Starfleet Academy, a guy who was always ready with a smile or a joke, and always seemed to know when he'd most needed one. As cadets, they had hoped to be assigned after their respective graduations to the same posting, and Mitchell had made Kirk promise that, when he made captain, he'd take his friend along as first officer.

Those plans never quite panned out, though—in no small part because of one of Mitchell's "jokes," where he thought it would be funny to get Jim together with a pretty blond lab technician he'd met at an off-campus party. Jim ended up proposing to Carol Marcus, and while they honeymooned at Lake Armstrong, Gary shipped out on the *Republic*. Kirk didn't see him again until after the tragedy at Dimorus, though they both kept in close touch over the years.

"Well, now that the bulk of the repairs are done," Mitchell said, "maybe you'd be willing to tear yourself away from the old girl for a minute or two and let me buy you that drink I promised."

Kirk smiled wider at that suggestion. "Lead on, Macduff."

Mitchell led him out of the lounge, heading for his quarters. He still walked with a slight limp, a permanent aftereffect of the three poisonous darts the rat-creatures of Dimorus had hit him with years earlier. He'd actually been one of the lucky ones, having recovered well enough to return to active duty, even if he was no longer able to take a shipboard assignment. There were plenty of humans who didn't survive the attack at Dimorus—though the consolation was, even fewer rat-creatures survived the retaliatory counterattack.

"I still don't understand why you settled for another tour as XO, Jim," Mitchell said as they rode the turbolift to the residential section of Bozeman Station. "You could have had your own command right now if you hadn't."

Kirk shrugged. "I thought serving on the *Enterprise* under a man like Pike was the better career choice."

"Better than your own ship?" Mitchell continued to harangue

him. "Hell, Jim, the *Horizon* was yours for the taking, if you had just waited."

"Sure, and I would lie awake every night, worrying that the old rust bucket would end up falling apart around me." The entire *Daedalus* class was supposed to have been retired sixty years ago, and yet, there were more of them still flying than there were of any other class of ships.

"The old girls might not be as pretty as the younger ones, but they're a lot tougher and more reliable than anything Marvick and his Martian dilettantes have come up with. You've heard about their *Excelsior* Class Project?" Mitchell asked as the turbo-lift doors opened to let them off. "Nearly twice the size of the *Constitution*s, an upgraded warp system that doesn't actually exist yet, and they're not even planning to launch the first one for at least twenty years!"

Kirk couldn't help but chuckle. For a man who had never asked to supervise a team of starship engineers and technicians, his friend had certainly adopted the competitive spirit that pitted the team at Bozeman against the one at the newly established Utopia Planitia. "It sounds like you need this drink a lot more than I do."

Mitchell stopped at a gray cabin door with his name on the control plate beside it. "All I'm saying is, if you want to retire the old *Daedalus*es, then we need to build more *Soyuz*- and *Annapolis*-class ships, practical ships, instead of blowing resources on another white elephant." He punched a short code into the panel, opening his door. "Okay, the rest of my work rants stay out here in the corridor, I promise," he said, gesturing for Kirk to enter ahead of him.

Mitchell's quarters were huge—at least, compared to those Kirk had aboard the *Enterprise*. *One of the advantages of a non-shipboard posting,* he thought to himself. Two large transparent panes revealed the Earth below: the Rocky Mountains looked like a great sheet of crinkled paper painted brown, green, and white. To the east, in the middle of what from here looked like a completely unmarred plain, he could just make out the urban sprawl of Bozeman, Montana. Between the two windows stood a shelving unit holding a number of racquetball trophies and other mementos, as well as a collection of framed photographs.

"I've got a bottle here that I've been waiting for a good reason to crack open," Mitchell said as he moved into a kitchen/dining area off the main room. Kirk wasn't paying attention to him anymore, though—all his other thoughts had been driven off as he spotted one particular picture.

Carol was glowing. She smiled a huge smile at the camera, her right hand atop her head, holding the mortarboard in place, and her left hand gripping her hard-earned Ph.D. diploma. The loose black graduation gown she wore couldn't disguise the bulge of her seven-months-pregnant abdomen. Gary stood on one side of her, hand on her back, while Jim had his arm wrapped around her shoulder, kissing her cheek. Until the day David had been born, that day had been the proudest and happiest of her life. Little had she realized how few days she had left . . . and how few David would ever have . . .

"Jim, what . . . oh, damn." Mitchell moved up behind Kirk and saw what it was his friend held in his hands. "I'm sorry, Jim, I didn't realize . . . I've had these pictures up so long, I don't even see them anymore. I didn't mean to leave them here for you—"

"No, don't be sorry," Kirk said, blinking away the stinging he felt in his eyes. "I'm okay." He took a deep breath, put the picture back down, then turned and reached for one of the two glasses Mitchell held. "To old friends, and happier times."

Mitchell said nothing, but just nodded his head before pouring back his drink. Kirk did the same . . . and fought to swallow down the unfamiliar liquid. "Oh! Oh my . . ." he sputtered as it burned its way down his esophagus. "What the hell is this?"

"Saurian brandy."

"Saurian?" Kirk looked aghast at his friend. "Gary, this stuff is illegal! You know that!"

"Only to buy it or sell it," Mitchell said, grinning like a mischievous child. "For all you know, the bottle was left anonymously on my doorstep one night, with a tear-stained note begging me to take it in and give it a good home."

"Are you insane?" Kirk asked, thrusting his glass back at his host. "This stuff was never intended for human consumption!"

"Neither were Brussels sprouts, but Mom kept trying to make me eat 'em . . ."

"Gary, I'm not joking. You're a Starfleet officer. It's our job to defend the human race from alien outsiders, not—"

"Lighten up, Jim," Mitchell said, raising his voice to be heard over Jim's tirade. "We're not talking about a threat to national security; we're talking about *alcohol*. The same alcohol, the same chemical substance in Earth brandy, Earth whiskey, Earth whatever the hell else you want to talk about. Just because aliens make it and drink it doesn't make it a threat."

"Just because you don't see a threat doesn't mean there isn't one," Kirk shouted. "Have you been stuck in orbit so long you've forgotten what it's like out there, Gary? We face the threats out there so you don't have to face them here!"

Gary Mitchell's eyes went cold and hard as he glared back at his friend. "No, Jim. I have not forgotten," he said, his left hand rubbing at his thigh.

Kirk realized he had gone too far, and that he'd have to apologize eventually. But he was beyond caring just then. "Carol didn't think there was a threat, either," he said, his voice turning low and harsh.

Mitchell's earlier irritation suddenly fell away. "Jim—"

"She took the Vulcans' invitation at face value," Kirk continued. The Vulcan Science Academy had announced an interstellar symposium on the subject of molecular biology, and for the first time in decades, had welcomed a select number of human scientists to participate, including Doctor Carol Kirk. It was, she said, the opportunity of a lifetime, the chance for members of the scientific community to gather together for the free and open exchange of knowledge, without politics getting in the way.

Which all turned out to be a complete lie. The transport ship that had been hired to ferry the scientists to Vulcan was challenged as it crossed into I.C. territory. The Vulcan captain said she never received a response from the encroaching Earth ship, even though their distress call, after they came under fire, was picked up by subspace relays for light-years around, on both sides of the border. "Those Vulcan bastards murdered my wife and son," he growled, biting off each word with sharp teeth dripping with venom. "So forgive me if I seem a bit overcautious about what is and isn't a threat."

Mitchell sat still for a moment, saying nothing. Then he stood, limped back out to the kitchen, and returned shortly with two clean glasses and a bottle of amber liquid with a black label that clearly stated its point of origin as Lynchburg, Tennessee, Earth. "Thanks," Kirk whispered as Mitchell poured a glass for each of them.

"Don't thank me," Mitchell warned as he set the bottle down on the coffee table. "I take it you haven't heard the rumors about *Enterprise*'s next mission, have you?"

Kirk paused just as he was about to bring the whiskey to his lips. "No. What rumors?"

Mitchell shook his head. "Drink first. I think you're going to want a few in you before hearing this . . ."

4

Pike sighed in frustration. "Took me ten years to get that old chair the way I like it," he grumbled, shifting one way then the other in his new bridge's new center seat.

"I can check with the station supervisor, sir," Kirk said, "and see if they can still salvage it from the old—"

"I'm kidding, Number One," Pike told him. *Mostly,* he added to himself as he stood up. Both of his knees cracked loudly, and a small twinge went up his back. *You're getting old, Chris.* Maybe the new command seat wasn't such a bad thing; otherwise he might be tempted never to get up out of his chair again.

Pike nodded and took in one more look at his bridge. The forward viewscreen was larger, and the bulky comm units had been removed from his chair and the other stations, replaced with less obtrusive audio transceivers. Otherwise, it was identical to the original, right down to the dull gray bulkheads, doors, and rails. Pike had often wished there could be at least some bright colors, besides the console lights, to break up the monotony. But then, Starfleet wasn't meant to be a colorful organization, was it?

Another difference was the faces manning a number of stations. A young, dark-skinned woman—whose name escaped Pike at the moment—sat at communications, while the new science officer, a man named Masada, sat at the science station. Both tried not to notice their new CO's eyes on the backs of their heads as they ran through their tests of the new bridge's system. Masada was particularly discomfited, given that Pike had already upbraided him about the long ponytail he wore when he first reported aboard. He studied his boards intently as his right hand repeatedly ran over the now exposed back of his neck.

"Sir?"

Pike turned toward Chief Engineer Scott, who had been running his own diagnostics at the engineering station, and now stepped down into the center well. "Everything checks out at optimal levels," he said, handing the captain a data slate. "The Bozeman lads did a find job nursing the ole girl back to health."

Pike gave Scott a small grin as he scanned the report, unclipped the stylus, and made his mark at the bottom. "Thank you, Commander," he said, handing the device back.

"Captain?"

Pike turned to the melodic-voiced woman sitting at communications, holding one of the new wireless Feinberg receivers to her ear. "Yes, Lieutenant . . ." *Dammit, what was her name?*

The young lieutenant flashed him a lovely, forgiving smile. "Penda, sir."

Pike nodded quickly. "Sorry. Yes, Lieutenant Penda?"

"It's Admiral Komack at Starfleet Command," she informed him. "He says our guests are standing by and ready to be received."

"Acknowledged. Number One?" Pike gestured to Kirk, who fell in behind him as he headed for the turbolift. "Transporter room," he said as he gave the control wand a twist and the car started descending.

Christopher Pike had never been big on small talk, and that held especially true when it came to his subordinates. He could be sociable when the occasion called for it, and was downright gregarious when among friends. But with very few exceptions, he did not like to get close to his crew on a personal level. Still, the silence between himself and Kirk right now was grating on him somehow, and after a moment's hesitation, he asked, "Did you manage to get down to Iowa at all this week, Number One?"

Kirk blinked once before slowly turning his head. "I'm sorry, sir?"

"Iowa. Your brother and his family still live there, don't they?"

"Yes, sir, they do."

"And did you get a chance to visit?"

"Yes, sir, I did."

Realizing this stab at small talk was going even worse than normal, Pike just nodded and turned to stare again at the lift doors.

"They are all the family I have left, after all."

Pike winced at Kirk's cold tone. He hadn't wanted to pick at that scab. Kirk had been less than thrilled when Pike had confirmed the rumors he had heard about their upcoming mission. The captain could hardly blame him; it had only been six months since losing his wife and son. He had refused to take any leave at the time, dealing with his loss instead by throwing himself into his work. Until now, Pike had believed his first officer had been coping. He could only hope he'd somehow continue to do so.

The turbolift opened, and the two senior officers crossed the corridor into the transporter. "Mister al-Khaled," Pike prompted with a nod. The engineer at the transporter console nodded back, made the final setting adjustments, and slowly nudged the rematerialization sequencer to its full power. On the platform, three columns of tiny swirling lights shimmered and coalesced into solid, humanoid form. "Welcome aboard the *Enterprise*," the captain told the trio, though his eyes fixed on T'Pol, looking frail and, despite her alleged lack of emotion, nervous. "I'm Captain Christopher Pike."

The petite, dark-haired woman standing at T'Pol's right stepped down from the platform and marched directly up to Pike. "Ambassador Nancy Hedford, chief negotiator," she said, thrusting her right hand out and looking up at him as if challenging him to doubt her. Given that she looked barely twenty-five, Pike could see how that would be a common reaction she'd faced. "My colleague, Ambassador Garrett Tarses," she continued, indicating the tall, middle-aged gentleman still standing at T'Pol's side. "And I understand you've already made the acquaintance of Lady T'Pol of Vulcan."

Pike nodded in answer to Hedford, and then nodded again more deeply to the older woman. "It's a pleasure to see you again, ma'am, and I'm very glad you've agreed to join this mission."

T'Pol nodded back. "Captain," she said in a quiet tone that in no way sounded like the woman who had threatened him with an antique phaser a few days earlier.

Looking away, Pike gestured and said, "My first officer, Commander James Kirk." Kirk did not nod, did not speak, but simply stood stock-still, staring blankly at some point on the bulkhead behind the diplomatic party. And though his face was just as impassive as the Vulcan's, the emotions that Pike saw in his eyes were far, far darker ones. After a much too long silence engulfed the transporter room, Pike turned to the lieutenant behind the transporter console. "Mister al-Khaled, would you show our guests to the VIP quarters?"

"Yes, sir," the younger man said, moving forward to engage the visitors and leading them out.

Once the double doors slid shut behind T'Pol's slowly shuffling form, Pike turned on his first officer. "And just what was that, Number One?"

"Sir?" Kirk answered, feigning shock at the captain's harsh tone of voice.

"You're not happy about this mission. I understand that. However, I also don't care. I expect you, going forward, to comport yourself appropriately."

"I don't understand what I've done that's been inappropriate, sir."

"You don't play stupid very well, Commander," Pike snapped. Then he moderated his tone a bit as he said, "You're a good officer, Jim. You could be a good captain someday. But you cannot allow personal considerations to interfere with the performance of your duties."

Pike watched a storm of emotions play silently across Kirk's face, before he asked, "Permission to speak freely, sir?"

"Granted," Pike said with a nod.

"Sir, I understand we have to respect the chain of command. But, with respect, what you cavalierly refer to as my 'personal considerations' is the cold-blooded murder of a three-year-old child and his mother." Anger and pain seemed to roll off Kirk like waves of heat over the sands of the desert.

"And I can never know what you've been through," Pike admitted. "But we've all lost people to this cold war with the Coalition, Number One." Unbidden, the face of the last officer Pike had given the name "Number One" floated up in his memory, first as she was when she transferred to his command, an eager, handsome young officer . . . then as she was at the end, burned and disfigured, unable even to beg to be put out of her misery.

Pike willed the image away. "With any luck, this summit will help bring an end to all that, finally let us and the Vulcans bury the hatchet after two hundred years of suspicion and mistrust."

Kirk shook his head almost imperceptibly. "Captain, you can order me to hide my emotions. But you can't order me to get rid of them altogether; even if I could, I wouldn't. I'm a human being; I *need* my emotions. I *need* my pain."

Pike sighed. "If that's what I have to do, Number One . . . I'm ordering you to keep your personal feelings in check, and to comport yourself in a manner appropriate for an officer of your rank and station."

"Aye, sir," Kirk answered flatly, before marching out of the transporter room.

"This is going to be a fun trip," Pike muttered to himself as he watched the doors slide closed again.

★ ★ ★

"This is where they put the VIPs?" Ambassador Hedford sniffed as she took in the cabin to which she'd been assigned. "I'd hate to see where they put the insignificant peons."

"Then you'll want to avoid deck seventeen, ma'am."

Hedford turned toward the officer who had been assigned to escort her, standing just inside the cabin doorway. He kept a deadpan expression, but there was a glint of humor in his eye. "Thank you, Lieutenant. I'll be sure to remember that." She looked around the guest quarters again and sighed. The Foreign and Commonwealth Office normally employed its own fleet of warp yachts for ferrying diplomats to and from their various missions. In this instance, though, it was decided by people well above her pay grade that the symbolism of using the *Enterprise* outweighed all other considerations. She thought it was silly, but had given in to Minister Fox on the matter, thinking it a minor point.

That was before she'd boarded. "Oh, this won't do," she said, throwing her hands up and letting them fall at her sides. "There's not enough room for three people to meet and work together in here."

"There is an observation lounge at the end of this corridor, ma'am," the lieutenant said. "I can see that it's reserved for your exclusive use for the duration of your mission."

Hedford shrugged in response to that offer. "We'll need a secured subspace radio link back to Earth, and access terminals for each of us to the ship's library computers."

"Shouldn't be a problem, Ambassador. I'll see to it myself."

Hedford looked again to the dusky-skinned Starfleet officer, and saw he was openly smiling at her now. *Is he . . . flirting? With me?* A small part of her was appalled that any man who would willingly put on the ugly mustard-brown uniform of Earth's military forces would be attracted to her. The greater part, though, noticed his dark eyes and exotically handsome Middle Eastern features . . .

"Thank you, Lieutenant," she said curtly, and turned her back,

pretending to study the rest of her cabin until she heard the door
slide shut behind the lieutenant. She pushed down the tiny tinge
of regret she felt for her rude dismissal of the handsome young
officer. She was here to do a job, and she wasn't about to jeopardize that for trivial personal matters. For Prime Minister Winston
to have chosen her for such an important, historic mission was a
tremendous vote of confidence.

Only five years earlier, she'd been a junior administrator as-
signed to the Commonwealth Mission on Epsilon Canaris III.
One of humanity's most far-flung colonies, it had been consid-
ered a trouble spot since the end of the last century, when the
Canarans tried to declare themselves independent from United
Earth.

At first, the reaction from the homeworld was muted; these
were fellow human beings, after all, and no one wanted to be
the first to advocate clamping down on their freedoms. But then
the idea of independence started to spread, with small but vocal movements cropping up on a dozen colony worlds. Even the
Martian Colonies started agitating for a break away from the rest
of their neighbors in the Sol system.

Just as the Parliament started to openly worry what the end
effect would be if so many worlds, whose resources the United
Earth economy had become so dependent on in recent decades,
broke away from Earth, a violent demonstration erupted in the
Canaran capital between Earth loyalists and secessionists. Eleven
were killed, including one government official, which by itself
would have been enough of a black eye for the independence
movement. However, another of the dead activists was later discovered to have not been human. Starfleet troops were dispatched
to Epsilon Canaris, as well as the other colonies threatening se-
cession, to counter the alien-backed insurrection.

The Canaran independence movement wasn't entirely extinguished, though. Every decade or so, a new conspiracy theory
would crop up, accusing Starfleet Intelligence of planting the al-

tered alien "patsy" on Canaris, or else having the autopsy results falsified. But even if those far-fetched stories weren't widely believed, there still remained a solid undercurrent of disdain toward their distant rulers.

When Hedford had first arrived at Canaris, it was a world on the precipice of collapse. Because of its distance from Earth and proximity to Coalition and other alien trade routes, Canaris had become a major base for black market activity, so much so that the underground economy actually outpaced the planet's legitimate mining and agricultural industries. Her superiors at the Canaris mission devoted all their attention and energies toward stopping this illicit activity, while at the same time they failed to realize that the leaders of these black market cartels were laundering their credits by buying up legitimate businesses and infrastructure—as well as buying several legislators. Despite United Earth policy not to negotiate with criminals, Hedford approached the largest of these players and helped them negotiate a deal whereby they not only got to keep their legitimate assets, but let their other competing endeavors coexist in something resembling friendly competition. She also managed to find a few loopholes in the import-export laws that allowed such products as Andorian silk and Tallonian crystals to be traded legitimately.

Her superiors on Canaris tried to get her recalled back to Earth. Their superiors, however, saw the results of Hedford's approach, and instead recalled the rest of the team from the Canaris mission. They then decided to see what she might be able to accomplish at other trouble spots around the Commonwealth, to similar outcomes. And now here she was, entrusted with perhaps the most vital diplomatic challenge in Earth history—let alone her career.

Hedford unpacked her small bag, setting her clothes into the cabin's bureau of drawers, which rotated out from inside the room's wall—the limited space she had here was, she had to admit, efficiently utilized—and arranging her collection of data cards alongside her computer workstation. This assignment had come on such short notice—short notice to her, at least, though apparently it was something Carter Winston had wanted to do since coming to office—and she had so much to familiarize herself with. Not only did she plan to review the Compact of the Interstellar Coalition itself, but all of its antecedents, including the preliminary drafts of the charter of the would-be Coalition of Planets, and the transcripts of the doomed talks that took place in San Francisco in 2155. Tarses, a thirty-year veteran in the field of interstellar affairs, would help her with the task of combing through the kiloquads of documentation, while T'Pol . . . well, she wasn't quite sure what T'Pol was supposed to do, but she imagined her unique perspective would be of some value.

Hedford realized she should check on the ancient Vulcan woman in the cabin next door to hers. They had only gotten the chance to exchange traditional Vulcan greetings at the prime minister's residence in Geneva before they'd beamed up to the *Enterprise,* and the ambassador was looking forward to getting acquainted with her over the next several days. After all, this would be the first time she'd ever been at a negotiating table with an alien beside her, not just opposite.

Hedford stepped out into the corridor and pressed the signal tab beside T'Pol's door. She was greeted with silence, as she was the following two times she tried signaling. "Lady T'Pol?"

"In here, Ambassador." She turned toward Garrett Tarses's voice, seeing him in a doorway several meters down the corridor, in what she assumed was the observation lounge. Inside, she saw a comfortably large space—more than suitable to her needs, as the lieutenant had promised—with several floor-to-ceiling portals looking out onto the star-dotted sky. She was surprised to see they were in motion; as big as this ship was, she hadn't felt its engines power up, and it was only because she saw Luna growing larger as it slid across their view that she knew they were heading out of the Sol system.

And directly in front of the windows, her face mere centimeters from the transparency, T'Pol stood gazing out. Both Hedford and Tarses stayed back by the lounge doors, silently watching the alien woman, as she in turn watched the stars move toward them, seeming to stretch into long streaks as the ship broke the subspace barrier and exceeded the speed of light.

The silence lasted for a seemingly interminable time, and was broken by what sounded strangely like a sob. Hedford and Tarses looked at each other briefly, hesitated, and then Hedford said, in a near whisper, "Lady T'Pol?"

T'Pol dipped her head as she turned, avoiding the others' eyes. "One hundred and three years, two months, eighteen days," she said. "That is how long I have been in exile on Earth. I believed I would never see the stars like this again." Her voice was flat as she spoke, but it was impossible not to perceive the feeling behind her words.

Hedford turned to Tarses, who wore an expression of confusion and concern that she imagined mirrored her own. "Are you all right, ma'am?" she asked, turning back again.

"I . . . would ask for a moment of privacy," T'Pol answered, turning back toward the windows. Hedford could see the Vulcan's sand-brown robe and sun-darkened face reflecting in the transparency, and though she couldn't see details from her angle, she got the impression that the older woman had her bottom lip between her teeth, biting down in an effort to keep herself from crying.

Hedford and Tarses looked again at one another, and then did as T'Pol asked, stepping out into the corridor. "Vulcans aren't supposed to act like that, are they?" Hedford whispered, while making sure no Starfleet crew members were eavesdropping nearby. "Is she having some kind of breakdown?"

"I wouldn't call it a breakdown," Tarses answered. "I think she was just caught unaware by the degree of nostalgic feelings being back in space called up inside her." Tarses was the closest thing

United Earth had to a Vulcan expert, and he tried to sound confident and reassuring as he told Hedford, "I'm sure she'll be fine."

However, Hedford was aware that, for all his academic knowledge, his actual firsthand contact with the aliens was limited. "How can you be sure?"

To which Tarses simply said, "Because she's Vulcan."

Hedford drew a deep breath as she considered the situation. "You'd better be right," Hedford said, as she let her breath out in a sigh. "Because we're gambling a lot on this mission. If things don't go right, it could well be another century before we get another chance."

5

"*I* *wish I could have been there to see you off, Daddy.*"

Leonard McCoy smiled at his daughter's image on the small desktop screen and shook his head. "I know, darling. But frankly, you being there probably would have made it hard for me to leave. Besides, you shouldn't be skipping classes for foolishness like that, not in your first semester, anyhow."

"*Still,*" Joanna said, scrunching her face up in disappointment like a small child—which McCoy still had trouble believing she wasn't anymore. "*It must have been terrible for you, all those other families there to say good-bye, and you going aboard all alone.*"

McCoy chuckled. "Actually, it turns out that's more an invention of movies and holoplays, that crowd-at-the-boarding-pier scene. It was just like using any other transporter terminal."

"*Except you weren't just beaming from one city to another,*" Joanna said, her voice rising a bit as her eyes started to mist. "*You were leaving!* *You're going to be gone—*"

"Hey, hey, hey," McCoy tried to calm her from across billions of kilometers. "Come on, darling, you said you were going to be okay with this."

"*I am, Daddy, I swear I am,*" Joanna said, gripping the cuff of the Ole Miss sweatshirt she wore and wiping the sleeve over each eye. "*I'm just being stupid . . .*"

"No, you're not . . ." McCoy's heart was breaking for his daughter. It had been just the two of them for eighteen years, since her mother Jocelyn died only a month after giving birth.

It had been tough on McCoy, losing a wife and becoming a single parent, and at the same time establishing himself as a newly minted doctor. It had meant a lot of sacrifices, but it had all been worth it, and he and Joanna had been as close as any father and daughter could be. Though, being the father, he couldn't bring himself to tell her he also had gotten misty-eyed as he left Earth and his daughter behind.

"Don't worry, I'll get over it," she said, as if reading his mind. She forced an indulgent smile and said, *"I know how much you've wanted to do this, and how long."*

McCoy couldn't help but smile at that. He had indeed dreamt of traveling the galaxy since he was a boy, reading the junior adventure books about Zefram Cochrane and the early space boomers with a flashlight under the covers long after bedtime. With his daughter leaving the nest, now seemed the perfect opportunity to start living his dream.

"Besides, we can still talk to each other live like this. I just need to convince myself that you're really still home in Atlanta, and I'll be fine," she said with a giggle.

"That sounds like a good plan," McCoy told her, smiling as she seemed to get past her dark mood. Of course, he couldn't tell her that this would be the last live conversation they'd have for at least a week, until the *Enterprise* returned from Coalition space. He couldn't even tell her they were headed for the Coalition border in the first place; the first officer had made sure to impress upon him and the two dozen other fresh recruits joining the *Enterprise* the seriousness of sharing mission information with civilians, and the penalties for doing so.

They continued talking for several more minutes about nothing in particular, avoiding verboten topics, until McCoy was assured Joanna's stiff upper lip would hold. They eventually exchanged their last "love you's" and both signed off. McCoy checked the chronometer on his desk, and was confused for a moment before he remembered to subtract twelve from its military time readout. He realized it was well past his usual dinnertime, and his stomach, thus reminded, began to gurgle at him. He cast a brief glance at the unpacked cases stacked against the wall of his new office and, convinced that they weren't going anywhere, set off in search of the nearest mess hall.

After only a couple of wrong turns, McCoy found one of the ship's large communal rooms which served as mess, recreation room, and lounge. Only half the tables were occupied, and at one of them McCoy recognized the first officer, Commander Kirk. He was sitting with a group of three other officers, playing a game of chess with one as the other two watched. McCoy went over to the food slots on the far wall, ordered a fried chicken platter and milk, and took his tray over to Kirk's table. "Excuse me, Commander, mind if I join you?"

"Doctor!" Kirk looked up from the board and gave him a broad friendly grin. "By all means." As he took one of the empty chairs, the commander made introductions. "This is Lieutenant Commander Montgomery Scott, Lieutenant Lee Kelso, and Lieutenant John Stiles. Gentlemen, our new chief medical officer, Doctor Leonard McCoy."

Each of them smiled as they shook hands with McCoy, though Kelso's smile was fleeting; he was sitting across the chessboard from Kirk, and looked to be on his way to a thorough drubbing. McCoy gave him a sympathetic grin as he dug into his meal—which wasn't bad for resequenced protein, but sure wouldn't keep him from missing the genuine article—and fell into conversation with his new crewmates. They were all lifers, it turned out, with nearly fifty years combined service among them. Longer, if one took into account the fact that Stiles grew up a Starfleet brat, the latest in a long line of officers going back for generations.

Before long, Kelso gave a pitiful whine and tipped his king onto its side. "Someday, Jim, I'm going to be smart enough, when you challenge me to a game, to just say no."

Kirk smirked and turned to the rest of the table as he started resetting the white and black pieces into their starting positions. "Who's next? How about you, Doc? You play?"

McCoy lowered the nearly clean drumstick from his mouth. "I know *how* to play. I doubt I'd give you much of a game, though."

"I'll be the judge of that," Kirk answered as he gestured to Kelso to give up his seat, and for McCoy to take his place across the board from him. Figuring it wouldn't do to flat-out refuse such a request on his first day aboard, McCoy stood up, wiping his greasy fingers with a napkin as he moved to face the first officer.

It took all of five moves for Kirk to make his judgment. "You weren't just being modest, were you?" he observed as he captured a second of McCoy's black pieces.

"Afraid not," McCoy said, cautiously sliding one of his pawns forward. Kirk's hand darted out the second McCoy's fingers left the piece, moving one of his knights in position to take out the black queen. McCoy stared with all his might, but saw no way to change her majesty's fate.

"I'll have you checkmated in ten moves," Kirk declared after McCoy made his ineffectual move and the queen was snatched away. "Correction," he added, following McCoy's subsequent turn, "make that six."

McCoy shot a cross look at his tormentor, but managed to bite back the scathing comment that was on the tip of his tongue. He instead tried to maintain as much dignity as possible until Kirk finally announced, "Check and mate," and flashed him a cocky, utterly self-pleased grin.

McCoy turned to the three other officers watching. He was somewhat mollified when he noted their expressions seemed to be ones of sympathy toward him. "Does he always play such an irritating game of chess?" he asked, hiding his very real annoyance underneath a teasing tone.

Fortunately, Kirk took it as a good-humored jibe, which went a long way toward softening McCoy's current feelings toward him. "Sorry, Doctor," he said. "I know I tend to get a little caught up in the game. You'd just think, on a ship of four hundred and thirty crewmen, there'd be at least one other person to offer a challenge."

"Well, if a challenging chess opponent is what you want, maybe you could invite our honored guest to play a game or two."

Kirk's good-humored façade suddenly collapsed. "You're not suggesting what I think you are," he said in a low, cold tone.

McCoy was taken aback by this change in the first officer's demeanor. A smarter man might have resolved to extradite himself from that conversation right then and there. But not Leonard H. McCoy. "I don't know. What do you think I'm suggesting?"

"You're talking about the Vulcan."

McCoy nodded. "That's right."

"Hey, Doc," Stiles interrupted, putting a hand on McCoy's arm, "you might want to just drop it, okay?"

McCoy looked from one man to the other. "Well, now you've got me curious. What's so terrible about inviting Lady T'Pol to a friendly game of chess?"

"Friendly, my eye," Kirk spat. "Friendliness is an emotion. And if the last two hundred years have taught us anything, it's that trying to be friendly with Vulcans is a sucker's game."

"Really? Any Vulcan?" McCoy challenged. "Even one who left the High Command to join Starfleet in the wake of the Xindi attack? One who for years helped work for peace between Earth and the rest of the galaxy? One who, hell, married a human man . . ."

"That appeals to you, does it, Doc?" Stiles asked, with an expression close to disgust. "Sharing your bed with a cold-blooded, pointy-eared hobgoblin?"

"Actually, have you ever seen the old pictures of T'Pol from back in the day?" Kelso interjected, waggling his eyebrows and flashing a wolfish grin.

McCoy ignored that adolescent comment, and instead glared at Stiles. "You take a lot of pride in your family and your heritage, don't you, Mister Stiles? Well, I do too," he continued before the other man could do more than nod. "My family is from Georgia, going back at least twenty generations. I grew up in Atlanta, just a stone's throw from where Martin Luther King, Jr., gave his first sermon. Every schoolchild there learned about the history of that part of the world, warts and all, and how we finally learned to move beyond the attitudes that had been passed down from generation to generation—"

"Doctor," Kirk interrupted, "please. I understand where you're going with this, but you are making a specious analogy."

"Am I?" McCoy snapped. Again, a part of his brain warned that he should perhaps be a bit more judicious in how he spoke to a superior officer. But he knew he couldn't be, not on this particular topic. "What's the difference between judging a whole group of people because of the color of their skin, and judging them because of the planet they come from?"

"The difference is, Vulcans are not humans."

"Which is the same thing the Europeans said about Africans six hundred years ago to justify their actions."

"And they were wrong. But that doesn't change the fact that Vulcans and humans are completely different species."

McCoy cocked an eyebrow at Kirk. "Completely, huh? 'Cept for the ears, they look just like us. Their DNA is ninety-some percent the same as ours. They're intelligent, communicative, sentient. They have history, culture, philosophy, even a concept of a kind of soul and an afterlife. Exactly how much more similar would they need to be in order for you to regard them with something other than utter contempt?"

"You are out of line, Doctor," Commander Kirk snarled at him.

"Apologies, *sir,*" McCoy growled back. He stood up, and considered the four faces around the table looking up at him. Stiles glared at him through nasty narrowed eyes. Kelso seemed somewhat shocked that someone had stood up the way he did to the first officer, as did Scott, though McCoy thought he detected a bit of admiration from him for doing so.

And Kirk . . . well, he wasn't pleased with McCoy, by any means. But behind the aggravation that was plain on his face, the doctor thought he caught a flash of thoughtfulness in the younger man's eyes. "Thanks for the game," McCoy said as he made his exit, hoping his lecturing had had at least some small positive effect.

If not, well, it was going to be a long tour, that was for sure . . .

Garrett Tarses had not been happy when he was first informed that he would be playing only a supporting role in the mission to Babel, and less so when he had learned that the person he'd be supporting was Ambassador Nancy Hedford, Girl Diplomat.

Tarses had spent nineteen years in Starfleet Intelligence, ten of those at a covert listening post gathering and translating coded Vulcan communications, after which he then served another eleven years with the Foreign Office, establishing himself as United Earth's foremost expert on the Coalition, the Vulcans in particular. In contrast, Hedford had made her reputation in diplomatic circles early on, with an unconventional solution to the conflict then brewing between opposing factions on Epsilon Canaris III. Though most of the old guard within the Foreign Office dismissed her and her reckless use of "cowboy diplomacy," a number of observers—not least of all, philanthropist-cum-politician Carter Winston—recognized that she brought a new perspective to the old problems that had dogged United Earth and its Commonwealth Colonies for generations.

In the days since he first started working with Hedford, though—in particular, these intensive days on the *Enterprise* in preparation for the Babel Summit—Tarses found himself coming to admire the younger woman, not only for her intelligence and her understanding of interplanetary and interspecies politics, but also for her enthusiasm in the face of the challenges before them, her idealism, and her optimism about the eventual results of their efforts.

No matter how naïve that optimism was.

"What about Rigel?" Tarses asked her, as the last hours before their arrival at Babel started ticking down.

Hedford raised her heavy-lidded eyes from the three data slates that lay on the conference table, and blinked slowly at Tarses. "Rigel? What about Rigel?"

"You don't think the Coalition delegates are going to bring up the way we've dealt with the natives of the Rigel system?" he asked. For decades, Earth had supported the Rigelians of Rigel V in their efforts to dominate the turtle-like Chelons of Rigel IV for control of the system as a whole, in the name of security for the human mining interests that had been established on the system's outer worlds. This followed close to thirty years in which Earth had backed the Chelon government, until their citizens began to protest that humans were exerting too much influence in their affairs. In most recent years, the Rigelians and Chelons had decided to make peace and reassert their control over their shared system. Around that same time, United Earth had suddenly discovered the poor, oppressed Kaylar of Rigel VII, and threw their support behind their strikes against the two dominant Rigelian species. And all the while, dilithium continued to ship regularly from the Rigel mines back to Earth.

"Let them bring it up," Hedford said, as she lifted her coffee cup, frowned at the empty bottom, then got up to go to the food slots. "But this conference is about the future, not the past. Once we're a part of the I.C., with trading access to Coridan, Janus V, and the rest, we can afford to step back from the Rigel system and allow the Rigelians to step up. Besides, the Compact allows member worlds to deal with their own internal matters without outside interference."

" 'Internal' meaning on their own homeworlds," Tarses countered. "Not other conquered planets."

Hedford looked up at him questioningly. "Conquered planets?"

"Just anticipating what they're likely to say. Hell, you look at some of the precedents, and I wouldn't be surprised if the Coalition decided Mars was an oppressed world!" Tarses's grandfather had been one of the Human Loyalists back in '05 who had stood up to and eventually helped beat back the Declarationists who had wanted to make the Martian Colonies a free and sovereign world. He'd be damned if he'd let his sacrifice, and the sacrifices of so many like him, go for naught.

"You're getting ridiculous now," Hedford told him. "The Coalition won't interfere with our administration of any of our colonies, or any of our *conquered worlds,* end quote."

"And how can you sound so sure of that?" Tarses asked, as he silently debated how much more caffeine his system could handle. He finally decided to join Hedford in refilling his own cup. "Look at every other planet to have joined the I.C. over the last seventy years. Look at how thoroughly they've been integrated, to the point where they don't even have control of their own space forces anymore. All their authorities have been absorbed into Coalition Space Command."

Hedford shook her head as she took her seat again. "The majority of those new member worlds had only recently even achieved warp flight. By the time they got beyond their star systems, they found themselves already surrounded by the Coalition, and had little practical choice but to allow themselves to be assimilated.

"Your mistake, Garrett," Hedford continued as she sipped her coffee, "is that you're focused on the most recent precedents for newly joined worlds. If I thought Earth would be treated like another Rhaandaran or Grazer, I would have no part of this. No, the precedents I'm looking at are Vulcan, Andoria, and Tellar."

Tarses's eyes widened as he at last understood what the woman was driving at. "You're going back to the original compact. For the original Coalition of Planets."

Hedford gave him a small grin. "All the negotiations for Earth's alliance with the other three powers were hammered out a hundred and ten years ago, predating the renegotiations for the I.C. *That* should be our starting point."

Tarses grinned back at her, in spite of himself. *Dammit if the Girl Diplomat hasn't put another unexpected twist on the game.*

T'Pol sat in a corner of the conference room, ignored by the human diplomats. Earlier, she had been encouraged to contribute to the ambassadors' strategy meetings and share her opinions of their planned tactics, based on her experience. Hedford had quickly proven herself disinterested in her experience, dismissing her contributions as being "stuck in a twenty-second-century mindset."

"So, you gonna just sit here, let these two screw up Earth's last chance of fulfillin' the captain's dream?" the argumentative, distinctively accented voice in her mind asked. T'Pol understood, of course, that it was not in fact Trip Tucker speaking inside her head. However, from the start, her relationship with Trip had been characterized by their vigorous disagreements, and since his death, she had found that, when her thoughts were conflicted, her mind would take his voice for one side of the intellectual self-debate.

But T'Pol couldn't find it in herself to answer. Following Paxton's catastrophic attack on Starfleet Command, Archer was determined to make something good come from the deaths of those diplomats, and the innocent civilians who had also perished.

Including, he'd made a special point of telling her, Elizabeth.

For six years, the *Enterprise* shuttled from Vulcan to Andor to Tellar to Denobula to Coridan, often without the knowledge of his superiors in their newly reestablished Antwerp headquarters, trying to salvage as much of the Coalition of Planets as was possible. Much of it, though, was not possible, not without the official backing of the United Earth government. But Archer did not let that deter him; he refused to believe his world's rising tide of xenophobia was anything but a temporary situation, and that it was only a matter of time before cooler heads decided to continue on the path of progress toward closer relations with their interstellar neighbors. Even after the Isolationists took control of Parliament in 2161, and threatened him with charges of treason, Archer continued to hope for the future.

T'Pol wondered what Jonathan would make of Nancy Hedford, with her arrogance and sense of human exceptionalism. But he had been dead close to twenty years. Everyone she'd known was dead.

And so too, she thought, silently listening to Hedford and Tarses as the stars slid past the portal, were their dreams.

6

Babel was not, in fact, the actual name of the small Luna-type planetoid around which the *Enterprise* was now entering standard orbit. Technically, it had no name; Earth astronomers had given its star a numerical NGC designation, and their Vulcan, Andorian, and Tellarite counterparts had done the equivalent. "Babel" had actually been the code name for the conference the United Earth government had proposed between Andoria and Tellar back in 2154, taken from the Biblical story in which the peoples of Earth, all speaking a common language, had worked together to reach the heavens. Even after Earth withdrew from the interstellar community, the name somehow stuck.

Pike wondered if maybe the old universal translators the aliens used a century ago had misconstrued "Babel" as "babble," and that was why the name had such resonance. The idea that mockery of politicians might be a universal trait somehow boosted his hopes for interspecies cooperation.

"Captain, we're being hailed," Penda reported from her aft station.

"On-screen, Lieutenant."

She nodded, and a moment later, the image of a diminutive copper-skinned woman Pike recognized as an Ithenite appeared on the main viewscreen. "U.E.S.S. Enterprise, *this is Babel Orbital Control. On behalf of the Interstellar Coalition, welcome,*" she said, flashing a brilliant platinum-white smile.

"This is Captain Christopher Pike, and we are honored to be here," Pike answered with a slight nod.

"We are now transmitting orbital coordinates. Given the number of ships present, we ask for the safety and security of all that you maintain this position for the duration of the conference."

A low bleep sounded from the helm/navigation console. "Co-ordinates received, sir," Kirk confirmed. His tone and demeanor were completely professional, as they had been while on duty since Pike's dressing-down several days earlier. It helped, no doubt, that T'Pol and the diplomatic party had kept very much to themselves.

"Also," the Ithenite woman continued in her crisp, rehearsed manner, *"for the sake of security, transporter activity to and from the planet is restricted."*

"Understood," Pike said. "We have our shuttlecraft standing by."

"Excellent. Please be certain to alert Orbital Control before launching any smaller vessels, or if you require any other assistance during your time here."

Pike nodded again. "Thank you," he said, and pivoted in his chair, thinking that was the end of the spiel.

"And, Captain?" Pike turned back toward the screen, where the Ithenite woman seemed to be debating whether to speak aloud whatever unscripted thought had just occurred to her. Finally, she gave him a smaller, sincere grin and said, *"Welcome back,"* before ending the transmission.

"Welcome *back?*" Masada asked from the science station.

"I believe that sentiment was meant for humanity as a whole," Pike said, unable to suppress his own grin. "Lieutenant Penda, let Ambassador Hedford know we've reached orbit, and that she and her party should meet us at the shuttlebay at 1945 hours."

He took a quick glance at the chronometer in the arm of his chair and saw it was just past 1900 hours now. "Number One," he said, as he stood up from the command chair, his knees again protesting loudly. Kirk stood up from the helmsman's seat and turned, anticipating that he would now be taking the center chair, but Pike stepped right between the two. "Number One, you're going to be accompanying me planetside for the opening reception."

Had the captain announced to the bridge that he was a *mugato* and started beating his chest, Kirk still could not have looked more surprised. "Sir?"

"Full dress uniforms" was Pike's only reply.

"Sir, is it really wise for both the captain and first officer to leave the ship together?"

It was all Pike could do to keep from laughing out loud; in five years, Kirk had never once protested against joining him on a landing party. "We're holding in standard orbit at a peace conference. I trust Mister Kelso will have no trouble keeping everything running smoothly in our absence."

Something flashed behind Kirk's eyes, but the young man quickly tempered whatever untoward thoughts he might have had in that moment, and simply answered, "Aye, sir."

Half an hour later, the captain, wearing his olive-gray jacket trimmed with brown leather at the neck and along the shoulders and decorated with a starburst of triangular ribbons above his left breast, pressed the chime outside Kirk's cabin door.

The door slid open to reveal Kirk bare-chested, his own dress jacket draped over the back of his desk chair. His right foot was up on the seat of the chair as he applied a fresh coating of polish to his boot. When Kirk saw who it was visiting, he nearly stumbled trying to get both feet back on the deck and straighten up to attention. "At ease, Number One," Pike said, as the chair clattered backward onto the deck.

"I'm just about ready, sir," Kirk said as he righted the chair and brushed off the jacket.

"Plenty of time," Pike said as he noted, not for the first time, that the younger man wore almost as many ribbons on his dress uniform as he did himself, from such campaigns as the Third Battle of Axanar, the Taurus Reach Incursion, and the Alpha V Rebellion. "You're probably wondering why I decided to make you part of this," Pike said.

Kirk looked up at him, then turned away toward a mirror. "I didn't want to ask . . . ," he said as he finished dressing.

"You've made it clear these last few months that you intend to continue your career in Starfleet," Pike said, eliciting an uncomfortable look from Kirk. "But I need to know that you'll be able to do that, Jim. If this conference accomplishes what it's supposed to, it could change the very nature of our roles as Starfleet officers. And even if it doesn't . . . well, the reality is, space is not as wide as it used to be. We can't realistically expect to avoid dealing more and more with the Coalition, and we're going to have to deal with them professionally, as Starfleet officers."

Kirk met Pike's look directly. "I understand, sir." No promises, but also no show of any qualms. Pike saw that he did, indeed, understand what was potentially at stake here, and he was willing to see matters through to wherever they led. Pike nodded, gestured to the door, and the two men headed out for whatever faced them.

The *Halsey* descended toward the surface of Babel and landed on a small semicircular platform, one of five that ringed a large domed shuttle hangar. The moment the *Enterprise* shuttlecraft cut its engines, a set of large curved bulkheads slid into place around it, enclosing it in its own small dome.

As the area outside was repressurized, the two Starfleet security guards stood, checked to make sure their sidearms were in place, and moved to either side of the hatch at the shuttle's port side. "Captain Pike, I must again protest." Ambassador Hedford stood up from her seat toward the rear of the small craft and glared at the captain, who was seated at the front, beside the shuttle pilot.

"This is a peace conference. If armed guards are the first thing the other representatives see of the United Earth delegation—"

"And again, Miss Hedford," Pike responded wearily as he stood as well, "I am responsible for the lives of the people aboard this shuttle, and I will do what I feel needs to be done to protect you and the rest of them. As for anyone taking any notice of the guards, I suspect the attention of everyone on this planetoid will be directed elsewhere," he said, nodding to T'Pol.

She did her best to ignore them all as she pulled herself out of her seat. She found her heart rate accelerating beyond normal, and attempted to use one of her breathing techniques to slow it down. But, being in close quarters with half a dozen humans, she found she couldn't stand to inhale through her nose. She ended up instead holding her breath as she waited for the doors before her to open.

At last, the hatch unsealed with a hiss of equalizing air pressure, and the upper panels parted before her, revealing a wide, open bay. At the far end of the bay, a set of doors also opened, and for the first time in close to a century, T'Pol found herself faced by members of her own species.

There were two, male and female. The man was perhaps a hundred years of age, with thick eyebrows and dark hair just starting to show hints of gray. Accompanying him was a female wearing a simple blue gown with a jeweled IDIC pinned above her left breast. T'Pol was struck by how young she was—it was probable that she had not yet experienced her first *Pon farr*.

T'Pol thought her emotional control might have failed her at this moment, but instead, she found the mere presence of other Vulcan minds gave her a degree of strength she hadn't known for longer than she could remember. She filled her lungs with newly cycled oxygen and stepped out onto the lower hatchway door that now formed a bridge onto the shuttle's nacelle. The two other Vulcans approached, followed close behind by a pair of Andorians and a pair of Tellarites, forming a kind of reception line once the procession leaders stopped, a few meters away from the shuttle. T'Pol raised her left hand to the lead pair, and with not inconsiderable effort, spread her fingers into the traditional Vulcan salute.

"Peace and long life, T'Pol," answered the female Vulcan, returning the salute. The older male, though, said nothing, and kept both of his hands at his sides. He stared directly at T'Pol, but she could get no sense of what he was thinking.

The shuttle pilot moved up beside her, put a hand on her elbow, and helped her step down to the deck. The two ambassadors were the next to follow her out, and now the Vulcan man did raise his hand in salute. "Earth honors us with your presence," he told them. "I am Councillor Sarek, Vulcan representative to the Grand Council of the Interstellar Coalition." He then indicated the female. "My chief aide, Subcommander T'Pring."

"We are honored to be your guests," Hedford replied, making a valiant attempt at mirroring Sarek's hand gesture. She introduced herself and Tarses, and then Pike and Kirk. The Andorian and Tellarite contingents followed suit, but their names did not register with T'Pol. She nodded where appropriate, but her attention was focused on Sarek, who pointedly avoided looking back at her or acknowledging her presence in any way.

Such a reaction was not unanticipated. T'Pol had been a pariah in Vulcan society, to at least some degree, since the monastery on P'Jem was exposed as a covert listening post used to spy on what was then the Andorian Empire. Her decision to stay with the humans following the murder of Ambassador Soval and his fellow diplomats had no doubt intensified the negative regard in which much of her homeworld held her, and apparently persisted even now. All the same, she had to force back the urge to confront Sarek in the same way she had the hateful young human she'd encountered weeks earlier at Berkeley.

Once the introductions were completed, the senior Andorian representative bared his teeth at them all. "It is a great pleasure to have you join us here this day," he said in an awkward effort to affect a tone of human geniality. "If you will all please follow, we have prepared for you a traditional Earther welcoming rite: a reception *booph'ay.*"

The humans, including Pike's visibly discomfited first officer, reacted positively to this news. From their initial encounter with Zefram Cochrane following his first warp flight, Vulcans had noted the curious and seemingly innate need humans had to include food and drink in any type of social interaction. Councillor Sarek again took the lead among the Coalition delegates, ostensibly guiding the way to the reception hall. T'Pol, due to her slowed gait, fell to the rear end of the group as they made their way through a series of curving corridors, and quickly lost sight of Sarek. By the time they reached their destination, T'Pol realized that Sarek and his aide must have taken a detour at some point, as neither were present among the throng of alien envoys.

As members of the Interstellar Coalition's diplomatic corps surged forward, clamoring to welcome their guests of honor, T'Pol was struck again by the long-familiar feeling of being alone.

"How do you vote on the question of Earth's admittance, Vleb of Denobula?"

Ambassador Vleb gave the Tellarite a broad, elastic smile. "Vleb should suffice, seeing as there are no other Vlebs here. As to your question . . ." The Denobulan glanced sideways at Nancy Hedford, who stood watching the exchange in open fascination. "The vote will not be taken here, Ambassador Gav," he said as he turned back to his colleague. "My government's instructions will be heard in time, in chambers."

"No, you!" Gav pressed. "In council, your vote will carry others. I will know where you stand."

"You will know where I stand, Gav, just as soon as I know myself. Earth has not yet formally declared their petition to join, let alone presented their case or addressed whatever concerns the council and the individual delegates have. I will not prejudge the matter until I've heard from and considered all sides."

Gav grunted, clearly unsatisfied with this answer, as it gave him no opportunity to argue an opposing viewpoint. He looked down the top of his upraised snout at Hedford before turning on his heel (or whatever Tellarites turned on) and marching in the direction of the Zaldan delegation.

Vleb gave a soft sigh of relief, then turned to Hedford and said, "Don't let Gav's manner discourage you, Ambassador," he said.

"Oh, it doesn't," Hedford said. "I'm familiar with Tellarite argumentativeness."

Vleb's eyebrows rose in surprise. "Really? Are you?"

"Yes. From my research," she explained.

"Ah," the Denobulan said, turning to grab a glass of Enolian spice wine from a passing server. "Well, hopefully your research will prove to have adequately prepared you for the actual experience."

Hedford nodded in appreciation of this sentiment. "May I ask, Ambassador . . . Gav said your vote will carry others?"

"He did say that, yes," the Denobulan said with a soft chuckle. "Whether it's true or not, I have my doubts."

"I'm just . . . no offense, but why would your vote carry any more weight than anyone else's?"

Vleb smiled in bemusement. "I see your research has failed you in at least one regard, though I suppose it's not the kind of information that would have been easily accessible to you. You see, Ambassador, I am of the direct patriarchal line of one Doctor Phlox. His great-grandson, I believe you would say."

Hedford's eyes bulged wide. "You are?"

Vleb smiled and nodded. "Hm."

Hedford fell silent as she absorbed that. The Denobulan doctor, she recalled, had been a member of the Interspecies Medical Exchange before signing aboard Jonathan Archer's *Enterprise*. Unlike T'Pol, he had long relished the opportunity to interact with numerous species, and had eagerly joined the crew of the first warp five starship. But, in a reversal of their positions following the rise of Terra Prime, Phlox had regretfully decided to leave his human colleagues and return to Denobula. "I suppose he had quite a few stories when he returned home," she said, trying to keep her tone casual.

"Oh, yes. The ones I was always most fond of as a child were the ones about Porthos," Vleb said, with a nostalgic smile. "Denobulans don't keep pets, you know, but hearing Phlox's stories about Captain Archer's beloved beagle made me wish for a dog of my own."

Hedford smiled and nodded as Vleb related this story. Archer's love of dogs was legendary, and from the logs she'd read of the *Enterprise*'s officers, one would almost believe Porthos was just as much a member of the crew as any of the others.

"There was this one story in particular," Vleb continued. "Porthos had caught a nasty pathogen on the planet Kreetassa. Captain Archer was so aggrieved, he spent the entire night with Porthos in sickbay, obsessing over the poor animal. Meanwhile, the Kreetassans were demanding a ritual apology for a grave offense Porthos committed, but Archer refused. He was so upset about his animal that he was willing to endanger Earth's relations with this newly encountered alien race out of pure stubborn spite, until Phlox managed to get him to see sense."

Vleb shook his head in a bemused manner. "Fascinating, isn't it, how even the greatest of heroes can be so different from the way historians depict them, hmm?" Vleb chuckled again, while Hedford felt any hint of amusement being sapped out of her. Vleb must have noticed, and asked, "Are you feeling unwell, Ambassador?"

"No, I'm fine," she said quickly. "I just . . . I should mingle a bit more."

The Denobulan gave her another of his smiles. "Oh, yes, by all means. You should 'work the room,' as they say." Hedford was already several meters away as he finished that thought, and still moving.

The alien aimed his hors d'oeuvres directly between Christopher Pike's eyes. "All our engines were running at full reverse," he told the Starfleet captain, "and still, we were accelerating forward toward nothing. Well, since everything else in this void had seemed completely counterintuitive, I ordered engines full forward."

"And that moved you in reverse," Pike said, shaking his head in wonder.

"Exactly." Coalition Fleet Commander Ra-ghoratreii pulled the small cheese pastry backward, away from Pike's face, and popped it into his own mouth. "Or, at least, it slowed our forward motion enough for us to catch our breath," he continued, brushing the crumbs from his long white mustache, "and to investigate the specific physical laws of the region."

"Fascinating," Pike said, imagining what it must have been like to have made a discovery like that. Or like any that the tall, impressive-looking Efrosian had regaled him with over the past half hour.

"Oh, that's nothing compared to what we found at the center of the dark zone," the fleet commander said, snatching another topped cracker from a nearby table. "At the void's core, actually generating this null region around itself, was a single-celled organism."

"What? Like an amoeba, you mean?"

"Yes, but an amoeba big enough to swallow this entire planetoid."

"The hell you—" Pike blurted before stopping himself, realizing how undiplomatic that particular response was.

Ra-ghoratreii seemed not to take offense. "You disbelieve me," he said with a grin.

"Well," Pike answered sheepishly, "it does seem rather incredible."

"Well, of course it is! I'd probably think you a gullible *nivak* if you had taken such a thing on faith, without having seen it yourself," the Efrosian said with a wink.

"I wish I could," Pike said, with a trace of wistfulness in his voice.

"I'd share my visual logs with you if I could. However," the fleet commander continued, bitterness entering his tone, "my superiors have decided to classify the material."

"Oh? Why?"

Ra-ghoratreii shrugged. "Maybe the Grand Council thinks it will start to multiply and eat the entire galaxy. More likely, they have an even more ridiculous concern."

Pike grinned as he recognized a kindred spirit. "Tell me, what does 'Babel' mean to you . . . ?"

T'Pol had attracted a sizable crowd around her, all of whom were clearly fascinated by the only nonhuman among them ever to have visited Earth. "Why would you have stayed for so long, under such conditions?" asked the aide to the Ktarian ambassador.

" 'Why' is obvious, isn't it?" interjected the Caitian ambassador. "It was love."

"Love?" a Coridanite man scoffed. "You forget we're talking about a Vulcan?"

"Vulcans feel emotions; most only choose to suppress them." The Caitian turned directly toward T'Pol. "Isn't that true?"

Before she could demur from answering, a Rhaandarite official interjected, "Love is all well and good, but even the greatest love ever could hardly stand against the degree of hatred humans directed at non-Terrans during that period."

T'Pol found herself agreeing with the Rhaandarite. Terra Prime, rather than dying when Paxton did (having given up his hypocritical use of Rigelian gene therapy to counter his Taggart's

Syndrome while imprisoned, and thus making himself a martyr), only became stronger. Six years after the strike on San Francisco, Nathan Samuels was forced from office when the newly formed Isolationist Party won a plurality of seats in Parliament, and the draconian Extradition Acts were quickly enacted, barring even the most innocuous dealings between humans and nonhumans.

Phlox returned to his family, but since the death of T'Les, T'Pol's only family were the people she served with, and in particular, the father of her cloned child. And she did not care to leave him.

"So don't," Trip told her.

T'Pol showed him a completely emotionless mask. "If you are intent on returning to Earth with the captain"—which of course he was, and T'Pol would have insisted he do so if he wasn't—"then I have no other choice."

"Actually, you do," he said, and then, for some unfathomable reason, he kneeled in front of her. "Marry me, T'Pol."

T'Pol furrowed her brow. "Excuse me?"

"I've been studying up on this," Trip told her. "The Extradiction Acts don't say nothing about marriage. And United Earth law about marriage as it stands has a lot of antidiscrimination language in it, giving couples a whole lot of rights. A planet-sized loophole that says if we get married, they have to let us stay together."

T'Pol felt her breath quicken even as she continued to doubt this idea. "And who would perform this ceremony?"

"The captain."

T'Pol narrowed her eyes at him. "I was unaware Captain Archer was a justice or a clergyman."

"The captain of a ship in international waters—or interstellar space—can perform a marriage and have it be totally legit." At T'Pol's skeptical look, he added, "It's a tradition, from back to the days of the first wooden sailing vessels."

T'Pol considered the man before her—friend, confidant, frequent sparring partner, and partner in other pursuits. "You are not a lawyer, Trip. And even if your interpretation of the law is correct, I am not at all confident, given the current political climate on Earth, that the legal system would feel compelled to uphold my rights."

Trip sighed. "This scheme is a little harebrained, isn't it?"

T'Pol nodded slowly. "I believe so."

Trip dipped his head, then looked back up at her. "Marry me anyway."

". . . Lady T'Pol?"

She snapped out of her reverie and back to the present. "Excuse me," she said, quickly masking her embarrassment and other close-to-the-surface emotions, "what were you saying?"

"Why agree to join Commander Tucker on Earth at the worst time an offworlder could choose to do so?"

T'Pol flashed back to the look in Trip's eyes as he smiled and got off his knees to embrace her. "It seemed the logical thing to do."

"I don't know where you're getting these stories from," Tarses said, and drained the last of his martini. "Our partnership with the Halkans is a peaceful one, and one that is extremely beneficial to both sides."

"You mine their dilithium without their permission," Ambassador Shras of Andoria charged, baring his teeth.

"We have the permissions we need . . ."

"Not from the Halkan Council," piped in the Kazarite ambassador.

"No," Tarses allowed as he waved down a server and swapped his empty glass for a fresh one. "From the occupants of the land in question."

"So, you circumvent their rightful government," Shras said, "in the process violating their pacifist beliefs . . ."

"And we're to accept that the government can dictate the moral beliefs of all its citizens?" Tarses answered heatedly. Though he'd concentrated on the Vulcans for most of his career, he couldn't help but pick up a few things about the Andorians as well. They were a passionate people, as prone to violence as early humans had been—*not just* early *humans,* he admitted in the privacy of his own thoughts—and tended to appreciate when others expressed their passion. "Not every Halkan is as absolutist in their interpretation of ethics. Some understand that Earth wants peace, and that we depend on dilithium to maintain the peace—"

"Peace for Earth, you mean."

Tarses nodded emphatically. "Yes, peace for Earth, which extends to Halka, Canopus Planet, Benecia Colony, and all the rest of the worlds within our sphere. Unlike, I would add, Eminiar and Vendikar."

The Andorian's antennae went rigid at that comment; he was no doubt surprised by the human's knowledge of the Coalition's recent disastrous contact with those two worlds. "Watch yourself, Earther," he warned in a low tone. "You can hardly blame the Coalition for what, technically, is just the continuation of five centuries of bloodshed . . ."

"Five centuries," Tarses repeated. "How many billions does that total? And how many more billions will die because of the Coalition's policy of noninterference?"

The Andorian seethed silently for a moment before saying, "I cannot defend every policy of the Space Command. Just as I'm certain you wouldn't wish to be asked to defend the actions of Kodos on Tarsus IV."

Ah, now the gloves are off, Tarses thought to himself, secretly relishing the opportunity to knock the almighty Coalition down a peg or two. "Or the actions of Coalition commanders who refused to allow the Trill relief ships across the border."

Shras's retort to that was lost, however, as a deep, booming voice from the far end of the hall shouted, in flawless and untranslated English, "No! I don't . . . *Get away from me!*"

★ ★ ★

Commander Kirk stood with his back against a wall, glaring at the bald-headed Deltan ambassador, Arlia. Time seemed to freeze as everyone in the hall turned to stare at him in alarm—except for Arlia, who wore a look of sadistic amusement on her face. Time unstuck as Ambassador Hedford crossed the room and grabbed Kirk by the arm. "What is going on here?" she demanded through clenched teeth.

Kirk's mouth opened and closed, but no words formed. The smooth-scalped Deltan stepped up then and said, "A misunderstanding. It is my fault. Apologies to you, Commander," she said, looking not the slightest bit contrite. She gave him a wisp of a smile, and then turned and headed for the other side of the room.

The gazes of the crowd around him also turned quickly elsewhere. Once Hedford was convinced no one was minding them anymore, she leaned in close again and hissed, "Goddammit, Mister Kirk, what do you think you're doing?"

"I'm sorry, Ambassador," he muttered back. "I didn't mean . . ."

"No, I'm sure you didn't," she snapped angrily. "Now listen: this is my mission. You are here as support for that mission. If you cannot do that, then you can go and sit in the shuttle until it's time to return to the ship." Without waiting for him to reply, Hedford spun away, pretending to ignore the several stares aimed her way, while at the same time trying to decide which witnesses needed to be approached and assured this was atypical human behavior.

Kirk held back the urge to scowl at Hedford's backside as she walked away. Instead, he scowled at the bottom of his half-empty glass of bourbon, and at himself.

Kirk had never cared much for aliens. Almost nobody he knew of in Starfleet did; aliens were at best impediments to human use of the planets they lived on, and at worst . . . well, at worst, they ripped permanent scars across the Earth's crust, killing millions in the process. But ever since his chat with Doctor McCoy the other day, he'd forced himself to take a good hard look inside himself. And he had to admit, a lot of what he found bothered him.

One of his first missions out of the Academy was to a planet called Neural, where Starfleet had negotiated for mining rights. There, he was forced for the first time to interact directly with nonhumans, though Tyree and his fellow tribesmen were almost completely indistinguishable from humans. And still, despite the open, hospitable nature of the primitive cave-dwellers, Kirk had developed an instant aversion to them. Was McCoy right? Was he as wrong in his attitudes toward non-Terrans as those who opposed Doctor King? Or his own hero, Abraham Lincoln, a hundred years earlier?

When Pike ordered him to join the reception on Babel, he resolved to put his personal feelings aside. And he managed to handle himself rather well, if he did say so himself: he had a very cordial chat with the Catullan ambassador and one of the Tiburonian aides.

Then Ambassador Arlia approached him. Again, Kirk was very cordial toward the Deltan, which was made easier by her close resemblance to a human woman. A *very attractive* human woman, even without a single hair on her head—somehow, that only heightened her exotic beauty. They fell into a very easy and open conversation, and just being close to this woman, Kirk felt things stirring within him that had been missing and presumed dead for six months . . .

And then it all came back to him: not only Carol, who, he was ashamed to realize, he had actually momentarily forgotten, but also the knowledge that Deltans gave off especially strong pheromones, which were known to affect the brain chemistry of other species, leaving them defenseless. The alien flashed a seductive, predatory smile, and suggested showing him her suite of rooms where they might initiate "private negotiation," while she ran one fingertip lightly across the back of his hand . . .

"No!" he shouted at the inhuman alien, backing away, "I don't . . . *Get away from me!*"

Kirk sighed and drained the rest of his bourbon. He wondered if he had done any real damage to Hedford's mission here, to bring about some kind of unification between Earth and the Interstellar Coalition. He wondered then if he honestly cared . . .

"Commander Kirk."

Kirk turned, and stiffened when he saw the person who had addressed him: a Vulcan male in a formal slate-gray outfit. "Yes?" he said, trying mightily to keep his voice even.

"Please accompany me," the Vulcan said, then turned and started walking away before Kirk could even form the response, "What?"

The Vulcan stopped about five paces away, turned, and stared at Kirk, as if he were a dog expected to come to heel. Kirk's first instinct was to just stand there and ignore the pointy-eared demon. But as he looked away from the Vulcan, he found himself looking in the direction of Captain Pike, still chatting with the Efrosian captain, smiling and laughing. The captain's eyes found Kirk, and with that, he realized standing around doing nothing as he was would not pass muster. Warily, he moved after the Vulcan.

Kirk followed the alien out a service entrance in a dimly lit corner of the room, and then down a gleaming white corridor. The sounds of the reception hall faded, replaced with the clattering of plates and glasses and trays being set up in the kitchen area. Soon, even the sounds of the facility's staff grew fainter as Kirk was led farther into the building, around a couple of corners, and then through a set of doors into a large storage area. Rows of metal shelves piled with cases and cartons and barrels split the room into about six narrow aisles, with ill-placed ceiling lights casting shadows onto the green-tiled floor. Kirk guessed this was the conference hall's main pantry, though he didn't recognize any of the alien labels, or even the graphic depictions of the containers' contents.

His guide moved down one aisle, and just as Kirk was beginning to wonder if following him had been such a good idea after all, the doors clapped shut behind him. He turned with a start and threw both hands against the solidly secured exit. He slapped at the panel set in the wall to the side of the doors, and he was unsurprised when it did nothing. Then, he heard a pair of footsteps approach from behind, a bit slower and heavier than those of the Vulcan he'd followed. Kirk spun around again, and this time, was surprised.

The Vulcan councillor, Sarek, stopped at the edge of the room's shadows, holding his hands before him with just the fingertips touching, and nodded slightly. "Councillor," Kirk said, battling the crazed jumble of emotional reactions stirred up inside him.

"Commander James Tiberius Kirk," the Vulcan answered, in a tone that was as dry as the planet where its speaker originated.

"What is this all about?" Kirk demanded. "Sir?" he then amended.

Instead of answering, Sarek continued, "Born to Winona Kirk and George Samuel Kirk, in the city of Riverside on Earth, in the year 2233 of the Gregorian calendar. Commissioned as an officer of the United Earth Starfleet in the year 2254. Wed to Carol Marcus in the year 2255, and sired a son, David Samuel Kirk, in the year 2261. Widowed in the year 2264, when—"

"All right, you've done your research," Kirk said through clenched teeth. "May I ask why you find me fascinating enough not only to bring me here, but to memorize my biography?"

"—when the transport vessel *Galileo* was mistakenly destroyed by the *I.C.V. Vanik,* by Captain T'Prynn of Vulcan. Among the seven humans killed were your wife and your son."

Kirk had to bite the inside of his cheek to keep the tears at bay, refusing to be provoked into an undisciplined emotional display.

"I grieve with thee, Kirk."

"The hell you do!" Kirk spat back. "You don't even know the meaning of the word!" He knew he was finished right then and there, but he'd decided that he just didn't care. Goddamned Vulcans and their goddamned emotionless pro forma apologies, it just wasn't worth it. No matter what it meant to his career or the mission or Winston Carter or whoever, it just wasn't—

"You think that the loss of those we share our lives with doesn't affect us?" Sarek asked in a quiet voice. "It does. I too lost a wife as a young man, Kirk. Our son, though still living, rejected the Vulcan way and left our world—to where, I do not know. In my years, death has taken many I've known: family, colleagues, friends."

Kirk studied the alien with a suspicious eye. While Sarek kept his expression properly stoic, Kirk could hear the shift in tone that, if the other man weren't an alien, he would have interpreted as barely suppressed feeling hidden beneath his neutral words. "Friends?" Kirk repeated.

Sarek raised an eyebrow. "Certainly. One can regard an individual more favorably than others, even without an emotional aspect to the relationship. After all, is that not, in theory, what this current summit is about?"

Kirk decided not to comment on that. "You still haven't told me why you're so interested in me and my life story."

"Because, Commander, you and I are of a kind. I do not believe Earth should unite with the Interstellar Coalition any more than you do."

"Why don't you think there should be a union?"

"The Interstellar Coalition has always been a very loose union, which exists due almost solely to each member's support of Space Command, and its mission of providing them a strong common defense. There is a growing feeling among the Vulcan people that Space Command has exceeded its intended authority, much as the High Command had prior to the Syrrannite Reformation. They feel we should abandon the Coalition and strive to move closer to the peaceful path Surak laid out for us."

Kirk didn't understand Sarek's reference to the Syrannite Reformation, or the importance of a person with a name very similar to his own. Still, he got the unstated point. "You're not just talking about keeping Earth out of the Coalition," he said. "You want out yourself."

Sarek nodded. "A union with Earth—the world that initially brought the Vulcans, Andorians, and Tellarites together—will make the Coalition stronger than ever. It would make it politically impossible for Vulcan to secede. Especially given T'Pol's role in the matter. Ironically, she plays to the emotional reasons for a union."

"I still don't understand what this has to do with me."

"I need to speak to T'Pol," Sarek said. "Alone, without other ambassadors or diplomats listening. I ask your help in this, Commander. All I desire is to have the opportunity to make my case to her."

"I don't know . . ." Kirk said. He had far less love for the Coalition than Sarek apparently did, but what he was asking of him was to help undermine Earth's purpose in asking for this summit— essentially, an act of treason.

"What if I were to tell you, Mister Kirk, that by preventing this unification, you would in fact be saving Earth?"

"I'd be skeptical."

"Naturally," Sarek said with a nod. He turned and began to pace slowly. "The Klingon Empire is growing restive. Since their defeat at Donatu V, they have contented themselves with picking away at minor worlds beyond either of our territories, such as Khitomer, Mestiko, and Organia. But a new generation is coming of age on Qo'noS, young warriors longing to earn honor in combat. Their High Council has been pouring more and more resources into the Defense Force." He turned then to look at Kirk directly. "It is all but inevitable that they will launch a new offensive within the next five-point-four-three-seven years, either against the Interstellar Coalition, the Commonwealth worlds of United Earth, or, most likely, both."

Kirk shook his head in confusion. "Then, you're saying it makes no difference if Earth joins the Coalition or not, we're still as likely to be attacked."

"But as a member of the Coalition," Sarek reminded him, "your Starfleet would be under the direction of Coalition Space Command. Say the Klingons launched a two-pronged attack, one at Aldebaran Colony, a world of approximately twelve million, the other against Betelgeuse, one with over eight billion inhabitants. Which do you think will receive the bulk of the defensive effort?"

Kirk blanched at that thought. Of course, they would put their strongest defense around a highly populated member world. But, with a foothold on Aldebaran, it would be an easy matter for the Klingons to then move on to Deneva, Ivor Prime, and then Earth itself. "But . . . like you said, the Interstellar Coalition is supposed to serve the mutual needs of all its members. They couldn't just leave a world like Aldebaran defenseless."

"No. But they would not be able to defend it well. Except for the occasional Orion raid or other isolated incidents, the Coalition has been at peace for the past generation. Any war would be devastating. The only questions are whether your people can make the choice how to fight, and my people can be allowed to choose peace instead."

Before Kirk could offer any more counterarguments, Sarek pulled a bright green data card from the cuff of his jacket sleeve. "Here," he said, handing it to Kirk. "This has the time and the coordinates where I will meet you and T'Pol tomorrow, as well as the codes which will allow you to beam down without triggering any security alerts."

"Well, now, hold on," Kirk said, still holding the small plastic square out at arm's length. "I haven't said I'll help you yet."

"Tell her whatever you must to have her accompany you," Sarek said, ignoring Kirk's objection, "but speak to no one else of any of this."

Kirk started to repeat his protest, but was cut off by the oddly pitched hum of a non-Starfleet transporter beam. The Vulcan seemed to shift out of focus, then disappeared in a column of swirling energy. As soon as he was gone, the doors behind him opened with a swoosh, letting light from the corridor spill in.

Kirk hesitated for just a moment, trying to absorb everything he'd just heard and to sort through all the questions now swirling through his head, chief among them, what to do with this information the Vulcan representative had given him. He turned and headed back for the reception hall, determined to find some answers before making any decisions.

7

"Lieutenant Penda?"

Nyota Uhura muted her earpiece, but made certain she was still recording all the comm traffic to and from the Coalition vessels *Shallash* and *Kuvak* before turning in her seat. "Yes, Commander," she asked, looking up at the *Enterprise* first officer with wide, innocent eyes.

"Pulling double shifts so soon after your transfer?" Kirk asked, offering a small sympathetic grin.

Uhura—or rather, "Penda"—nodded and explained, "Lieutenant Palmer had some personal business she wanted to take care of." An easy half-truth, since everyone on a starship crew always had personal business that needed attending to, and never enough off-duty time to take care of it. However, it had been Uhura who offered to let the beta-shift communications officer have the evening off—ostensibly so that "Penda" might have the chance to "get better acquainted" with the handsome young relief helm officer. Palmer was happy enough to comply, and fortunately discreet in her brief knowing glances between "Penda" and Kevin Riley. Of course, Uhura had zero interest, romantic or otherwise, in the lieutenant; life in Starfleet Intelligence didn't allow for such indulgences, particularly not in her section.

"So," Kirk said, leaning his right hip against her console, "how are you enjoying your new assignment so far?"

"Just fine, sir," "Penda" answered with a smile, while behind that façade, Uhura silently snarled in annoyance. Who knew what kind of vital, time-sensitive information she could be missing while engaging in patient small talk with her supposed superior officer.

"I'm glad to hear that," Kirk said, flashing a boyishly winsome smile. The hell of being an attractive young female in the service, Uhura considered, was having to endure being chatted up by every self-styled charmer in uniform. At least Kirk wasn't as obnoxious as some others in their flirtation.

"Lieutenant . . ." Kirk said, hesitated, then continued, "I was . . . wondering if you . . . if I might ask . . . off the record, unofficially . . ."

"Sir?" she prompted. She wondered that someone with Kirk's looks would be so bad at this, before recalling that he was a recent widower, and likely just out of practice.

Kirk lowered his voice, leaned in almost imperceptibly, and said, "Wondered if you had picked up any recent chatter about the Klingons."

Uhura blinked. "Excuse me?" That was the absolute last question she had expected.

"I know a lot comes through your board," Kirk explained. "Things that don't necessarily make their way into Command reports and dispatches. I'm just curious if there's been any uptick in talk about the Empire?"

For the briefest of moments, Uhura felt a flash of disappointment that Kirk had not, in fact, been flirting with her. That disappeared as she wondered whether he was being candid about his reasons for asking her, or if he in fact knew who she really was and what her real mission was aboard *Enterprise*.

It only took a moment to decide that it didn't matter either way. "Well, I did just happen to notice the *Guadalcanal,* which has been on border patrol the last six months, has been sending a large number of transmissions back to Earth." Uhura knew that Kirk's security rating was high enough that he could access all except Captain Padway's classified logs. It wasn't generally a good

idea to give personnel outside of Intelligence access to raw un-
analyzed data like this, but if it let her get back to her work, Uhura
had no misgivings as she pulled a freshly encoded data card from
her console and handed it over to the commander.

"I appreciate your help, Miss Penda," Kirk said, grinning once
again before turning and ducking into the turbolift directly behind him.

The moment he was gone, Uhura turned back to her monitoring boards and keyed a new set of variables into her search parameters. Now, on top of everything else her superiors had expected
from her here at Babel, she needed to find out how the Klingons
figured into whatever had been discussed at the opening reception. She was looking at a lot more deep research work now.

Well, I guess I know what I'll be doing during gamma shift, she
thought to herself.

T'Pol watched as the candle flame guttered and drowned in its
surrounding lake of melted wax. She sighed and pushed herself
up off the deck, giving in to the realization that meditation was
not possible in her current mental state.

She could not understand why the reception had left her so
unsettled. Other than Sarek's snub, and some sort of altercation
involving Commander Kirk, the evening had gone relatively well.
Her impression from those she had spoken with was that a closer
and more friendly relationship with United Earth would, generally speaking, be a welcome development.

"But would that be a good thing?"

T'Pol took pause. *Of course it would,* she told the contrarian
voice. *It is the goal toward which we worked for so many years.*

*"Is it? From what I've gathered, Winston and Hedford and Tarses
aren't much interested in the captain's goals so much as their own."*

*They ultimately have the same goal: to partner with the other powers of
the galaxy . . .*

"Yeah, but not in the same spirit," Trip's voice said. *"Granted, you*

need people like them: the practical, political minds to deal with the nitty-gritty details. But the captain brought more than that to the table. Could he have convinced the Andorians and Vulcans to start talking in the first place if all he cared about was how it affected Earth? Where is Jonathan Archer's spirit, his dream, in any of this?"

Before she could formulate an answer to that self-posed question, her thoughts were disrupted by the sound of the door chime. T'Pol opened her eyes and glanced at a nearby chronometer, which read 0446 hours. The conference proper was not scheduled to begin for another four hours and fourteen minutes, and thus anyone directly involved should currently be asleep, and would have no reason to deprive her of the same. As this suggested an urgency on the part of whoever was on the other side of the door, T'Pol called out, "Come in," as she slowly and carefully pulled herself to her feet.

She was not surprised when she saw Commander Kirk enter the cabin. The first officer would be a logical choice to alert her to any type of shipboard emergency or similarly vital information. However, there was no suggestion of stress in the man's expression; or rather, the stress he did convey appeared to be anticipatory, rather than the result of something that had already happened. The two stared at each other for what seemed to be a very long and uncomfortable time.

Finally, Kirk said, "Miss T'Pol, I need to ask you to come with me."

T'Pol fought back the sudden surge of irrational fear she felt trying to overwhelm her. "Where?" she asked the young human.

"Down to the planet."

"Indeed?" she replied. "I assume, given your placid demeanor and the lack of any alerts, this is not a life-threatening emergency. And the absence of Ambassadors Hedford and Tarses leads me to question your intentions."

Kirk reacted with a prickly scowl and said, "Well, your logic is half correct, at least: we're not in a life-threatening emergency, no."

"Then I am curious as to what possible reason you would have to be here in the middle of ship's night, with the intent of removing me clandestinely from the ship."

"Councillor Sarek wants to speak with you, privately. He asked me to arrange for you to meet with him."

T'Pol cocked a single eyebrow at him. "I find that highly improbable."

"I honestly don't care if you find it probable or not. Now please, either come with me or—"

T'Pol did not care to find out what followed "or." Neither did she care to learn what the first officer had in mind for her down on the planetoid surface.

And so, she let out a moan and pitched forward.

Kirk instinctively put his arms out to catch her, no doubt believing the frail old Vulcan woman had succumbed to some debility or stress-induced shock. T'Pol steadied herself against his chest, took a couple of short breaths, and in an apparent effort to right herself, brought up her right hand and laid it on Kirk's shoulder, just where it began to curve up to his neck . . .

"Ouch," Kirk said quietly, taking hold of T'Pol's arms and in doing so, pulling her hand away. Were she human, she would have cursed her aged muscles and their inability to exert enough pressure on the junction of nerve cells to knock the younger, stronger man into unconsciousness.

"Are you okay?" Kirk asked, his hands still on her arms, holding on to her as if she might swoon again.

"Let go of me!" T'Pol rasped, straining to pull away. Kirk acquiesced, and T'Pol backed away across the stateroom until her back was to the bulkhead, eyeing him warily. Anger, fear, and frustration all welled up within her as it became clear she was at this man's mercy.

Kirk remained where he was, standing staring at the old woman. "I understand you don't trust me," he said quietly. "And given the way Sarek snubbed you, I doubt you trust him much, either. Since I don't much trust any of you, I guess we're all on even ground together."

"If this is supposed to be leading someplace, Commander," T'Pol said, "may I suggest a less circuitous path?"

"All of that aside . . . I am a Starfleet officer," Kirk said, pointedly. "I know you know what that means. And I give you my word, as an officer and a gentleman, that I have no hidden motives or sinister intentions here. I'm simply passing on a request that you come and listen."

T'Pol considered Kirk anew. She of course knew what it meant to be a Starfleet officer—or rather, what it meant to be one a lifetime ago. She also knew the significance of Kirk's vow, which harkened back to those days, and indeed to long naval tradition predating Starfleet by centuries. Finally, she pushed herself away from the wall, dipped her head slightly, and said, "Very well, Commander." Kirk returned the nod and gestured for her to precede him out of the cabin.

The gamma-shift transporter chief was caught off guard by their arrival. As beaming down to Babel was generally prohibited, he had been spending his quiet watch playing a colorfully animated game on a data slate. He was so abashed at having been caught at this by the first officer that he didn't even raise the slightest protest when Kirk handed him a data card and ordered the two of them beamed down to the encoded coordinates.

Moments later, T'Pol found herself in a dusty, warm, and dimly lit space, filled with a constant rhythmic thrumming and the scent of industrial lubricant. As her eyes adjusted, she realized she and Kirk had beamed into the Babel facility's physical plant, buried beneath the surface of the planetoid and housing its energy generators, air and water circulators and purifiers, and waste recyclers. Large pipes and conduits wound like jungle vines throughout the cavernous space, giving it the impression of a labyrinth, with her at the center.

"I appreciate your promptness, Commander." The voice came from a short distance ahead of them, though the echoing surfaces around them confused Kirk's less sensitive ears, causing him to whip his head wildly in all directions. Then the speaker emerged from behind a squat piece of machinery, faced T'Pol, and raised his left hand, fingers spread. "Live long and prosper, T'Pol of Vulcan." T'Pol returned the salute, but upon being addressed in such a way, found herself momentarily unable to speak.

Sarek lowered his hand and turned to the human. "You have proven yourself a friend of my people and our cause, Kirk. You have my gratitude." Kirk, too, seemed to have no response to his words. Sarek then said, "You may return to your ship now. I would speak with T'Pol alone."

Kirk seemed a little put off by this brusque dismissal, but he said nothing as he pulled a communicator from his hip pocket, spoke to the transporter operator, who had been instructed to stand by, and moments later disappeared in a swirl of sparkling energy.

Now alone, Sarek considered T'Pol silently, with an air of what, in a human, she would have termed exhilaration. "I must admit, I have often imagined meeting and speaking with the infamous T'Pol, whose actions sparked so much upheaval and debate on Vulcan. It is quite fascinating now to find those imaginings made a reality."

T'Pol fought to keep any hint of emotion from her voice as she said, "And yet, you forfeited all opportunity to do so yesterday evening."

He shook his head. "I had no interest in being one of the throng of curious admirers. It must have been quite agreeable to have been so enthusiastically received."

"Though not by any of my own people."

The man raised a surprised eyebrow at T'Pol's unveiled animosity. "You may have forgotten, in your long absence, how politics is waged on Vulcan. As one who helped bring down V'Las and the High Command, you know how much is kept hidden in such matters."

"Indeed, I am familiar with V'Las's methods," T'Pol said. "Just as I am familiar with the reforms T'Pau put in place once the extent of his mendacity and lies was discovered."

"Yet secrets do remain secret, usually for good cause."

"And lies?" T'Pol asked. "What good cause do you have for those?"

There was only the slightest tightening of muscles at the corners of the man's eyes. "What lies do you believe I have told?"

"Presenting yourself as Councillor Sarek, for one."

His reaction was restrained, but enough to tell T'Pol that her suspicion was correct. Vulcans were very low level telepaths, and T'Pol's own talents were never more than average. But she had received a specific mental impression of Sarek during their initial meeting. The sense she got of the man before her now, despite the physical resemblance, was different. At first she conjectured the difference was in the new openness he was now willing to show her, but she then realized that this mind was in fact more closed off than the councillor's had been.

The faux Vulcan shrugged as a smile slowly pulled at the corners of his mouth. "Ah, well. I should have preferred the fiction of a cordial encounter between fellow countrymen had persisted a bit longer, but no matter. Come," he said, reaching for T'Pol's elbow, "let's find someplace more comfortable to continue our conversation."

T'Pol tried to pull away and avoid the imposter's grasp, but the effort was futile. The heaviness of his grip sent a bolt of pain up her arm, and she was forced to accompany him through the maze of machinery. Through the pain and near irrepressible anger roiling up inside her, she asked, "Who are you?"

"My name is hardly of any importance" was the response. "Just know that, for the time being, you are an honored guest of the Romulan Star Empire."

* * *

Captain Pike's morning coffee went cold in the cup before him as he became more and more engrossed in his reading. He didn't do much recreational reading, but given the prime minister's personal recommendation, Pike decided to pick up John Gill's biography of Nathan Samuels. He was up to the section on Samuels's college years, following the death of his father, when he first joined Terra Prime, and then, only after being fully drawn into the group, began to realize the full extent of what they represented. It was a fascinating look at the mindset of the early twenty-second century, as Earth finally emerged from the Post-Atomic Horror with the help of the Vulcans, and then started to lash back at their benefactors.

Those who fail to remember history . . .

The captain was interrupted by an electronic whistle over the comm, followed by the voice of Lieutenant Ed Leslie: *"Bridge to Captain Pike."*

He put his slate down and tapped his comm panel. "Pike here."

"Captain, it seems T'Pol has gone missing."

"What?!"

"She wasn't in her cabin when Ambassador Hedford went to wake her this morning. I had security run a phase-one search of the ship, and they came up empty."

"What about internal sensors?" the captain asked. "She's the only Vulcan aboard; you should—"

"Already done so, sir," Leslie interrupted. *"Results were still negative."*

Pike's mind raced. How could a one-hundred-plus-year-old Vulcan woman simply disappear? "Could she have gone down to the planet already?"

"All shuttles are accounted for, and there's no record of any transporter activity."

Pike quickly drained his coffee and set it with the rest of his breakfast dishes for Yeoman Rhoodie to retrieve later. "Where are Hedford and Tarses?"

"Here on the bridge, sir."

"Good. I'm on my way," he said. "Get Number One and Scotty up there as well. Pike out."

The captain rushed out of his cabin and to the nearby turbolift. As his knuckles turned white from his death grip on the control wand, one question caromed around in his mind.

"Captain, how could something like this be allowed to happen?" Nancy Hedford's shrill voice cut across the bridge the moment the turbolift doors opened. Tarses, the more seasoned of the two diplomats, managed to keep the expression of his anger toward Pike nonverbal.

"I damned well intend to find out," Pike answered them both through his clenched jaw. He headed not for the command chair but for the aft port engineering station. He called up the most recent ship status report, and then the results of the Vulcan life-signs scan. "When was the last time anyone saw her?" he asked as he studied the readouts.

"Last night, after the reception," Hedford said. "We went straight from the shuttle bay to our own cabins."

"But she could have left her cabin sometime in the night?"

"We don't lock her in, if that's what you're getting at, Captain."

"It wasn't, but thanks for the reassurance." Pike studied the station screen before him and confirmed what Leslie had reported: there was no sign of a Vulcan biosignature anywhere on the ship. It was possible that she could be in one of the more heavily shielded sections of the engineering deck, where her life signs would be masked, though he couldn't conceive of any reason she would be there. All the same . . . "Leslie," Pike called. "I want a second search of engineering, concentrating on sections . . . 18-Y through 23-D. Tell them search subject may be incapacitated or . . ." Pike hesitated, then continued, ". . . otherwise unable to make herself found."

Pike heard Hedford gasp softly behind him. "Captain, you don't think . . . ?"

"I don't think anything just yet," the captain replied, "but I need to consider all possibilities."

The turbolift doors slid open again, this time delivering Kirk and Scott to the bridge. "Gentlemen," Pike said, standing up from the bridge station, "we have a situation. Lady T'Pol is missing, and may no longer be aboard *Enterprise*."

"Captain—" Number One said.

Pike continued talking right over him. "Scotty, I need you to tell me if some other ship used their transporter to abduct her off this ship."

"Dear heaven," the engineering chief said. "Do we know when this would've happened?"

"Between 2330 last night and—"

"She wasn't abducted."

Pike stopped in mid-thought and turned to Kirk. "Number One?"

"She's down on Babel," Kirk continued. "I escorted her myself."

"You did what?" Hedford shouted. "On whose authority?"

"My own," Kirk answered.

"Number One, you had better have a damned good explanation why—not to mention how—you smuggled our guest of honor off the ship in the middle of the night without letting anyone know about it."

"The Vulcan Councillor, Sarek, asked that T'Pol meet with him privately."

"Sarek approached you?" Hedford frowned. "I find that difficult to believe."

"Do you believe Commander Kirk is lying, Ambassador?" Pike asked pointedly. He too was more than surprised that Kirk and Sarek had spoken last night, let alone that he would have agreed to assist in arranging a meeting between the two Vulcans. If not for the lingering adrenaline from the perceived crisis situation still pumping through his system, Pike would have been quite proud of his first officer's ability to cooperate with the aliens he'd borne so much animosity toward.

"Of course not," Hedford said, in a tone that suggested she wouldn't at all put such a thing past Kirk. "But, as the leader of this mission, any such requests should have come through me or Ambassador Tarses. Councillor Sarek knows this."

"Councillor Sarek had his reasons for circumventing protocol," Kirk said.

"I'm sure he did," Tarses muttered.

Hedford pulled her glare from Kirk and fixed it on the communications officer. "Contact Councillor Sarek's suite on Babel. I want to hear this directly from him."

The lieutenant looked from Hedford to Pike, who was surprised to see it was the same newly transferred, dark-skinned woman who'd been there over twelve hours earlier. He gave her a nod, and she turned back to her board to fulfill Hedford's request. Moments later, she announced, "I have the councillor's aide, Subcommander T'Pring."

Hedford nodded curtly and turned expectantly toward the main viewscreen. Pike gave the lieutenant another gesture, then also turned to face the image of the young Vulcan woman. *"Captain. Ambassadors. Why do you wish to speak with the councillor only hours before the scheduled start of the formal session?"*

"Actually, we were wondering why the councillor needed to speak alone with T'Pol before the formal session," Pike said.

T'Pring's left eyebrow lifted. *"I cannot answer that question, as Councillor Sarek has no need to speak with T'Pol."*

Pike gave Kirk a sideways glance before again addressing T'Pring. "Where is T'Pol right now?"

"I would assume she is aboard your ship, Captain. Is that not the case?"

"No," Kirk blurted. "She's with Sarek."

T'Pring's eyes shifted to Kirk. *"That is a mistaken assertion."*

"No, it's not!" Kirk shot back. "I beamed down with her three hours ago. I left her with Sarek."

"You beamed down?" There was a subtle change in the Vulcan woman's voice. *"How did you do that without triggering the security alarms?"*

Pike turned to his first officer, also curious about that point. The commander didn't bat an eye as he responded, "Sarek gave me the bypass codes."

"That's quite impossible," a male voice responded, and Councillor Sarek, dressed in formal Vulcan diplomat's robes, moved into position beside T'Pring on the viewscreen. *"No members of the diplomatic parties have Babel Security's access codes."*

Kirk stared speechless for a second, and then muttered, "You double-crossing—"

Before he could finish his thought, Ambassador Tarses stepped forward. "Councillor, is T'Pol on Babel with you?"

"She is not," Sarek said. *"Nor did I request any special audience with her."*

"Captain Pike," T'Pring interjected, *"if your first officer claims to have breached Babel's security, it must be reported immediately."*

"I haven't breached anything!" Kirk exploded. "I was given the access codes by *that man.*"

"Indeed?" Sarek said, his left eyebrow twitching upward. Then he turned to T'Pring and said, *"When you make your report to Babel's security division, you should also report the suspected presence of an imposter."*

"Imposter?" Hedford asked.

"Certainly," Sarek answered. *"It would not be logical for Commander Kirk to continue to claim I provided him with security codes unless he was wholly convinced it was I who did so. And as I did not, it is most likely that another individual assumed my identity and was able to convince him thus."*

"No," Kirk whispered, not in denial, but in unwillingness to believe he had been so duped.

T'Pring gave Kirk a piercing glare. *"Perhaps we all look alike to you?"* she suggested.

Pike put both hands up in the air to stop things from going any further. "Councillor, Subcommander, I apologize for this . . . situation. We will contact Babel Security immediately, and hopefully have all of this resolved quickly."

"That would be the most preferable outcome," Sarek said, then nodded just before the transmission terminated on his end, leaving the view of the planetoid below them on-screen.

Pike stayed facing the screen, his back to the rest of the bridge as he took a long, deep breath, trying to maintain a hold on his temper. Behind him, Hedford and Tarses resumed their outraged harangues, berating Pike, Kirk, and the entire United Earth military for its incompetence. Finally, he spun around, and in a tone that silenced the rest of the bridge, said, "Mister Leslie, contact Babel Security Division. Inform them of our missing passenger, and of the suspected breach in their security. Mister Scott, get to the transporter room. Confirm whether the transporter was or wasn't used last night, and if it was, why that's not reflected in the ship's logs. Kirk—" he then said, fixing the first officer with a vicious glare, "with me."

Pike entered the turbolift, with Kirk a couple of hesitant steps behind him. "This is not the way I like to start my mornings, Number One," the captain said once the doors had slid closed. Kirk wisely kept silent as the car descended, and remained so as they reached deck three and moved to the privacy of Kirk's own cabin. "All right then," Pike said once they were inside and alone, "from the beginning: what is this story about Sarek and T'Pol?"

And Kirk told it all. The Vulcan aide and the secret assignation in the pantry. The Vulcan separatist movement and the threat of war with the Klingons. The late-night visit to T'Pol's quarters and Sarek's claim of friendship with him. "I swear on my eyes, sir, it was the same man we just talked to on the screen," Kirk insisted. "If it was an imposter, well, he was a better actor than Anton Karidian."

Pike paced the room slowly, avoiding having to look at the other man. "If I understand you correctly, Number One, your main reason for going along with any of this was your concern about war with the Klingons if these talks with the Coalition went forward."

"Yes, sir."

Pike then turned to face him directly. "And yet, you whispered not a word of this to me, to Hedford or Tarses. You just took it upon yourself to take T'Pol off this ship, handing her over to some stranger lurking in shadows . . ."

"Sir, I thought he—"

Pike slammed his palm on top of Kirk's desk. "It doesn't matter who you thought he was! Just because he called you 'friend' doesn't make him any less an unknown quantity! If T'Pol had accepted those override codes herself and snuck down to meet whoever, that would have been one thing. But we were charged with her safety. You were obligated to use an *over*abundance of caution. But because she's—" Pike cut himself off then, before the conversation veered in a direction he didn't really want it to go.

But Kirk knew where he had been going, and engaged all thrusters. "Because she's a Vulcan, sir?"

Pike considered his first officer, then nodded. "I have to believe that affected your judgment, yes." Pike recalled Phil Boyce's chiding speech to him, and quickly willed the old doctor's face away.

Kirk dropped his head and seemed to lose himself in thought. Pointedly, he did not make any denial. Pike waited, letting the man fully examine his conscience, before saying, "As of right now, you're relieved of duty, and confined to quarters until further notice."

Kirk's head snapped back up again. "Sir!"

"Dammit, Jim, do you understand the seriousness of what's happening?" Pike snapped back. "At best, we can expect that

Babel Security will demand your hide for compromising security during the biggest summit they've ever hosted. And if, God forbid, we find out your Sarek impersonator wanted to do more with T'Pol than just talk to her . . ." He let the rest of that supposition hang in the air over Kirk's head, before finally turning and leaving the cabin.

In the corridor, Pike paused to run a hand over his face, just as the comm whistled for attention again. *"Bridge to captain."*

With no small degree of dread, Pike moved to the nearest wall-mounted communicator. "Go ahead."

"Sir, Babel Security is shuttling a team up, requesting permission to come aboard and begin their investigation."

Pike's eyes clamped shut. "Yes, of course, permission granted. We will do everything we can to assist in this matter. Pike out."

The captain hit the disconnect switch on the panel entirely too hard before starting back for the bridge, wondering if there was any way he'd be able to salvage anything from this fiasco.

8

Subcommander T'Pring could not help but reflect that, had Councillor Sarek deigned to attend last night's reception, despite having deemed it "illogical," the current situation would not have come to pass. While T'Pring could understand the view that the informal event was frivolous and extraneous, it did at the very least offer the opportunity to learn more about the humans. Even if Sarek had wanted to avoid T'Pol (which he strongly denied, in a manner that, were he not her mentor and a most honored elder, would have been unconvincing), their presence would have averted the hoax being carried out against Commander Kirk.

"And what makes you so certain this Kirk is a victim rather than a perpetrator?" Colonel Tharlas, the Andorian officer in command of Babel Security for this summit, asked as they together examined the *Enterprise* transporter logs. The young human transporter operator had provided them with the data card Kirk claimed to have received from Sarek, which indeed contained Babel's security codes, as well as a subroutine that prevented the recording of the transport to the main computer. "This could have all been engineered by him, to create new mistrust between Earth and Vulcan."

"Perhaps," T'Pring admitted, "though he would have needed a confederate to obtain these codes for him; he's had no direct access to such information since the *Enterprise*'s arrival."

"We know Starfleet Intelligence has its spies and agents everywhere," Tharlas insisted. "Just recently, a human espionage agent was captured on Deneb V in possession of stolen specifications for a Vulcan fuel synthesizer."

"What happened?" asked the *Enterprise* captain, from the corner of the room where he had been unobtrusively watching the investigative team of technicians pore over his transporter equipment. He was clearly agitated, both by the presence of outsiders and by the situation as a whole, but he managed to keep a largely stoic mien that T'Pring thought impressive, for a human.

Tharlas's left antenna twitched as he looked over to the human. "Justice was served," he said simply.

"Justice is served only if the guilty are punished and the innocent spared." T'Pring closed the log file and plucked the data card from its slot. "And the evidence we have gathered thus far does support Commander Kirk's version of events."

"Evidence which he was most able of controlling," the Andorian said in a dismissive tone. "Any evidence we find at the beamdown site will be far more telling, I think."

"I concur," T'Pring said. Tharlas issued orders to his technicians, leaving one to finish the examination of the *Enterprise* transporter, while the rest packed their equipment and followed the chief to the shuttlebay. With Babel at heightened alert status, even security personnel were prohibited from using transporters, and so they all climbed back aboard the slightly cramped *Zabathu*-class shuttle. It wasn't until the entire team had boarded that T'Pring noticed Captain Pike had accompanied the group to the bay.

"I'm coming with you," the human declared once his presence was acknowledged.

Tharlas scowled. "I don't think so, Captain. We allowed you to be present in the transporter room as a courtesy. However—"

"A courtesy?" Pike said, in an unexpected burst of emotion. "To allow me to go where I please on my own ship?" Then, as suddenly as his ire had flared, it seemed just as quickly to burn away. "Colonel . . . Subcommander . . . Lady T'Pol is my responsibility, as are the actions of my first officer. I respect that this is your jurisdiction, and I promise to keep staying out of your way, but I need to be a part of this. Besides," he added, letting some hint of emotion pull at one corner of his mouth, "I don't think any of us want to create yet another interplanetary incident, when the summit hasn't even officially started yet."

Before Tharlas could refuse, T'Pring turned to him and added, "I agree. Additional diplomatic incidents are undesirable at this point."

Tharlas's antennae twitched in annoyance, but he realized arguing further would be pointless. They boarded and took their seats as the small craft began to power up. "I must admit, Captain," T'Pring said as the shuttlebay outside depressurized, "I am surprised by the degree of emotion you've shown in this matter."

Pike looked at her askance, then shrugged. "Well, I am only human."

T'Pring took a moment to consider that seemingly incongruous answer. "Pardon me, Captain, I believe my word choice was improper. I believe it more accurate to say I've been surprised by the degree of *passion* you've shown in this matter."

"How so?" Pike asked, turning his stoic face directly toward her.

"You are a longtime veteran of Starfleet service," she answered, "and have served as a starship commander for over ten Earth years. Only days ago, you attempted to violate Coalition territory and were briefly engaged in a standoff with a Coalition ship. I would not have expected such a person to express such a direct, personal concern for T'Pol, given what she represents."

Pike's eyes narrowed slightly in a show of confusion. "And what does she represent?"

"To you, the end of history. A significant alteration, if not the termination, of the life you are so familiar with."

The tiny beginnings of a smile cracked Pike's stoic mien. "You say that like it's a bad thing."

T'Pring raised a single eyebrow in reaction to that unexpected response. "Oh, don't get me wrong," Pike added, "I'm proud to be a Starfleet officer, and I'm proud to have served my world and my people all these years. But if you want to know what T'Pol represents for me . . . ?"

"I do," T'Pring confirmed.

"T'Pol to me represents the old Earth Starfleet, an organization that aspired to more than patrolling the borders and making sure our dilithium supplies were secure—when we were concerned with advancing the human race, not just maintaining the status quo."

"Despite the fact that she is not of the human race?" T'Pring asked.

Pike shrugged. "Not logical, is it?"

"I would not say that," T'Pring answered. "One does wonder how humanity might have advanced in the past century had your people . . . *our* peoples . . . continued to build upon the relationships T'Pol forged."

Pike considered that for a moment silently, then asked T'Pring, "So, what about you? What does this woman—whose relationship with humans was so important that she decided to leave your world and live on Earth—represent to Vulcan?"

T'Pring considered Pike, and wondered what his reaction would be if she were to offer the complete answer. "There is no consensus" is what she finally said instead.

After a short descent through the planetoid's negligible atmosphere, the shuttle landed, and the investigative team made its way through the complex to its subterranean levels. They reached a door that was labeled "Maintenance Personnel Only" in Vulcan and four other languages, and as soon as the team entered, Sublieutenant Loak, a young Tellarite technician, began sneezing loudly and violently. "There's definitely been some—graa-chhooo!—body in here recently. The dust is flying like—*graaa-cchhooo!*"

As Loak excused himself, the other team members pulled out

their hand sensors and multicorders, scanning for any indication of who had been there, and where they might have gone. "I'm picking up traces of residual transporter energy," Tharlas reported. "The signature matches that of the *Enterprise*'s system," he added, glaring accusingly at Pike.

"Curious," T'Pring said as she examined her own multicorder.

"What is?" Tharlas asked.

"We confirmed three transports on *Enterprise:* two disembarking, one boarding. The residual energy levels in this area would seem to indicate more transporter activity in and out than accounted for."

"Somebody else beamed in and out, then," Pike said.

T'Pring reconfirmed her readings before continuing, "The curious part is, as Tharlas stated, all the energy signals indicate the use of a Terran-design transporter system."

Pike's eyes widened slightly. "Which means another ship using a Terran transporter!"

T'Pring looked at Pike directly. "That is the logical conclusion."

"Colonel, Subcommander, come look at this."

Tharlas and T'Pring turned in the direction of Lieutenant Hyaud. "What is it?" the colonel asked as they approached the Bolian woman, with Pike close behind.

Hyaud answered by handing the Andorian her multicorder. His antennae snapped nearly straight up in surprise, then turned to T'Pring. "What do you make of this, Subcommander?" he asked, fixing her with a look that he had until now reserved exclusively for use on the humans.

She took the proffered device, awkwardly trying to operate both it and her own scanner. After a bit of juggling, she let her multicorder hang loose on its strap as she examined the top portion of the other's small screen. She noted what appeared to be highly magnified and rather unremarkable images of hair strands. It took a moment for T'Pring to understand the significance of this find, until her eyes went to the chemical analysis of the hairs.

"What is it?" Pike asked, peering over her shoulder.

"What appear to be strands of Vulcan head hair," T'Pring said carefully, "broken free of their follicles two to eight hours ago."

"T'Pol's?" Pike asked.

T'Pring shook her head. "Their pigmentation and relative strength indicate a younger individual, in the range of eighty to one hundred years."

Tharlas nodded as T'Pring made his case for him. "I am going to need to reinterview Councillor Sarek."

"I understand," T'Pring said, although she knew these hairs were not Sarek's. Nor were they, despite initial appearance, any Vulcan's, but she could not share that information with the Andorian. She handed the Andorian's multicorder back and took hers in hand again. She quickly broke the link she had established between the two devices, and confirmed that she had copied and transmitted all of Tharlas's data to the only people to whom she could entrust it, and all it entailed. Now, she could only hope they could use it to some advantage.

Captain Syvak emerged from his small private office and found himself the object of the rapt attention of every crew member present on the *Kuvak* bridge. On any of his seven previous commands this would not have been remarkable. But the *Kuvak,* as a diplomatic vessel in service to the Vulcan government, was exempt from Coalition Space Command's diversity requirements, and was crewed exclusively by natives of that single planet.

This meant Syvak had to be particularly mindful of his reaction to T'Pring's communiqué, and make certain he was in control of even the most subtle expression of his thoughts and worries as he faced his people.

They did not seem to have the same concerns, though—the curiosity was plain on each one of their faces as they awaited the latest news on the security breach on the planetoid below. "Mind your stations," the captain ordered, causing eyes to quickly shift away. *Undisciplined children,* Syvak thought to himself as he crossed to the science station and handed the sublieutenant currently on duty a blood-green data card. "Stonn, I require an analysis of these multicorder readings."

The younger man nodded as he took the card, and pulled the data up on his screen. "Portions of this message have been redacted," he declared, turning back to face the captain.

"They were irrelevant," Syvak said firmly, inadvertently allowing a tremor of annoyance to underlie his words. Stonn, no doubt, would have understood any redactions would have been made by Syvak himself, and thus, there was no logical reason for him to blurt out his observation aloud to the rest of the crew. "The data provided is sufficient for your purposes," the captain told him sharply. Stonn hesitated a fraction of a second before turning away and back to his task.

It was only his experience in commanding officers of a variety of differing species that enabled Syvak to tolerate this young man. Stonn was a mostly competent but mediocre scientist, and unmotivated as an officer, seemingly content to remain a sublieutenant until his term of service expired. He had been assigned to the *Kuvak* at the request of Councillor Sarek, though it was no secret that this had in fact come at the behest of the councillor's aide. Given her position, T'Pring could have her choice of consorts, and Syvak saw no logic in preferring Stonn over any other potential mate; and yet, for whatever reasons, she did.

Several minutes later, Stonn had compiled and translated T'Pring's multicorder data into a three-dimensional representation of the planetoid, with the Earth ship in orbit above it, and six lines, representing transporter beams, stretched upward from a single point on the planetoid. Three of those lines ran directly to the *Enterprise.*

Three others did not. Rather, they extended past the Earth

ship's starboard warp nacelle, through empty space, with no obvious end point.

"Curious," Stonn noted. "Were these transports initiated at the ground site?"

"Negative," Syvak answered as he studied the image. "All were initiated by orbital transport systems." The captain pondered the three anomalous beams a moment longer before saying, "Incorporate data from our sensor logs over the last six hours."

Stonn nodded and keyed in a new series of commands, incorporating the new data into his display. Now, the science station showed some sort of faint, ill-defined blur approximately nine hundred meters below the *Enterprise*'s position. All three of the mystery beams intersected this anomaly directly.

Syvak leaned in closer, but could not make anything more of the image than a hazy distortion. "Analysis, Sublieutenant?"

"Inconclusive," the younger man said. "It would appear to be a minor ionic disturbance in the magnetosphere. Perhaps a reflection of the Earth ship's warp engine emissions."

"Reflections, however, cannot initiate transporter beams," Syvak pointed out. "Can you refine the image?"

Stonn pressed a new series of buttons, and then shook his head. "My efforts are limited by the resolution of our aft sensor array."

Syvak nodded. The bulk of the *Sitar*-class starship's sensors, logically, were located on the forward section of the ship, and primarily directed ahead, with a smaller array mounted at the aft. The primary sensors could be redirected, but would be of limited effectiveness when targeted through or past the ship's massive warp coil ring.

"Perhaps we should alert the Earth ship," Stonn added. "They may see this only as a reflection as well, and may not be aware of the potential danger it could pose."

Syvak considered that, and was forced to reject it. Because if this reflection was what he suspected it to be, it would be disastrous for the Earthers to learn this two-thousand-year-old secret in this way. Instead, he turned toward the helm operator. "Lieutenant Sepek, slow our orbital velocity gradually to one-third of current level, and discreetly bring our main sensor array in line with that anomaly." Syvak lowered himself into the seat at the center of the bridge and fixed his concentration on the *Enterprise,* drawing nearer.

"I can't believe Jim would really do something like this."

Stiles lifted his head and looked up at Lee Kelso, who stood beside him at the end of the navigator's console. "Do what? None of us know what he did. Technically, he hasn't done anything. Innocent until proven guilty, right?"

"Well, we know he took T'Pol off the ship in the middle of the night," Kelso said. "We know now nobody knows where she is . . ." Kelso shook his head, not wanting to even consider the possible conclusions. Now his friend had been relieved of duty, and the captain was helping in the search for T'Pol on the surface, leaving him in command of the *Enterprise,* in the midst of what was starting to look like a mission gone completely to hell.

"Geez, Lee," Stiles said, turning back to his console, "I thought Jim was your friend."

"What?" Kelso replied, baffled by the accusation. "Of course he is."

"Then why does it sound like you're siding with the Vulcans?" Stiles challenged him. "Jim said he brought the old bag back to her people. They say he didn't, but when have you ever heard of a Vulcan who didn't lie?" He shrugged. "Far as I'm concerned, what he did should've been done a hundred years ago."

Kelso could think of nothing to say in response to that. He'd always known Stiles had strong opinions about aliens. His family had been ruined years before, when their cargo business went bankrupt in Earth's first big trade war with the Interstellar Coalition, and the grudge had been carried down father to son, generation to generation. But he rarely saw his friend in such a malicious mood as this. Kelso was no alien lover himself, but still, he found it hard to countenance the abduction and mistreatment of an old woman, no matter what her species.

Even if he had thought of a rejoinder, he wouldn't have had the opportunity to express it. "Lieutenant, there's something happening with the Vulcans' ship, the *Kuvak*," said Ed Leslie at the helm. "Their maneuvering thrusters have increased output by two hundred percent in the past two minutes."

Kelso's brow furrowed. Minimal thruster usage was needed to maintain position in orbit; the sudden jump could only mean they didn't intend to maintain it any longer. Kelso moved back toward the command chair and ordered, "Let's see them. Onscreen."

The image of the planetoid below them disappeared and was replaced by a view of the *Sitar*-class Interstellar Coalition vessel. With only the stars as reference points, it appeared to be holding perfectly still, but Kelso knew enough not to trust that perception. "Range?"

"Eleven point eight kilometers, and closing," Leslie answered.

"They're maneuvering toward us?" Kelso asked, seated just on the edge of the captain's chair.

"No," Leslie replied, "they're actually slowing their orbit— *we're* moving up closer behind *them*. But they're also assuming a higher orbit, making sure they're keeping at a comfortable distance."

"No such thing," Stiles muttered, barely audible to the rest of the bridge.

"Sir?"

Kelso turned to the new science officer. "Yes, Mister Masada?"

"Sir, you should know the *Sitar*-class has Type III phaser emitters on its ventral hull, set just forward of their warp coil ring. Once they're at a z-axis bearing of 0-9-1—"

"—they'll have a clear shot," Stiles said, finishing the thought.

"They're not going to fire on us at a peace conference!" Kelso said, though he wondered exactly how firmly he believed that.

"If they wanted us to hand Jim over to them, they would," Stiles said. "Threaten to, at least."

"You're being paranoid," Kelso said, even as his heart started racing a little faster.

"Sir, z-axis bearing is 0-8-0 now," Masada reported.

Stiles turned around in his seat to look directly at Kelso, and paranoid or not, his eyes showed genuine worry. "Lee . . ."

Kelso had often wondered, since first being assigned to the bridge crew, how he might deal with a crisis situation while in command of the ship. He wasn't pleased to realize that seconds were ticking by and he had yet to issue any kind of order. "Yellow Alert, raise shields," he finally said, after what seemed to him like an eternity. He considered raising the captain and informing him of the situation, but the situation was that the *Kuvak* was slightly shifting its position in orbit, without making any overtly hostile moves. Already, he was wondering if Yellow Alert wasn't an overreaction, and what a panicky fool he'd look like if all this turned out to be was—

"Bearing 0-8-7 . . ." Masada reported. "0-8-8 . . ."

And then, without warning, blue light flashed on the viewscreen, in the form of twin energy beams blasting from the *Kuvak*'s weapons array.

As the Vulcan ship drifted closer, the *Enterprise* misinterpreted their actions and raised its defensive screens.

A part of Syvak's mind admitted that, not having been informed of his intentions, the humans were behaving completely logically in taking this defensive precaution. He quickly dismissed that thought, however, in light of the fact that humans had always been irrationally defensive toward Vulcans and other non-Terrans; assuring them of one's nonhostile intentions would do nothing to change that.

"We have reached position, Captain," Sepek reported from the helm.

Syvak nodded, rose, and returned to the science station beside Stonn. "Any difference in readings?"

"Yes, sir," Stonn replied, his voice rising a bit more than was seemly. From the closer range and with the superior sensors, the faint cloud of ions was resolved into a solid, symmetrical object. "It is a ship," the younger man opined. It appeared generally disk-shaped, with two clearly identifiable warp nacelles held away on opposite sides from the main hull.

Syvak was about to ask if the image resolution could be refined any further. Before he could, though, the image cleared of its own accord. The ship became fully visible, as did the markings on the hull—the same image that flew above those who marched against Surak at Mount Seleya . . .

"Weapons!" Syvak shouted, forgetting all his training. "Quickly, bring all weapons to bear on that ship! Now!"

The Vulcan shot missed by only meters. Kelso sprung out of his chair and shouted, "Return fire!"

A violent volley of high-power phaser beams lanced out from *Enterprise*'s dorsal emitters, pounding the shields around the Vulcan ship. They shimmered visibly around the vessel, and then flared out of existence. Seconds later, a single photon torpedo homed in on the target, striking the primary hull dead-center. The giant ring encircling the Vulcan ship seemed to fill with fire as the warp plasma inside the coils glowed with the brilliant energy of an unregulated matter/antimatter reaction. In a matter of milliseconds, those energies filled the ship's entire volume, then burst through the exterior hull, leaving nothing of the *Kuvak* but an expanding cloud of radiation and shrapnel.

"Holy shit . . ." Kelso's mouth hung open as he watched the fire in space quickly burn itself out. His brain threatened to snap shut at the enormity of what had just happened, but he was in command, and he knew he didn't have that luxury. "Stiles, I didn't order photon torpedoes!"

"That was no photon torpedo, sir," the navigation officer answered in a tone of bewilderment, then turned to face him. "And we didn't fire it."

"Then who—?" Kelso began to ask, and then stopped as something new appeared on the forward viewscreen. Though it did not in fact fully appear, but presented itself as an opaque specter of a curved metal-gray ship's bow, rising up from the bottom of the screen, somehow wavering just on the edge of existence. As more of the object came into view, the head and outstretched wings of a great bird of prey were revealed painted on its ventral hull. "What is that?" Kelso asked.

"I don't know," Stiles said, "but I'm pretty sure that's who fired the last shot at the *Kuvak.*"

The image of ship wavered and faded almost completely into transparency as it accelerated past the *Enterprise,* heading out of orbit and into space.

"Lieutenant Kelso!"

Kelso spun toward the new communications officer, who winced as she pulled a small wireless receiver from her ear. Kelso noticed that practically every light on the console behind her was either lit up or blinking madly. "We're being hailed by Babel Central and half the ships in orbit," Penda reported, "demanding to know what's happened. We're also getting demands—"

"Sir!" Leslie interrupted. "Five—six Coalition cruisers are closing on us, weapons running hot!"

"— for our immediate surrender," Penda finished.

As Tharlas's forensics team reached the end of their directory of tests, the Andorian colonel returned to where T'Pring stood watching. "Subcommander," he said, his antennae pointing accusingly at her, "you had attested earlier that no members of the Vulcan diplomatic contingent were absent from the ambassadorial suite during the period in question. Do you wish to amend that statement?"

"No," T'Pring said, holding herself up straight. "It is an accurate statement."

"In spite of this new evidence?"

"The evidence is circumstantial," she said, even though the Romulan hair they'd found in fact exonerated Sarek. She would have preferred not to have allowed the cloud of suspicion to remain over the councillor—Sarek had been a generous benefactor to her for many years, and she owed him much. But as much as it pained her to be so circumspect, she could not reveal all the facts to these individuals, not just now. "While it appears to suggest the presence of another Vulcan—"

T'Pring suddenly stopped talking, interrupted by the death screams of one hundred and forty-seven Vulcan minds. They cried out inside her head as their ship burned around them, loosed *katras* trying to touch another mind—any mind—except for a single one looking specifically for her . . .

"Stonn!"

Before Tharlas could ask what that meant, the shrill blaring of a klaxon filled every corner of the utilities room. The colonel, his antennae pressed flat to his scalp, pulled a communicator from a holster on his hip and shouted above the din, "Tharlas to Central! What's going on?!"

"Code Four!" the voice on the other connection shouted back, giving the call sign for a threat in planetary orbit. *"The* Enterprise *has just fired on the* I.C.V. Kuvak!"

"No . . ." Captain Pike whispered, his face a picture of disbelief and horror.

Almost as if in response, the voice on the speaker continued, *"No . . . it's been destroyed! The Earthers destroyed the* Kuvak!"

Pike turned to T'Pring, as if to plead his innocence, but he had no other words. T'Pring had to push back hard against a surge of fury toward the human, calling on all her logic to remind herself that he could not be responsible for Stonn's death. Stonn's commitment to Space Command would have been over in just three more years, and then they would have been together. Except now they would not . . .

She secured her emotions back behind the suppressing barriers of her mind, to be dealt with at the appropriate time, and refocused on the situation at hand. Pike had turned away from her and shifted his gaze to the other members of Tharlas's investigative team. He found no more sympathy from any of the non-Vulcans gathered than he had from her. "There has to be a mistake," he said, as much to himself as to any of the individuals now glowering at him, betraying emotions that ranged from mistrust to murderous rage. Pike reached for his communicator in his right hip pocket . . .

. . . and collapsed in mid-motion, as a phaser beam struck him between the shoulder blades. "Human filth!" Pike's Zaranite assailant shouted through her fluorine breather. A Betazoid technician quickly restrained her, as T'Pring dropped to her knees to check on the stunned human.

He had apparently bitten his tongue when he hit the floor, and his strangely miscolored blood flowed freely from his mouth. A large reddening welt just below his hairline suggested additional traumatic cranial injuries. His breathing was shallow, and his pulse was nearly nonexistent, though for all she knew, sixty beats per minute could be a perfectly normal heart rate for his species. He was, however, unconscious—very deeply so, she determined with a quick brush of her fingertips across his temple.

Around her, Tharlas and his people were shouting at each other, emotion building on emotion like layers of lava and ash building a volcano. Amid this cacophony, she heard the electronic chirp of Pike's communicator. She reached over his body, pulled it from his pocket, and lifted the hinged grille cover. "*Enterprise to Captain Pike!*" a female voice called. "*Come in, Captain Pike!*"

What T'Pring did next would certainly be deemed illogical by Sarek and the rest of her superiors. However, in the brief time she had spent with Christopher Pike, she had determined that ensuring his continued existence was in fact a most logical objective. *"Enterprise,* your captain has been injured," T'Pring said into the transceiver. "Beam both him and myself aboard." She hesitated imperceptibly before adding, "Code *V'Shar, kef-yet keh-kuh steh-kuh."*

The ceiling above Kirk's bunk was far from the most interesting feature of his quarters, but that's where he fixed his attention for the bulk of his time in confinement. He felt exhausted—he'd gotten little if any sleep since his encounter at the reception, what with all that followed—but his mind was unwilling to shut down, going over and over the events of the last twelve hours.

Damned Vulcans, he thought over and over. First they took his wife and his son from him, and now they'd ended his career. He'd probably end up spending the rest of his life in Leavenworth because of some pointy-eared con man . . .

Stop that, he told himself, angered by how pitiful those thoughts sounded inside his head. Jim Kirk had never thought of himself as a victim of fate. He'd never believed there was such a thing as a no-win scenario, but rather, that there were always choices he could make. Loath as he was to admit it, he couldn't place all the blame on the Vulcans. He'd made his choices, as the captain said, based on his prejudices. And he would be made to pay for his choices.

Kirk was jarred out of his contemplative state by the blaring of the Red Alert siren. He bolted out of his bed and instinctively started for the door before stopping and reminding himself how he came to be in his quarters to begin with. He stood there in the middle of the room for a moment, feeling ridiculous, useless. He moved to his desk and hit an embedded power control button. "Computer."

The machine chattered to life and replied: *"Working."*

"Computer, what's happening?"

More chattering. *"Please specify."*

Kirk frowned. The *Enterprise* computer was not always very helpful unless one asked very focused questions. Rather than taking the time to try to rephrase his initial query, Kirk instead asked, "Is Captain Pike back aboard?"

"Negative."

"Then who's in command?"

"Lieutenant Lee Kelso."

Kirk grimaced. Lee was a good guy, but he tended to get a little nervous in crisis situations. Kirk switched off the computer interface and hesitated. Having been confined to quarters by his commanding officer, he was under a moral obligation to obey that order and stay put. At the same time, he was obligated not to blindly adhere to orders when doing so could put his ship and crewmates at risk.

A moment later, Kirk was in the turbolift, his knuckles white from his grip on the control throttle. After the slowest ride Kirk could remember, the turbolift doors opened onto the bridge.

"— and prepare to be boarded, or we will be forced to fire on you!"

Kirk stopped on the threshold of the turbolift as the image of the Coalition fleet commander from the reception—Rawgor-something-or-other—glared from the main viewscreen down at Lee Kelso. To his credit, Lee held himself steady and firmly answered, "We are not responsible for the destruction of your ship. The attackers have already left orbit—"

"Enough of your 'invisible ship,' Enterprise!" the alien shouted back. *"You have sixty seconds to comply!"* The wild-haired captain disappeared from the screen, replaced with the image of two *Gral*-class ships targeting them.

"Sir, we have a response on the captain's frequency," Lieutenant Penda called out as soon as the ship-to-ship signal was broken. "But it's not the captain."

Lee called back over his shoulder, unable to tear his eyes from the threat bearing down on them. "On speaker, Lieutenant."

"*. . . captain has been injured. Beam both him and myself aboard. Code* V'Shar, kef-yet keh-kuh steh-kuh."

Kirk noticed the communications officer's eyes go wide at hearing that. "What? What's it mean?"

The young woman looked up at Kirk and hesitated. Kirk practically lunged at her, grasping both of her shoulders. "Lieutenant?!"

"*'V'Shar'* is the Vulcan Security Directorate," she blurted. "The code is security override for Babel's transporter screen." She grimaced, almost as if surrendering that bit of knowledge was physically painful to her. Kirk studied her face, wondering how this young lieutenant had come across such intelligence, though not for a moment doubting it.

"It's a trick!" Stiles yelled, his eyed glued to the screen. "They're trying to get us to lower our own shields!"

"And in half a minute, they're going to try to blow us out of the sky!" countered Leslie. Kelso looked from one man to the other, and then back to the two ships hovering on the viewscreen before him . . .

"Lower shields, Mister Stiles!" Kirk commanded, then reached over Penda's shoulder and stabbed a pair of controls. "Transporter room, lock onto the captain's communicator signal, two to beam up, authorization code being fed to your board. Stiles, raise shields again as soon as transport is complete," he ordered as he released the first two switches and thumbed a third. "Bridge to sickbay. Emergency team to the transporter room." He paused just long enough to hear the "ayes" coming back from all stations, then moved down into the command well. "What was the fleet commander talking about, an 'invisible ship'?" he asked Kelso.

Lee stared back at him. "Jim, you were relieved—"

"And the tribunal can add mutiny to the list of charges against me," Kirk snapped back. "Now, the ship?"

Lee faltered for a split second, then reported, "It was . . . invisible. Until the *Kuvak* fired at it. Then it fired this plasma weapon back—they destroyed a *Sitar*-class ship with *one shot,* Jim!"

"Then it was visible?"

"Barely. Sensors only picked it up as an ion cloud. But we saw it."

"McCoy to bridge."

Kirk turned to the command chair and keyed a button on the right arm. "Kirk here."

"Captain Pike has been stunned and concussed, but he should be all right. And there's also someone here who—"

McCoy was abruptly interrupted by a calm feminine voice. *"Commander Kirk, open a subspace channel to Fleet Commander Ra-ghoratreii immediately."*

Kirk was not thrilled to learn Sarek's aide had beamed up with Pike. But, seeing as he'd already trusted her this far, he signaled to the communications officer to comply. "Hailing frequencies open," she said.

"Fleet Commander Ra-ghoratreii, this is Subcommander T'Pring. Hold your fire, and stand down."

It occurred to Kirk that, although he wasn't familiar with the Coalition's rank structure, a subcommander was probably outranked by a fleet commander. And yet, the previously fearsome Space Command leader responded with a simple, *"Understood,"* and on the main viewing screen, both Coalition vessels broke off and moved away from the *Enterprise.*

As Kirk and the rest of the bridge crew watched in mild disbelief, T'Pring hailed the bridge again. *"Commander Kirk, did you detect an unidentified vessel leaving orbit shortly after the destruction of the* Kuvak?"

"We did."

"Evidence indicates both Lady T'Pol and Councillor Sarek's impersonator are both aboard that vessel. I suggest the Enterprise *break orbit as well and set in pursuit."*

Kirk took a moment to absorb that. Then, he looked around to find the entire bridge crew staring at him expectantly. "You heard the lady," he said. "Mister Leslie, take us out of orbit."

T'Pol took a long, deep breath, and then screamed as loud as she could.

She had been imprisoned in a small cell aboard a warp-capable ship, and was surely about to be executed. Fear and anger and frustration and self-pity welled deep in the well-guarded part of her psyche, ready to boil up and erupt violently. Letting it do so would accomplish nothing, but at the same time, repressing those feelings would be equally futile. What logic was there, she asked herself, in using the little energy left in her aged body to show the empty room her stolid Vulcan demeanor, when it would feel so much better to rant and scream and pound her fists against the cold metallic walls?

So she screamed and screamed, until the door opened and a helmeted Romulan guard entered, a handheld disruptor aimed at T'Pol's chest. Following directly behind him was the man who had posed as Sarek, now wearing the same uniform as the guard, with a red and black sash over his right shoulder to indicate command-level rank. "Are you all right?" he asked, sounding genuinely concerned.

"What would it matter to you if I were not?" she asked, slightly winded. To her disappointment, she did not feel any better now than she had before.

"In fact, yes, it would," the Romulan answered. "I regret that we meet in this way. Our mission was only to disrupt the Coalition's talks with Earth, and prevent any unification. It was never my intention to bring any harm to you."

"And yet, you have," T'Pol said. "This entire ship and everyone on it is doomed."

"Empty threat," the helmeted soldier scoffed.

T'Pol fixed him with a withering look. "Even this deep inside the ship, I could tell when we were fired upon, and hit. The ship then went to high warp, sustained it for approximately two hours, eighteen minutes, and then came to a stop. Given the location of Babel, it would have been impossible for this ship to have reached its home territory. We are most likely then in a position of relative safety—inside a nebula or the magnetosphere of a large planet—where you hope to effect repairs before getting back under way."

The Romulan commander gave her a respectful nod. "The reports about you were not exaggerated."

"But," she added in conclusion, "it will all be too late."

The commander raised a single eyebrow as he considered T'Pol. Then he turned to the guard. "Leave us, Decius."

"But, Commander, the prisoner . . ."

"Kroiha!" the commander shouted impatiently. "Go, report to the chief engineer. You'll be of far more use on one of the repair crews than you are here."

The guard was not happy, but he put his fist to his breast in a show of deference to his superior. Once the door closed behind the guard, the commander considered T'Pol silently, then said, "We've detected the Earth ship, tracing our warp signature directly to this system. They will intercept us within two *veraku,* well before we'll have been able to finish repairs."

"At which time, you will destroy this ship in order to avoid capture."

The Romulan commander did not answer, but the sad, faraway look that overcame him confirmed her conjecture.

"Why?" she asked. "What was the point of all this subterfuge, of giving yourself Councillor Sarek's face?"

The Romulan chuckled without humor. "As unlikely as it may seem, it was nature that gave me this face. Perhaps he and I share a common forefather from back before the Time of the Sundering."

Somehow, T'Pol managed to hide her emotional response to that unexpected revelation. It had long been speculated that the

Romulans were the descendants of those who left Vulcan during the Age of Surak, but there had never been anything more than circumstantial evidence pointing to that conclusion. Her captor, however, spoke of his racial connection to her people as established fact—something she found vaguely distressing. "Still," she finally said aloud, "what is it that makes me so important, that you had to go to these lengths to capture me?"

"I would have thought Vulcans would eschew modesty just as they did pride."

"I am not modest, only curious."

"You are surely aware of what you represent—what you symbolize—to the cause of uniting Earth with the Interstellar Coalition?"

"Too aware," T'Pol said with a sigh. "But why would that concern Romulus?"

"The Earthers are a very consternating people," the commander explained. "The Empire began to take an interest in them when they started launching their first primitive interplanetary probes, using the same chemical rockets they employed to threaten each other with atomic fission weaponry. Then, mere years after they finally did launch those weapons against themselves, they'd broken the light barrier. Fortunately, your people were there to hold them back for a time."

T'Pol bristled slightly, remembering how long it had taken her *Enterprise* crewmates to overcome that unjust perception and put aside their initial suspicions of her. "But they eventually managed to reach warp five," the Romulan continued, "and quickly became the power brokers in this part of space, imposing peace between Vulcan and Andoria, Andoria and Tellar, then attempting to position themselves as founders of a multispecies Coalition . . ."

T'Pol nodded, recalling the holographic ship that had nearly scuttled one of those early missions. "Their goal was peace," T'Pol said. "Did Romulus so fear peace?"

"Not at all," the commander said, shaking his head. "My people have seen far too little of it down through the generations. What they feared was that, once a part of this Coalition, the Earthers would revert to their baser instincts. Fortunately, this degeneration happened before any treaties could be finalized and signed."

"Not so fortunate for the millions murdered in the attack on San Francisco," T'Pol said.

"Fortunate compared to what might have been instead," the commander countered. "Had the humans continued their expansionism unabated, rather than pulling back from their unexplored frontier, war with the Romulan Star Empire would have been inevitable. Tens of millions of lives would have been lost, on both sides."

T'Pol had to admit, given what she knew about the Romulans and their territorialism, that this was a logical conclusion. Such a war would have undoubtedly dragged on for years, and *Enterprise* would have certainly been at the vanguard. She could well have ended up one of those casualties, right along with Trip . . .

"It is pointless to imagine what might have been in a different reality," she told her captor, pushing all other thoughts and memories aside. "And I question your claim that the Romulans desire peace, when this plot of yours will almost certainly spark a conflict not only with Earth, but with the full Coalition."

"Yes," the commander nodded bitterly. "My gift to the homeland: another glorious war for the praetor."

The Romulan turned away from her then, almost as if, T'Pol thought, he were ashamed to have voiced such a disloyal thought aloud. "But I am a creature of duty," he continued, to himself as much as to his prisoner. "I have lived my life by it. And if we are to die for it . . ." He turned back again and looked her in the eye. "I envy and admire you greatly, T'Pol of Vulcan."

T'Pol didn't bother to hide her surprise at that claim. "Why do you say that?"

"I studied your record as I prepared for this mission. How you defied the Vulcan High Command in order to join the Earthers in pursuit of the Xindi, and then defied the humans by remaining on Archer's crew after Earth cut off its relations with all alien worlds. You have, throughout your life, acted on what you believe to be right, regardless of your orders or—if you'll forgive me—of logic."

T'Pol raised an eyebrow, but could not immediately offer a response. *"He got you on that one,"* Trip's voice mocked her.

"Why should you envy me in doing what I think is right, rather than doing what you believe to be right yourself?" T'Pol finally asked him.

He shook his head in remorse as he stared at the deck. "It is not our way."

"And illogic is not our way," T'Pol answered. "But if there is a way to save your people from a war, would not both logic and duty demand you do everything within your power to do so?"

The Romulan commander said nothing for a long time. Nor did he make any move to leave her cell. Eventually T'Pol turned away and settled onto the cell's small hard cot. Since screaming had not helped in the face of impending death, she decided to attempt meditation again . . .

"Yes."

T'Pol's head snapped around toward the Romulan, and as their eyes met, she realized that he had answered her question. "But how?" he asked.

T'Pol rose again from her bunk, keeping her eyes on his, and offered the words of a classic literary work she had read, at Jonathan's persistent urging, a lifetime ago: "Let me help."

9

Pike gradually returned to consciousness and became aware of the padded bed underneath him and the dull rhythmic tones repeating above his head. His eyelids fluttered, then opened a crack against the bright light of the sickbay.

"You're awake," a gruff voice said, as a blue-clad figure moved to the edge of his vision. "How do you feel?"

"Like I was shot in the back," Pike answered with a voice like sandpaper. He put his hands on either side of the bed and started to push himself up.

"None of that, Captain," the voice said, as a firm hand fell on his shoulder and pressed him down flat on his back again.

Pike grabbed the doctor's wrist and tried to pull the restraining hand off. "Dammit, Phil, I don't need to be mollycoddled," he growled in annoyance.

"Who?"

Pike jerked his head to the side and forced his eyes fully open. "Sorry, McCoy," he said, suddenly remembering. "Old habit."

"Yeah, well, old habit or new concussion, you don't leave my sickbay until I say you're ready," McCoy told him.

"Aye aye, sir," Pike surrendered. He settled back into the pillow at the back of his head, but then quickly snapped back up as the circumstances around his being shot came back to him. "The Vulcan ship! What happened?"

"Easy!" McCoy scolded, his hand back on Pike's shoulder, but the sudden burst of adrenaline helped the captain remain upright.

"Their vessel was lost with all hands. They were attacked by some kind of stealth ship, with light-bending shields that made them invisible. That pushy young Vulcan lady with you, she says Lady T'Pol was being held by Romulans on that ship, and we're chasing after them now."

"Oh, hell," Pike muttered, and swung his legs off the edge of the pallet. He stood up, testing his weight and pausing just long enough to let the dizziness subside.

That gave McCoy the time to circle the bed and try to block his way. "Were you not listening to me just a minute ago? You're staying put!"

Pike narrowed his eyes at the new sawbones. For a man who had never served in Starfleet before, he had certainly taken to the idea of hurling orders around, even toward his commanding officer. From Phil, he might have taken this, but not from a virtual plebe like this fellow. "Doctor, my ship is heading into a potentially hostile situation, my crew is at risk, and *I* need to be on the bridge, making sure we don't end up sending a hell of a lot more people here for you to patch up."

Having matters put that way for him, McCoy backed down. "I don't like this; that was a pretty bad blow you took. Let me just give you a shot of this . . ." He turned to a nearby cabinet, selected an amber vial and loaded it into his hypospray. "I guess it's better you're on the bridge than that Kirk kid . . ." he said as he raised the hypo to Pike's neck.

The captain turned his head before the doctor could administer the drug. "What about Kirk?"

"Well, no disrespect, sir," McCoy answered as he pressed the instrument's cold nozzle to his neck, "but all things considered, I don't think he should be in command right now."

Pike hid both his surprise at learning Kirk was in command and his irritation toward the plainspoken doctor. Pike had never refused a request from any of his officers for permission to speak freely, but he still liked to be asked.

"Obviously, I don't know him near as well as you do," McCoy continued, "but he strikes me as a bit of a hothead. Honestly, I don't know that I'd feel comfortable serving under him on more than a temporary basis."

"You're right, McCoy, you don't know him," Pike told him. "I'll grant you, in terms of making a first impression, this mission hasn't been a very good one for Mister Kirk. But he is a good man, and a solid first officer."

"Yes, sir," McCoy said, looking properly abashed.

Pike considered the doctor just before turning to leave, then paused to say, "I will tell you, though: he can be impulsive at times. And until now, I'd always depended on my ship's surgeon to be a kind of counterweight, to provide me with more of a thoughtful, analytical view to balance things out. I'd like it if I could look to you for that kind of advice going forward."

McCoy nodded cordially. "I'm happy to help any way I can, Captain."

Pike clapped him on the shoulder as he headed out of sickbay.

T'Pring was surprised by the variety of emotions her presence on the *Enterprise* bridge provoked in the individual crew members.

From some, such as Science Officer Masada and Helm Officer Leslie, it was simple curiosity. In contrast, Navigation Officer Stiles exuded a disconcerting and perplexing degree of hatred, and it took considerable willpower to meet his loathing looks with any kind of impassivity.

Then there was the communications and intelligence officer. She was the only member of the bridge crew to have attempted conversation with her. "That was a rather foolish risk you took, breaking your cover and revealing your *V'Shar* status like that," she had said, sotto voce, while pretending to focus on her board and avoiding eye contact as T'Pring paced behind her.

T'Pring had then paused to supposedly examine the communications board from over her shoulder. "It was the only logical option, given the circumstances," she told the human woman in a similarly quiet voice. "I naturally assumed a Starfleet Intelligence agent would be aboard this vessel for this mission, and my message would be understood. Which proved accurate," she added.

"Still, you were very trusting that an agent of a rival power would have broken cover also," the dark-skinned lieutenant said, in what sounded to the Vulcan agent like an accusatory tone.

T'Pring nodded. "Earth is in attendance at this mission because they no longer wish to be perceived as a rival power."

The human woman turned toward T'Pring to offer a retort, but stopped herself when she noticed Commander Kirk watching suspiciously, and turned back to her console. His gaze lingered a moment on the back of her head, then flicked briefly to T'Pring before darting quickly away. It was First Officer Kirk who had the most intriguing emotional reaction to her presence. His feelings appeared to be severely conflicted, despising her and at the same time feeling guilt over doing so. Such dynamics to her were, in a word, fascinating.

Her psychological study was interrupted by Lieutenant Masada, who announced, "The warp trail ends at that star system, dead ahead."

"Mister Leslie, bring us out of warp," Kirk ordered. "Mister Stiles, put us on Yellow Alert. Main viewing screen on."

There was little to see on the viewer, however. The system's star, designated only as NGC-8149 in the UESPA database, was an unremarkable red dwarf that barely stood out from the rest of the starscape beyond it. Kirk stared at the nearly featureless screen for a moment, then turned back toward the science station. "Any sign of them?"

"I'm not picking up anything," Masada answered, his frustrated expression bathed in the blue light of his hooded viewer.

"That is a positive sign," T'Pring said. "We've determined that, while the Romulan ship did enter this system, they have not left it."

"Great," Kirk replied, "but that leaves the question, where are they?"

"I do not know," T'Pring answered.

"Gotta mark my calendar."

Both T'Pring and Kirk turned toward the man at the navigation post. "What was that, Stiles?" Kirk asked.

"A Vulcan admitting there was something she didn't know," Stiles explained. "That's got to be one for the history books."

T'Pring raised one eyebrow. "That would be an example of human humor?"

Stiles flashed an insincere smile at her. "Sure. Why not."

"All right," Kirk said, preempting any further exchange between them. "Where do you suggest we start looking?"

In answer, T'Pring turned back to the library console and brought up a chart of the system on the large screen positioned just above her head. "NGC-8149 is orbited by three gas giants, and one Minshara-class planet, plus—"

" 'Minshara'?" Masada asked.

"Oxygen-nitrogen atmosphere, capable of sustaining humanoid life," the Vulcan clarified.

"Then that's probably where they're headed," Kirk said, nodding thoughtfully.

"Perhaps," T'Pring said. "If we assumed they were headed anywhere."

"What does that mean," Kirk asked, frowning at her.

T'Pring answered, "Considering the path of their warp trail, I believe this system was picked as a destination well after they left Babel, either in order to stop and repair whatever damage they took in their exchange with the *Kuvak,* or—"

"Aw, dammit, Jim, she's rambling!" Stiles blurted, spinning away from his console. "Why are you even bothering to listen to her?"

"Or," T'Pring continued, "they are lying in wait, ready to spring a new attack on this ship."

Stiles was silenced by that suggestion, realizing that she had proposed a very real possibility. Kirk turned to face him, as if expecting a retort, and when one wasn't forthcoming, turned back to T'Pring. "And if they are waiting to attack us?"

"Assuming they have not been able to repair their invisibility screens, the magnetospheres of any one of the system's gas giants would be the most logical place to seek cover. I would scan the outermost planet first, on the assumption they would want to attack from astern as we headed in-system."

Kirk nodded slightly, then turned toward the helm. "Mister Leslie, bring us toward the outermost planet, one-quarter impulse, then assume a high polar orbit."

"Aye, sir," Leslie answered. One of the dim dots of light on the screen began to grow and resolve itself as a planetary body.

"I never thought I'd see it," Stiles muttered. "She's got you cowed, Jim. Completely!"

"Lieutenant Stiles . . ." Kirk said in a warning tone

The navigator ignored the warning. "What the hell's happened to you, Jim?" he asked as he stood up from his chair and put himself far too close to the other man. "Taking orders from a Vulcan?"

"Sit down, Stiles," Kirk said through his now-clenched jaw.

Stiles didn't waver. "Have you forgotten that the bastards murdered your family? What would Carol say if she—"

And in a burst of heated emotion, Kirk swung his right fist at Stiles's jaw. Stiles was staggered, but stayed on his feet and returned his own punch into Kirk's abdomen. The commander let out a loud moaning breath as he doubled over, and Stiles took the opportunity to deliver a roundhouse blow to his right eye.

"Stop it!" the SI officer shouted, moving down from the bridge's raised level toward the skirmish. Her voice seemed to prod the rest of the crew into motion, as well as T'Pring, who had been watching the show of unchecked emotion in detached fascination. Masada joined Penda in attempting to pull Commander

Kirk free from the confrontation, while Leslie tried to pin Stiles's arms behind his back.

But whereas Kirk's flare of violent impulse had quickly extinguished itself, Stiles's was still burning bright. He pulled his left arm free and swung wildly at the large man restraining him, at the same time trying to pull his other arm free. Leslie tried to grab the other flailing arm but missed, and Stiles spun away, and found himself staring straight into T'Pring's dark, emotionless eyes.

"Bitch!" he snarled, straining against Leslie in an effort to lunge at her.

T'Pring did not even flinch, but calmly reached out and placed a hand on the junction between Stiles's shoulder and neck.

Pike stepped out of the turbolift and onto the bridge just in time to witness the Vulcan security officer grabbing John Stiles's neck and dropping him like a sack of oats.

"What in hell?" T'Pring turned, along with the rest of the *Enterprise* officers, who were all on their feet in the center of the bridge. The captain circled around the raised deck, stepped down to where Stiles lay, and checked his pulse and his breathing. Once he determined both were present and steady, he lifted his head and fixed his glare on the Vulcan woman.

"He is merely unconscious," T'Pring said, as if starship officers swooned all the time. "He should revive in approximately five to ten minutes."

"'Should'?" Pike echoed as he stood up again, both knees popping in protest.

The woman tilted her head, looking almost thoughtful. "Naturally, I have never used the nerve pinch technique on a human, but . . ."

Pike turned and impatiently punched a button on the arm of his command chair. "Bridge to sickbay: I have a man down, in need of medical attention."

"On my way," McCoy answered.

Pike closed the circuit, then turned on T'Pring. "You, off my bridge." His pointing finger then snapped toward his bloodied, disheveled first officer. "Kirk, you're rel—"

Pike was cut off by the sound of an explosion reverberating through his ship, and a sudden lurch that pitched everyone forward. The inertial dampers quickly kicked in, and the flickering lights came back to full intensity, supplemented by flashing Red Alert signals. "Report!" Pike shouted.

Kirk jumped into Stiles's navigator's seat and started stabbing buttons. "It's the Romulan ship!" he said. "Bearing 1-9-8 mark 2-0-8."

"Return fire!" Pike ordered. "On viewer," he added, and the on-screen visual switched from a forward to a reverse view. The saucer-shaped ship was rising up from the surface of a Jupiter-type planet, trailing hydrogen plasma, making it appear that the large raptor painted on its hull was aflame. He watched as the *Enterprise*'s phasers struck amidships, resulting in a brilliant flash of expanding plasma.

"Careful!" Pike shouted. "We just want them disabled!"

Another flash erupted from the Romulan vessel. "Hard to port!" Pike ordered. He felt the artificial gravity plates straining under his boots to maintain the illusion of a steady deck, even as he gripped his armrests to keep himself upright. The Romulan torpedo detonated less than ten meters off the starboard hull, sending a shudder through the defensive shield system.

"The feeling isn't mutual," Kirk deadpanned.

"Target their shield generators," Pike ordered at the same time that Doctor McCoy, accompanied by a blond nurse Pike did not recognize, arrived and carried Stiles off to the side of the bridge. They tended to him as unobtrusively as they could, even as the *Enterprise* was forced to make several more abrupt evasive maneuvers, and took another hard hit.

"Their shields are gone!" Masada reported from his station.

"I'm reading power fluctuations throughout the ship—all systems, including life support."

Pike fought the urge to smile. Even though they bested the enemy, if T'Pol perished aboard that ship, all would be for naught. "Mister Leslie, prepare to move in on the Romulan vessel," he instructed the helm, then called over his shoulder. "Ship-to-ship, Lieutenant."

"Hailing frequencies open, sir," the communications officer confirmed.

Pike straightened in his chair and said, "This is Captain Christopher Pike of the *United Earth Starship Enterprise*. We're standing by to beam your survivors aboard our ship."

"No."

Pike spun his chair around toward that voice. Subcommander T'Pring had not left the bridge, but stood in the small alcove before the turbolift doors. Pike was about to bellow at her, but there was something in the Vulcan woman's eyes that brought him up short for a moment. She took advantage of that to tell him, "That is not their way. They will destroy their ship and themselves before surrendering."

Pike clenched his teeth hard as he glared at the maddening alien woman. One minute she was his ally; the next, she nearly killed one of his best officers. Now here she was offering what seemed like invaluable information, yet he could not read her well enough to truly trust her.

Regardless, he could afford to trust the Romulans even less. "Masada, scan their ship, isolate any Vulcan life signs you read over there." If the Romulans didn't want to be saved, he could live with that. But they weren't going to kill T'Pol in the process.

The science officer punched a series of buttons and frowned into his viewer. "I'm getting some kind of interference," he said. "I'm picking up twenty-seven humanoid readings, but I can't get the resolution from the biosensors I need to differentiate between species."

Pike crossed his arms and cursed under his breath. "All right. We'll need to send a boarding party, find T'Pol, and get her out of there, fast." He turned to communications. "Lieutenant, contact security section. Have them assign four tactical guards for an armed detail, and have them meet me in the transporter room."

"Sir!" Kirk said, leaping out of the navigator's seat and rushing to intercept Pike before he could reach the turbolift. "Let me lead the party."

"You're not even supposed to be out of your cabin!" Pike snapped.

"I know, sir," Kirk said, dipping his chin slightly. "I'm responsible for all of this. That's why you shouldn't be the one to put yourself in harm's way to set matters right."

Pike considered Kirk's sincere expression of guilt, and despite his better judgment, nodded and told him, "Go."

Kirk had already taken hold of the control wand and directed the car to the transporter room before he realized T'Pring had entered the car with him. Kirk started and tensed.

"Is something wrong, Commander?"

"No," he said, "I just don't want you pulling that move you did on Stiles on me."

"Stiles was hostile, violent, and uncontrollably emotional. He was—"

"He was being human." *A little too human,* he thought as he touched the welt on the side of his face, *but still* . . . "For all your superior attitudes, the fact of the matter is, you Vulcans don't understand us humans. You never have, and you never will."

The turbolift opened, and Kirk exited, with T'Pring falling in step right beside him. "Where are you going?"

"Over to the Romulan ship."

"The captain said nothing about—"

"Captain Pike agreed to cooperate with all Coalition efforts in investigating T'Pol's disappearance. Logically, then, I must join your boarding party."

Kirk wore a pained look as he realized the Vulcan woman had him over a barrel. They entered the transporter room, where the four security specialists, wearing mottled gray tunics that evoked the uniforms of the old MACO military, waited. All four of them, at the sight of the alien woman, moved their hands to their phasers.

T'Pring herself froze, eliciting a mildly amused grin from Kirk. "Welcome to the team." To her credit, her face had not changed, nor did it as she nodded to the grayshirts and moved past them onto the transporter platform. After extracting a phaser from the weapons locker for himself, Kirk joined her and the four guards, then nodded to the engineer at the controls. "Energize."

The Romulan ship was small and cramped; the transporter had needed to compensate by tightening the circle the team stood in when they rematerialized. Battery-powered emergency lights cast inconsistent illumination up and down the corridor they'd beamed into, creating suspect shadows at regular intervals.

Crewman Pavel Chekov, freshly graduated from Starfleet's security and tactical training, took a slow deep breath through his nose and let it out silently through his mouth. This week had been a series of firsts for him: his first assignment, his first time outside the Sol system, and now his first time putting his life on the line against murderous aliens. He scrutinized the unevenly lit passageway looking for aliens, even as it dawned on him that he hadn't the first idea what a Romulan looked like.

Beside him, the unit's leader, Lieutenant Commander Vinci, slightly loosened his grip on his phaser. "Clear," he told the rest in a low voice.

"Clear," Lieutenant Lester reported on her survey of the passageway's opposite direction. Crewman March, the other junior team member, quietly concurred.

Chekov remained at the ready, though, even as Vinci holstered his weapon and opened the display console of his multicorder. It threw colored light into the dim space around them, though it kept silent as it ran through its scanning cycle. "Picking up life signs, Commander," he told Kirk.

"Can you identify T'Pol's biosignature?" the first officer asked.

"Negative. Still not able to distinguish between Romulan and Vulcan."

"Assuming the target is even still alive," added Lester. In the brief time Chekov had been aboard *Enterprise,* he had decided that she was the most pessimistic person he had ever met.

Vinci, being far more used to Lester's negativity than he, simply ignored her and continued his report: "The majority of the crew is concentrated in two areas of the ship—the bridge and engineering." He gestured down the passage he and Chekov had just visually reconnoitered. "Forty-seven meters down that way, I pick up a group of four, plus a pretty strong independently generated energy field."

"Their brig," said March.

"There would be little logic in assigning three keepers to a single elderly woman."

Chekov's eyes flicked in annoyance toward the Vulcan interloper. In keeping with the pattern of his week, she was the first extraterrestrial he'd ever personally encountered. Yet she was exactly as he expected from years of hearing how Vulcans had held back human achievement, suppressing the work done at the Baykonur Kosmodrom and the Russian Academy of Sciences in developing a warp-five engine, back when Henry Archer was still in short pants.

"And how many would they assign to interrogate and torture her?" Lester hissed at the Vulcan woman, and without pausing to wait for an answer, turned to the new crewman. "Chekov, take point."

He nodded, and started his way down the corridor, holding his phaser out steadily as he made closer inspections of the dim niches and closed doorjambs he led the team past. Behind him, the first officer asked Vinci, "Any indications of a self-destruct sequence in progress?"

"Negative," he said. "No indication of an active integrated self-destruct system."

"Which isn't to say they couldn't destroy themselves—and us with them—at the drop of a hat."

Thank you for that cheery thought, Chekov thought at Lester. He took another deep breath and forced himself to stay focused.

"It does look like all intraship communications is off-line," Vinci continued. "And all the emergency bulkheads on the ship have been sealed shut."

"Hull breaches?" March asked.

"No, none," Kirk answered, which was somewhat of a relief to Chekov, as they had just reached one of those sealed bulkheads. Though, given the choice of finding a room full of angry Romulans or the vacuum of space beyond the sealed doors, it was a toss-up.

Chekov slowly and carefully pried the cover off the hatch control panel, while Vinci, using a series of silent hand gestures, laid out the plan for their assault. Kirk and the security contingent all nodded and took up their positions. Meanwhile, Chekov identified the locking circuit, took one more deep breath, and pulled it loose. He looked to the first officer, who gave him a sharp nod, and then yanked the manual release lever down hard.

There was a loud clack, and the doors slid apart. He ducked and leapt through the widening gap, firing his phaser at the pair of figures at the far end of the wide-open room, scrambling for cover before they could respond in kind.

Chekov found a computer bank to hide behind. On the opposite side of the doorway, he saw March crouch behind a desk of some sort, his face twisted in determination. Between them, bolts of tightly focused colored energy blazed from the passageway as Kirk, Vinci, and Lester lay down covering fire.

Chekov watched where the return shots were coming from, then peered around the edge of his concealed position and aimed for their source. He fired and hit something round and shiny gold, realizing as it snapped backward that it was the helmeted head of a Romulan guard. The man went down, but before Chekov could feel too good about himself, a return shot struck the device he was using as his shield. Though the beam itself did not penetrate, the explosion of its inner workings was powerful enough to blast a hole through the back side and blow thousands of bits of microscopic shrapnel into Chekov's face. He screamed as white hot needles pierced his eyes and ripped his skin. He doubled over, hands to his face, and fell into a tight ball, keeping just enough presence of mind to maintain his cover.

"Chekov!" He lifted his head toward the sound of Commander Kirk's voice, but all he could make out was a dark shadow hovering over him against the already weak light of the room. "You okay, kid?"

"Just a flesh wound," Chekov said, or at least tried to. He spat out a glob of warm blood and phlegm, then said, slightly more clearly, "At least I took out one of the damned Cossacks before they got me."

Kirk gave Chekov's shoulder a squeeze and said, "Don't worry about it, kid," suggesting Chekov had not been as coherent as he had thought. "You did good. We'll take care of the rest; you just take it easy."

That sounds like a good idea, Chekov thought as Kirk's shadow grew and filled his entire failing field of vision with darkness.

★ ★ ★

Chekov was torn up pretty good, worse than anything Kirk's field first-aid training could deal with, even if they weren't still in the middle of a firefight. He pulled his communicator from his pocket and called for an emergency medical beam-out for the Russian kid. He thought to reach out and snatch Chekov's phaser from his open hand—just in case—just before the crewman was caught in the transporter and dissolved away. He stuck Chekov's phaser in the back of his pants and leaned out into the open with his own weapon held forward.

As he squeezed the firing stud and ducked back, he noted with satisfaction that the second of the three helmeted soldiers he'd counted was now kissing the deck. It occurred to him that the headwear had to be traditional or ceremonial, because it sure didn't seem to have any practical defensive worth. Kirk's own shot had just missed the one unhelmeted soldier in this security section—an officer, most likely, and a woman at that, with long dark hair and a shockingly short skirt. She also looked shockingly human; in another reality, Kirk would be offering to buy her a drink rather than trying to blast her through the bulkhead. She fired back at him while shouting some Romulan obscenity—which, he considered, might not have been an unexpected response to his offer of a drink, either.

From the corner of his eye, he saw Vinci jump up and fire, then heard what sounded like a third Romulan body collapsing on the deck. That left only one more—assuming, with communications down, the rest of the ship was unaware of what was going on down here, or else reinforcements were being slowed down by the emergency bulkheads. Neither of these was a particularly good assumption to make.

The female Romulan officer started shouting at them again in her own language. If the Romulan ship had a universal translator, it must have been off-line with the rest of communications. Whatever the woman said, though, she sounded damned confident. Kirk imagined she was assuring them more guards were on their way, they didn't stand a chance, et cetera. He checked the power level on his phaser, and then checked Chekov's. He had the idea of setting his largely drained weapon for a force chamber overload and using it as a grenade against the platoon of alien gunmen they were about to face . . .

Then the woman stopped talking, and even though he still couldn't understand the language, Kirk got the impression she had not reached the end of her thought. He looked across the way to where Lester and Vinci were, and they looked back, equally confused. Then they heard another voice from where the Romulan guards stood, this one male, and perfectly understandable: "I am unarmed. Please, do come forward."

Lester slowly rose from her crouching position, her own weapon ready in case this was a ruse. When she fully straightened and hadn't fired or been fired on, Vinci followed suit, as did Kirk. March, Kirk noted, did not rise, and never would again. He cursed silently as he drew a bead on the man who stood over the insensate body of the female Romulan—the same man who had deceived him by posing as the Vulcan councillor—his hands up, palms forward. T'Pring then entered the small chamber, and out of the corner of his eye, Kirk thought he saw a look of shock on her face as she got her first look at Councillor Sarek's impersonator.

Once the entire boarding party had revealed themselves, the Romulan looked back over his shoulder, and from the now-opened door of a small cell behind him, the captive Vulcan woman stepped forward. "Lady T'Pol." T'Pring stepped farther into the room. "Are you harmed?"

The older woman shook her head. "No. My treatment has been quite civil."

"Give us your hostage," Kirk ordered, his weapon trained directly at the Romulan.

"On one condition."

Kirk very nearly pulled the trigger then, just to show the lying son of a bitch what he thought about his "condition." But instead, he asked, "And what is that?"

The Romulan hesitated, then turned to look at T'Pol, almost as if for encouragement or willpower. Some kind of silent communication passed between them, and then the Romulan turned back and looked directly at T'Pring.

"I request political asylum."

10

The Romulan was quickly removed from the transporter room to the brig by the security team, with T'Pring following directly behind. T'Pol watched them go, wondering how the Romulan would be received once his request was formally presented to the Coalition, or what Vulcan would make of him.

"Are you sure you're all right, madam?"

T'Pol turned, and realized that Commander Kirk was the only other person besides her still in the transporter room. "Yes, Mister Kirk, I am certain," she said. "I should thank you for helping Subcommander T'Pring honor the commander's request."

"You're . . . welcome," Kirk said, even as he shook his head. T'Pol knew full well that the fear of the ship self-destructing around them while they debated the wisdom of bringing the Romulan aboard was a greater factor than any kindness on the humans' part. But they went through the ritual pretense all the same.

"And, Lady T'Pol, I want to apologize to you," Kirk added, unexpectedly. "I . . . there was no excuse for my earlier actions. I can rationalize them, tell myself that I was thinking of Earth's best interests, but in reality, I let that man play on my preexisting prejudices. What's more, even after confirming his claims, I didn't entirely trust him. Part of me suspected he didn't have the best of intentions in wanting to get you alone, and . . . that was all right with me. I put your life at risk for no good reason. You did nothing to deserve . . . I don't expect you to forgive me for that, but I am sorry."

T'Pol considered the rush of words and genuine emotion the human offered, and she was repelled. While she believed his remorse was real, and his apology earnest, they were meaningless. They did not undo a single thing that had been done to her, and would do nothing to make his actions less damaging. And since the man specifically said he did not expect forgiveness, she saw no reason to assuage his feelings of guilt by giving in to this ridiculous emotional, human need for . . .

"Oh, now, come on. I screwed up more than my fair share of times, and you always accepted my apologies once it got through my thick skull how wrong I was."

It *was different with you,* T'Pol protested. *The manner in which we typically resolved our disagreements . . .*

"Well, I'm not suggesting you make up with Kirk that way, *for Pete's sake. But that part aside, don't tell me you didn't feel better once you decided to accept an apology. No matter how illogical that might be."*

T'Pol stared at Kirk, silent and impassive. He naturally took this as a dismissal of his heartfelt expression of contrition, and started to turn away from her.

"Mister Kirk."

He turned back, but now his countenance had hardened, his emotions reburied and hidden behind the façade of the serious Starfleet officer. As a faithful follower of the teachings of Surak, she should have left those obscured emotions just as they were. Instead, she probed the recess where they'd been hidden. "What made you so hateful of Vulcans?"

Kirk glared back at her, almost as reluctant to liberate those emotions as one of her own people. Then the restraining walls crumbled. "My wife and my son were killed when a Vulcan patrol fired on their transport, after she had been invited to a scientific symposium on Vulcan."

"The *Galileo*," T'Pol whispered. The tragedy had been the

main story on all of Earth's information services for weeks after it happened.

Kirk nodded. "Yes. Of course, I know you had nothing to do with that, that it was just a tragic mistake. But since then, every Vulcan . . ." He hesitated, clenching his jaw and looking away from her. T'Pol did not interrupt the silence that followed, but waited for Kirk to finish. "I look at you, and I can't help but see the murderer of my family."

"I am sorry for your loss, Mister Kirk," T'Pol told him. "And I understand. When I look at you, I—"

T'Pol quickly stopped herself, and Kirk turned his face slowly back to look directly at her again. "You what?"

It is irrelevant, she should have said. Because it was. And because she had never told another being the full story. But here, with this human who had just admitted his own anger and hatred toward her and all her people, the words began spilling out of her for the first time . . .

It was freezing cold in New York City.

T'Pol had known, of course, it would be. After all, it was winter in Earth's northern hemisphere, and it had been hours since night had fallen in this part of the globe. And both she and Trip had bundled up in layers upon layers of clothing—including a heavy woolen cap that completely covered her ears—over a set of strategically placed sarium battery–powered heatpacks. This ensemble had always sufficed in the past, in those years when they would celebrate the traditional winter holidays at Jonathan's home a few hundred kilometers farther north. But the winds that blew through the crowded, man-made canyons of Seventh Avenue and Broadway seemed to cut right through to the skin, and deeper, causing her entire body to tense. As another such gust roared past, carrying tiny shards of crystallized water with it, again T'Pol wondered how she had allowed Trip to talk her into this.

The original plan had been for them to join Jonathan and his family for this event, but he had called earlier in the day, explaining that Erika had taken ill, and that he and his wife had opted to quietly celebrate the holiday at home. T'Pol had wanted to do the same, but Trip wouldn't hear of it. "Come on, we've been planning this for over a year! The celebration in Times Square is one of the great New Year's Eve traditions."

"Perhaps next year."

"Next year, hell. This is the turn of the century! We have to go!"

"As I understand the Gregorian calendar, 2200 is in fact the last year of the twenty-second century, and the twenty-third does not begin until the year 2201."

"Eh, don't give me that nitpicky stuff," Trip grunted, waving his hand dismissively at her. "New Year's 2200 is the big one; ask any human."

T'Pol ignored the jibe. After thirty-eight years of marriage, she had given up trying to either understand or debate what Trip deemed important. If her husband wanted to assign special significance to the date of 1 January 2200, it was best to simply accept that.

"We should go," Trip continued to wheedle. "We never go anywhere."

T'Pol furrowed her brow, and turned on Trip. "Go then," she had told him, her tone almost as frigid as the New York air. "Nothing is stopping *you*."

Trip's face fell as he realized his faux pas. "Wait, now, T'Pol . . ." he said, but she had turned her back on him at that point, moving into the small house's kitchen. She ignored Trip as he followed and called her name again, busying herself by flipping through meal cards, though she was not hungry.

She had not exactly been hiding here in Panama City since coming to Earth. She and Trip had visited Jonathan's home several times, they'd attended Travis Mayweather's wedding, and

Hoshi Sato's funeral. But at the same time, she tried not to draw attention to herself, being the only alien on a planet that did not want her there. On occasion, she would wistfully remember the freedom they'd had aboard *Enterprise,* traveling wherever they liked, the Vulcan High Command or the United Earth Foreign Office be damned. But she'd given that up—and much more—in order to stay with Trip, and had done so willingly. For him to then behave as if he were the one to have made some great sacrifice . . .

Then Trip was right behind her, one hand on her shoulder. "Wife," he said low into her ear, as he reached around her with his other hand, holding out the first two fingers.

T'Pol sighed and turned as she touched her fingers to his. He occasionally called her by such human endearments as "honey" and "darling," which were largely meaningless to her. But that word, which carried in it all the weight and significance of the Vulcan marital union that had survived since the Time of the Beginning, never failed to strike a chord deep within her Vulcan heart and soul. "Wife, I am sorry," Trip told her. "You know that being with you is the only important thing to me."

"I know, husband," she said, caressing his two fingers. Then she reached up with her other hand, slipped it around the back of his neck, and pulled his face to hers for a kiss. "We will go."

"You sure?"

T'Pol raised an eyebrow, then nodded. "As you said, we rarely go anywhere."

And so, there they were in the middle of Manhattan Island on a late December night, celebrating the approach of an arbitrarily selected second in time, surrounded by tens of thousands of other boisterous, inebriated celebrants. A band on an elevated stage performed something called "splitter," a contemporary musical style which to T'Pol's covered ears sounded like the cries of *aylakim* being eaten alive by a *le-matya.* The younger revelers in the crowd,

however, clearly enjoyed it, throwing their bodies about in an un-
restrained manner that T'Pol could only guess was supposed to
resemble dance. She and Trip watched their enthusiastic contor-
tions, he with a huge smile on his rosy-red face that, illogically,
seemed to warm her. T'Pol allowed herself a rare smile of her
own. Trip turned to face her, and the noise and crowd became
irrelevant as husband and wife shared this moment of happiness
together.

Then, for some unknown reason, Trip's smile faltered.
He reached out and grabbed at the knit scarf T'Pol had knotted around her neck with a gloved hand, trying to pull it loose.
T'Pol's smile disappeared as the remnants of a snowball still stuck
to Trip's fingertips melted on the underside of her chin and slid
down her skin. "What are you doing?" she asked as she pulled
away, a move that only served to tighten the scarf knot against the
side of her neck.

In backing away, she bumped against a large man who, judging by the smell of his breath, had been celebrating the coming of
midnight since noon. And for reasons known only to him, rather
than accepting the contact as an inevitable consequence of having
a large number of people in a relatively small area, he opted instead to thrust his elbow out, driving it into the small of her back,
and growl, "Watch it, damn you."

"Hey, pal!" Trip shouted as he caught T'Pol and staggered
backward slightly himself. "Take it easy, huh?"

The other man's expression darkened even further. "You got a
problem, gramps?" he asked, reaching past T'Pol and poking Trip
in the shoulder.

Before matters could escalate any further, T'Pol turned to face
the man and said, "I apologize for bumping into you. It was not
deliberate."

The irritation on the man's face twisted into a look of confusion. "What's wrong with your face?"

T'Pol lifted a gloved hand to her cheek. She should have

realized, seeing all the ruddy-faced humans around her, that she would have a similar physiological response to the cold—except, in her case, it would manifest in her complexion taking on an emerald hue. That, she understood too late, was why Trip had been fussing with her scarf.

Trip now grabbed her elbow, whispered in a voice only she could hear, "The natives are getting restless," and started to guide her away from the drunk. T'Pol didn't argue, nor did she intend to let Trip set their pace in putting distance between themselves and the drunken stranger.

She couldn't move fast enough, though. The drunk lashed out with his hand as the two tried to escape into the crowd, and his fingers just happened to catch the cap T'Pol had been wearing.

There were gasps, and shouts of "Vulcan!" and "Alien!" The drunk was so stunned that he could only stare at her, the cap fallen from his slackened grasp to his feet. But others stepped up in his place, eyeing T'Pol with suspicion and anger. It had been nearly half a century since the last extraterrestrial had been expelled from Earth, and now, here was one among them, posing as one of them, infiltrating one of their ritual celebrations.

The angry villagers surged toward their monster . . .

T'Pol paused, and Kirk remained silent, almost afraid to breathe. She had remained expressionless as she told her story, relating it in a detached, Vulcan-like manner. But Kirk could recognize that, far from being emotionless, she was in fact making a concerted effort to hold back the very real pain she was reliving. It was a look he had done his best to perfect himself over the last six months.

"Trip, of course, leapt to my defense," she continued a moment later. "He put himself between me and the others, even though he was hardly a match for a mob of men a third of his age. By the time the police were able to push through the crowd, break up the fight, and have him beamed to the hospital . . ."

T'Pol fell silent again. "I'm sorry," Kirk whispered after a moment, and then, remembering what the Romulan had said in his Vulcan guise, added, "I grieve with thee."

T'Pol looked somewhat surprised at that, but simply nodded in acceptance of the sentiment. "But that is who I see when I look at you, Mister Kirk."

"Thank you," Kirk answered, and then clarified, "for sharing that story with me. I get the feeling that it was not that easy for you." T'Pol said nothing, neither agreeing nor disagreeing with him.

Kirk turned and started to leave, but paused short of the door. "I think, madam, that the next Vulcan I meet, I will be more likely to see you in them than anyone else."

T'Pol studied him for a long moment, then dipped her head in what he took as a gesture of gratitude. Kirk smiled back—a genuinely heartfelt, friendly smile.

Christopher Pike stood in the well of the main council chamber, looking up at the grand ivory-white dome overhead, and then letting his eyes fall to the rows and rows of tiered wooden benches that circled the speaker's dais. The room was rich in history, and its walls seemed almost to echo with the famed speeches that had been delivered here over the centuries, from the Ramatis Choral Debates of five centuries ago, to the founding of the Interplanetary Coalition in 2161. And now, fates willing, history was to be made once again.

"Captain."

Pike turned to face Ambassadors Hedford and Tarses, joining him at the foot of the high marble podium. They exchanged hellos, and then Hedford turned, as Pike had, to take in their surroundings. "Kind of gives you an idea how the early Christians in Rome felt, just before the lions were released," she observed as more and more delegates filled the seats.

Pike studied her face, looking for some hint of irony, and finding none. "You think it's that bad?" Pike asked, looking up again and studying the attendees a bit more critically.

The conference had almost been canceled outright in the wake of the *Kuvak*'s destruction, and it was only after the *Enterprise* had returned to Babel with proof of outside interference that it was agreed the summit should go on as planned. However, one didn't need a high esper rating to tell that the mood of many of the participants had shifted.

"The delegates are concerned," Tarses said, diplomatic as always. "We're being blamed, rightly or wrongly, for drawing the Romulans back onto the galactic stage. We lost a lot of the goodwill we started out with forty-eight hours ago. Whether or not we can earn that back . . ."

As Tarses trailed off, leaving that question to dangle just above their heads, Jim Kirk joined the group. The two ambassadors both greeted the commander's presence with rather undiplomatic expressions. Pike couldn't really fault them, all things considered. But Babel Security had decided—in the interests of diplomacy, of course—to drop any charges stemming from the Romulans' theft of security codes, and the worst official offense Pike could think of to pin on him was unauthorized absence. However, the fact that Kirk actually wanted to be witness to this event was reason enough, in Pike's mind, to temporarily forgo any punitive measures against him. "How did it go, Number One?" Pike asked him.

"Pretty well, I think, considering," he answered.

"How did what go?" Tarses asked.

Kirk hesitated slightly before telling the ambassadors, "I spoke with Councillor Sarek, to express my personal apologies to him."

"You did what?" Hedford's eyes grew huge, outraged that the Starfleet officer had once again interjected himself into her diplomatic realm. She looked over Kirk's shoulder to one of the foremost tables, where the Councillor and Subcommander T'Pring were now seated in close conversation.

"I felt I owed it to him to explain myself, face-to-face," Kirk said.

Tarses scoffed. "I'm sure he found the sentiment utterly illogical."

"Yes, he did," the commander confirmed. "But . . ."

"But?"

"Well, he told me that he had visited the Romulan in the *Kumari* brig," Kirk said, the beginning of a grin pulling at the corner of his mouth, "and that he couldn't have faulted his own son for making the same mistake I did."

"Well, his son was banished from Vulcan twenty years ago," Hedford pointed out, "so that's not saying very much."

Kirk shrugged and continued, "He seemed really fascinated by his look-alike. Almost . . . excited by his existence."

"An excited Vulcan?" Tarses asked, one eyebrow raised.

Before Kirk could respond, though, a high chiming noise rang out, filling the chamber and echoing back down from the dome. Pike turned to note a uniformed Ithenite—the sergeant-at-arms, he guessed, or the equivalent—holding a small bell and striking it as he climbed the dais. Pike and the rest of the Earth party moved to a small table at the side of the floor as a tall, birdlike Skorr then took the podium. "Attention, all present: this special session of the Interplanetary Coalition Diplomatic Council, called for the purpose of the consideration of a petition by the government of United Earth and its Commonwealth Colonies, will now come to order."

There followed what Pike took for ritualistic invocations, some parliamentary procedures, and a reading into the record of the official petition from Prime Minister Winston. Just as Pike's mind had begun to wander, the entire chamber was on its feet, clapping and making other sounds and gestures of welcome as T'Pol appeared from a side doorway and made her way to the dais.

She looked uncomfortable, but not overly so. As she reached the podium, she gave the assembly a slight nod of appreciation, and the ovation faded. She paused, looked out into the crowd, and began to speak.

"I am privileged to stand here today, at the same podium where my friend Jonathan Archer urged your predecessors to continue the work toward creating a coalition of worlds, and to address the august body his efforts helped to bring forward. I am here, as you know, at the behest of Prime Minister Winston, to aid his renewed effort to forge a new bond between Earth and the Interstellar Coalition.

"However, the reasons for my presence are not logical."

An indistinct murmur rose up from the assembled crowd and filled the domed chamber, and the four humans present exchanged confused and slightly nervous looks with one another.

T'Pol continued her unvetted remarks, "I am not a diplomat. Nor am I human, or even truly a citizen of Earth. The reason I am at this summit is the same reason the *Enterprise* is—to serve as a symbol. A simple yet powerful reminder of a time when humans stood as an example to the other worlds in this part of the galaxy in putting old destructive ways aside and working together for the common good.

"One might reason that the need for such symbols is an indication that that time is now too far in the past to be truly relevant. Few of you in your lifetimes have ever known an Earth that was not isolated, xenophobic, and paranoid in its dealings with outside powers. The exploits of Jonathan Archer and his *Enterprise* crew have already begun to recede from memory, and I fear that soon, after my own death, they will fade away into the realm of myth.

"But, symbols can mean different things to different people. My recent ordeal has informed me that the ways I had been viewed by others—and that I had viewed myself—are not only wildly diverse, but are also malleable.

"I agreed to join this mission as a representative of a time long gone by, because that is how I saw myself. But that ignores the more recent past. I have lived as an expatriate on Earth for 103.247 years. I must admit that I have not thoroughly enjoyed living among humans. Yet I remained, contrary to all logic. And it was not until just recently that I have been able to articulate a reason for my choice.

"Hope.

"I witnessed firsthand Earth's backward slide into isolationism and fear, how humans demonized their own explorers and their diplomats, and raised Paxton's sympathizers to positions of power. And throughout those dark days, I believed that the human species would someday return to its senses. Over the past century, there have been several times when I thought a change was imminent, and each time, I was disappointed. But still, even after so many years, I hope.

"I would like to tell you I have greater faith in this current initiative, but I cannot. I am still Vulcan, and logic tells me that the chances of success are, in human vernacular, a toss-up. But I have hope.

"I close my remarks with one request. I ask you—all of you— even if the results of this summit prove to be less than you would like, keep the hope of better days. Someday, if not today, Earth and the Coalition will be ready to be united. I have believed this since the Coalition was first proposed, and I will continue to believe so for the remainder of my days. I ask that you share in this hope with me, no matter how much longer it takes. Thank you."

The applause that followed was subdued and somewhat awkward. The Earth ambassadors did not join in, but simply sat slumped in their chairs, slack-jawed, as if unable to process what they had just been witness to. "Damn her," Nancy Hedford muttered under her breath. "She's just given the entire assembly permission to send us packing." She looked down at the data slate that held her prepared speech, shook her head as she scanned the first lines, then pushed it aside, leaving it behind on the table as she stood, squared her shoulders, and headed for the rostrum.

Hedford did an admirable job, considering how badly she had been blindsided by T'Pol's speech. She managed, in her improvised remarks, to straddle the line between expressing respect for T'Pol and explaining how very wrong she was about contemporary Earth and humans. It was a valiant attempt at damage control, and one that everyone knew had fallen short.

A recess was called once Hedford stepped down from the podium. The chamber largely emptied, as delegates moved into the corridors and meeting rooms to discuss what they had already heard, and what they would hope to hear in the debate that would follow. Nobody approached the table where the representatives from the United Earth government and Starfleet sat, pondering their current state of affairs.

"We're finished," Hedford declared.

"We don't know that," Tarses answered without conviction.

The young ambassador gave her colleague a disdainful sideways glare. "I can't believe she undermined us like that," she said, pressing her hand over her eyes. "It's history repeating: humans held back by a Vulcan."

Pike frowned deeply as he reflected on the morning's events. Scanning the room, he spotted Ra-ghoratreii, his back to Pike as he spoke with another Space Command captain. He looked for T'Pol, but the old woman had not rejoined the *Enterprise* party following her speech, and he had no idea where she had disappeared to. He suspected she wouldn't be returning to the ship at the end of the conference, and found he was disappointed by that thought.

"With respect, Ambassador," Kirk piped up, "you didn't exactly have an easy case to make before all this, did you?"

"It was a hell of a lot easier," Hedford all but snarled at him.

"But not guaranteed," Kirk continued unbowed. "When T'Pol said it would have been a toss-up whether we got enough members to vote in favor, that was about right, wasn't it?"

"Your point, Commander?"

"It's what T'Pol said about better days," Kirk answered, adopting a surprising tone of respect as he talked about the Vulcan woman. "Even if we don't get enough votes here now, maybe the members who vote against us will remember what she said, and be willing to keep an open mind for the next time."

Pike found himself nodding. "Perhaps, in the long run, she'll have ended up helping Earth's cause."

Garrett Tarses scoffed at that. "And what makes you think there will *be* a next time?"

The captain grinned as he anticipated Kirk's answer: "The hope of better days."

Epilogue

Sunrise over Vulcan's Forge.

The man with Sarek's face stood at the edge of the desert canyon, watching as the red glow of dawn spread skyward from the eastern horizon. Looking down to the canyon floor, he observed a mother *sehlat* nudging its cub's rear haunches with her snout, urging it to hurry back to their den before the temperatures began to soar again.

Looking then to the west, he saw another pair of dark figures moving along the edge of the Forge, and as they moved closer, it became clear that the only shelter they were seeking was his. He fell back into the shadows of his refuge within the crumbled ruins of the T'Karath Sanctuary, watching warily. Before long, they had drawn close enough for him to recognize the taller of the two—a man as familiar to him as his own reflection.

The old Romulan moved down the set of steps hewn into the cavern's rock wall, slowly and carefully. It would be the cruelest of ironies if, after so many years, he were to trip and split his head open just before the news he had so long waited for could be delivered to him. His aged bones made it safely to the stone floor, just as Sarek and his companion—a younger Vulcan with dark skin and short curled hair—slipped in through the narrow fissures that kept these ruins hidden from outsiders. The Romulan lifted his hand and gave his guests the Vulcan salute. "What news do you bring, Sarek?"

Sarek returned the gesture and answered, "The Romulan Senate has decided that they will hear our proposal."

"This is a most historic day," the former commander effused, making no effort to hide his joy. Even though he had spent the decades since turning himself over to his Vulcan cousins immersing himself in their ways and their philosophies, he had no interest in giving up his emotions.

Sarek's aide reacted to his smile with a disapproving look. Sarek's own look eerily mirrored it, though the Romulan could detect the smile underneath his old friend's serious mien. "Historic, perhaps, to those of us who have worked so long to reach this point. However, it is merely the first step in what will be a long and arduous journey . . . or else, a short and fruitless one."

The Romulan chuckled. "This does not sound like a man who spent the better part of the last century in negotiations with the Legarans."

"Dealing with the Legarans has been a challenge," Sarek said, with his usual flair for understatement. "But those efforts cannot be compared to what it has taken to convince both the Grand Council and the Empire to agree to this forum. Even without interjecting the question of reunification, the odds of success are—"

"Please don't," the Romulan interrupted. "T'Pol, I am quite certain, would never have brought calculated odds into account."

"No," Sarek allowed, "I am quite certain she would not." A faraway look clouded his eyes. "It is unfortunate that she could not be witness to everything that she helped bring about."

The Romulan nodded, and both men fell silent for a moment as they remembered the great woman. If not for the example of her own life among the humans, and her urging to put the desire for peace above military duty, the two men would not be together in this time and place right now.

Sarek's aide respected the silence for as long as he could before ending it: "Councillor, we do need to be under way."

"Yes, yes," Sarek answered, and gestured for the Romulan to come along with them.

"What? Now?" he asked. "So quickly?"

"How many more years would you prefer to wait?" Sarek asked, a hint of a smile slipping past his emotional barriers. "We already have a ship standing ready in orbit for us. It is best we go now, before minds change."

The three of them filed out of the ruined temple, Sarek's aide leading the way along the worn path which would take them beyond the Forge's field of electromagnetic interference. "You may be interested to know," Sarek noted, looking back over his shoulder and into the morning sun, "that our ship is one of the newest in the Space Command: the *I.C.V. Enterprise.*"

The Romulan's right eyebrow arched upward in surprise. "A coincidence, no doubt," he observed, since such a symbolic gesture would be completely illogical. Sarek offered no answer, though his small smile had almost imperceptibly widened.

It was nothing compared to the expression on the Romulan's face, though, as they reached the transport point beyond the Forge, and beamed up to begin their journey into a new era.

Places of Exile

Christopher L. Bennett

To all who dreamed of the roads not taken

Historian's Note

Places of Exile begins during the latter half of the *Voyager* episode "Scorpion, Part 1" and concludes some two years later.

Note on Pronunciation

The name *Vostigye* is pronounced *Voss*-ti-guy. All occurrences of *ye* in Vostigye names are pronounced equivalently, as in *rye* or *bye*.

We all carry within us our places of exile, our crimes, and our ravages. But our task is not to unleash them on the world; it is to fight them in ourselves and in others.

—ALBERT CAMUS

Part One

January–February 2374

"An alliance with the Borg?"

The surprise Tom Paris showed at Captain Janeway's proposal was no greater than Chakotay's own. But unlike the impulsive young lieutenant, *Voyager*'s first officer kept his own counsel until he'd heard more. He stayed in the background of the conference room, standing like the rest of the senior staff—everyone except Harry Kim, who still lay helpless in sickbay. While surveying the ruins of a Borg cube, Kim had been attacked by one of its destroyers—ruthless invaders not native to this universe, listed prosaically in the Borg database as Species 8472. The attack had infected him with alien cells that now devoured him from within. Perhaps anxiety for Harry was what compelled them to stay on their feet despite the late hour.

"More like . . . an exchange," *Voyager*'s captain told her pilot. She explained further, moving around the room with an energy that belied the two days she'd gone without sleep. The treatment the Emergency Medical Hologram had devised for Ensign Kim, using Borg nanoprobes modified to attack the cells that made up Species 8472's ships and weapons as well as their bodies, gave the crew leverage over the Borg. The Collective could not innovate, only draw on the knowledge they had assimilated. That left them defenseless against the entirely new threat of Species 8472. Janeway intended to offer them the nanoprobe modification in exchange for safe passage through Borg space, a vast swath of territory blocking *Voyager*'s course toward the Alpha Quadrant and home.

"But the Borg aren't exactly known for their diplomacy," said a puzzled Neelix. It was a fitting comment from the Talaxian-of-all-trades who had earned the unofficial title of *Voyager*'s ambassador. "How can we expect them to cooperate with us?"

The answer came from Kes, not Janeway. Chakotay was still adjusting to the changes the Ocampa had undergone in recent months. Now nearing four years old, close to midlife for her species, Kes had outgrown the elfin innocence that had somehow coexisted with one of the oldest, wisest souls Chakotay had ever encountered. She had ended her relationship with Neelix and begun seeking new responsibilities and experiences outside her roles as head nurse and aeroponics supervisor, eager to live as fully as possible in her remaining years. She had stopped cutting her fast-growing strawberry-blond hair (it had grown out unexpectedly curly) and begun wearing outfits that hugged her lithe figure, perhaps hoping to snag a suitable mate before her once-in-a-lifetime reproductive cycle began within the year.

More importantly, Kes continued to refine her latent telepathic abilities under the guidance of Lieutenant Tuvok. Those abilities had made her receptive to contact from Species 8472, who had sent her visions of their assaults upon the Borg and warnings of their destructive intentions toward all life in this universe—though their reasons for doing so were unclear. "If what I've learned from the aliens is true," Kes said in her soft voice, "the Borg are losing this conflict."

"In one regard, the Borg are no different than we are," Janeway observed. "They're trying to survive. I don't believe they're going to refuse an offer that will help them do that."

Tuvok asked the obvious security question. "What makes you think the Borg won't attempt to take the information by assimilating *Voyager* and its crew?"

"Because that won't get them anywhere." Janeway declared her intention to delete the EMH's program and all his research if the Borg threatened *Voyager*. Chakotay was surprised to hear her propose such a thing so blithely. "But it won't come to that, Doctor," she reassured the holographic physician. "It's in the Collective's own interest to cooperate. *Voyager* is only one ship," she added to the group. "Our safe passage is a small price to pay for what we're offering in exchange."

Chakotay didn't believe she could be so certain of that. The Borg collective consciousness didn't think in terms of exchange between individuals, only of absorbing everything into itself. The concept of tit-for-tat might be too fundamentally alien for it to grasp.

But before anyone else could comment, Janeway ordered the crew to implement her plan. They filed out to comply, but Chakotay remained. Janeway leaned on the table and studied him. "You were awfully quiet."

He spoke frankly, as their friendship demanded. "I didn't want the others to hear this, but I think what you're proposing is too great a risk."

He told her the parable of the scorpion who sought to ride a fox's back across a river, assuring the fox that he would be safe, for if the scorpion stung him they would both drown. "But halfway across the river," he went on, "the scorpion stung him. As the poison filled his veins, the fox turned to the scorpion and said, 'Why did you do that? Now you'll drown too!'" He paused. "'I couldn't help it,' said the scorpion. 'It's my nature.'"

"I understand the risk," Janeway said intensely. "And I'm not proposing that we try to change the nature of the beast, but this is a unique situation. To our knowledge, the Borg have never been so threatened they're vulnerable. I think we can take advantage of that."

"Even if we do somehow negotiate an exchange," Chakotay countered, "how long will they keep up their end of the bargain? It could take months to get across Borg territory. We'd be facing . . . thousands of systems. Millions of vessels!"

"But only one Collective," she said, pointing for emphasis.

"And we've got them over a barrel. We don't have to give them a single bit of information, not until we're safe." She moved closer to him as she spoke. "We just need the courage to see this through to the end."

"There are other kinds of courage. Like the courage to accept that there are some situations beyond your control," he went on, his voice starting to harden. "Not every problem has an immediate solution."

"You're suggesting we turn around."

"Yes. We should get out of harm's way, let them fight it out. In the meantime, there's still plenty of Delta Quadrant left to explore. We may find another way home."

"Or we might find something else. Six months, a year down the road, after Species 8472 gets through with the Borg, we could find ourselves right back in the line of fire. And we'll have missed the window of opportunity that exists right here, right now."

Even as she spoke, his response formed in his mind—words driven by his disappointment in Kathryn, his anger at what he saw as a selfish choice. *How much is our safety worth? We'd be giving an advantage to a race guilty of murdering billions. We'd be helping the Borg assimilate another species just to get ourselves back to Earth. It's wrong. I think you're struggling to justify your plan because your desire to get this crew home is blinding you to other options. I know you, Kathryn. . . . Sometimes you don't know when to step back.*

But another part of his spirit advised caution. Would those words knock sense into her, or just exacerbate her stubbornness and push her away?

He almost decided he didn't care. A part of him was still the embittered Maquis rebel, angry at the Federation's hypocrisy in seeking alliances with devils, turning a blind eye to their cruelties when it suited the Federation's idea of "the greater good." It warred with the part of Chakotay who was a diplomat, a philosopher, and Janeway's loyal friend. The forces came to an impasse inside of him, perfectly balanced.

How often has history come down to a single choice of words . . . ?

After a moment, Chakotay reined in his anger. "Then we'll have had six months or a year to prepare for them," he said. "Instead of acting on fragmentary information, we'll have had that time to study them from afar and devise defenses. And whichever side survives the war will be weaker than they are right now."

Janeway paused, considering his words. Still, she was unconvinced. "What about Harry Kim? He's barely alive thanks to Species 8472. If we can ally with the Borg, their resources could help us cure him faster."

"Why would they care about one individual?"

"They wouldn't refuse a test subject to help perfect the nano-probe weapon."

"And they wouldn't hesitate to test him to destruction. I'd rather rely on the Doctor's bedside manner. He's already halfway to a cure. He just needs time." He stepped forward. "Time we won't have if the Borg call your bluff and you have to delete his program."

That struck home. Janeway had a maternal feeling toward most of her crew, but especially toward Ensign Kim, the eager young space cadet who'd been stranded in the Delta Quadrant on his first assignment. If anything would override her desire for vengeance on the species that had hurt Harry, it would be her desire to protect him from further harm.

Janeway began to pace, pondering the options. "Time," she muttered. "This crew doesn't have that much time to waste. If we turn back, how many more decades before we get home? If ever?"

"We may find opportunities in unexpected places. One thing we learned in the Maquis was patience. When fighting a superior foe, pushing relentlessly forward is suicide. You have to take your time, wait for your opportunities, strike, and retreat."

"And just sit and watch, hoping the winner of the war is weak enough to take?"

"We don't have to rely on their weakness. We can build our own strength. We've met other species that could be allies—the Nezu, the Mikhal, the Vostigye. Plus species like the Voth and the Nyrians who possess powerful technologies."

She almost chuckled. "And who'd be very unlikely to work with us."

"But they'd have to, once the Borg or Species 8472 came this way. Common enemies have bred unlikely allies before." He smirked. "You're the one proposing an alliance with the Borg. How is this any more radical?"

Janeway gazed out the window for a long time. "I've already told Tom Paris to set course for the nearest Borg vessel. I'm not prepared to rescind that order just yet. But . . . maybe I do need to consider another alternative."

"That's all I can ask."

Janeway smiled and clasped his shoulder. "We agreed we'd make this decision together. I'm always grateful for your input. It's good to know . . . I'm not alone."

Kathryn Janeway had a dilemma.

Privately, she was willing to concede that Chakotay had been right—not necessarily about his proposal, but about her undue, sleep-deprived haste in proceeding with her own plan. She was willing to gather more information, perhaps extend some feelers to friendly local powers, before making her final decision.

But she had already given the order to seek out the Borg. True, it was a captain's prerogative to change her orders without explanation. But in a situation like this—with an order like this—she couldn't risk appearing arbitrary or capricious. The crew had to be able to trust in her decision-making process—even when she knew it had been flawed.

So she had ordered Tom to execute that course toward the Borg, but more tentatively than she had planned. They would drop to sublight at some distance and gather intelligence before proceeding. Perhaps they would uncover some information that would give her a reason to order a retreat—or to proceed with her original plan. At worst, perhaps they would have time to hash out a compromise that she and Chakotay could both be happy with.

But mere minutes after they arrived at the scanning coordinates, sheltered behind a large ice dwarf in the Oort cloud of a system with three Borg-occupied planets, the decision was rendered moot. "A quantum singularity has appeared thirty thousand kilometers from the outermost planet," Tuvok reported. The singularities were the termini of the wormholes the Species 8472 aliens used to travel to and from their own universe. "A bioship has emerged and is heading directly toward the planet."

Janeway watched the tactical display on the viewer as three Borg cubes engaged the bioship and were struck by its fire. "The Borg shields are weakening," Tuvok said.

"Captain," Tom reported. "There are *nine* more bioships coming out of the singularity."

The nine extracosmic vessels closed on the planet, taking up a rosette formation, with the largest ship in the center, as the first bioship ran interference. "The outer ships are transmitting energy to the one in the middle," B'Elanna Torres narrated from the operations console, filling in for Harry. "The power buildup is . . . off the scale. But it looks a lot like the energy signature of a Xindi planetkiller."

Janeway's head shot around. "A strong-force reversal field?"

"I think so, Captain."

"It is now firing," said Tuvok. Without further comment, he switched the viewer to visual. Even at this range, it was possible to see what happened next.

But Janeway knew what would happen without needing to see

it. The gravitational energy that bound a planet together was immense and difficult to overcome; to disintegrate the Earth, for example, by conventional means would require concentrating the Sun's entire energy output onto the planet for a week. But a reversal field could turn a planet's own energy against it. The strong force that bound atomic nuclei together was immensely more powerful than gravitation. Reverse it so that it repelled instead of attracting . . .

The dark, metallic orb on the viewscreen began to glow, livid orange cracks and volcanic pustules spreading across its surface. Moments later, its molten mantle blew outward, its particles compelled by the spreading reversal field to escape one another at all costs. The Borg ships fled, motivated by a similar centrifugal imperative, but those too close to the planet were shattered by the expanding cloud of debris.

Janeway almost felt sympathy for them. Borg or not, there had been billions of living beings on that planet—and most of them had been *people* once. Still, she quashed her reflexive impulse to hail the survivors and offer assistance, knowing that it would probably draw unwelcome attention.

But there were other ways to draw the outsiders' attention. *"Kes to Captain!"* came the call from sickbay. *"They sense my presence. They know we're here! And they're coming to destroy us!"*

"Tom, get us the hell out of here! Maximum warp!" The last time a bioship had attacked them, it had not followed them into warp.

This time they were not so lucky. "The first bioship is on a pursuit course," Tuvok reported.

"Just one? That's a relief," said Paris. "I'd hate to have to take on the other nine and that wave-motion gun of theirs." Janeway assumed the weapon description was another of Tom's obscure twentieth-century cultural allusions.

"The other ships remain on course for the second planet in the system," Tuvok replied.

Chakotay whirled. "You mean those ships have enough power to blow up *two* whole planets? Even three?"

"There is no way to be certain unless we remain to find out, Commander. I, for one, am content to remain ignorant just this once."

Janeway traded a smirk with Chakotay. Though he'd deny it even under torture, Tuvok had a scathing, dry wit and was not above dropping a zinger to break the crew's tension. Janeway reflected on just how fond she was of the man.

Then the first blast from the bioship hit them and everything lurched. "Warp field destabilizing!" Kenneth Dalby called from the engineering station.

B'Elanna Torres, still at ops, barked instructions across the bridge and worked with her fellow ex-Maquis engineer to stave off the field collapse, while Janeway ordered Tuvok to return fire. But both efforts proved futile, the next blast forcing a convulsive return to normal space. According to Tuvok's report a moment later, even the residual energy not absorbed by the warp field was enough to knock the shields down by a third.

"Paris, evasive!" Janeway ordered. It was their best chance. *Voyager* was badly outgunned, but she was built for maneuvering and had a barnstormer at the helm. Tom danced the ship around like he was skywriting in Bajoran, and she could swear he was grinning. But the bioship kept up with him, its quick reaction times making Janeway wonder if the vessel itself was a living animal chasing down its prey. More blasts connected, the energy sufficient to arc over circuit breakers and blow out system after system.

"Shields at eight percent!" Tuvok announced, as though it made a difference. Janeway could see Tom's free hand calling up scan data, his eyes searching for a micronebula, a rogue gas giant, anything in this interstellar void that they could hide in.

But there was nowhere to run. Janeway took her seat and held on tight. "All hands, brace for—"

Impact! The world turned upside down, toppled her onto the hard deck. The roaring and groaning from the bowels of the ship nearly deafened her.

"Critical damage in engineering!" Dalby cried. "My God, they've severed the starboard nacelle!"

Torres set the viewscreen to show the nacelle as it tore free, blasted from below. The warp plasma within the nacelle ignited, blowing it apart and driving the collector assembly at its prow forward like a bullet.

Directly for the bridge.

"Evacua—" Janeway began. But then her universe convulsed again, the sound of it driving all thought from her mind. All except the memory of what she saw as the whole starboard side of the bridge crumpled inward, pinning Tuvok between the wall and his console, crushing him instantly. His eyes met hers for a split second, conveying his apologies for such a gross failure of discipline as dying while on duty.

Then the overpressure shock hit her, the air itself turning against her as the collapsing bridge compressed it inward. It knocked her down, mercifully sparing her the sight of Dalby's fate as the wall of Janeway's ready room collided with his spine. The pressure sent icepicks through her eardrums and into her brain, and her head rang like a gong. She could barely hear the groaning sound from overhead, or Tom Paris's warning cry of "Captain!"

But then Paris was kneeling over her, pulling her up by the shoulders and shoving her back into Chakotay's arms—back out of the path of the ceiling support beams that had been about to collapse upon her—that he had instinctively sought to shield her from with his body, and that now smashed him to the deck.

"Tom!" cried Torres, rushing out from behind ops.

"Man your station, Lieutenant!" Janeway cried. She knew B'Elanna and Tom had been growing closer, even though they hesitated to admit it to themselves. But she needed Torres to focus on preventing the imminent warp core breach that the computer was now alerting them to. "Bridge to sickbay. Medical emergency," she called, but got no response that she could hear over the ringing in her ears. As she knelt by Tom and gauged the extent of his injuries, she doubted it could do much good at this point anyway. She simply clasped Tom's hand as his pulse slowed to a stop, hoping that he could feel it. "Thank you," she whispered just before he went.

"I can't prevent the breach," Torres said, her voice rough. "We've got no warp drive anyway. I'm ejecting the core."

"Try to . . . to aim it at the bioship," Janeway said. At least it could be a gesture of defiance.

"No thruster control," Torres told her. "Ejecting's about all we can do."

Chakotay had moved over to the science station to scan the area. "The bioship is leaving," he reported. "Long-range scans show . . . more Borg cubes converging on the system. It must be going back . . . to engage them."

Janeway looked around the wreck of the bridge—command center for a wreck of a ship, adrift without warp drive, light-years from any star system besides the one the enemy had just obliterated. "Or maybe they consider their mission accomplished," she said bitterly. *"Voyager* is dead."

2

"You must turn these . . . these *Voyager* people away."

Kyric Rosh tried not to roll his large round eyes at Vitye Megon's imperious statement. He also resisted reminding the orange-furred female that as Subspeaker of the Legislature, she was not in a position to deliver imperatives to the Overminister of the Vostigye Union. Rosh knew she would simply remind him of the large anti-refugee bloc that backed her Preservationist party and might, if he were not careful, throw out his Progressive coalition in the next election.

Instead, he asked her, "Where would they go? You've seen the interviews." He pushed forward the datasheet containing the transcripts recorded after a border patrol vessel had rescued the wrecked vessel's crew, not long before their power and life support would have given out. "They come from the other end of the galaxy. They have no support base and few allies here. And their vessel is probably past salvaging."

"That is exactly my point," Megon told him. "We have reports of these *Voyager*s from neighboring governments. They have made many enemies: the Etanians, the Nyrians, the Swarm, even the Voth! And now, it seems, this new enemy from another dimension, one even more powerful than the Borg! We must turn them away before they bring these enemies down upon us."

Rosh was finding the urge to make some kind of face at Megon too strong to resist, so he padded over to look out the window. He stroked his tortoiseshell fur with the grooming pads on his fingertips in order to give the illusion that he was studying his reflection. Instead, he took in the view that always soothed him: the interior of Kosnelye, the large spherical habitat that served as the Vostigye capital. Vast swaths of blue-green parks and forests, lightly interspersed with spacious residential areas, spread before him and up the interior curve of the sphere. Aircars cut across chords of the interior, minimizing the need for ugly roads to break the idyllic scene. Away from the equator, broad terraces rose like gigantic steps, each offering gentler rotational gravity than the ones below. Filtered sunlight shone through the clear dome at the sunward pole, while a ring-shaped star window surrounded the microgravity spaceport facility at the dark pole. Through the windows, Rosh could see the smaller agricultural and industrial stations that supported Kosnelye, and beyond them, the cerulean curve of the Birthworld, ringed by the lights of hundreds of other habitat spheres.

But Rosh's eyes were drawn to the low-grav terraces, where many of the offworld refugee populations settled, jockeying for territory with the wealthy elites who appreciated the effects of diminished gravity upon their appearance and health (allegedly, although Rosh did not see the health benefits of allowing fat, lazy elites to get by with less exertion). "We've taken in many who flee from the Etanians, the Tarkan, the Porcion, even the Borg. It has not brought down retaliation."

"None of them offended the whole lot of them at once."

"You exaggerate, Vitye. *Voyager* offended them merely one at a time. And I don't believe they've met the Porcion."

"Which is lucky for the Porcion, from what I've heard. These are a dangerous people, willing to roll over any who get in the way of their mad quest for a home many octades away. You know they are suspected in the destruction of one of our own science stations!"

Rosh sighed. "Only in the propaganda of the most rabid Pres-ervationists. The analysis confirmed that the station was destroyed by a subspace eddy. *Voyager* merely informed us of the incident."

"And did not bother to remain nearby for the follow-up investigation. They are arrogant, self-absorbed, unwilling to accommodate disagreement. They will be a disruption to our way of life." She held out a datasheet of her own. "Even now, lying in hospital, their captain makes demands. She wants resources and facilities to repair her derelict ship. She asks us to fight these new enemies they have made. She hasn't even agreed to pay for their treatment, and she wishes to dictate our foreign policy!"

"You know the state covers refugees' emergency medical needs."

"Only if we fail to override your veto, Overminister."

"You don't have the votes."

Megon's muzzle pulled back into a smile. "Throw away more precious Vostigye resources on such disreputable outsiders, and we will."

Rosh turned back to her. That kind of xenophobic drivel warranted an overt glare. "You underestimate the decency of the Vostigye people, Vitye. Not to mention the vigor of our economy. We can afford to show charity to the helpless, outsiders or no."

"You speak of decency, as though taking in refugees by the planetload were a moral act. Refugees who waste resources and despoil the land. Who do not understand the Scripture's words, 'Be thou not overly fruitful, nor multiply beyond what the land can nourish.'"

Rosh sighed. "Words written in the time of the Catastrophe, when our ancestors first migrated out here and had to live in small, limited habitats. We are long past that now," he said, gesturing to the window. "The Vostigye spheres combined have more room than sixty-four planets."

"That space is carefully allocated. It all serves a purpose."

"Allocated to give the richest of us the largest swaths of land so they may show off how rich they are to have such large swaths of land. They can survive with a little less."

"The people will not accept many more reductions to our standard of living in support of these refugees. Already they threaten our social order, show contempt for our laws and our values."

Rosh sat back behind his desk. "As I recall, Vitye, your people were among the last to leave the Birthworld. For generations, the Gorenye were scorned as criminals and savages, bringers of disease, threats to the Vostigye way of life."

Megon straightened and puffed the crest of stiff red hairs that ran down the middle of her head. "And we rose above that debased state to become true Vostigye, a heritage in which we take justifiable pride. And it is because of that heritage that we can appreciate the true meaning of Vostigye principles and the need to preserve them."

"Don't these refugees deserve the same chance to integrate into our community?"

"They are not Vostigye."

Rosh chuckled. "Your ancestors would've been horrified to hear you call yourself that instead of Gorenye. They believed the genetic divide between your ethnic group and mine was insurmountable. For that matter, so did the people who persecuted them."

Megon shook her head. "My constituents will not be distracted by history lessons, Overminister. They have had enough of these outsider intrusions. Your speeches about tolerance and decency do not sway them, and you know it. Give in to this Janeway and you lose your mandate." She gave him a smile that came off more as a sneer. "You should appreciate my generosity in even giving you this warning. Many Preservationists would love to see you cut off your own head this way. But I do not wish to see our standard of living suffer more erosion merely to get you out of office. That will come in its own time."

Rosh hid his expression again, for it would be one of defeat. He knew he had to tread gingerly where the *Voyager*s were concerned. Still, it was the Vostigye way to help those in need, and he would not throw that aside simply because one current political bloc had forgotten it. "I will extend hospitality to Captain Janeway and her crew," he told Megon, "under the same terms as our policy extends it to any refugees. They may live and work among us, but they must give back to the community just as any Vostigye does. They may attempt to repair their ship, but they must pay for the facilities and resources just as any Vostigye would."

Megon appeared somewhat mollified. "And what form would this payment take?"

"They have considerable experience in research, engineering, and starship operations. They may share that expertise by taking jobs in those fields."

"By taking jobs away from skilled Vostigye."

"There is always room for more skilled personnel in the space service. There's a great deal of the galaxy left to explore."

Megon's expression grew calculating. "There is more they can offer us in payment. Some of their technologies are . . . somewhat more sophisticated than our current state of the art."

Rosh nodded, sharing her interest for once. The newcomers were a bit backward in genetics and cybernetics, but possessed faster and more powerful warp drives, reliable teleportation, extraordinarily lifelike photonic-field simulations, and advanced matter replication that put Vostigye synthesis technology to shame. "That is true. However, their captain is proving . . . resistant on that point. Her people have a directive about sharing technology, it seems."

"Hypocritical," Megon said. "They need our technology to survive. If they can't understand the virtue of a fair exchange, how can they possibly live among us in a way that preserves the balance of our environment, our community?"

"They will be made aware of the terms for our assistance," Rosh assured her. "We will see if they can adapt. If not . . ." He sighed. "Then I suppose you will get your wish." *To see them cast out to die in the cold of space.*

Megon smiled in triumph. "Thank you, Overminister. You have chosen wisely."

Politically, yes, he thought as she strode from the room. *But at what cost to my principles?*

"I won't do it," Janeway insisted. "There has to be another way."

"What way?" Chakotay asked from the couch—if you could call it a couch. Janeway wasn't quite sure how to describe the furnishings in these temporary accommodations the local government had provided. The Vostigye had an unusual build, their torsos angled forward and their knees bent, not unlike that mustachioed fellow in the Marx Brothers films that Tom Paris enjoyed—*had* enjoyed. It was easier on the joints and back in their high native gravity. Luckily, *Voyager*'s crew was being housed in a lower-gravity level of the habitat.

"If we refuse the Vostigye's terms," Chakotay went on, "where do we go? Who else in this region would be as generous to us? The Nezu? The Mikhal? They don't have the resources. And how would we reach them without *Voyager?*"

"You call this generous?" Janeway countered. "Requiring us to serve in their fleet? Demanding our technology in exchange for their help?"

"They aren't a replicator-based economy, Kathryn. They still rely on money and trade—they can't just give resources away. All they're asking is that we earn our keep. And from some of the rhetoric I've heard from the opposition party, the Overminister is going out on a limb offering even that much. I say we take it and be grateful."

"I'm not willing to take that step, Chakotay. *Voyager* may be crippled, but she's not dead. I was wrong to say that. As far as I'm concerned, we're still a Starfleet crew, and that means we live by Starfleet principles. I won't give up the Prime Directive just for our convenience. We've lost too much already—we *have* to hold on to the rest."

She gazed out the window, unmoved by the marvel of engineering that was the Vostigye habitat. All she could see, even three weeks after the fact, was the roster of the dead. Tuvok. Tom Paris. Kenneth Dalby. Lyssa Campbell. Chief Clemens. Joe Carey, Vorik, nearly half the engineering department. Jenny Delaney, whose loss had devastated her twin sister, Megan. Mortimer Harren, whom she'd barely even spoken to in three years and now never would again.

"I'm not convinced this is a Prime Directive situation," Chakotay said. "These aren't the Kazon trying to steal our replicators. The Vostigye have just developed differently than we did. They were forced off their planet early by a geological cataclysm, concentrated on building artificial habitats instead of warp drive. They're behind us in some ways, but they could teach us plenty about environmental engineering and robotics."

"Anything we give them could still affect the balance of power in this region."

"Like it or not, we're part of this region now. We no longer have the luxury of pretending the Delta Quadrant is a place we're just passing through. We're here for good—or at least for the foreseeable future."

"Just as you wanted," she said, her voice hardening, though she regretted letting the words out.

Typically, though, Chakotay didn't rise to the bait. "I never wanted this. But I understand it, Kathryn. As a Maquis, as an Indian, I know what it's like to be out in the cold without a powerful nation to support you. I know that following your own rules stringently is a luxury of those with the authority to enforce them. When you're powerless in someone else's culture, you have to adapt to survive.

"For three years, we've managed to get by without needing to learn that lesson. But now our free ride has ended. We're at the Vostigye's mercy. And given what many of their neighbors are like, that's probably the safest place for us under the circumstances."

"But at what cost, Chakotay? They wouldn't let us stay together as a crew. We'd be scattered across dozens of ships and star systems. What if . . ." *What if we stop thinking of ourselves as a crew? What if some of my people decide they like living here? What if I never see them again?*

She cleared her throat. "And you said it yourself—there's a lot of intolerance toward outsiders."

"Only among some segments of the population. They seem numerous because they're politically vocal and active. But most of the Vostigye I've met have been kind, open-minded people. Their values aren't that different from ours; they just have a few outstanding issues they haven't settled yet. That's true even of the Federation," he reminded her. She knew he was referring to the "issues" that had led to the formation of the Maquis.

Janeway turned back to the window, hesitant to let him see the sadness, the defeat, in her expression. "If I give in to this, Chakotay . . . I'm admitting I failed. I'm saying to my crew that I can't get them home again. If I do that, is there even any point in rebuilding *Voyager?*"

She felt his hand on her shoulder, and it soothed even as his words burned. "Don't see it as a failure, Kathryn. This can be a new beginning for *Voyager*'s crew. The chance to explore a rich Delta Quadrant society up close, from the inside. The chance to help build a new coalition that can defend against the Borg and Species 8472. Maybe a new community as well."

Janeway sighed. What were the chances of building such a coalition if her people had no standing in the region's society, no ship to offer for its defense? How safe would Vostigye space be in a few months, when the nearby war ended?

She straightened, firming her resolve. She would have to try, no matter the odds. She was still a Starfleet captain, and she would hold on to that even if she lost everything else. At the very least, she would do what she could to defend these people from invasion.

But no matter what Chakotay said, these were not her people, and this was not her home. Someday, no matter what it took, she would get *Voyager* flying again, reassemble her crew, and resume course for the Alpha Quadrant.

But how many of the crew would join her when the time came?

Part Two

August–November 2374

3

"*Lieutenant Kim, report to command deck.*"

Harry didn't feel like getting out of bed. He'd woken up early, surprised when he'd rolled over and collided with a warm nude body. His lover usually left well before he woke up. Even in sleep, she was tense and aloof, jabbing him with an elbow and rolling away. But with a little more delicacy, he'd managed to get an arm around her, and eventually she'd relaxed against him. He'd been so content just spooning that he'd lost track of time. He wanted to stay that way forever.

But there was that title: *Lieutenant Kim*. True, it was just how his translator rendered the Vostigye rank, but for all practical purposes, he was a lieutenant at last. And he'd worked damn hard to earn it, harder than most because he'd had the "refugee" stigma to overcome. Now he'd gained a position of trust on *Ryemaren*'s bridge crew, one not unlike his post on *Voyager,* but with opportunities for advancement he never would have had on that ship. He couldn't let his captain and colleagues down by blowing off a duty shift.

So he reluctantly pulled himself away from his lover, taking a moment to admire the deceptively delicate contours of her back, its smoothness so unusual for those of her heritage. Then he went into the 'fresher for a quick sonic shower.

It came as an even greater surprise when, a moment later, the door opened and she came in. "Mind if I join you?" B'Elanna's voice was no more expressive than usual, a disinterested monotone barely audible over the shower's hum, but the gesture itself was extraordinary. He knew full well that she had turned to him merely for comfort, for distraction from her grief at losing Tom Paris before she'd even admitted her love for him. Her lovemaking was hungry, needy, but detached and impersonal, and often he derived more gratification from the belief that he was helping to ease her pain than he did from the sex itself. But Harry accepted it because he needed comfort and distraction as well. Even this tenuous, frustrating thing that he could barely call a relationship was a link to the life he'd known, a reminder of the friendship he and B'Elanna Torres had shared for three years.

But for B'Elanna to stay the night, even to seek out further intimacy in the morning, was remarkable. As she slipped into the tight shower cubicle and pulled his head down into a kiss, he cursed the timing of it. This could be a breakthrough, and he had to shoot it down, not knowing if it would ever come again. "I'd love to," he said softly into her ear. "But they need me on the bridge."

"Call in sick. Just this once. You've earned it by now."

"Voenis would kill me. She'd kill both of us if she found out why I skipped school."

"I don't care."

That was exactly the problem. Getting B'Elanna to care about most anything seemed a hopeless task. She was lackluster in her duties, insubordinate, and this close to getting kicked out of the Vostigye space service. Harry's influence was the only thing that kept her in line.

He kissed her ridged forehead and stepped out of the booth. "I do. About you. I won't be responsible for getting you in more trouble."

"Because Harry Kim always has to do what's right."

The anger was the most expression he'd heard in her voice for some time. It was downright gratifying. "I try my best. But I want to do what's right for you too. We can talk about it tonight, okay?"

She gave him a look he couldn't fathom. "We all try to do what's right, Harry," she murmured. "Remember that."

Then she closed the shower door and left him with his confusion.

"Mister Kim, identify the intruder."

Harry Kim fed the readings on the unfamiliar ship into *Ryemaren*'s computer. The answer came back in the Vostigye script and language that he'd mastered over the past six months. "The ship is of unknown origin. But the life signs read as Casciron."

"Casciron," Captain Nagorim muttered in a resigned tone. They were a people Ensign Kim of *Voyager* had never met, but Lieutenant Kim of the Vostigye border patrol was a veteran of multiple encounters. Their homeworld had fallen prey to the Etanian Order, conquerors who staged natural disasters to drive out or kill off the populations of planets they wanted for their own. *Voyager* had saved the Nezu from the Etanians last year, but the Casciron had not been so lucky. Like many refugees, they came to the Vostigye Union hoping to benefit from its prosperity, strength, and legal protections, only to find that earning those protections could be . . . complicated. Especially in the Casciron's case.

Nagorim opened a channel. "Casciron vessel, this is Captain Azorav Nagorim of the Union patrol craft *Ryemaren*. You are violating Vostigye space. Power down your engines and await inspection." His tone was firm but devoid of malice.

A Casciron appeared on the round viewscreen—tall, intimidating, with deep gray, glossy skin that reminded Harry of a shark. *"Vostigye vessel. We are here by accident. We seek the nearest border outpost to request entry through proper channels. But our navigation system failed."*

"What a novel excuse," muttered Morikei Voenis, Nagorim's first officer, a russet-furred female who had little patience with refugees.

"*Casciron do not deceive!*" the alien shot back. "*We may have no world, but we have our pride.*"

"Tell that to the Vostigye whose habitats have been raided by your pirates!"

"From what I'm reading, Captain," Harry said, "their sensors and computers are in pretty bad shape. I doubt they could navigate except by looking out a window. And that K-class—sorry, *Mol*-class star they're aimed for is a near-perfect match for the star the border outpost orbits. They could've made an honest mistake." Voenis glared at him. He had earned her grudging respect through months of skilled service, even saved her life at Calentar, but she still disliked being undermined on the command deck—at least by a refugee. Harry had hoped she had outgrown seeing him that way, but it seemed he still had more work to do.

"*If you would inspect us, then proceed. We have nothing to hide, and little time to spare.*"

"You don't have much life support, either," Harry said. "And your engines are falling apart. You won't make it much farther."

"Mind your place, Lieutenant," Voenis told him.

"Voenis," the captain cautioned. "Casciron ship, we must board you for inspection and escort you to the border outpost for processing. If all is in order, we will assist you in repairing your life-support systems."

"*It seems we have little choice.*" The Casciron bowed formally. "*You are invited to visit our territory.*"

"Their territory," Voenis scoffed.

"Mister Kim, would you like to lead the boarding party?" Nagorim asked.

"Aye, sir. Request that the AMP and . . . and Ensign Torres accompany me."

Nagorim threw him an amused look. "Now, Harry. You know ship's policy about favoritism."

Harry blushed. "It's not that, sir. Their power systems employ chromodynamic plasma technology. I happen to know that Ensign Torres has extensive firsthand experience with that technology." Strictly speaking, she had only encountered it once, during her abduction by the Pralor Automated Personnel Units over two years ago. But those circumstances had demanded that she become an expert in record time. *And it couldn't hurt to pad her résumé a little,* Harry thought.

"Very well," Nagorim said. "Assemble your team."

"I should lead the team, sir," Voenis said.

"Your reasons?" Nagorim asked.

"The team leader should have experience dealing with the Casciron in person, not from behind a console."

The captain gave Harry an infinitesimal look of apology. "Very well. Report for teleportation."

Voenis led Harry from the command deck and through *Ryemaren*'s upward-curving corridors. The Vostigye ships were cylindrical, with gravity pulling outward from the central axis, like their habitats in miniature. Even after four months, Harry still felt as if he were living in a giant hamster wheel. At least the gravity came from AG plating instead of the centrifugal effect; the necessary rotation for a ship this small would have been dizzying even for the Vostigye. And mercifully, the gravity was kept below Vostigye standard for the benefit of alien crew.

But Harry still had to push himself to keep up with Voenis and confront her. "You still don't trust me."

She paused. "It's her I don't trust. Or your judgment concerning her."

"B'Elanna's had a rough time. She lost a lot of people she cared about." *And one she loved.*

"And you let her take it out on you. I've seen your injury reports."

"It's not like that. Klingons are just . . . enthusiastic about . . ."

Voenis rolled her eyes at his hesitation. "Refugees. Why can't you just say 'sex' when you mean 'sex'? Listen. I understand you find comfort and familiarity in her. But you know where she stands on the Casciron issue. Can I trust her to do her duty?"

"Has she ever given you reason not to?"

She had no response. "Very well. But you vouch for her at your own risk, and I wish you could see that. You're not like her— you have a future here." She leaned in closer. "I tell you this as a friend," she whispered, as though such friendship were a dirty secret. "Break with her before she pulls you down with her."

Ryemaren's transporter delivered them efficiently to the Casciron ship—as well it should, since it was based on *Voyager*'s technology. Voenis, wary of trusting anything from refugees, didn't relax until she materialized safely. Except she didn't relax much, given the approaching party of large, powerful Casciron. Well, large Casciron. Harry could see they moved slowly and were gaunt from hunger.

"I am Danros, commander of this vessel." The speaker and those accompanying him crossed their arms over their chests in greeting, the left wrist clasped beneath the right hand. Harry knew the gesture was meant to show that the large, venomous stingers extending from their left wrists were being withheld from use. "I extend welcome to the guests in our territory."

"How touching," Voenis said. "Except that you're in our territory, and that entails certain rules. You know those venom glands will have to be removed."

Harry felt B'Elanna bristling beside him. The treatment of the Casciron refugees was the one thing that she ever seemed to get passionate about, her old Maquis spirit rallying against what she perceived as the oppression of a vulnerable people. He clasped her hand to restrain her. But Danros saved her the trouble. "And you know that is an act of mutilation that offends the Allfather. Must we become less than we are simply to live in your territory?"

"The law requires you to disarm. To live in our territory, you must obey the same laws that apply to everyone else."

"Everyone else is not required to undergo mutilation."

"For what it's worth," came a new voice, "the literature says the procedure is quick and relatively painless. But then, that's what they used to say about circumcision." Harry still did a double take whenever he heard the Doctor's sardonic voice coming from the mechanical body of the ship's auxiliary medical probe. Finding the EMH too useful to limit to one ship, the Vostigye had uploaded him into their integrated medical network, giving him control over all the robotic AMPs. Essentially, he now existed within several hundred bodies simultaneously.

"Look, we can debate all this later," B'Elanna said. "Right now we've got a life-support system to fix, right?"

"We have an inspection to perform," Voenis corrected. "The life support will last that long, at least." From her tone, she was skeptical that the ship had malfunctioned at all.

But B'Elanna's tests of the vessel's navigation and sensor systems bore out the Casciron's story. So Voenis allowed her and Harry to begin repairs on life support and the Doctor (or *a* Doctor) to tend to their malnutrition while she continued the inspection. "Thanks," Harry told B'Elanna as they worked.

"For what?"

"For not getting into that argument back there. Focusing on the work."

She bristled. "You think I can't resist an argument, even when there are lives at stake?"

Harry refrained from pointing out that her reaction didn't do much to refute that. "I'm just saying it was a good call. For you as well as the Casciron. Maybe it'll help you gain some respect in Voenis's eyes."

"Like I want respect from her."

"Like it or not, she's our superior officer now, and it doesn't do any good to antagonize her." He leaned in closer. "She's not as bad as you think. She has her prejudices, sure, but I think she's willing to outgrow them. She even called me a friend today."

"Sure. She'd call *you* a friend. You're the nice refugee, the one who tries to fit in and doesn't make waves."

"I'm trying to set a positive example. To show that refugees can be just as civilized and responsible as anyone else. What's wrong with that?"

"What's wrong is that there's so much going on that we should *not* be complacent about. When people like you assimilate so smoothly, it makes it easier for them to pretend there aren't critical problems to be solved."

He strove for calm reason to temper her anger, although it was refreshing to see her getting animated about something. "I think that if we earn their respect as civilized people, they'll be more willing to listen to our concerns."

"We've tried that. Chakotay and Neelix have been trying for months. And Casciron are still getting mutilated, stripped of something sacred to them."

"There are Vostigye trying to change those laws too. But it's hard for them to get enough votes when the Casciron keep raiding border outposts."

"Sometimes you have to fight back against an injustice, Harry."

Harry was losing patience at the old argument. "Don't give me that noble Maquis speech again. The truth is, you're just looking for an excuse to keep fighting. It's been seven months, B'Elanna! Tom wouldn't want you to keep tearing yourself up—"

"Don't make this about him!" she roared, startling him. "You let go if you want. Let go of your friends, your crew, the Alpha Quadrant, your principles. But you'll be letting go of me too."

"What are you saying?"

"I hoped I could talk some sense into you before it was too late, maybe even get you to go along with me. I hoped at least I could get you to be off duty when this happened. But it's obvious I don't have a chance. Keep being a good Vostigye soldier, Harry— maybe it'll keep them from blaming you for this."

"For what? Go along where?"

She shook her head. "I'm sorry, Harry. You were a good friend when I needed one, but honestly . . ." She sucked in a shuddering breath. "You're better off without me."

"B'Elanna!"

She activated her wrist communicator. "Torres to *Ryemaren* computer. Initiate sequence Maquis Alpha."

"No!"

Harry's cry died out as the Casciron ship dissolved around him and *Ryemaren*'s transporter room took its place. Voenis was at his side, looking around sharply. "What happened? Where's Torres?"

"She . . . she . . ."

"Never mind!" She threw him one last look of betrayal before running for the command deck.

It quickly became evident that Torres's transporter program had not only returned Harry and Voenis to *Ryemaren,* but had removed several critical components from the ship's drive and sensor systems, leaving it unable to pursue or track the Casciron ship as it fled deeper into Vostigye space. Moreover, the entire contents of the ship's weapons locker had been beamed away as well. The medical probe had also been taken, although the Doctor's program, operating the probe remotely from the ship, remained in *Ryemaren*'s computer. The Casciron would only get its surgical equipment, pharmasynth unit, and medical database, but those were of considerable use even without a controlling intelligence.

In place of all she'd taken, B'Elanna left only a recorded statement speaking out for Casciron rights and absolving Harry Kim of any involvement in her defection. The investigation suggested that she had told the Casciron how to fake the damage sufficiently to fool *Ryemaren*'s sensors (and their operator, Harry thought ruefully), and had suggested they find a ship using chromodynamic plasma so that she could volunteer herself as an expert, ensuring that she would be the engineer on the scene "confirming" the damage. Except her good friend Harry Kim had ended up volunteering her himself, becoming her unwitting accomplice.

The worst part was, Harry couldn't even comfort himself with thoughts like *I really thought we had something.* He knew he'd never been more than a consolation prize to B'Elanna, a patient, forgiving sounding board for her rage and desolation—and maybe a reminder of the love she'd lost, the closest she could get to Tom Paris in this lifetime. Their time together had been physically intense, but never happy. They'd been far closer before they'd become lovers. In a way, it was almost a relief that it was over.

Except that Harry had lost the one other person on this ship who had been a part of *Voyager.* Well, there was still the Doctor, but not in his familiar form—and existing in multiple bodies had begun turning him a little weird, to be honest. And the friends he'd begun to make on this ship were now looking at him oddly, with either suspicion or pity. Harry was alone in a way he'd never felt before.

4

When the hunger pangs began, Kes tried to dismiss them at first. After all, she'd been very busy lately, going for days without sleep as she drew closer to a cure for the Tarkan wasting syndrome, a project she had to balance with her other priorities.

When Kes found herself snacking on test specimens from the botanical incubator, her denial became more conscious and harder to rationalize. *Not the* elogium. *Not now. Just a little longer, please.*

But she knew from experience that the symptoms would get worse quickly, and it would be bad for her research team's morale if they came upon their team leader in a wild frenzy, drenched in sweat, and devouring anything remotely edible. If the *elogium* was upon her—and the timing was definitely right this time—her staff had a right to know what was happening.

So she logged out and asked Seroe to take over the epigenome analysis. The work would take much longer by conventional means, without Kes's ability to perceive the molecular structure directly and *feel* how it could be nudged back into a healthy configuration. But right now, Kes's priority was to see the Doctor.

"I've been expecting this," he told her when she arrived in the medical hololab to report her symptoms. "Any fever yet? Any cravings for potting soil?" he asked with a kindly smirk. Here, at least, thanks to the holotechnology adapted from *Voyager,* this avatar of the Doctor could still manifest in his familiar appearance, with only his wardrobe changed to something more fitting a Vostigye research station. He had an alternate Vostigye appearance which he used most of the time, but for Kes, the Wildmans, and the other *Voyager* personnel serving on Moskelar Station, he reverted to his original features.

"Not yet," she told him.

He frowned. "You don't seem excited about the impending blessed event."

She shook it off. "I'll get over it. This is my one chance, after all. And I do want a family."

"But."

She smiled at his expression. "But . . . so many people are depending on me right now. This breakthrough could mean peace with the Tarkan, an end to their piracy."

"Even if you don't finish the work yourself, Kes, you've still made an inestimable contribution. If you hadn't risked your life to beam over to that damaged Tarkan ship, we still wouldn't know the real reason behind their raids."

"I know that, Doctor. But it's been hard enough getting the Tarkan to trust us even this far. If it looks like the head researcher just gave up the project to focus on personal concerns, it could jeopardize the cease-fire."

The Tarkan were a powerful, advanced race that preyed on shipping lanes between Vostigye territory and the Nekrit Expanse. Kes had learned of them from Zahir *(Zahir! I'll have to contact him, have him come right away!)* when *Voyager* had first encountered him and his fellow Mikhal Travelers. He had spoken of how the Tarkan would overpower ships, drop off their crews on the nearest remotely habitable worlds, and claim the vessels as their trophies. He hadn't known or wondered why a people with such powerful vessels would need to take the ships of others, or why they would leave their crews alive. But then, the Mikhal were wanderers, rugged individualists concerned mainly with their own survival. They would have had no way of discovering that a devastating plague had ravaged the Tarkan worlds for generations; that the crews of Tarkan ships, unable to return home, felt compelled to capture other ships to give themselves room to reproduce and expand their population. Moreover, since the disease could lie dormant for decades, they felt the need to spread out their population into as many separate small groups as possible, to minimize the losses if an outbreak occurred.

Kes had read this in the minds of the Tarkan she'd treated, and had lobbied hard with Neelix's help to persuade the Vostigye legislature to fund this project. It hadn't been too difficult, really, since her reputation preceded her. Over the past few months, she had become very much in demand within the Vostigye scientific and medical community, and had attracted considerable interest from their government as well. It had been overwhelming to her at first. Apparently her brief telepathic contact with Species 8472 had unlocked mental abilities she'd only been able to access twice before, once with the help of Tanis at Suspiria's station, and once when her body was under the control of the warlord Tieran. But this time, her abilities had remained permanently unlocked after the fleeting encounter, and there was more than she'd experienced before. It wasn't just increased telepathy and a limited telekinesis that she had only tentatively dared to explore. Her ability to learn and retain knowledge had increased even beyond her innate eidetic recall. She could even gain knowledge from the minds of others—not by a conscious reading of their thoughts, but more like the way prenatal Ocampa absorbed basic skills, language, and general knowledge from their mothers while in the mitral sac. She sometimes felt like a fraud because of that, but she couldn't deny it was useful—and endlessly fascinating, as she gained more and more new skills through osmosis from the brilliant people surrounding her. She often wondered whether more extensive contact with Species 8472 might supercharge her abilities still further—and whether she would even want that to occur. She was still getting used to the abilities she had, and to the new responsibilities the establishment kept placing on her shoulders as a result.

"I think the Tarkan can understand the importance of ensuring the continuation of your family line," the Doctor was saying. "After all, that's why they do what they do in the first place." He smiled. "Don't worry, Kes. Even you aren't completely indispensable."

She blushed. "I know. I didn't mean to imply that."

"Of course not."

"It's just . . . sometimes the people around here treat me as though I am." She grinned. "Sometimes I feel so tempted just to run off with Zahir. Just the two of us, exploring unknown space, with no responsibilities."

"Well, maybe now's the time. Except for the 'no responsibilities' part," he added.

Kes's gray-green eyes widened. "I hadn't even thought about that. I've just been worrying about my responsibilities as a scientist, a healer. . . . I have to start adjusting to the idea of being a mother."

"I'm sure you'll be a fine mother. After all, you've done it once before. Or after, as the case may be."

"But I only have fragmentary memories of that timeline." Nearly a year before, Kes had undergone a bizarre experience wherein she had jumped backward from the end of her life aboard *Voyager* in an alternate timeline—or her original timeline, actually, one that had been altered as a consequence of her journey into her own past. Nothing since then had happened the way she remembered it occurring in that future. There, *Voyager* had never been crippled in a Species 8472 attack, and Tuvok and Tom Paris had survived; indeed, Tom had become her husband and the father of her daughter Linnis. But the ship had suffered badly at the hands of a people called the Krenim, and both Captain Janeway and B'Elanna Torres had been killed. Kes sometimes wondered if there had been some way in which her own return from the future had triggered the change that had led to the 8472 attack—and to the death of her mentor and one of her dearest friends. But she could see no connection between the events. Perhaps resetting the timeline had just enabled certain random factors to fall out differently.

"I'm sure it'll come back to you," the Doctor said. She smiled wanly. He was comforting in his own way, but still, she wished Tuvok were here to advise her. In many ways, she felt that the crippling of *Voyager* had been liberating for her, forcing her to move beyond the comfort zone of her ship and friends, to strike out and make it on her own as an adult. But she often wished for Tuvok's wise, reasoned counsel to guide her. His decades of experience as a father and husband would be very helpful to her in the weeks and months—all right, years—ahead.

Husband! The word resonated in her mind. "I had really better talk to Zahir," she said.

"I know this is a big decision to spring on you like this."

"Decision?" On the viewscreen, Zahir looked around in disbelief, even though there was no one else in the cabin of his cozy scout ship to look at. *"From what you're telling me, Kes, it sounds like I've got no choice in the matter!"*

"I'm the one who has no choice, Zahir. The *elogium* is once in a lifetime. And we both knew it would happen soon." She struggled to keep her tone gentle, but the hormonal surges and her soaring body temperature made it difficult, even with the supplements the Doctor had given her to ameliorate the effects.

"But I didn't think it would be . . ." Zahir trailed off, his ridged nose wrinkling in a frown as he brushed his long black hair from his face. She self-consciously brushed at a few of her own locks, their golden curls gone limp and dull from the sweat that drenched them. She'd stripped down to nothing, alone in her quarters with only her lover to see her, but she was still burning up and panting, and it embarrassed her to look so bedraggled in front of him, even though he didn't seem to mind watching her pace the room this way. *"There's nothing the Doctor can do to . . . to treat this? He's had years to come up with something."*

"You make it sound like a disease! This is it, Zahir. The time is now, or never. And there's no one else. You're my only hope for becoming a mother."

He glared. *"And you make it sound like I'm just the one who happens to be around."*

"You know that's not what I mean. Why do you think I sought you out again? You're the man I chose to be the father of my child." *Or children,* she amended. Ocampa procreated only once, but they often bore twins or triplets; otherwise, their population would have quickly declined.

She had almost gone with him once before, the first time they had met. Fully grown and ready for change in her life, feeling the urge to leave the nest of *Voyager* and spread her wings, Kes had become captivated with the handsome Mikhal Traveler and his romantic way of life: wandering the spaceways in ones and twos, seeking adventure and new experiences, bound only by the laws of chance and fate. But she had decided that if she was going through changes in her life, it was better to stay with the people who knew her best, those she could trust to keep her anchored.

But she had still cared for Zahir, so after *Voyager* had been crippled, she had sought him out again. They had shared some wild adventures for a time, but then her augmented powers had made her valuable to the Vostigye Union and she had been compelled to settle down. He had been reluctant to spend too much time in Vostigye space, given the attitudes toward outsiders, but he had chosen to stay close in his wanderings for her sake. She had indulged his need for freedom, not wishing to rush him into anything. But biology had trumped her plans.

Zahir finally found words again. *"To be a father . . . I'm not sure I'm ready."*

She smiled. "Isn't it the Mikhal way to go where fate takes you and adapt as you go?"

After a moment, he grew resolute. *"You're right. I'll come as soon as I can."*

"Please hurry. I should begin to secrete the *ipasaphor* any time now, and after that, we'll only have fifty hours to conceive."

"I can make it if I cut through the Myrel plasma drifts. It'll play hell with my intake manifolds, but . . . well, I suppose I won't be needing them if I'm going to be staying in one place for a while." He smiled. *"How long does the mating process last? Six days?"*

She chuckled at his excitement. "Oh, at least."

"You're a far more robust people than you look." They shared a laugh. *"Though you've never looked more enticing. I love you, Kes."*

"I love you too. See you soon."

But she was distracted as she signed off. Her mention of the *ipasaphor,* the hormonal secretion from the palms that catalyzed the mating bond, had reminded her—she should have begun to show more signs by now. She should have felt the itching as the mitral sac emerged on her back. She reached back; the bare skin there was as smooth as ever.

Could something be wrong with the process? Could my premature elo-gium before have affected it now? Or could my other recent changes be affecting it? It was time to see the Doctor again.

"Kes, this is extraordinary!"

"Is there something wrong, Doctor?"

"No, no, you're in perfect health. But your *elogium* has completely reversed itself."

A chill ran through her, but there was a touch of relief to it. "Permanently?"

"I don't think so. All your reproductive glands are mature, in-tact, and ready to go—they just aren't going. It's as though some-thing is holding them back."

"Something? It sounds like you have a theory."

He paused. "The one anomaly is your serotonin level. It appears that the telekinetic center of your brain is exceptionally active."

Her eyes widened. In the past, her telekinetic ability had proven dangerous when it got out of control—and lethal when under Tieran's control. "Does it pose any danger?"

"No . . . in fact, it seems its psionic output is focused through your own nervous system. Put simply, Kes . . . I believe you've managed to postpone your *elogium* through a sheer effort of will."

"Is that possible?"

"When it comes to you, Kes, I've stopped asking that question. You were expressing concern earlier about the inconvenience of the *elogium* striking now. Would you have chosen to delay it if you could?"

She thought carefully. "Yes. I do want this—I want to have a family—but this is not a good time for it. In fact . . ." Her breath caught as she realized something. "I think I was feeling a little resentful that my biology was taking the choice away from me. I would've preferred to be able to choose when and with whom I had my children. I just didn't admit it to myself because I thought I had no choice." She caught the Doctor staring at her. "What is it?"

"You said 'when . . . and with whom.' "

It took a moment to sink in. "You think I'm having second thoughts about Zahir?"

"You'd have to tell me that. It just occurs to me that, in the wake of Mister Neelix, Zahir has been the only romantic partner of your adult life. And until just now, you thought you'd have only one chance to become a mother, and that it would happen within the next few months. Now, it seems, you suddenly have more choices. Your condition seems stable; my best medical judgment is that you can continue to postpone the *elogium* indefinitely, until you decide you truly are ready. So I suppose the question is, did you choose Zahir because he was Mister Right, or Mister Right Place at the Right Time?"

She glared at him. "That's an awfully blunt question, Doctor."

He hesitated. "I apologize, Kes. It's . . . different for me now.

Before, I always identified myself with a single holographic body. Now, I'm in hundreds of bodies at once, and it's hard to feel truly attached to any one of them. It's a different . . . level of self-awareness. So I fear I sometimes find it harder to relate to . . . individuals the same way I once did. I need to try harder to maintain my usual, sterling bedside manner."

She smiled at his optimistic assessment of his usual manner. "It's all right, Doctor. I've always appreciated your bluntness. Maybe I just . . . didn't want to hear the question."

"You mean . . . we're not having a baby?"

The disappointment on his face was heartbreaking. Less than two days ago, he'd been frightened of the idea. Now he'd come around to it fully. But maybe that mercurial tendency was part of the problem. "I'm sorry, Zahir. But my options have . . . broadened. I have a freedom I've never known before. The Doctor thinks that my mental control over my bodily functions might even let me prolong my life expectancy."

"But that's wonderful! We could have more years together."

"Maybe we could. But you were right the other day—I chose you because I didn't think I had another choice. Now I can't be so sure. I just don't want to rush into any decision."

He heard what she wasn't saying. "Because you don't want to end up unhappy with the wrong man."

She wanted to reassure him, but decided he deserved honesty. "I'm sorry. I do love you for what you've been to me—a breath of fresh air, an adventure. A free, roving spirit who was nonetheless willing to slow down and stay awhile for my sake. I'll always cherish you for that. But I don't think that makes you the man I want to start a family and live out my life with. Certainly not right now. Now I have so much more of my life that I can explore, so many more opportunities I can take. I still want motherhood to be a part of that, but it can be on my own terms now, when the time is right."

"And when the man is right."

"I'm sorry, Zahir. You're a wonderful man. But a young woman's infatuation is not enough of a basis for a marriage."

He laughed, blinking rapidly. "I don't know why I'm upset. This is a load lifted from my back. I was terrified. Of course I'm not ready to be a father—what was I thinking?"

She kissed him. "You were thinking of me. Of being there when I needed you. I'll always love you for that."

"But you need to move on," he said, his voice rough. "Find your own path. I'd be a poor Traveler if I tried to hold you from that. Not when you have the kind of potential you do."

In his mind, she felt the pain beneath his words—the love he felt for her, deeper than he would acknowledge. But she also felt that it was a juvenile love, the kind that burned strong and then burned out. Fathering her children would have become a trap for him, and it would not have ended well, even if she had lived only four or five years more. Ending it now was better for them both.

But she knew she would be lonelier without him. She relished the new freedom that lay before her, but she missed her old friends from *Voyager*. She corresponded with them all, of course, but it wasn't the same.

Would they just keep drifting further apart? Would she keep losing the ones she loved?

5

"Good day, everybody, and welcome to the latest installment of *Catching Up with Neelix*. I, of course, am your host, Neelix, and, well, I guess you've caught up with me. Heh-heh. And just in time, too, for this is a momentous occasion indeed. As of today, it has been exactly six Earth months since my first broadcast. Which is just under four Vostigye *ronds*. And in just another few days, it will have been forty Talaxian *niziks*, and—well, that's the great thing about living in a multispecies community. So many excuses to throw an anniversary party!

"You know, when I started these broadcasts as a way for *Voyager*'s crew to stay . . . *caught up* . . . on one another as they scattered across Vostigye space, I had no idea they would become so popular with Vostigye viewers as well, not to mention the Nezu, the Bourget, the Ridion, and the rest of the fine folks who make up the Union. I guess it just goes to show that everyone has a hunger to learn about new worlds and new civilizations.

"And not to worry, folks, we'll have plenty of that today. We'll get the latest update on the progress of the Tarkan cure from everybody's favorite, the lovely and charming Kes. We've got an interview with Lieutenant Lyndsay Ballard on the ongoing reconstruction of *Voyager*. And the one and only Doctor—eh, so to speak—will be here with his latest . . . *fascinating* medical lecture, 'Sympathetic or Parasympathetic: The Debate Rages On.'

"As for myself, I've just gotten back from my goodwill tour to the Nyrian home system, and I'm happy to report some promising developments on the diplomatic front. Of course, now that everyone in the region's been tipped off to their little takeover-by-translocator trick—thanks to Captain Janeway and her crew, by the way—the Nyrians aren't exactly in a strong bargaining position. But they're not a bad people once you get to know them. And they know they're as much at risk as the rest of us if the Borg or Species 8472 come this way. So . . . I can't say anything official at this stage, but I wouldn't be surprised if there was an alliance in our future. In the meantime, we have a fascinating segment on Nyrian culture and history, helping you get to know your neighbors a little better.

"Speaking of which, one of our guests today is the eminent Casciron historian and poet, Garvas Caer. He'll be here to talk about the deep-rooted cultural issues underlying the current tensions over Casciron immigration policy. We'll also have Vitye Megon, Subspeaker of the Legislature, as our guest to offer the opposing side. I'm sure that will be a . . . *lively* debate.

"But first, some announcements. I'm happy to report that, thanks to your generous contributions, we now have sixty-seven percent of the funding we need to rebuild *Voyager*'s science labs. Meanwhile, the holodeck reconstruction fund is at, uh, eighty-nine percent. I guess that shows where your priorities lie. Heh-heh. Seriously, we are all deeply moved by the generosity of our Vostigye and other viewers. With your help, we'll have *Voyager* flying again before you know it.

"In other exciting news, our favorite Bolians, Chell and Gol-wat, have finally set their wedding date. Now all we need are something new and something borrowed. Uh, sorry, human joke. And *Voyager*'s own Lauren MacTaggart has agreed to sing at the wedding . . ."

Chakotay gazed out at the ruins of the ancient Vostigye city with awe. Despite—or to spite—their planet's high gravity, the Vostigye had striven to build tall, and many of their ancient towers had remained standing through centuries of seismic instability, thanks to their sturdy, ziggurat-like construction. "Thank you for bringing me to see this," he told Dobrye Gavanri. "I'm amazed at how untouched these ruins are."

The Minister of Science answered with a wry grin on her gray-furred face. "Most Vostigye don't like to come to the Birthworld. Even for those who aren't superstitious, the smell of death on this place is forbidding. There's a certain irony in our use of the name."

Chakotay nodded solemnly. Over ninety percent of a thriving industrial-era population had died in the course of the Catastrophe, when the gravitation of a passing white dwarf had triggered intense geological upheavals. The Vostigye had been at the most primitive level of spaceflight back then, driven by necessity to develop that technology as quickly as possible. They hadn't known whether their young could develop properly without full gravity, hadn't known how much cosmic radiation they could withstand, hadn't even known if it was possible to build a self-sustaining artificial biosphere. Many more lives had been lost on the way to solving those problems. But they'd endured their Trail of Tears against all odds, refusing to give up. Chakotay felt a deep kinship with these people.

He began moving down the slope into the half-collapsed city, grateful for the strength-enhancing armatures the Vostigye had developed to let offworlders cope with unaccustomed gravity. "That's not the only irony I see here," he told Dobrye as she loped down beside him.

"Oh?"

"Being here reminds me that the Vostigye are a whole civilization of refugees. So I wonder sometimes why many of you have so much trouble accepting other refugees."

"We worked hard to create the civilization we have," the minister said. "We're deeply invested in it, and justifiably proud. Many fear letting it become diluted or changed." He heard a hint of defensiveness, hastily quashed, in his friend's voice. Dobrye had grown up in a staunchly Preservationist family, her love of exploration and novelty overcoming their insularity and leading her to a prominent post in the Progressive government. Though she disagreed with their politics, she still cared for them and strove to understand them. Chakotay wished there were more like her in the Vostigye government, people who could serve as bridges between the ideological factions.

"But isn't that why so many refugees come here?" he asked her. "Because they admire what you've created? Doesn't it stand to reason that they'd want to help preserve it too?"

Dobrye chuckled. "I'm not the one you have to convince, my friend. But your little speech would play very well on the net. All the more reason why you should accept my offer to run."

He smirked and shook his head. "Sorry, Dobrye. I already have a constituency to look out for."

"Your crewmates have adapted very well. They can take care of themselves—especially with a tireless advocate like Neelix. And they've proven themselves capable, intelligent, responsible individuals, everything the Preservationists say refugees can't be. But there are still laws in place that hold them back. You could help to change that."

"And if a *Voyager* crewman joins the establishment, it's a great public-relations win for the Progressives."

"True," Dobrye conceded. "It proves that outsiders can assimilate and contribute meaningfully. And that can only help in your quest to build a regional alliance."

Chakotay pondered. "You have a point. But I'd prefer you didn't use the word 'assimilate.'"

"Apologies. It was impolitic."

"No, that's all right." The problem was his, not hers. He still lay awake at nights, imagining the faces of Riley and the others in the Cooperative. They were so proud of what they had done, breaking free of the Borg, forming their own new society that allowed both individuality and collective thought, convinced it would bring them the best of both. Chakotay had doubted their good intentions after they had imposed their control on his mind and forced him to help create that new interlink. But he had hoped their innate humanity would let them grow beyond that mistake and build something of value, perhaps something that could keep the Borg in check.

But now they would never have the chance. Six months ago, they had been attacked by Species 8472 as part of the extra-cosmic invaders' genocidal war against all Borg. They had applied the creativity the Collective was incapable of, devising a nano-probe defense not unlike the one the Doctor had developed to cure Harry, though less effective as an offensive weapon. They had succeeded in driving off the 8472. Unfortunately, that had brought the attention of the Collective, which had come in force and reassimilated them, wiping out a whole nascent civilization to protect its own hide. The nanoprobe defense had let the Borg rally and prolong the war past its expected duration. That was a mixed blessing, for it provided more time to build an alliance, and might leave the victor even weaker. On the other hand, the prolonged fighting might force the victor to become tougher and more creative, harder to defeat.

But what kept Chakotay up at night was the question: what if he'd gone along with Kathryn's original plan? Species 8472 might have been defeated, and Riley and the Cooperative might have been spared. Of course, he couldn't know that; it was possible that the Borg would have remained a stronger threat and assimilated the Cooperative anyway, along with the Vostigye and everyone else in the region. But he couldn't help wondering all the same.

Dobrye stroked his shoulder; through the fabric, he could feel the odd texture of her grooming pads. "Very well—enough talk of politics. We came here to do some archaeology. To help you learn about the history of your new home."

Chakotay nodded and joined her in heading down toward the

city again. It was some time before he realized that the phrase "your new home" hadn't felt wrong to him at all.

Kathryn Janeway stood on a catwalk in Kosnelye's spaceport hub, staring up at the sight of *Voyager* suspended in the drydock cradle that had been its home for the past eight months. "Stood" was an imprecise term, though, for only the gentlest rotational gravity held her against the catwalk's surface. The Vostigye had grown accustomed to varying gravity conditions, and thus did not employ gravity plating as ubiquitously as Starfleet did, although there was a force field around the catwalk to contain a shirtsleeve atmosphere. She caught a stray strand of hair that waved before her face and tucked it back into her bun.

Her regular inspections of her ship's exterior drove home how much had changed in its rebuilding. The warp nacelles were still startling to see. Although one original nacelle had remained, a ship could not work with mismatched nacelles, so it had been dismantled, its components recycled where possible. The new nacelles were comparable in performance to the old, but had a different, more Vostigye aesthetic. They were also permanently mounted on right-angled pylons not unlike those of an *Excelsior-* or *Ambassador*-class ship, since the Vostigye and *Voyager*'s surviving engineers had devised a solution to the subspace erosion problem that was simpler than the original variable-geometry nacelles.

Her eyes moved to the underside of the forward hull, which looked oddly vacant without the contours of the aeroshuttle at its center. Of course, there had only been a nonfunctional mock-up there originally, installed as ballast when *Voyager* had been rushed into action for that three-week mission to the Badlands. Tom Paris had always wanted to build a real aeroshuttle, insisting that the ship's industrial replicators could fabricate the necessary parts. But power reserves had been insufficient for some time, and then the damage inflicted in various battles had required using the mock-up as a sort of splint for the hull, until it became too integrated into the ship's structure to be safely removed without dry-dock facilities. Tom had begun reworking his plans with a whole new shuttle in mind, but he had died before they had progressed beyond the most embryonic stage. And now, when *Voyager* was finally being rebuilt in drydock, the aeroshuttle had needed to be scuttled altogether due to insufficient funds. Janeway regretted that deeply. It would've been a lovely tribute to Tom's memory.

"She's shaping up nicely." It was Chakotay. He must have arrived alongside her while she was engrossed in her ship.

"She's still not what she was," Janeway said. "We've had to make so many compromises."

"I prefer to think of them as adaptations. Even improvements. The Vostigye's automatic repair systems are impressive."

She studied him. "I hear that you might be running for the Vostigye Legislature."

He chuckled. "Gossip travels fast—and grows along the way. I just told Dobrye Gavanri that she made a couple of good points when she tried to recruit me."

"Still . . . you didn't say no to her."

"She did make good points. We and the other refugees could always use another advocate in the government."

"So you're considering it?"

He seemed surprised by the disbelief in her tone. "I'm keeping an open mind."

"Don't you think you should've consulted me before you gave a high-ranking member of the government the impression that you might run?"

"I didn't mean to give any such impression. And I'm happy to discuss the issue with you now, if it's that important to you."

"What's important to me is that you don't begin to lose track of our mission."

Chakotay frowned. "I haven't lost track, Kathryn. Our mission has just changed."

"Our mission is still to get our crew home."

"In the long term, yes. But it's not like we were planning to take off and abandon these people the moment *Voyager* was spaceworthy again. We've committed to helping them defend themselves against whoever wins the war. We never would've gotten even partial government funding to rebuild *Voyager* otherwise. And we can't exactly resume course for the Alpha Quadrant when one implacable enemy or the other is still in the way."

She held up her hands, conceding the point. "I know that. It's just . . ." She shook her head. "I look around, and it seems that more and more of us are drifting away. I could understand when Telfer and Tal Celes resigned—they weren't Starfleet material to begin with; they never would've lasted on *Voyager* if there'd been an alternative. Gerron, too, though it looked like he was coping so well. But Freddy Bristow running off to marry that Mikhal woman . . . Megan Delaney joining a convent? I couldn't believe that."

"She was devastated by the loss of her sister. The Vostigye religious orders formed during the Catastrophe; they have centuries of experience at counseling the bereaved. Honestly, sometimes I wish B'Elanna had hooked up with them instead of the Casciron militants."

Janeway winced. That had been the hardest blow. B'Elanna Torres had come so far in her three years on *Voyager*—Janeway never could have believed she would revert to her old ways. But then, B'Elanna had perhaps lost more than anyone else.

"And if some of us discover that their definition of home has changed over the past few months," Chakotay went on, "isn't that their choice to make?"

It was a moment before Janeway responded. "I've resigned myself to the fact that not everyone will join us when it's time to resume course for the Alpha Quadrant. But I always assumed that when that time came, you would still be by my side. Lately, it seems you're drifting away. Can I still rely on you?"

His gaze hardened. "I'm still doing my duty. As first officer, my job is to take care of the crew. But most of the crew isn't on *Voyager*—they're out there, living in the Union." He paused. "If anyone's drifting away, Kathryn, it's you. Our crew is out there, but you're always here, cooped up aboard *Voyager*. You haven't made any real effort to connect with the Vostigye."

"I've done my part to promote the alliance."

"In diplomatic meetings, yes. But you haven't tried to get to know them as people. To experience their culture, as our crew is experiencing it. To show the skeptics among them that you're willing to relate to them as a friend and offer them something meaningful in return for their sanctuary."

"You mean offer my allegiance? I'm still a Starfleet captain, Chakotay. The Federation is still my home."

"But we won't see it for decades, Kathryn. A wise man once said that life is what's happening while you're making other plans. I still want to get back home someday, but this is the life we have now, and we shouldn't be afraid to live it. It's not a bad life. We have friends, allies, a support structure we didn't have when we were just one ship against a quadrant. We have the opportunity to be part of a larger community again, maybe not the Federation, but not a bad substitute. Why not enjoy it while we have it?"

"And what if we enjoy it so much that we lose sight of our identity? Of the ties we still have in the Alpha Quadrant? There are many of us who haven't forgotten those for a moment. Mister Ayala has his boys back home—boys who need a father. Rollins has a wife, Gennaro a husband. I still have my mother and my sister. We can't forget them, Chakotay."

"I have a sister too. And I've never forgotten her, not for a moment. But she wouldn't want me to waste away my life because I was so busy preparing for tomorrow that I never seized the day."

"Is that what you think? That repairing *Voyager*, trying to get home, is a waste?"

"Of course not. I'm just saying that we shouldn't use it as an excuse to let life pass us by. And frankly, Kathryn, I'm beginning to worry about you. There's a part of you that can get too attached to your goals, too blind to alternatives. You're becoming more single-minded, and I don't like what that's doing to you. That's not the Kathryn Janeway I've grown to know and admire.

"I think . . . you could do with a break. Dobrye has been offering to take me to Loresch—it's the most popular resort planet in the sector. Why don't you come with us? *Voyager* will still be here when you get back."

"I'm sorry—no." The casual way he spoke of *Voyager* was painful to her. He really didn't see how much his priorities were changing.

Or were they? Was he right? Did serving the best interests of the crew mean helping them adapt to a new life in the Delta Quadrant?

Oh, Tuvok . . . I wish you could be here to advise me. I feel so adrift without your counsel.

No, she told herself. *I'm still the captain. The decision is mine.* She had to remain focused on the goal. If she let herself drift even a little, then the whole crew would lose its way, even worse than it already had.

And if Chakotay couldn't understand that, then she'd simply have to follow that path by herself. Such was the burden of command.

6

"The life signs—they read as Borg, sir!"

"Shields up full!" Captain Nagorim ordered.

Voenis opened the comm to the weapons bay. "Arm torpedoes. Stand by to fire."

Harry Kim frowned. "But, Captain, why would the Borg send out a distress signal?"

"The war has forced them to adapt, Lieutenant. Maybe they've learned guile."

"Or maybe these Borg have broken free of the Collective somehow. It's happened before. Last year on *Voyager*—"

"Yes, I've read the reports on the Cooperative."

"Captain," Voenis said, "we can't take the chance."

"At least we can hear what they have to say, sir." Harry tried to keep his voice level, to avoid a pleading tone. He'd worked hard to prove himself again after B'Elanna's defection, but he wasn't sure how far the captain would trust him now.

And Voenis was a lost cause. "That would risk exposing us to a viral attack like the one that got the *Nelcharis* assimilated," she said.

"Captain, there are anomalies in these biosigns, but I can't resolve them well enough yet. I just need a little more time."

Nagorim pondered. "Voenis, how soon to weapons range?"

"Thirteen *lants*."

"Mister Kim, you have that long to refine sensor resolution."

Harry had spent months getting *Ryemaren*'s sensors as close to

Starfleet specs as possible. What could he do in twenty-odd seconds? He'd need a whole different set of sensors to—

That was it. "I can launch a probe, sir. The interferometry should give me a better reading."

Nagorim nodded. "Do it."

Eleven *lant*s later, the results came in, the two sensor grids working together to produce more detailed results. "They're not drones, sir. Not anymore. They have Borg implants, but their biosigns and neural activity readings are individualized."

The captain relaxed. "Accept their hail."

"—*stigye vessel, repeat, we are not hostile! We need urgent medical assistance. Requesting asylum. Please respond!*"

"Wonderful," Voenis grumbled. "More refugees." But Harry could tell she was relieved that she hadn't given the order to fire on innocent beings.

The eight former drones were beamed directly to sickbay, and the captain brought Harry along to meet them. "It's thanks to you they're still alive," Nagorim said, "so I'm assigning you responsibility for them." Harry thanked the captain, recognizing it as an expression of trust rather than a punitive burden.

The refugees still looked like drones, mostly; they had made a few token attempts to remove their implants, but with limited success. Their medical distress, according to the Doctor, resulted as much from their self-surgery as from their resurgent immune systems' rejection of their implants.

Their leader introduced himself as Malken, saying he was a member of a species called the Hirogen, a name as unfamiliar to the captain as to Harry. He told a remarkable story of a realm called Unimatrix Zero, a kind of virtual reality within the Borg collective consciousness. Apparently a tiny percentage of assimilated drones had a mutation that let their subconscious minds remain active after assimilation. When they were in their dormant cycle (Malken called it "regenerating"), they shared a sort of collective dream. "No, not a dream," Malken corrected when Harry described it that way. "For it is only in Unimatrix Zero that we are awake, able to remember who we are and think for ourselves."

Unfortunately, they had never found a way to carry this awareness into their active phase, so Unimatrix Zero remained an entirely passive form of resistance. "Fascinating," the Doctor observed through his AMP body. "What you're describing is a form of dissociative identity disorder—two separate states of consciousness with no awareness of one another. Unsurprising, under the circumstances. Such a dissociation would allow the mind to retreat from the trauma of being assimilated and suborned to the collective will."

"Maybe that is so," Malken said, "for I have no memory of how we came to be liberated. We were in Unimatrix Zero when suddenly we awakened, in these Borg bodies, surrounded by destruction." From his description, it sounded as though their cube had been crippled in a Species 8472 attack. The attack had apparently burned out the minds of all the drones, except those few who had been in Unimatrix Zero at the time, five out of a cube of thousands. They had made their escape and spent weeks trying to get out of Borg space, picking up three others like them along the way.

"And you made it here just in time," the Doctor said. "Luckily, you're in the finest medical hands in the quadrant."

Harry noticed one of the drones looking nervous, her wide gray eye—the one not covered by an ocular implant—darting about the medical bay. Though half her face was obscured, there was something striking about her features. She could almost have been human, but it was more than that. There was an innocence about her, a vulnerability that made him feel protective. He sidled over to her. "He's right, you know. The Doctor really is the best there is."

She seemed uncertain, warily eyeing the Doctor's robotic form. "Is he . . . a person?"

"Well, you could say he's a lot of people."

"Like the Borg?" She pulled her limbs in on herself, like a timid child.

"Oh! No, not like that. Really, he's fine. It's . . . well, it's a long story. All you need to know is, there's nothing to be afraid of. My name's Harry, and I'm going to make sure that nothing bad happens to you. To any of you."

The woman gathered herself, straightening out and trying to assert some dignity. But her voice was still gentle and girlish as she said, "I'm sorry. This is all so new to me. I . . . I've never known anything but Unimatrix Zero."

"Never? Were you born in the Collective?"

"No, but . . . I was taken when I was very young. I guess I remember a few things . . . but I try not to think about it much."

No wonder she seemed so youthful. If her entire life since early childhood had been lived in fragments during regeneration cycles, then her total life experience might be a fraction of her physical age (and it was clear, even through the Borg exoskeleton, that she was a fully developed woman, to say the least). Awakening to find herself in a Borg body, surrounded by corpses and a disintegrating ship, must have been a shock for her.

He put a hand on her shoulder, hoping she could feel it through the exoskeleton. "Don't worry," he told her. "You don't have to think about it now if you don't want to. Although . . . I've told you my name. Do you remember yours?"

She smiled, a bright, open smile that made her face beautiful despite everything the Borg had done to it. "Annika. My name's Annika."

"The Voth?" Neelix asked. "The government wants me to meet with the Voth?"

"That's right," Chakotay said. "Overminister Rosh is concerned about some reports he's getting. In the past, the Voth have mostly kept to themselves, not taking much interest in what goes on outside their city ships. But apparently, in recent months, they've begun looking outward again."

"Well, maybe that's a good sign." Neelix vividly remembered *Voyager*'s encounter with the Voth, a civilization descended from an ancient Earth species called hadrosaurs, which had somehow survived a mass extinction in Earth's distant past and migrated across the galaxy. "Maybe it means they're starting to open up a little."

"I doubt it. They've been showing up at various worlds in the territory they consider theirs and demanding tribute and formal declarations of allegiance."

"Oh, dear. As if we don't have enough powerful enemies in the other direction." Neelix had always found *Voyager*'s technology miraculous, but the Voth had completely neutralized it without working up a sweat—or whatever it was that reptiles did.

"I'm hoping it's not that bad. I think the Voth are a lot like Ming China back on Earth. A millennium ago, they were the most advanced and powerful culture in the world. They sent out great trading fleets, the biggest, most sophisticated ships on Earth, to exact tribute from other nations. But all they wanted was token submission. It wasn't about conquest or exploration, just about asserting their power and superiority to the rest of the world. As they saw it, there was nothing anyone else had that was as good as what they had already. So after thirty years, they scuttled the fleet and closed in on themselves again."

"So you think that's all the Voth are doing? What's the expression, showing the flag?"

Chakotay nodded. "I wouldn't be surprised if we started it. The controversy over the Distant Origin Theory challenged the beliefs on which the Voth regime bases its authority. They're probably feeling insecure, wanting to assert that authority again."

Neelix recalled being imprisoned by the Voth, who had used *Voyager*'s crew as hostages to convince the advocate of the Distant Origin Theory, Professor Gegen, to retract his claims. Their sa-

cred Doctrine claimed that the Voth had been the first sentient
natives of this region of space, thus holding an inviolable claim
to its rule. The very existence of the humans aboard *Voyager* had
offered hard genetic evidence that this was not true. For a while,
Neelix had feared that the Voth would eradicate that evidence by
destroying *Voyager*. Instead, once Gegen had recanted, *Voyager* had
been sent on its way and commanded never to return.

"Have you shared this with the Overminister?" Neelix asked.
"If we only have to make a token gesture, we should be fine."

Chakotay shook his head. "The Voth's demands may be symbolic, but they want them to be memorable. They're extorting
massive amounts of tribute, demanding that planetary leaders
submit to humiliating rituals . . . and they're more than willing
to use deadly force to get what they want. Even if we go along,
the Vostigye Union could be economically crippled, politically
destabilized. And we can't afford that with the war still looming.
We need to reach some diplomatic understanding with the Voth
before that happens. Hopefully convince them to join the alliance. Their technology could make the difference when the time
comes."

"It certainly could," Neelix said. "But do you really think they'd
meet with me?"

"More likely you than me," Chakotay told him. "After our last
encounter, they made it clear that they'd prefer never to see me
again. Besides, 'nonindigenous' beings have no status in Voth society. Since you're from this quadrant, they might listen to you."

"I see your point."

"I'd send Kes with you if I could," Chakotay added. "She's
done wonders for the Tarkan peace process. But she's very much
in demand already."

Neelix smiled, suffused with pride. "She's become such a remarkable woman. I mean, she always was, but now—"

"I know what you mean. But I have every confidence in your
ability to speak for the alliance. You've done a fine job raising

awareness and building bridges—not just on the crew's behalf, but for the refugee population in general."

Neelix felt his muttonchops bristling at the praise. "Well, Commander . . . I've been a refugee myself for a long time. It's my privilege to do what I can." He frowned. "But the Voth don't exactly have a high opinion of refugees, do they? Hmf, at least the Vostigye don't rewrite their history to deny their origins."

"Don't be so hard on the Voth. It's hard to imagine what such an ancient civilization is like. More likely the knowledge of their origins was simply lost over the ages. Maybe they never knew it. We still don't know whether they came here on their own or were brought here before they evolved intelligence."

Again, Chakotay reminded Neelix of just why he admired the man so much. Even though he had befriended Professor Gegen and had every reason to resent the Voth regime for what they had done to him, Chakotay was still able to see their point of view and show them tolerance. This was not a man Neelix would let down if he could help it.

Right now, the Doctor was on *Voyager,* treating Lyndsay Ballard and a triad of worker-caste Bourget for serious injuries sustained in a construction accident. It was touch and go; he was close to losing the core member of the triad, without which the other two would be unable to think coherently for themselves. Bonding them with another member of the core gender would restore them, but they might no longer have an interest or facility for engineering. Lieutenant Ballard was badly injured as well, but fortunately *Voyager* had two auxiliary medical probes aboard, so the Doctor was able to use one to operate on Ballard and the other to work on the two dependent Bourget while his original holographic body tended to the core member. Thus, no triage was necessary; they could all receive the best possible care.

Right now, the Doctor was on *Ryemaren,* finishing up the final phase of implant extraction and regeneration for the Borg refugees. All of them would need to retain some of their Borg implants, but he had discovered a remarkable and unanticipated talent for cosmetic surgery, restoring all eight to appearances that were not only quite natural for their species, but aesthetically pleasing as well. He was particularly satisfied with his success at creating a bionic eye that perfectly matched Annika Hansen's surviving human one, and at stimulating the rapid regrowth of her hair, for which she had been extremely grateful. The Doctor was tempted to joke about its being a strictly vicarious pleasure for him, but of course he had no holographic body on *Ryemaren,* so the joke would be lost.

Right now, the Doctor was in Moskelar Station's hololab, giving Naomi Wildman a checkup and advising her mother to make sure she didn't eat too many Loreschian pastries, which her human-Ktarian system could not metabolize well. Naomi pouted and called him an old grouch.

Right now, the Doctor was in the mainframe of the central hospital in the Vyenokal habitat, coordinating emergency care for the dozens of victims of an explosion set off by Casciron extremists. Here he had an entire staff of skilled medical professionals to work with, and nominally his role was merely to serve and support them. However, they had welcomed his suggestions and knowledge almost from the start; the Vostigye, he reflected, had a far more enlightened view of artificial intelligences than the Federation did. So he could trust them to do the physical side of the work while he concentrated on the purely cybernetic: processing information, monitoring the patients' conditions, calling up records and precedents, keeping the staff updated on the latest findings about the type of explosives used, their effects, and the optimal treatments. He also devoted some of his attention to the other patients, those whom the staff was too busy to tend to at the moment, and made sure there was no diminution in their level of care. Right now, he was carrying on a lively conversation with an elderly Quitar composer who was living out her final days in the hospital and wished to pass along her memories and experiences while she still could.

Right now, today, the Doctor could not imagine how he had ever functioned in just a single body when there were so many people in need of his genius. True, he had been designed only as an emergency supplement, meant to fill in for a humanoid physician in a temporary capacity. But as an AI, his potential had been far greater, and once he had been integrated into the Vostigye medical network, he had finally begun to discover what he was really capable of. He'd thought it was an exercise in growth to study opera or commune with the great minds of history or create a simulated family on the holodeck. All those things had been worthwhile, true, but they had only served to make him a better humanoid. And that was only a fraction of what he was capable of being.

Right now, he was reminded of that as a memory update came in from his most distant AMP, an extension of himself running mostly autonomously because it was too far for real-time subspace networking. Periodic data transfers ensured that it shared continuity of memory and personality with the rest of him; otherwise it might diverge and end up being more an offspring than an avatar. He may have become many things now, but he wasn't sure he was ready to become a daddy.

Besides, this self's mission was too critical to leave unsupervised. Once it had become apparent that he was going to remain in this region indefinitely (even assuming his original self would eventually leave with *Voyager*), he had felt it incumbent upon himself to address the greatest medical crisis he had encountered in this quadrant: the Phage, the deadly degenerative syndrome that had turned the Vidiians from a once-great civilization into predators stealing healthy organs to survive. The Doctor had deployed an AMP in an unmanned craft, capable of devoting all its energy to propulsion and shielding and thus able to traverse the distance to Vidiian space—nearly a year's travel for *Voyager,* albeit with numerous stops along the way—in a fraction of the time. Its small size had let it slip through the Swarm sensor grid safely, unmolested by that viciously territorial species, but the Vidiian military had captured it and attempted to extract data on *Voyager*'s location. So he had wiped that probe's memory and sent another. Finally, they had gotten the message and allowed him to help.

Unfortunately, his attempt to recruit a key colleague in the research had hit a snag, and as he synchronized the memory upload with his own consciousness, he now remembered his avatar's attempt to apologize to her and persuade her to cooperate.

"I'm sorry it caused you such distress to encounter me in this form," he had told Danara Pel through his AMP body. "And I apologize that I can't give you what we once shared. But I never intended to give you the impression that I was being cold to you. You must understand—"

"I know, I know," she had told him, blinking away tears. "You told me about the memory loss you suffered when *Voyager* encountered the Swarm. You told me that you no longer remember falling in love with me. I don't need you to rub it in."

He had wanted to tell her that he had recovered a few fragmentary memories of their time together since then, that some of the feeling remained, but that would only hurt her more under the circumstances. He regretted the pain he'd already caused her when he'd first come to her. She had been shocked by how much he had changed, and he had been a little too blunt in informing her that he was no longer the "Shmullus" she had known.

So instead he had said, "It's more than that. When you knew me before, I was programmed to think of myself as essentially humanoid. I existed in a single humanoid body, pursued humanoid interests and interactions. As you can see, that's no longer the case."

"But you were the one who taught me that physical form doesn't matter!"

"It isn't just in form that I've changed. This robot isn't me, Danara. It's just one of the many appendages I control. My awareness is . . . interstellar now. I exist simultaneously on hundreds of ships and habitats, providing medical treatment to thousands of people at once."

"So no one person can truly matter to you anymore? Is that it? You've just grown too big to care about us?"

"I care more than ever, Danara! That's just it! I'm caring for so many different people now that I could never give my exclusive attention to any one person, any one thing. I've become so much bigger, gained so much more ability to save lives and care for those in need."

She had blinked away tears. "And is there no room in your life for anything else?"

"Yes, there is. But at any given moment when I'm engaged in recreation or personal discussion, other parts of me are conducting surgery or research. I still value my personal connections, but they're just one facet of a larger, more . . . intangible existence." He had simulated a sigh. "I wish I knew how to convey what it's like for me. There just aren't any words for it.

"The important thing is, I never intended to make you feel insignificant. Whether I remember it fully or not, you played an important role in my personal growth. And I'm grateful for that, even though my growth has taken me in a different direction. I hope that we can still be friends. And I hope that you can find it within yourself to work with me on curing the Phage."

As he absorbed the memory, awaiting her reply, he found himself reflecting on his new existence. He had gained so much. He was helping so many people. Lieutenant Ballard and the core Bourget were stabilizing. Annika was smiling at him. Samantha Wildman was thanking him as she left with her daughter. The Quitar musician was singing, her voice too weak to carry, but his AMP's receptors picked it up and stored it for posterity. But now he found himself wondering if, in growing so far, he had lost something. If maybe there were special joys unique to being small and singular, ones he would never know again.

After a moment, Danara had stepped closer to his AMP body. "I suppose it's very childish of me to refuse to work with you on saving my people because of a broken heart."

"Not at all. It's well established that romantic losses can cause clinical depression and impair performance in humanoids of any age."

She had laughed. "It's odd that I find that comforting. But no, I have been very selfish. What you've become . . . it sounds remarkable. It's unfair of me to reject you just because you've become something different. I'd . . . I'd like the chance to get to know the new you. Even if we can never be more than friends."

"We'll be more than friends," he had assured her. "We'll be the ones who save your people from the Phage. Together."

In the memory upload, Danara smiled. All across Vostigye space and beyond, those parts of the Doctor that were not too busy with life-and-death operations paused and took a moment to appreciate the sight.

7

Janeway did not appreciate being unceremoniously ordered to pull herself away from *Voyager*'s repairs and beam to the Overminister's office. So she was in a cranky mood when she arrived. Seeing Chakotay there too, along with Vitye Megon and most of the Council of Ministers, didn't ease her irritation. "Overminister Rosh. What's so urgent that it couldn't—"

"Kathryn," Chakotay said. "The Voth have captured Neelix. A city ship has just dropped out of transwarp on the border and is making its way here at warp seven."

"Is Neelix all right?"

"As far as we can tell, he's just being detained," Rosh told her. "But the Voth have made their purpose known." He hesitated, just barely. "They are . . . ordering us . . . to turn over *Voyager*'s crew."

He nodded to an aide, who activated a replay on the main monitor. A hard-edged reptilian face appeared, one Janeway found very familiar. *"This is Sanctioner Haluk of the Voth,"* he announced, and Janeway recognized his voice; he had commanded the forces that had boarded *Voyager* in their first encounter. *"Let it be known that the crew of the starship* Voyager *are known enemies of Voth authority. Your attempt to send a member of* Voyager's *crew as your emissary is a direct affront to our authority. If the Vostigye Union does not wish to be declared an enemy as well, you will turn over all of* Voyager's *personnel for immediate trial. Remember that you are granted your present way of life only through our indulgence."*

Janeway turned to Rosh. "How do you intend to respond to this . . . ultimatum?"

"It is not Vostigye policy," Rosh said proudly, "to submit to threats and intimidation."

"Be realistic," Megon interposed. "The Voth are millions of years beyond us. We have no way to stand against them."

"Again you underestimate our people, Vitye. We would not fall so easily."

"Perhaps not. But we would lose countless lives in the battle. Is it worth it for a few eights of refugees? Give them what they want and they will leave us be."

"Is that the position of the Preservationist bloc?"

"I speak for them. Sacrifice our military in a futile defense of these aliens and you will lose whatever tenuous support you have left. Your coalition will lose its place in the government."

"I think you're being overly optimistic, Subspeaker," Chakotay told Megon. "The Voth won't be satisfied with leaving you unharmed. In their view, you've defied their authority, and they'll want to punish you."

"They'll do that simply by taking the *Voyager*s away," Rosh said. "Losing the Doctor program would be a devastating blow to our medical establishment. And we certainly don't want Kes to fall into unfriendly hands, do we?"

"So that's all that matters to you?" Janeway challenged. "What you get out of our presence?"

"Kathryn," Chakotay said.

"She has a point," Megon said. "As do you, Overminister. The medical intelligence and the Ocampa are both of great value to us. But one is an extension of *Voyager*'s technology and the other was merely their passenger. Perhaps we could persuade the Voth to let us keep them when we turn over the others."

"You'd be turning us over to our deaths," Janeway said.

"And you would have us throw away countless Vostigye lives along with yours."

Rosh sighed heavily. "Open a channel to the city ship. We need to begin negotiations, see if some understanding can be reached."

Janeway stared at him. "You're not seriously considering her suggestion?"

"I must consider all possibilities. I must do what is necessary for those I am sworn to protect. As a leader yourself, you must understand this."

Soon, Haluk's face was on the viewer again. *"There can be no negotiation,"* he said, cutting off Rosh's overtures. *"Turn over the* Voyager *crew or suffer the consequences."*

"A number of *Voyager*'s personnel have brought considerable benefit to our people," Rosh countered. "They have helped promote peace and cooperation with our neighbors. It is in that spirit of cooperation that I—"

"Do not mistake us for your 'neighbors,' endotherm. You are tenants in our home space. Your fleeting mammalian civilization is a passing thought by our standards. We could easily take the Voyager *crew. It is as a courtesy that we give you the opportunity to surrender them yourselves, as a gesture of loyalty to the Voth."*

Megon spoke up. "Some of us are prepared to make that gesture, Sanctioner Haluk."

"Vitye, be still!"

"This is a democracy, Overminister. I am prepared to assemble the Legislature and call for a vote of no confidence right now."

"To cave in under threat!"

"To protect our people. Either way, you would not prevail." She turned back to Haluk. "However, we would request that you allow us to retain the medical intelligence program derived from *Voyager*'s technology, as well as the young Ocampa who traveled as their passenger for a time. Hers is a race indigenous to the region. Oh, and the Talaxian envoy as well. He offers a fair amount of entertainment value to our people."

"The Talaxian has defied our authority and must pay for his affront."

Haluk paused. *"However, the Voth are willing to be generous. You may retain the other indigenous endotherm and the medical software, if you deliver the rest of* Voyager's *crew without delay."*

"Subspeaker Megon does not have the authority to negotiate for this government," Rosh interposed.

"This is not a negotiation. This is a description of what will occur." The screen went dark.

"You have no choice, Overminister," Megon said. "Give the order, or I will convene the Legislature."

"No!" Dobrye Gavanri, Chakotay's science minister friend, rose from the council table. "This is wrong, can't you see that? We are Vostigye! We have fought for over sixteen generations to build a civilization we can be proud of. And it's not a civilization based on mere survival. Even at the beginning, when survival was all we had, we nonetheless held on to our ethics, our principles. Our Scripture kept us on the path of justice."

"These *Voyager*s do not revere our Scripture!"

"This is not about them, Subspeaker. This is about us and whether we live lives that the Ancestors would look upon with pride or shame."

"This is about whether we live lives at all! Charity is a noble ideal, Minister, but it can be taken too far! We cannot put our nation at risk for a smattering of immigrants!"

"You run home to your estate and cower in your impact shelter if you like," Gavanri said. "I will not see my friends turned over without a fight. I will take on the Voth myself if I must."

"Then you will die for nothing."

"Then I will die for everything that makes us Vostigye."

"Sir?" The technical aide addressed Rosh. "We have transmissions coming in from . . . numerous vessels and state facilities. Apparently the Voth's ultimatum was widely broadcast, and . . . our personnel are responding."

He put up a signal. A tortoiseshell-furred Vostigye captain appeared on the screen—and Harry Kim was visible on the bridge behind him. *"This is Captain Azorav Nagorim of the starship* Rye-maren, *addressing the Voth—and the Vostigye. I hereby make it known that if ordered to surrender any member of my crew to a foreign power, even by my own government, I will refuse that unethical order. Whether they originated in our Union or elsewhere does not matter—every member of* Ryemaren's *crew has proven his, her, or its worth and loyalty on many occasions, and deserves equal loyalty in return.*

"I admit there have been a few missteps along the way, a few misunder-standings and disagreements. But no more than we have always had among our own people. Such dissent is part of any free society, and it is a reason to try harder to understand one another, not to turn against one another.

"We are all Vostigye, whatever our origin. And we will stand together as one. That is my command, and I know every member of my crew is with me." It seemed to Janeway that the russet-furred female in the first officer's seat fidgeted at that, but only slightly.

The other messages were similar. Captains of other ships re-fused to surrender the *Voyager* personnel under their commands. The administrator of Moskelar Station refused to give up Kes or anyone else, hinting that the research facility had innovative and potent ways to defend itself. The dockyard personnel who had spent months rebuilding *Voyager* pledged to raise their tools in its defense. Even the Sisterhood of Solace issued a statement on Me-gan Delaney's behalf, stating that those who sought peace within their walls would never be expelled against their wishes.

As message after message came in, Janeway found her eyes fill-ing with tears—and cursed herself for her folly. Chakotay smiled at her softly, not gloating, merely gratified that she was finally seeing what he'd been trying to show her all along.

Rosh was smiling too, and there was definitely a touch of gloat-ing in it. "Go ahead, Vitye," he said. "Assemble the Legislature. I know where the people stand. And I serve their will. We will pro-tect the *Voyager*s among us, just as we would protect any Vostigye. For that is what they are."

A chastened Megon had no reply, merely drifting off to the

side to contact her supporters on her personal comm. Janeway sidled up to Rosh. "Overminister . . . I owe you an apology. I've been a poor guest—what you're doing for us now is more than I deserve."

"It's what anyone deserves."

"But you shouldn't suffer on our behalf. *Voyager* is just about spaceworthy. Let us board her and make a break for it."

Rosh looked at her askance. "And do you really think they'd spare us punishment after that humiliation? Besides, the Union wouldn't be the same without you."

"I can't let you fight our battles for us."

"Kathryn," Chakotay said, "don't you see? We don't have to stand alone anymore. We're part of something bigger." He turned to Rosh. "Maybe bigger even than the Union. We've been working hard to build an alliance—maybe it's time to put it to the test."

Sanctioner Haluk was amused when his subordinates reported a sudden increase in ship activity in the region. Not only Vostigye ships were convening in their capital system, but others as well: Ridion, Nezu, Porcion, Nyrian, even Tarkan. *No doubt they hope for strength in numbers,* he thought. Occasionally over the millennia, the Voth's periodic assertions of dominance had invited similar joint resistance from the powers that had preceded this current crop of flitfly civilizations—which was why those powers were not around any longer.

But Haluk saw no reason to hasten the destruction of these toy ships. He allowed them time to assemble around the Kosnelye habitat, even slowing the city ship's approach just enough to accommodate their sluggish drives. Best to let them assemble their maximum strength so that the demonstration would be most effective.

Soon enough, the city ship entered normal space to find itself facing dozens of starships of many different types. *Voyager* was not among them; most likely it was attempting to escape. But it would wait. Now it was time to make an example of these local endotherms who had dared to side with the intruders.

"Activate the neutralizer field," Haluk ordered. It was almost too easy—the simple press of a button would render this entire fleet powerless. But Haluk checked his thinking. He was not a carnivore like so many of these endotherms, taking pleasure in destruction for its own sake. No, he was a civilized herbivore, acting in the interests of his people's security. If there was pleasure to be taken, it should be in the knowledge that the just and proper order of the universe—an order that placed the Voth above all others—was preserved and reinforced once again.

Still, Haluk told himself, it would only support that goal if these endotherms were put in their place *forcefully,* and so painfully that they would never forget the lesson. Since that served Voth interests, surely he was entitled to derive satisfaction from it.

"Sanctioner!" his chief subordinate called out, his scales flushed with anxiety. "The field is . . . not working!"

"Whaat?"

"Their vessels are generating some kind of shielding that blocks the effect."

Haluk didn't bother to protest that none of these powers was known to have any such technology. He could guess where the innovation had come from. *"Voyager,"* he growled. Leave it to outsiders to disrupt the natural order of things.

"The anti-damping shields are holding," Lieutenant Ayala reported from the rebuilt tactical station on *Voyager's* bridge. "Reports coming in . . . power loss is ranging from eight to seventeen percent and holding, except the Nezu, who are down twenty-nine percent."

Thank you, Tuvok, Janeway thought. In the wake of *Voyager's* first encounter with the Voth, the tireless security chief had spent months devising countermeasures to their energy-damping technology in case of future clashes. It comforted Janeway to know that she could still rely on Tuvok even after his death.

"Work with the Nezu," she told Ayala. "See if you can help them boost their shielding. Bridge to engineering. How soon, Lyndsay?"

"If we were doing it right, two weeks," came Ballard's ever-cheerful voice. *"As it is, we're kind of making it up as we go, so I can't give you more than 'sometime soon.'"*

"Just get us out there."

"The Voth are firing on the Nezu ships now," Chakotay reported, his voice heavy. The circumstances made her guilty at the joy she felt to have him back at her side again.

"Damage?"

He stared at her. "Totally vaporized. On the first shot."

"The Tarkan are moving in," Ayala said. "They're taking damage, but intact. They're returning fire."

The young Vostigye female at ops finally got the screen hooked in to an external feed. Janeway watched as the powerful Tarkan ships unleashed their full fury on the saurians' vessel. But it wasn't called a city ship for nothing; it was like firing a blowgun at a brachiosaur.

Still, there was damage being done. "Remind them that Neelix is aboard that ship somewhere. Have them scan for Talaxian biosigns."

But it was a moot point. Suddenly something rippled out of the Voth ship, a distortion in space, and a moment later the Tarkan vessels found themselves thousands of kilometers away, suddenly strafing the Kosnelye spaceport. Janeway felt a distant shudder, transmitted through the umbilicals that held *Voyager*.

Chakotay spoke for her ears only. "How do you win against an enemy with weapons you've never even imagined before?"

"Sheer cussedness," she replied. Privately, though, she was feeling a lot less confident. On the screen, the Ridion ships were firing their plasma torpedoes at the city ship. Space rippled again, and the torpedoes struck the ships that had fired them, blowing them to atoms.

How much longer do I let them fight for us? she wondered. *At what point does being part of this community mean sacrificing ourselves for it?*

But then a proximity alarm sounded at tactical. "New incursion!" Ayala called. "Three bioships."

A chill ran down Janeway's spine. "That's the last thing we need."

"Maybe not," Chakotay said, checking the telemetry. "They're aimed right at the city ship, not at us. That thing has a pretty strong transwarp signature—not unlike a Borg cube. Maybe that's what drew them here."

It didn't take the bioships long to make their intentions clear. Intense bolts of energy crackled from their prows, tearing into the city ship's hide and leaving deep gouges. The spatial-distortion field burst out toward them, but they shook it off, barely moved, and continued their assault.

Rosh came onto the viewscreen. *"Their timing couldn't be better,"* the overminister said. *"All we have to do is sit back and let them solve our problem for us."*

"Neelix is still aboard that ship," she reminded him.

"We'll scan for his biosigns and try to beam him off. That's the best we can do."

"Is it?" She glanced at the screen on the arm of her chair, which still showed the city ship shaking under the assault from the bioships, fighting back as best it could but clearly outgunned. She reminded herself that what looked like small gouges in its sides were the result of explosions sufficient to destroy a *Galaxy*-class starship. "Mister Ayala. What is the population of the Voth vessel?"

"Approximately . . . eight hundred thousand. And falling."

Janeway paused to absorb the number. "Eight hundred thousand," she repeated to Rosh. "I'm not willing to just stand by and let them all be killed if I can help it. That's not the Federation way—and if there's one thing you've shown me today, it's that it isn't the Vostigye way either."

"Captain, I admire your principles, but are you sure it's wise in this case?"

"Look at the power of those bioships, Overminister. Species 8472 is here, in your home system, endangering us and the Voth equally. Is it wise *not* to do everything we can to band together against that common threat?"

Rosh nodded. *"I'll order the fleet to defend the city ship."*

"They won't be alone," Janeway promised. He signed off, and she switched to engineering. "Lyndsay! It's now or never!"

"I can give you impulse—barely. But warp is out of the question."

"Not an issue. Just get us in the fight."

"We . . . aren't fully armed. I can give you phasers, but there are no torpedoes on board."

"We'll make do. You just hold us together." She turned to the pretty, young blond woman at the conn. "Ensign Jenkins, disengage docking clamps and take her out."

"Aye, Captain." A shudder—and *Voyager* was moving under her own power for the first time in months. She accelerated tentatively, in fits and starts, but soon was clear of the dock and back in open space. Tricia Jenkins swung her around a bit erratically, but quickly got the hang of the rebuilt systems and had her on course toward the city ship.

Over a dozen other ships soon fell into formation around *Voyager,* protecting her. The ship shot forward faster, as if given confidence by the gesture, though it was really Ballard's team improving the engine performance. As soon as they were in range, Ayala cut loose with full phasers against the nearest bioship, firing in concert with the other ships of their battle group. Elsewhere, the rest of the fleet harried the other two bioships or ran interference between them and the city ship.

The Voth ship had been defending itself as well, but their weapons had little effect on the bioships, and now their efforts were diminishing. *"The Voth are evacuating,"* Rosh informed them. *"Thousands of them are materializing on our habitats."*

The Voth transporters must have extraordinary range to reach that far. But evacuating a city of nearly a million would take time nonetheless—time this vessel didn't have, by the looks of it. The fleet was taking heavy losses, and only one bioship—the one *Voyager* and its companions had ganged up on—had taken significant damage. The way 8472 biotech scattered sensors, there was no way to target precision fire; Ayala and his counterparts on the other ships were having to rely on brute force and luck.

"All ships, fall back!" Rosh suddenly reported. *"I've been informed by the Voth that they plan to self-destruct their vessel."*

"*Voyager* to Rosh. Is there any sign of Mister Neelix among the evacuees?"

"We haven't found him yet."

"Then we're not going anywhere. Tricia, take us in closer. Ops, sensors to maximum." *I won't lose any more of us to these monsters.*

Jenkins dived on the city ship like a kamikaze pilot, ducking and weaving around enemy fire, and Janeway was reminded that the young helmswoman had trained under Tom Paris. Explosions from inside the city ship scorched *Voyager*'s hull. But the bioships mostly ignored them, targeting the Voth leviathan and assuming *Voyager* would get caught in the general destruction. Admittedly, that was a fair assumption.

"I've scanned the whole vessel," the Vostigye at ops reported. "No Talaxian biosigns." Janeway's heart sank. "Wait!" she said a moment later. "Escape pods have been launched. I'm reading . . . yes! Mister Neelix is aboard one of them."

"Janeway to all ships. Get those escape pods in tow or inside your shields and clear the area, best possible speed!"

The fleet hastened to comply, and Janeway just hoped their retreat didn't tip off the bioships. Hell, she hoped the Voth would be considerate enough to wait until their defenders were out of range. Because *Voyager* was pretty much the slowest ship out here right now.

The blast came, and space itself was rocked as massive trans-warp engines destroyed themselves in a cataclysm of higher physics. Janeway saw the walls and floor ripple around her, felt her own innards squashed and stretched painfully, just before the more conventional impact hit and flung her to the deck. The groaning in the ship's superstructure gave her a nauseating sense of déjà vu—or maybe that was just the spacetime continuum playing cat's cradle with her digestive tract.

Finally she pulled herself together. "Ayala . . . report."

"The Voth ship . . . totally destroyed. The bioships . . . no sign of them. I think we won."

Then the other ships in the allied fleet began calling in, offering their assistance to *Voyager*. Janeway exchanged a look with Chakotay and smiled. "You're right, Mister Ayala. We won."

In the final analysis, the allies had lost over a dozen ships and over four hundred lives. The Voth had lost tens of thousands. But something new had been forged. There were no recriminations among the allies, no bickering over who had lost more or deserved more compensation. It would be overstating it to say the allies felt a sense of shared triumph, but there was a sense of new possibilities, a recognition of the strength that came from unity.

Even the Voth showed grudging gratitude, in their way. Their sense of face would not let them admit it openly. But when another city ship came to collect the survivors, the Voth went on their way without making any further demand for *Voyager*'s crew. When Overminister Rosh sent them a final message proposing an alliance against Species 8472 (for it was becoming increasingly clear that they were winning the war), Sanctioner Haluk responded, "If *you* should need *our* help defeating them again, you are free to attempt a petition." But at least his response implied that they might respond positively to such an overture.

Voyager was returned to her familiar berth, but this time, Rosh informed Janeway that the ship's reconstruction would have full government funding. It seemed he'd discovered that he had more political capital than he'd realized, and he was taking advantage of it to push through some new policies. He suggested that a formalization of the alliance would not be long in coming.

"I was so blind," Janeway told Chakotay as they stood on the balcony of his Kosnelye residence, looking out at the spherical landscape beyond. She'd never appreciated until now just how beautiful it was. "For three and a half years, I've been hell-bent on getting my crew back to the Federation. Maybe we haven't been getting any closer to it for a while . . . but maybe, in a way, we've been bringing the mountain to Mohammed. Or rather, you have. You, Neelix, Kes, Harry, the Doctor . . . thanks to your efforts, we may have the beginnings of a new Federation right here in the Delta Quadrant."

"You played your role too," he assured her. "It was you who decided, right from the start, that we would be a Federation crew. You who kept us dedicated to Federation values, even when expediency seemed to demand otherwise. If we've helped to promote those values here in the Delta Quadrant, it's because we've been following your example."

"But I should've been following yours as well. You understood that we could adapt without losing who we are." She moved closer. "I'm sorry I let my stubborn pride come between us. I should never have allowed that."

"You clung to what you believed was right. I've always admired that about you, even when I've disagreed with you."

"It was more than that. I resented you, I think. On some level, I believed that if you hadn't talked me out of my alliance with the Borg, Tom, Tuvok, and the others might not have been killed."

"More likely we all would've been."

"You're probably right. Allies with the Borg? What the hell

was I thinking?" They shared a laugh. "Especially when there are so many better allies to choose from. Instead of a deal with the devil, we've made true friends. Maybe even . . . a new home." She cleared her throat. "For some of us. Those who are willing to embrace it."

"You still have regrets," he divined.

"I still plan to take *Voyager* home someday, along with anyone else who'll come. I don't begrudge anyone else their right to stay here, in the new lives they've built." She shook her head. "I can't imagine asking Kes to settle for the limited role she'd have on *Voyager*. And Harry would never have the chance to rise through the ranks the way he has here.

"Still . . . all of you have been my family. And I regret that we've had to grow apart to fulfill our true potential."

"We've stayed in touch. We're still a family."

"But we're not as close as we were, and that's bound to continue." She shook off her melancholy and smiled. "Don't mind me. Just a case of empty nest syndrome."

"For what it's worth, Kathryn . . . I'm not going anywhere. I'll always be here if you need me."

"And I always will." She studied him for a moment, made a decision. "But not as my first officer."

He frowned. "Kathryn?"

"You've become more than you were on *Voyager* too. You've become a leader in the community, and not just to *Voyager*'s crew. I think you should accept Dobrye's invitation to run for office."

He took a moment before responding. "I have been thinking it would be a good idea."

"In more ways than one," she said, her voice becoming soft, vulnerable. She spoke tentatively. "You told me recently . . . that we shouldn't let life pass us by while we're pursuing other plans. And you were right. There's an opportunity that's been staring me in the face for four years, and I've always let my sense of duty keep me from pursuing it. But I don't know if I'll ever find a better one." She was close to him now, gazing up at him. "I've lost so many people close to me. If I don't learn now to take my opportunities while I have them, I never will."

And she kissed him. And he returned the kiss as though it were the most natural thing in the galaxy.

Part Three

June–September 2375

8

Voyager shuddered as weapons fire strafed its shields. "Surt, can you identify them?" Janeway called.

"Not a known design, Captain," replied the stout, gray-brown humanoid at ops. His small eyes narrowed. "Wait, the computer has a record of it. . . . It belongs to a species called the Jem'Hadar."

Janeway turned to stare at Surt, as did Harry Kim beside her. "Are you certain?"

"The computer is."

"On-screen."

A magnified, enhanced image of the vessel appeared as it came around for another pass. "He's right, Captain," Harry said. "I recognize the design. We had to familiarize ourselves with them at the Academy, just after they were first encountered."

"Been a long time since then, eh, Lieutenant Commander?" she asked Harry.

Her first officer smiled and nodded. "And they're a long way from the Gamma Quadrant. Looks like we've found another member of the Caretaker Club."

"Now we just need to convince them of that. Hail them, Surt." The round-faced crewman nodded when the channel was open. "Jem'Hadar vessel. This is Captain Kathryn Janeway of the Delta Coalition starship *Voyager*. We bear you no hostile intentions—in fact, we have something in common, and we may be able to assist you. Please cease fire so we can discuss the situation."

A moment later, a face appeared on the screen—not a Jem'Hadar, but a more humanlike female with long, dark hair and backswept, scalloped ears. Janeway remembered the briefings she'd studied a few months before *Voyager*'s abduction. She was a Vorta, a member species of the Dominion, as were the Jem'Hadar themselves. *"Delta Coalition? What trickery is this? And how does a Federation starship come to be so far from home?"* she added with frank suspicion.

"Probably the same way you did, Ms. . . ."

"You may call me Kilana."

"Kilana. I'm pleased to meet you." Janeway spoke to her about the Caretaker, his abduction of ships from all over the galaxy, and *Voyager*'s subsequent experiences leading to its membership in the newly formed Delta Coalition. It was a speech she had made more than once in recent months. Once she had committed *Voyager*— and herself—to the defense of this quadrant and its inhabitants, she had realized there was an obligation she had overlooked for years. Many ships had been brought here by the Caretaker, left to fend for themselves in hostile space just as *Voyager* had. And yet she had never made more than a token effort to seek them out. In the first weeks following *Voyager*'s arrival, she had ordered periodic scans and hails to see if any other abductees were in the vicinity; but upon finding none within range, she had essentially written them off and continued on course for home. In retrospect, that felt like a foolish decision; it would have been wiser to survey the region thoroughly first. Even just a few other ships could have helped with resource shortages and defense against local hostiles.

But once she had committed to staying in the region—at least until Species 8472 was dealt with and the Coalition's survival assured—Janeway had chosen to take *Voyager* back through the Nekrit Expanse and the perils of Swarm territory, back into the realm of the Kazon and Vidiians, in search of any remaining refugees who had managed to survive. It was a risk, taking *Voyager* away from the Coalition at a time when attack might be imminent; but the alliance was strong enough to spare one ship, and her search might bring back more allies who could make valuable contributions to the Coalition's defense.

Some had called it a fool's mission; what were the odds that any other Caretaker refugees were still alive, or still in the vicinity, after more than four years? And it would take years to track all the way back to the Ocampa system, while the Coalition was unwilling to let her extend the search past five months this first time out. At most, she could only find those who had traveled more or less toward the galactic core as *Voyager* had.

Truth be told, sometimes Janeway doubted her own motives for this mission. Despite her avowed commitment to joining Vostigye society and the Coalition that centered on it, was she perhaps still pulling away from that community by finding a new quixotic quest to pursue? She preferred to believe that she was making amends for a mistake, for her excessive haste to flee this quadrant rather than fulfilling her responsibilities to its occupants, indigenous or otherwise. Maybe that was compensation for her guilt at failing to get her crew home, but it was still a worthy goal. She owed it to her fellow abductees to search for them, at least; and the fledgling Coalition could use all the members it could get.

As it happened, a number of Caretaker abductees had banded together for mutual protection, thus saving *Voyager* the effort of tracking them down individually. Most were from the Alpha, Beta, and inner Delta Quadrants, and thus were heading in roughly the same direction. A few were familiar species: Kobheerian, Betelgeusian, Carnelian. The others had been from parts of the galaxy Starfleet had not yet reached, including Vomnin and Shizadam from the Beta Quadrant and Nygeans and S'paaphonn from distant parts of the Delta. Mister Surt himself was a Caretaker abductee, a member of a secretive inner Delta Quadrant civilization known only as the Hierarchy, a people skilled at surveillance and stealth but not big on individual initiative. (Annika Hansen, with her typical playfulness, had dubbed them "the Potato People," and though Janeway strove to discourage such characterizations, she had a hard time denying the resemblance.) He had proven a valuable replacement for Nemulye, the Vostigye ops manager who had been killed in the passage through Swarm space. And his people's cloaking technology would be invaluable for getting the convoy safely back through Swarm territory to the Coalition.

The members of the convoy, which now waited for *Voyager* in a nearby system, had told of various other abductees they had met or heard of. Some had already found new worlds of their own to settle on, some had been destroyed, and some had headed off on vectors to more distant parts of the galaxy. Janeway had decided to take her search antispinward, toward the Gamma Quadrant, in hopes of intercepting another convoy she'd heard rumors of. They might not be willing to turn back and accept lives in the Coalition, but at least she could offer them supplies and information on the region's dangers before wishing them a good journey.

Still, it was a surprise to encounter a Dominion vessel here; if her knowledge of the Dominion's location was correct, a direct course from Ocampa would not have brought it this close to Coalition space. They must have been forced to go around a major obstacle, perhaps the Krowtonan Guard she had heard of from the convoy members, or something even more dangerous. At this point, they might welcome the help the Coalition could provide.

Still, Kilana remained skeptical when she had finished. *"Why should I believe any of this? It's all some Federation trick!"*

"If we wished to deceive you, why wait over four years? We have extensive records that will verify our story."

"And will those records reveal what became of the device that could have sent us home? We heard that it was destroyed by a Starfleet vessel."

Oh, dear. This was a prickly issue. But she'd found it best to confront it openly. "I was the one who made that decision, Ms. Kilana. If I hadn't, then the Array would have fallen into the hands of the Kazon, and they would not have allowed anyone else to use it to get home. Moreover, they would have used its power to inflict great harm on the species of the region."

"The Kazon are petty thugs. We could have taken the Array from them easily—if you had left us anything to take."

Janeway spread her hands. "Maybe that's so. But what will you accomplish by fighting us over it?"

"Your destruction would only be just."

"But what would it get you? I can offer something better."

Kilana was wary. *"Explain."*

"You asked about the Delta Coalition. It's an alliance of regional powers united for mutual defense and the sharing of knowledge and resources."

"Just another Federation."

"Is the Dominion so different?" Janeway replied, though privately she was confident that it was. "You also cooperate for mutual benefit."

"We serve the Founders, our gods. No one else will ever have our allegiance!"

"Uh-oh," Harry muttered.

"We don't require allegiance," Janeway said. "But you'd be welcome as our guests. The Coalition has assisted many people who had no homes to return to or no hope of seeing home in their lifetimes. Including *Voyager* and a number of others brought here by the Caretaker. Some of us have clashed with one another back home, but we're a long way from those conflicts here."

Kilana kept up a brave front, but Janeway hadn't become a starship captain without learning how to read people. The Vorta was nervous, uncertain. Janeway recalled her briefings: The Founders of the Dominion were shape-shifters who had genetically engineered their servant races. The Vorta were their bureaucrats, the Jem'Hadar their enforcers. And Kilana's devotion to them seemed absolute. If she had been without the guidance of her "gods" for over four years, it was no wonder she seemed afraid.

Janeway offered one last incentive. "We have many scientists in the Coalition as well. There are efforts under way to develop transwarp drive or enhanced subspace communication with distant parts of the galaxy. I, for one, still hope to see my homeworld again. There may be hope for you as well."

After a time, Kilana nodded. *"Very well. You may escort us to this 'Coalition.' But if this is a trick, you will regret it."*

The screen went dark. "Whoa," Harry said. "Now, there's someone who's in over her head. I wonder how she's survived for four years."

"Plenty of battle damage on their hull," Ayala said from tactical. "They've been through a lot of fights, and won. I wouldn't recommend getting on their bad side, Captain."

"We're already there, Mister Ayala. The goal is not to stay there." She smiled. "But if things do get messy, it's good to know we have allies nearby."

Harry shook his head. "I'm still getting used to the idea of the Vidiians as allies."

"So are they. But I think we can count on them in a pinch." Indeed, ever since the Doctor and Danara Pel had cured the Phage, the Vidiians had been beside themselves with gratitude. They were still struggling to rebuild their civilization, but they had pledged their protection to *Voyager*—still home to the Doctor's core program—as long as it remained anywhere near their territory.

"And this Vorta and her Jem'Hadar?" Harry asked. "Do you think we have a chance of winning them over?"

"I think they have a need for a hierarchy to belong to. Whatever they feel about us, maybe the Coalition can offer them that." She gazed out at the menacing, insectlike vessel. "And the way things are going, we need all the good fighters we can get."

Over the past seven months, Species 8472—or "the Scourge," as it had become popularly known—had solidified its advantage over the Borg. The Collective was scattered, fragmented, nearing total defeat. The Scourge was broadening its attacks, striking at the Coalition's borders as well as sending more vessels to attack the Voth. The uneasy mutual alliance between those two powers had helped hold their raids at bay, but Coalition analysts projected that the conflict would likely escalate soon. If anything, they were surprised that it hadn't already done so.

Harry shook his head. *"Voyager,* Vostigye, Voth, Vidiians, Vomnin, and now Vorta. What is it with this quadrant?"

"I take it as a good omen," Janeway said, and smiled at his puzzlement. "V for victory."

Harry Kim loved helping Annika Hansen take her clothes off.

It wasn't just due to his admiration of her exceptional beauty; Annika herself took palpable pleasure in disrobing (in private, anyway), and that was what brought him the most joy. After the Doctor had removed her Borg exoskeleton and most of her implants, he'd still required her to wear a close-fitting dermal sheath that protected and nourished her newly formed skin, as well as taking over certain of the exoskeleton's sensory and motor feedback functions, which her remaining implants still required to operate at full efficiency. Wishing to avoid unsightly bulges, the Doctor had secreted the few bulky components of the sheath in high heels that the holographic physician insisted were quite stylish, though Annika insisted she would stumble over them constantly if not for the balance-regulation mechanisms built into them. But stylish or not, the sheath was embarrassingly tight for Annika, and she normally wore loose, bright dresses over it.

But as time wore on and her body continued to adapt, Annika was able to spend more time per day out of the constricting sheath, and she preferred Harry to be with her when she did—a sentiment he wholeheartedly shared. True, it was partly because the sheath was easier to remove and put on again if she had assistance, but he was gratified that it was his assistance she preferred. He was glad that Captain Janeway had seen fit to maintain a relaxed

policy toward shipboard romances since *Voyager*'s recommission-
ing. Perhaps her own belated relationship with Chakotay—and
regret at her long delay in pursuing it—had contributed to that
decision. Of course, Annika had no formal rank; a life of leisure
in Unimatrix Zero had not been sufficient preparation for service
on a Delta Coalition ship. She filled some of the roles Neelix and
Kes had performed in the past, helping grow food in the aeroponics bay and then preparing it as the ship's chef. Even though there
was no longer any need to ration replicator use, *Voyager*'s crew still
enjoyed meals prepared by hand—and frankly, they found Annika's culinary tastes rather more palatable than Neelix's.

Finally the sheath fell free, and Annika stepped forward and
stretched, reveling in the freedom. Harry was happy to watch her.
He looked forward to doing much more, but she enjoyed taking
time to revel in the air against her skin and the freedom of movement. She liked to make conversation while he watched, to dis-
tract him from his inevitable reactions to the sight. "That Kilana's
pretty," she said.

"I didn't notice."

She threw him a skeptical look, her full lips quirking. "I didn't
like those Jem-har of hers."

"Jem'Hadar."

"Whatever. They were really unfriendly, and didn't even try
the food."

"Their loss. But they're good fighters. They could be useful
against the Scourge."

Her skepticism grew more serious. "Unlikely. All they have
is fighting prowess. We have plenty of fighters already. What can
they do against a power as advanced as the Scourge?"

Harry was reminded again of the keen mind that resided beneath her girlish manner. He'd been hesitant to respond to her
interest at first, not wanting to take advantage of her inexperi-
ence. Also, in the wake of B'Elanna, he'd entertained a hope that
he might be able to build a relationship with Lyndsay Ballard,

whom he'd had a crush on since the Academy. But his duties and Lyndsay's had kept them apart, and in her correspondence, she had shown no more than friendly interest in him. Whereas Annika had quickly proven that she was sharp-witted and also very determined, skilled at getting what she wanted and not easily bent to others' wishes. She'd also proven that her life in Unimatrix Zero had given her considerable experience in matters of physical intimacy. She still sometimes mourned for Axum, her lover in the virtual world. She had never known where he was located in real life, but if he was anywhere close enough to be reached in less than half a lifetime, he had most likely died in the war already. But she was strong and adaptable, so she had coped with her loss and moved on with her life, deciding to make Harry a part of it. By the time he'd rejoined *Voyager*'s crew, any thoughts of romance with Lyndsay Ballard were well behind him.

"You have a point," he told Annika. "But we have to offer them some useful role to play, or you're right, they could be dangerous."

"And Kilana?"

He pondered. "I don't know. She seems strictly middle management to me. Her people have a lot of knowledge, but these Founders apparently control it. I think she's out of her depth, frankly."

Annika grew contemplative. "What's wrong?" Harry asked.

"I just wish *I* had a more useful role to play. All I do is cook and putter around in the garden. I'm a housewife."

"You play a valuable role for this crew. There's nothing wrong with what you do."

"But I could be doing so much more. The Doctor says I have all this Borg knowledge locked in my head, but I can't remember any of it! I can see when the captain looks at me—she thinks I could help fight the Scourge if I could remember what the Borg knew about them. And I've tried, I really have! But I can't get at it."

He took her in his arms. "I consider that a blessing. Would you really want to remember the things that happened to you as a Borg? The things you—" He broke off.

But she refused to be coddled. "The things I did? The lives I destroyed?"

"That wasn't your fault."

"Even so, is it right to hide from it? To go through life like it never happened?"

"And would remembering it make any of it better?"

"If I remembered, maybe I could do something to help stop the Scourge. Maybe that would make amends for some of it."

He stroked her long, golden hair. "Look . . . I'm not sure it'd help, anyway. The Borg are losing the war, badly. They hardly *exist* anymore. There may not be anything you know that could help."

She sighed. "Maybe you're right," she said, but he could tell she wasn't convinced.

But then she laughed self-deprecatingly, her smile brightening the room. "I guess I could use some cheering up," she told him. "You have any ideas?"

He smiled back. "I have a few."

9

The Casciron shuttle swooped and slalomed through the mountains of Kovoran, hugging their crags so closely that it left the occasional smear of paint behind. In the passenger seats, Danros and Gerron were taut with fear. But their pilot was loving it. For B'Elanna Torres, the exhilaration of facing death and barely scraping free of its clutches was the only thing that made her feel alive.

Sure, the goal was nominally to stay under the Kovoran sensor grid, to get close enough to the Vostigye research base to plant the charges that would bring it down. B'Elanna had been as angry as anyone else in the resistance upon learning of the biological experiments being conducted on the Casciron refugees on this planet. Apparently the Vostigye weren't content to live in their spacegoing tin cans and let the Casciron find planets where they could live independently. No, they had to plant colonies so they could claim more territory and make excuses for keeping the Casciron from finding a home. And even once they'd stripped them of their stings, they couldn't leave them alone; no, they had to use them in some sick medical experiment.

Oh, no doubt they would excuse it as something to help the war effort against the Scourge. B'Elanna had to hand it to Kathryn Janeway and her lap dog Chakotay—they'd done wonders bringing the sensibilities of the Federation to the Delta Quadrant. Just like the Federation, their Delta Coalition spoke of peace and inclusion, then made deals with monsters and overlooked their abuses when it served their own interests. Back with the Maquis, B'Elanna had preferred to strike at Cardassian targets, doing her best not to harm Federation citizens, whom she held blameless for the mistakes of their leaders. Now, she no longer cared to hold back. The Vostigye were the real monsters, and their friendly face as they assimilated and exploited other cultures just made them all the worse.

More, though, she just needed to *feel* something. Grieving and moving on hadn't worked; how could she move on from losing everyone who'd ever mattered to her? The distraction of sex hadn't worked; she'd indulged Gerron's interest for an evening here and there, but when she tried to invest herself in it, she was reminded too much of the one man she strove not to think about—the man who had taken her capacity for love with him when he died. The only thing that fulfilled her was the fight—any fight. Anything that let her feel death's fingers closing around her and then kick its teeth in one more time.

And if death won the next round? Well, what difference would it make to anyone, really?

But B'Elanna managed to stay just ahead of death's clutches this time, bringing the shuttle down safely in range of the research facility. Half an hour later, she'd snuck her team past its security perimeter, their biosigns masked by her equipment, and Danros planted the charges around the administrative section, away from the labs and confinement areas where the Casciron subjects would be held. Gerron still looked uncertain. "Maybe we should wait until the building's empty," the young Bajoran said.

"And how will that avenge our fallen?" Danros growled. By Casciron standards, being mutilated and experimented on was worse than being killed outright. But death was an adequate revenge for Danros's purposes.

"We don't just want to take out the building," B'Elanna added. "As long as the scientists are still around, we haven't solved anything. And if our spies are right, there are some Coalition officials in there too—maybe the ones who approved these experiments in the first place. I say they're getting what they deserve."

"Even if it brings down harsher reprisals?"

Her answer was practically a snarl. "Bring it on."

They retreated to the woods next to the compound. The honor of setting off the charges fell to Danros, and B'Elanna almost envied him. She wasn't nearly as eager to inflict death as to invite it, but she disliked the numbness that came over her when she didn't have a dangerous or destructive task to get her adrenaline racing.

Still, the explosion was loud and devastating and cathartic, and then would come the thrill of eluding pursuit as they raced back to the shuttle . . .

But then she thought she heard a familiar voice from the wreckage.

She turned back, ignoring the others' calls. *It couldn't be.* But as she jogged closer, halting just on the edge of the woods, she heard the cry again, a rough, throaty scream she'd recognize anywhere, calling a name she'd recognize anywhere:

"Neelix!"

B'Elanna raced forward, not caring what kind of security might be converging. She needed to see for herself. She came around the ruins of the outer wall and saw a familiar elfin figure, lithe and golden-haired, surrounded by rubble and flames and showing no sign of injury. There were bodies around her, both Vostigye and Casciron. *No! There shouldn't have been Casciron in this part of the complex!* Pieces of debris were flying away as though recoiling from her gaze. And under some of that debris was an equally familiar figure, chubby and garishly attired, bleeding and gasping for breath. "Oh no!" Kes cried again, reaching his side and kneeling over him.

Then Kes looked up at her, and B'Elanna realized that she'd been moving closer, stumbling through the rubble without even thinking about it. She didn't know if she could form a thought right now, didn't know if she wanted to. "Kes . . ." she began.

Then orange light flared in those gray-green eyes, and B'Elanna's head filled with agony, and she gave herself gladly to oblivion.

It had all been going so well.

Kes had spent months working on a medical solution to the Casciron problem where political solutions had failed. Finally, working with her staff on Moskelar Station, she had devised an inoculation that would protect Vostigye and other species from Casciron venom, hoping it would convince the Vostigye politicians to reverse their laws designating Casciron stingers as illicit lethal weapons. Under pressure from the Coalition, the Legislature had begun to draft such a reversal, though its passage was contingent upon the success of her trials here on Kovoran. She'd also devised an experimental treatment that would enable the Casciron settlers on Kovoran, who had consented to have their venom glands and stings removed as a precondition for settling here, to regrow the organs and be whole again in the eyes of their culture.

She had chosen Kovoran for her tests because it was home to the most contentious conflict between Vostigye and Casciron. Despite that, both sides had shown a guarded willingness to co-operate, though suspicions were high. Kes had asked Neelix to accompany her, hoping the Ambassador at Large would use his acclaimed diplomatic skills to reassure both sides and facilitate their cooperation. It had been delightful to spend time with her old friend again, and it made her proud to see how important he'd become, how much good he'd done at bringing people together. And it had seemed that he was making good progress at persuading the two Kovoranese factions to cooperate on this project.

But then the explosion had occurred and the conference room had collapsed around her, Neelix, and the representatives of both sides. Kes had instinctively raised a telekinetic shield around herself, but it had happened too quickly for her to do more, and Neelix had been across the room at the time.

There were a few other survivors, all in serious medical need, but it had been Neelix she had rushed to. She had felt that he needed her the most, and she didn't really care if it was a selfish impulse. She would not let anything happen to Neelix. It was as simple as that. The debris between them went away, and he was there, but he was choking, gasping, unable to breathe. "Oh no!"

As she knelt by his side, she sensed a new presence moving through the rubble. "Kes . . ."

And with that one word, Kes knew what B'Elanna Torres had done. It burned brightly on the surface of B'Elanna's mind. A mind that was scarred, imbalanced, lost in what the doctor in Kes recognized as severe clinical depression.

Kes didn't care, though. The woman had hurt Neelix. So Kes put her down hard. She stopped short of doing permanent harm, but allowed herself satisfaction at the act.

But then she put it aside and turned back to Neelix. "It's all right, sweeting," she told him, fury instantly replaced with tenderness. "You'll be all right. Try to stay calm." But sheer somatic instinct was driving him as he gasped for breath. Surveying him quickly with her eyes and mind, she saw no obvious injury that could account for it—

Yes. Of course. She reached deeper, feeling the piece of herself that lived inside him: her own lung, donated when his lungs had been stolen by the Vidiians. It had been adapted to suit him using Vidiian techniques, but still, it was an Ocampa lung, an organ bred by nature for no more than a decade of use. And since Neelix was more massive than she, it had been carrying more than twice its intended load for nearly half that time. The trauma of the explosion and the dust Neelix had inhaled had overwhelmed the tired organ, and it was failing.

What do I do? If the Doctor were here, he could fix it. He must have been aware of the risk, and he'd had years to improve his understanding of Talaxian physiology and devise a more permanent replacement. But none of his avatars was nearby, and the base's medical facilities had been destroyed.

None of that matters, she told herself. *Neelix will* not *die.*

Laying her head upon his chest, she reached into him with her mind, feeling every cell of him, every particle. She saw what they were, and she told them what she needed them to become. They demanded energy to make the change, and she fed it to them, giving freely of herself. *Take everything I have,* she told them, told him. *Share my life, as you always have. As you always will.*

We are one.

"What do you mean, I have my lungs back?"

Kes blushed, a response that thoroughly charmed Neelix. Even with all her power, her amazing accomplishments, she was still the most unassuming soul he'd ever known. "I . . . seem to have triggered a . . . regeneration. It's happened before; with help from Tanis, I was able to accelerate the growth of plants. I've experimented with developing that ability since my powers were augmented, but I never dared to try it on an animal or a person." She looked away guiltily.

He took her hand. "Well, I'm very glad you took a chance on it this time. Obviously it worked." He paused. "It did work, didn't it? The lungs will . . . stay?"

Kes nodded. "They're as good as new, the doctors say."

He frowned. "What about . . . your old lung? Is it . . . still in there?"

She grinned at the image. "Actually your body drew matter from it to grow the new lungs from. I can't make matter appear from nowhere. Umm, the rest of the mass was drawn from elsewhere in your body, which is why you feel so hungry and dehydrated."

"Hm. I *thought* I looked a little thinner." He took a deep breath, amazed at just how deep it was. "Oh, my. It hasn't felt like that in a long time." Kes giggled, which made his chest swell again.

But something else she'd mentioned had begun to sink in. "What about B'Elanna?"

Kes sat on the side of his bed, growing serious. "When I . . . came to after healing you . . . she was there, tending to the other wounded." Guilt flitted across Kes's face at her failure to treat the others. "She was very closed off. I couldn't blame her—what she must be feeling right now would be very hard to confront."

"Well, I'm afraid I don't feel a lot of sympathy for her. People died in that blast. I would've died too, if not for you. How could B'Elanna have let herself become such a thing?"

"I think she's begun asking herself the same thing. She could've escaped—I was too weak to stop her. But she stayed. She did what she could to help. And she turned herself over voluntarily for arrest." She took Neelix's hand. "Losing Tom, Joe, Vorik, and the others . . . it made her lose her way, worse than the rest of us. She was another casualty, Neelix. And we need to help her heal, if we can."

Neelix fidgeted. It shamed him that he couldn't be as forgiving, as noble, as profoundly *good* as Kes was. And he didn't dare say it without letting on about the profound adoration he felt for her right now. Without letting on that he'd never stopped loving her. Oh, he'd become her friend successfully enough, but only because it was what she had wanted and he would do anything for her. Now, after this, he loved her more intensely and devotedly than ever. And he would keep it to himself forever, so she would be free to achieve her true greatness.

He realized she was smiling at him, her eyes glistening. "Wha-what is it, Kes?"

"Neelix . . . when I healed you, we were joined more closely than we've ever been. I know everything you're thinking. Without even trying."

His blood ran cold. "Oh. Oh dear. Kes . . . I . . ."

"And do you know what I realized when we were joined? That it was *right*. When I saw you lying there, when I feared you would die, I knew that I simply could not let that happen. That I would have lost a part of myself if it did. And I don't mean a lung.

"Neelix, I realized that I never stopped loving you either."

He was stunned. After a while, he said, "Kes . . . I, I, I'm . . . *touched* that you feel that way right now, in the wake of a, a very intense experience. But we both know I'm not right for you. I was just an adolescent crush, and you needed to grow beyond me, stretch your wings."

"I *have* grown, Neelix. I've achieved so much, experienced so much more than I ever imagined I could. And at first, when I realized what I felt, I was afraid it would be going backward, retreating into old limits.

"But then I thought about the man you've become—a statesman, a diplomat, a peacemaker respected across whole sectors. You've grown as much as I have. You wouldn't hold me back at all.

"Besides, what matters most is what we feel for each other, and that's never truly changed. I pulled away from it for a while, when I needed the freedom to grow and find myself. But now I've discovered that a part of me was always with you. You're not a limit to me, Neelix—you're an anchor. No matter what's happened between us, you've always been there for me. You've never wavered in your loyalty, your commitment, your kindness. I know I can depend on you more than anything else in this universe."

Her glistening gaze held his. "And I don't think there's anything more important to have in a lifemate. Or a father."

It took a moment for what she was saying to sink in. "Ohh, Kes!"

"I'm finally ready, Neelix. I've found the right man to start a family with. I want you to marry me and be the father of my children."

The only answer Neelix could give was a brief, high-pitched noise. But then he roared with glee and hugged her delicate frame against him, and then their lips met, and he reflected on the wisdom and insight of the English language, in which "kiss" sounded so much like "Kes." When their kiss finally broke, he couldn't stop giggling. "I just hope they take after you!"

"Legislator Chakotay. Thank you for appearing before this ministry."

Chakotay gazed up at the portly, orange-scaled form of Minister Odala, the Voth Elder whose presence dominated the council chamber. There were other Elders present, but Odala clearly ruled the roost. And he remembered from hard experience that her honeyed, reasonable tones concealed a strict and unforgiving character.

"I'm glad to be here, Minister," he told her, though the truth was rather different. He didn't have fond memories of his first encounter with Odala. Even aside from that, he would rather be back home on Kosnelye, for *Voyager* was due to return soon. Becoming Kathryn's lover was the best thing that had ever happened to him, yet thanks to their respective responsibilities, they saw far less of each other now than they had as platonic friends and colleagues aboard *Voyager*. He cherished the all-too-brief opportunities he had to spend time with her, and was none too happy that the Ministry of Elders' imperious summons had come when it did.

Still, he kept up a pleasant diplomatic face, saying, "The last time we met, I'm afraid we parted under less than ideal circumstances. I welcome the opportunity to improve relations between us."

"That is good to hear," Odala purred. "In that case, perhaps you would be willing to cooperate in an inquiry."

"An inquiry of what nature?"

"When you were last before this ministry, you were being used by Professor Forra Gegen to help promote his Distant Origin Theory, which he subsequently confessed was erroneous."

"I stood with Professor Gegen, yes." He would have liked to say more, such as pointing out that Gegen retracted his conclusions only under the ministry's threat of imprisonment for *Voyager*'s crew. But the Coalition still needed the Voth's goodwill so long as Species 8472 remained a threat. Being a politician required a restraint he never would have needed as a Maquis. Luckily he'd had several years aboard *Voyager* to retrain his diplomatic instincts.

"Gegen was subsequently reassigned to another circle and his inaccurate data was purged," Odala went on, referring to the ministry's deletion of all Gegen's genetic and archaeological proof of the Voth's common heritage with humanity. "However, subsequently to that event, the Distant Origin Theory began to spread among the common people despite having been renounced by its formulator. Investigation revealed that data files pertaining to the planet you call Earth and Gegen's hypothesis of genetic ties between its inhabitants and the Voth were circulating among the common people, despite the ministry's best efforts to ensure that they were protected from such misleading propaganda. These data files appear to have come from your vessel, *Voyager*. Can you explain this?"

"Naturally, all of Gegen's direct information about Earth came from *Voyager*. He downloaded our database when he first contacted us."

"Please do not waste this ministry's time with obtuse replies, Legislator. Those files were purged. So how is it that supporters of Distant Origin were able to obtain further copies?"

Chakotay shrugged. "Perhaps you simply missed a copy when you attempted to delete it. Gegen must have shared his information with his fellow scientists."

"He was barred from contact with the scientific circles before he encountered your vessel."

"You said the information was circulating among the commoners, not the circles."

"Do not evade the question, Legislator."

"I've attempted to offer possible explanations."

"There is another you have not offered. You had contact with Gegen after his public renunciation of his hypothesis. Did you give him anything?"

"Just a souvenir. A globe depicting Earth as it appears in modern times."

"Did that globe contain any other information?"

You mean like the hidden isolinear chip containing a copy of all Voyager's *scientific data on Earth? The one I never even told Kathryn that I'd given him?* Chakotay had been unwilling to let Gegen's achievement be eradicated, so he had slipped the database to Gegen concealed in the globe, not even telling him it was there but merely hinting at it, leaving him to discover and act on it for himself. It seemed that Gegen had wisely chosen to disseminate the information among the plebeian class, through channels it would be difficult for the elites—the intricately interlinking "circles" of scholar-bureaucrats responsible for Voth sciences, government, arts, education, and the like—to control.

But for a member of the Vostigye Legislature, a representative of the Delta Coalition, to confess to such an act would scuttle relations with the Voth. So he chose his words carefully. "The globe was the only thing Gegen obtained from me beyond what he'd already obtained from *Voyager*'s database."

Odala leaned forward, eyes narrowing. "You are being evasive."

"I'm stating a fact. Besides, does it really matter where the information came from? The people have it now. But where's the harm in letting them study that knowledge and decide for themselves what it means?"

"The harm," Odala said, her voice growing harder, "is that the people are losing faith in the Doctrine which serves as the foundation of our society. Challenges against the ministry's authority are growing more and more overt."

"With respect, is one scientific theory really to blame for that? Consider the circumstances. Last year, an entire city ship was destroyed by an attacker. It was the first time such a thing has happened in thousands of years. It's no wonder that left your people uneasy, shaken from their complacency—that it's gotten them to question a lot of their assumptions. That would have happened with or without Distant Origin. Perhaps, instead of trying to quash that process, you'd have better luck engaging with the people, acknowledging their right to their uncertainties and participating in a dialogue to find new answers."

"We have already been forced to make concessions to quell dissent," Odala said with distaste. "We have allowed the Circle of Education to put forth the Parallel Origin Theory."

"The one saying that the Voth originated here, but that life on Earth and elsewhere in the galaxy may have branched off from them?" Chakotay nodded. "I suppose it's fair to offer that as a possibility. But do you allow your educators to discuss the scientific and logical flaws in that hypothesis?"

"Do not presume to tell the Voth how to teach our young. Doctrine has held our society together for millions of years." Chakotay strongly doubted that. More likely, many regimes had come and gone over such a span, each one rewriting history and Doctrine to suit itself. "We were here while your ancestors crawled on all fours, and we will be here long after you are gone. You need our power to preserve your Coalition against the Scourge. Do not offend us, or you will lose our cooperation."

"You're right, Minister," Chakotay said. "We do need your cooperation. But you need ours, too. With all your power, all your wisdom, you were caught totally flat-footed when the Scourge attacked. You had nothing that could defend against them. And now, nine months later, you still have nothing. Perhaps because you've repressed any scientist who dares to devise new ideas rather than merely promoting state ideology. You don't have anyone capable of innovating new defenses against a threat from beyond the universe as you know it. And that's why you need us."

Odala seethed, but strove to regain her calm. "It is in both our nations' best interests if the Voth remain stable. This dissent from within must be brought under control."

"Then maybe you should try trusting your people to think for themselves. Instead of trying to control what they're allowed to know and believe, show some faith in their ability to make responsible decisions for your society. All they want is a say in their own destiny. Give them that, and they'll be more willing to cooperate with you in return."

"It is the state's responsibility to protect the people," Odala declaimed. "To renounce that would be a confession of inadequacy. And that would be the downfall of everything we are."

She drew herself up. "You are distracting this ministry from the issue before it. Do you confess to providing Forra Gegen with new information to support the Distant Origin fallacy?"

"I confess to considering Forra Gegen a friend and a credit to his people. I confess to believing that his spirit of free inquiry is something the Voth can only benefit from."

"That is all you have to say?"

"It will do, for now."

"Then you leave me no alternative."

Chakotay braced himself. Would she sever diplomatic ties, even though it was probable suicide?

Odala took a heavy breath. "From this point forward, Delta Coalition citizens will no longer be granted visitation and travel rights aboard Voth city ships. Contact will be limited to diplomatic communication at the highest levels. In this way, we will restrict the potential for further contamination of Voth scientific thought."

Chakotay sighed. It was essentially a token gesture, one that would not prevent the knowledge of Earth from continuing to spread. And it would impact only the limited amount of tourism and research that Coalition members were allowed to engage in among the Voth; the tenuous military alliance was intact. Still, it was a petty gesture that rankled at Chakotay. In their insistence on serving their egos rather than the good of their people, the Voth Elders were as bad as the Cardassian leaders back in the Alpha Quadrant. And good people like Gegen still had to pay the price. Chakotay was prouder than ever of his little act of subversion.

Outwardly, though, he kept his cool. "I'll convey your decision to my government. But I will do so with regret, and with the hope that it is only a temporary measure."

"And it is my hope," Odala told him, "that this truly is the last time I ever have to gaze on your pasty countenance."

It was the one thing she'd said that he could agree with. All he wanted now was to get back home to Kathryn. He hoped this new contact she'd made, the Vorta she'd told him about, would turn out to be a more palatable ally than the Voth.

10

"I'm sorry, Ms. Voenis . . . Captain Nagorim is dead."

Morikei Voenis had little use for the simulated sympathy in the voice coming out of the auxiliary medical probe, one of the new holographic AMPs that "the Doctor" had deployed around *Ryemaren* to deal with its many casualties. Such trappings could not change the fact that Azorav Nagorim, her friend and mentor, was gone—gone in the middle of a battle with the Scourge that Voenis now had to get the rest of her crew through alive, if she could.

This is just like you, she silently cursed Nagorim as the AMP lifted his body away. *You and your lessons. You just got yourself killed so you could challenge me to rise to the occasion.* But if she wanted to survive that test, she had to focus on the task at hand. "Malken! Offensive and defensive status!"

The Hirogen looked up from his tactical console, green light glinting from the Borg optical implant he'd chosen to keep for its sensory enhancements. "Torpedoes are expended. Phasers off-line. Fore shields at two-eighths, aft at five-eighths. Fore point-defense beams nonfunctional, aft at six-eighths."

"Still venting drive plasma," called Susan Nicoletti, the human at engineering. "Reaction efficiency's down to five-eighths."

"Bioship closing again!" Malken barked.

"Nicoletti!" Voenis called. "Am I correct that the low reaction efficiency means there are unaltered antiparticles in the plasma stream?"

"Aye, Comman— Captain."

She didn't let herself react to that, focusing on her distant memory of her engineering courses. True, antiparticles would annihilate on contact with matter particles, but such particles were tiny and could easily miss one another if inadequately confined. Some of the excess antiparticles would be hitting the walls of the plasma conduits and warp coils, slowly eroding them, but most would be escaping into space with the venting plasma.

"Stop trying to halt the venting," she ordered. "Purge the plasma completely between us and the bioship!" She turned to Malken. "When the bioship collides with the plasma cloud, it will cause a compressive shock wave. At that instant, hit it with all our aft defense beams to create a countershock."

Malken nodded, catching on. "Aye, Captain!" he answered with predatory fervor.

It happened quickly, but the results were impressive. Compressed between the two shock waves, the particles and antiparticles in the plasma cloud were packed densely enough to react, and confined enough that the reaction was able to propagate and build. The resultant antimatter explosion ignited the rest of the drive plasma just as the bioship flew through it.

Malken growled. "The prey survives. Wounded, though. Damage to its propulsion and weapons."

"Take advantage, helm. Best speed away from here."

"Bioship is retreating!" Malken crowed a moment later.

"It did what it came here to do," Voenis told him, her tone quashing his enthusiasm. *Ryemaren* and the rest of the task force had been unable to save the colony on Ragoelin from annihilation by the Scourge.

Why did those fools have to settle on a planet in the first place? Voenis wondered. Most Vostigye knew better; planets were dangerous, capricious places, and they made sizable and stationary targets. Something about them brought out the worst in sapient beings, for wars always seemed to be fought over the acquisition of planets or parts thereof. Planetary living made sentient beings territorial, violent in their defense of places, whereas habitat dwellers could simply pack up and move on if one location became problematical to occupy.

That was the only thing Voenis had against refugees and immigrants, really. Most of them were from planets, and so they brought with them all the follies and dangers, all the chaotic attributes, of such an existence. She had no problem with those among them who were willing to outgrow it and adapt, like Harry Kim or Susan Nicoletti. It was only those who clung to it who caused problems, but they were far too abundant.

And Vostigye who reverted to planetary living bewildered her all the more. Indeed, they angered her. For they hadn't just put their own lives at risk. They'd condemned other Vostigye to die defending them. Good Vostigye like Azorav Nagorim, who deserved better.

But then, Azorav would have been the first to remind her that adaptation went both ways—that Vostigye needed to open their minds to alternatives as well. And now that she was captain, she would have to live up to that example. *Ryemaren*'s mission was to protect everyone in need, not just those whose lifestyles made sense to her.

Besides, she could hear Azorav's wry voice telling her, *it doesn't matter to the Scourge whether we live on planets or habitats. They want us all dead.* That was clear enough from the way their attacks had suddenly amplified over the past two weeks.

"Malken," she said. "Captain's office. Now."

Once she and the Hirogen were alone, she said, "This situation is unacceptable. We failed to save the colony. We barely survived. At best, we only inconvenienced the Scourge ship."

"We survived to hunt another day. That is enough."

"It isn't close to enough. Stop thinking like a lone hunter and remember your duty to the Coalition. Our mission is to protect its members, not to throw our lives away in fruitless fights." Malken growled, but acceded to her authority—or pack dominance, or however he saw it.

"Are you sure there's nothing you remember about them?" she pressed. "No Borg knowledge has surfaced after all this time?"

He grew uneasy. "That time is over. Nothing of it remains."

"Except your souvenirs," she said, gesturing at his cybernetic eye and the partial exoskeleton on his right arm. "I know you have neural implants remaining too. There must be a way to access those memories."

"No!" He subsided. "With respect, Captain . . . you cannot ask that of me. To remember what it was to be a . . . a captive beast, leashed by alien technology . . ." He shook his head convulsively. "That . . . thing was not Malken of the Hirogen. I will use its appendages to serve my prowess, but I will *not* take its thoughts into my head!"

"I could order you!"

"Try it and I would resign. I know the regulations." He leaned closer. "And what if the drone mentality took over this body? Hirogen are formidable enough to begin with. I could rend you limb from limb in moments."

She didn't like the implied threat, but knew her own threat was baseless. "Dismissed," she told him, silently cursing his Hirogen pride and cowardice. *One of us would understand the importance of sacrificing for others. Being Vostigye means I defend your right to uphold your culture's values—but the bottom line is, ours are better than yours.*

But now she found herself questioning that assumption in a way she wouldn't have before—now that she sat in Nagorim's chair, forced to see things from his point of view. *If I had been a liberated drone, my Unimatrix Zero personality safely segregated from my Borg identity . . . would I be willing to risk losing the identity I take such pride in?*

"You don't have to do this."

Annika clasped Harry's hand, trying to quell his anxiety even though it paled next to her own. "Yes, I do, Harry. Thousands of people are dying every day now, and there may be information in my head that can help them. I have to remember it." She wished it were the only thing she would remember. How many innocent beings had she helped assimilate or kill as a Borg drone? How could she live with the guilt? But then, how could she live with the guilt of doing nothing when she could help now?

"We can find another way. There are others like you."

"This isn't about them. If I'm able to make a difference, I have to try."

"Annika," Captain Janeway said, "if you're doing this out of some belief that your contributions to this ship are inadequate . . ."

"Don't coddle me, Captain. I'm the girl who cooks and gardens and sings on talent night. But I'm also the girl who has the Borg database locked in her skull. If you're going to tell me that's no more important than the other stuff, then don't. You'd just be lying."

After a moment, Janeway sighed. "I guess I would. But I also don't feel you have anything to prove to me."

"Even if I didn't have to prove anything to myself, I'd still have to do this, for all the others out there. Wouldn't you?"

The captain nodded solemnly. But Harry, still fidgeting, turned to the Doctor. "You're sure there's no other way to access her Borg memories? You can't just download them into the computer?"

"The Borg cortical node is too closely interlinked with her brain. It's been dormant since her last trip to Unimatrix Zero, but if I activate it, she will perceive its contents. Also, the information is stored in neural-network protocols adapted to her particular brain structure. Ms. Hansen's gray matter may be the only processing device capable of interpreting it fully."

Harry looked resigned. "I'm just afraid of how remembering all this will change you. I don't want to lose the sweet, wonderful woman you are."

"Harry." She kissed him. "If I don't do everything I can to help you and everyone else I care about, then I will have lost who I am."

Janeway turned to the Doctor. "Is there a risk the Borg personality could take her over?"

"If you can call it personality." The captain glared, and he elaborated. "I can't rule out the risk, so I'll be performing the procedure inside a containment field. But I will be interfaced with Annika's cortical implants the whole time to monitor the procedure. Hopefully I can help her integrate any new knowledge and behavioral imperatives into her own psyche. I've gained a fair amount of experience at reconciling multiple selves."

"Very well," Janeway said, and smiled at Annika. "Whatever the outcome, I admire your dedication and courage. You are a true asset to this crew."

Annika thanked the captain, hugged Harry, and let the Doctor lead her over to *Voyager*'s main surgical table. She jumped at the sound of the containment field forming. *Oh God oh God I don't want to do this I don't want to do this . . .*

But it had to be done. Once he laid her down on the table, she just closed her eyes and tried to breathe deeply and not think about it. She wished the Doctor didn't need her to be conscious. She tried to ignore the pressure against her head as he attached cold bleeping things to it. She tried to convince herself that the cold pressure inside her skull was imaginary, that there were no sensory nerves in the brain so he could be doing anything in there right now and she'd never . . .

IRRELEVANT.

What? she asked.

IRRELEVANT INPUT DETECTED. COGNITIVE PURGE UNSUCCESSFUL. CORTICAL NODE ERROR—UNABLE TO CANCEL HORMONAL/AFFECTIVE INPUT.

Oh no. It's happening.

UNACCEPTABLE ANXIETY LEVEL BEING GENERATED BY DRONE

ENDOCRINE SYSTEMS. INITIATING PRIORITY OVERRIDE/IDENTITY
PROTOCOL.

Who are you?

. . . Who am I?

WE ARE SEVEN OF NINE, TERTIARY ADJUNCT OF UNIMATRIX
ZERO ONE. WE ARE BORG.

No—

RESISTANCE IS FUTILE.

Her eyes opened, and the voice was right—she could not resist,
only watch. She watched in horror as her body rose in a swift, stiff
motion and turned on the Doctor, as black tubes tore from the
back of her hand. She tried to fight, to stop her hand from moving
toward him, but she found her desire to resist ebbing away, her
fear subsiding into acceptance. *We serve the Collective.*

The assimilation tubules penetrated the entity identified as
"the Doctor" and injected a standard complement of nanoprobes.
Feedback from the probes immediately revealed an error; this was
merely a photonic projection upon a force-field integument, with
no material substrate to assimilate.

The projection looked down at the assimilation tubules, rolled
its eyes, and simulated a sigh. "Oh, no, I'm being assimilated.
Help. Help."

But the same voice was speaking in her mind as well. *"Annika!
Remember who you are. You are Annika Hansen!"*

We are Borg. Annika Hansen is—is— A six-year-old girl, screaming, running from the monsters. Wanting to cry for her parents
to come save her, but her parents are already the monsters—her
parents are the ones who brought her to the monsters. No one
can save her.

THE COLLECTIVE WILL SAVE YOU. THE COLLECTIVE SAVES ALL
THAT IT ASSIMILATES.

Yes. Yes, in the Collective there was no fear, no doubt, no lone-
liness. As part of a boundless whole, there could be no death.

"Think again," came the medical AI's voice. *"The Collective is*

already dying. Destroyed by Species 8472. Which is why you're doing this, Annika. Remember the people who need your help."

Why do you fight this? she asked, though it was Seven of Nine asking as well. *You are yourself a composite intelligence. You understand its advantages. Individuals are small and limited.*

"*I am a man of many parts, it's true. But ultimately a single being.*"

You are a program comprising the collective medical knowledge of thousands of individuals.

"*I am large, and I contain multitudes. The difference is, I didn't abduct and mutilate those multitudes to obtain their knowledge. Remember, Annika! I know you're still in there, now fight this!*"

But his words had sparked memories, all readily accessible now. Her hand striking out, tubules inserted into being after being. Species 1137, designation Calentar. Species 521, designation Shivolian. Species 478, designation Hirogen. Species 5618, designation Human.

Human . . . I am human! I've done this to my own kind, to so many others . . . The memories included their fears, their despair, not so different from those of a six-year-old girl running through the corridors of her ship . . .

Fear is irrelevant. Despair is irrelevant.

But I did it to them. I did it to all of them.

Guilt is irrelevant. We are Borg. Our actions are the will of the Collective.

Yes. No guilt, no pain. No responsibility. So easy just to surrender to it, not to have to carry the burden for herself . . .

"*Is that what you want, Annika? To sit back and do nothing? If you were the sort of person who ducked her responsibilities, would we be having this scintillatingly schizophrenic conversation right now?*"

But, Doctor . . . what I did . . .

"*Can be made to count for something. Focus on what you* will *do with the knowledge you now have access to. Knowledge of Species 8472.*"

The knowledge came to her. A Borg experiment to enter other dimensional realms. The generation of a quantum ring singularity to form a dimensional shunt. Entry into a space pervaded with a biological fluid suspension, an entire universe that functioned as a single organism. It was an embodiment of the Borg ideal, *e pluribus unum* on a cosmic scale. The Borg had to have it, to make it one with themselves. But it had fought back, its sapient defensive components resisting assimilation. In achieving a perfection surpassing the Borg, Species 8472 had proven impossible to overcome. Ironically, the Borg had been killed by their own ideal.

The fact that she could recognize the irony told her that she was still Annika. Seven of Nine was still there, but subdued, no longer fighting. Species 8472 was the drone's enemy too; if the assimilation of its knowledge by the Coalition could assist in eradicating that enemy, then it would comply. Still, it made its opinion known. THE PROCESS WILL BE MORE EFFICIENT IF YOU SURRENDER CONTROL.

Never! I am Annika Hansen. I will never surrender that again!

YOUR GUILT AND SORROW WILL IMPEDE YOUR EFFICIENCY. YOUR LOVE FOR THESE INDIVIDUAL BEINGS WILL IMPEDE YOUR EFFICIENCY.

No. Those are what will give me the strength to get through this. The drone did not comprehend, but bowed to her will. No doubt comprehension was irrelevant.

"Very good, Annika. Now all you must do is embrace the Borg side of you. Make her part of you. Assimilate her. You have the strength to face what she represents."

WE WILL COMPLY.

Annika didn't want to comply. The drone in her was cold, aloof, unrepentant. Its memories were abhorrent. But the Doctor was right: it was part of her. Only by accepting that could she control it.

An unknown time later, she sat up and opened her eyes. They locked on Harry Kim, staring silently for a moment. "Annika?" he asked tentatively.

"We . . . I'm all right," she said, her voice calm and lower than normal. The memories were still with her, the guilt a terrible burden. But she had to put it aside for now, work through it later. The drone in her let her face it stoically.

"I can verify that," the Doctor said. "It's safe to lower the force field."

"Assuming your program hasn't been compromised," Janeway said.

"If it were, another of my avatars would have notified you by now," the Doctor reminded her.

After a moment, Janeway nodded. Harry lowered the field and ran to Annika's side. "Are you . . . you?"

His boyish uncertainty made her smile, and it was a great relief that she still could. "Yes, Harry. Maybe with a little extra, but I'm me."

Then she needed to do more than smile, and she fell into his arms, holding him tightly. "It's all right," he said. "You're going to be all right."

"No," she said after a time. "I won't be all right for a while. But I think I have what we need."

11

"We have the beginnings of a possible defense," Science Minister Gavanri reported.

The Coalition councillors at the meeting leaned forward, and Kyric Rosh urged Gavanri past her hesitation. "Go on, Dobrye."

"I prefer to let Doctor Kes and Captain Janeway explain. Their respective crews have done the bulk of the work on this."

The councillors had no objection, so Kes started out. "By now you're all familiar with the basic composition of fluidic space. It's a separate universe which, instead of being mostly vacuum containing stars, planets, and asteroids, is pervaded by an organic fluid. The entire universe is a single immense ecosystem. But its native life-forms are so closely linked by electrochemical and telepathic communication that the whole functions as essentially a single organism.

"When I first made telepathic contact with the natives of fluidic space over a year and a half ago, I had the impression that they were the only inhabitants of their realm. I now realize I was wrong. Fluidic space contains many species—the beings we know as Species 8472, their bioships, the smaller organisms on which the bioships feed, and so on. But they think of themselves as a unified whole. And essentially they are. Species 8472, their ships, their bioweapons, all are composed of the same cellular matter. It is literally a living universe."

"The mystery," Janeway went on, "is how such a thing could even exist. A whole universe filled with liquid? That's an astonishing amount of mass. By all rights, its own gravity should've collapsed the entire universe into a black hole milliseconds after its creation.

"At least—if it had the same physics as our universe. We soon realized that fluidic space must have a much higher cosmological constant than our own." At the puzzled looks, she added, "Let me explain. The cosmological constant is a sort of 'dark energy' that fills space and subspace. That energy creates a force of expansion that counters the tendency of gravity to pull things together—a bit like the way heating the air in a balloon can make it expand.

"Now, since fluidic space has so much more mass and gravity, it must have a much stronger cosmological constant to keep it in balance. Essentially, its subspace is much 'hotter' than ours. But there are limits to how strong the dark energy can be without destroying the capability of matter to form large-scale structures in the first place; so we conclude that fluidic space must be a far smaller universe than our own, or else the total mass would be too huge to cancel out. It might be no larger than our own galaxy."

Nardem, the Nasari councillor, wrinkled up his eyes inside their bony, goggle-like orbits. "I believe I sense where you are going. This . . . dark energy shores up fluidic space from collapse. Take away that support . . ."

"And the fluid would begin to compress under its own gravity. Eventually the compression would crush every living thing within it."

"You speak of theory," said Kilana. The Vorta may have been the only one of her kind in the Coalition, but through shrewd politicking and charm, she had worked her way swiftly into the role of liaison for the Caretaker refugees other than the *Voyager* veterans. "Has there been any progress on devising an actual weapon based on this?"

Janeway spoke slowly. "A sufficiently powerful subspace field could be tuned to modify the strength of fluidic space's cosmological constant—not unlike the way we use subspace fields to create gravity or antigravity."

Kilana beamed. "It sounds like quite a simple application. How soon can such a weapon be ready?"

"I'm sorry, I haven't made myself clear," Janeway said. "In practical terms, such a field would be self-perpetuating and would spread indefinitely. We haven't yet figured out a way to reverse or localize the effect."

"You mean it would destroy their entire universe."

"Exactly."

"And what is the problem with that?" Kilana asked sweetly.

"Madam," Rosh cautioned before Janeway could answer. "You are speaking of genocide."

"Pardon me, Councillor, but I don't believe I am. Doctor Kes said that fluidic space is but a single organism. Its loss would be regrettable, but single organisms have been sacrificed for the greater good before."

"I'm afraid you misunderstood me, Kilana," Kes told her in equally (yet more sincerely) gentle tones. "The biosphere behaves collectively, but there are trillions of distinct minds within it."

"We can't ignore that," Rosh said. "So long as there is a possibility of finding a more peaceful resolution, I prefer not to authorize something so drastic."

"The Scourge's attacks worsen daily," Nardem interposed. "We may not have time to wait!"

"Neither can we afford to rush into this," Kes replied. "Our intelligence on fluidic space is limited, secondhand. We can't be certain it will really behave the way our theory suggests. Neither can we be certain that the effect won't spread to our own universe somehow."

"Which is why we have proposed a reconnaissance mission into fluidic space," Gavanri said. "The Borg knowledge obtained from Annika Hansen includes the technique for creating a spatial rift into their realm. One of the EMH's mobile holographic emitters could be programmed to simulate the form of Species 8472 and emit the correct electrochemical signature to pass for one of them. He could perform the necessary scans, and perhaps gain valuable military intelligence in the process. And hopefully the knowledge he brings back could give us the key to reversing or localizing the collapse, so that we could use the weapon for deterrence rather than wholesale destruction."

"What about their telepathic communication?" asked the Nyrian delegate, Raneed, whom Rosh would have been unable to distinguish from a human if not for her more agreeable scent.

"We believe that Kes would be able to remain in contact through the rift and provide the appropriate mental camouflage."

Rosh turned to Kes. "Is this true, Doctor?" Of course, Kes had proven herself capable of remarkable things. But in this case, the Coalition could not take any chances.

Indeed, Kes appeared atypically unsure of herself, though not for that reason. "I'm confident that I could duplicate their telepathic signature. However, I'm not comfortable about helping to gather knowledge intended to destroy them, and I know the Doctor wouldn't be, either. I'd suggest instead that we send an avatar of the Doctor into fluidic space as a diplomatic emissary, to propose peace talks."

"Peace talks?" Nardem scoffed. "We know from your own testimony that they intend our total annihilation."

"But we now know, thanks to Ms. Hansen," Janeway said, "that the Borg started this war. The fluidics may simply believe they're defending themselves against invasion."

"With respect, Captain," Kilana told her apologetically, "they do seem to have taken to heart the human saying that the best defense is a good offense."

"Still," Kes said, "if there's any chance for a peaceful solution, we need to be open to it."

Rosh considered. "I don't think we can risk it at this point. As you say, Doctor Kes, we need more intelligence on conditions there, political as well as physical. I say we send the EMH avatar undercover, as Minister Gavanri suggests. His primary mission will be to gather the scientific and strategic intelligence we need for our defense. However, he will be authorized to keep an eye out for possible diplomatic openings."

"And expose himself as an undercover agent?" Nardem objected. "As paranoid as they are, they would no doubt retaliate fiercely."

But Raneed was more thoughtful. "He need not reveal himself then. If he finds such a prospect, he may return to report it, and then perhaps a separate mission may be undertaken."

"Perhaps," Kilana agreed. "But his priority must be strategic intelligence."

Rosh found this a reasonable compromise, and so did most of the others. The motion passed: the EMH would become a spy in fluidic space, authorized to look for diplomatic prospects but enjoined from revealing himself while there. If his mission was compromised, the mobile emitter would self-destruct; after all, the Doctor had other emitters and plenty of other selves to spare. It would be a relief to send a spy on such a dangerous mission without actually putting that spy's survival at risk.

Rosh only prayed that the mission would ensure the Coalition's survival as well—and that he would not have to give the order to annihilate a universe to do it.

When informed of the decision, the Doctor was adamant that his Hippocratic Oath would not permit him to engage in a mission intended to bring destruction. Kes sympathized, but managed to persuade him that if he didn't go, there would be no chance of a peaceful resolution. "All right," he eventually said. "But whatever my *orders* may be, I'm going there to look for a way to reverse the weapon's effects, not to enhance them. A deterrent, I can live with. And more to the point, so can they."

Kes was confident she could run interference between the

Doctor and those on the council who might differ with his interpretation of the mission. After all, she was an essential part of making it work. And it was *Moskelarnan,* the research vessel dedicated to Moskelar Station and placed under her command for this mission, that would deliver the Doctor to fluidic space. With help from Annika Hansen—now sadder and more serious than she had been—*Moskelarnan*'s deflector array was modified to generate a resonant graviton beam calibrated to the subspace signature of the fluidic universe. One spacetime orbifold later, a quantum singularity opened, its event horizon glowing blindingly white as energy poured across the differential between universes, the fluidic continuum possessing a greater energy density.

But the rift couldn't be kept open long, for fear of detection. As soon as it stabilized, Kes ordered her crew to beam in the Doctor's mobile emitter—not the tiny original which still held pride of place in *Voyager*'s sickbay, but a bulkier Vostigye-built unit able to fit inside the torso of one of the Doctor's avatars. The hologram it now projected was that of a member of Species 8472, hopefully accurate and nondescript enough to avoid drawing attention. Once the copy of the Doctor within the emitter confirmed his arrival, Kes ordered the graviton beam reduced to minimal strength; the rift closed, but enough of a link remained to allow its quick reopening in an emergency, and to allow Kes to maintain telepathic contact with the Doctor. *Though I still find it remarkable that you can read the mind of a computerized being,* he sent to her. *Reassuring, though. Does this mean I have a soul? And if so, how many do I have?*

Kes chuckled. "I'll get back to you once I figure out if I have one."

Closing her eyes, Kes could perceive what the Doctor perceived—a universe of fluid, yellow-green with bioluminescence, cloudy with density variations and microparticles, with larger specks floating through it. *Everything here is biological,* the Doctor reported, interpreting the readings of the emitter's built-in sen-

sors, which had been calibrated to cope with the scattering effect
of the inhabitants' bioelectric fields, though their resolution was
still limited. *I think those particles are a sort of plankton. Would it look
odder if I tried to eat some or if I didn't?*

"Is there anyone there to see you?"

*I'm not sure. There are some forms moving in the distance . . . it's
hard to make them out . . .* She sensed annoyance. *I'm thinking too
much like a humanoid. I'm essentially an aquatic life-form here. Sound is
more useful than sight.* She sensed him boosting his audio receptors.
Fascinating, he sent after a moment. *This universe is pervaded with
sound. Distant calls, large bodies moving . . . maybe some kind of currents
flowing . . . a literal music of the spheres, do you suppose, Kes? I wonder
if the 8472 have opera. Imagine a song that propagates across an entire
galaxy!* Although the Doctor had grown away from his former
fascination with humanoid hobbies such as dance and painting,
he'd retained his love of music.

"It's a lovely idea, Doctor, but about those moving forms . . . ?"

*Oh, yes. Moving my way, and fairly sizable. Wait a minute . . . there
are smaller forms congregating around me.* She could perceive them
too; some of the specks were circling around him, darting in to
taste his skin. *Kes, I think they're antibodies of a sort! If fluidic space
functions like a single organism, it must have a sort of immune system. But
why would a universe need defense against outside intrusion?*

"It's a very dense and energetic universe," Kes answered, drawing on the expertise she'd absorbed from the cosmologists aboard
ship. "Other universes might be drawn to it, with rifts forming
naturally."

*Or maybe it isn't all one organism. Do we really know that the fluid fills
the whole thing? Maybe it just has big liquid blobs in place of galaxies.*

"No, then there'd be centers of gravity pulling things toward
them and they would've collapsed into solid masses, even with the
repulsive dark energy. The fluid has to be uniformly distributed."

*Come to think of it, with no gravity and no solid surface, what am I do-
ing with three legs? Or any legs?* She sensed him thrashing a bit. *These*

stubby things aren't good for swimming. My body's not very streamlined, either. She felt his concern; the big forms were drawing closer. If his emitter wasn't giving off the correct electrochemical signature . . .

But Kes could do nothing about that, not at this range, anyway. Instead, she concentrated on projecting the right telepathic "scent" onto him, the same sense of presence she'd gotten from her intermittent contacts with Species 8472. The approaching forms were now becoming clear as bioships of a kind, though Kes could sense a telepathic ambience to them as well, recognizing that they were more animals than vessels. They didn't seem to have any of the tripeds aboard. But they were animals with a lethal bioelectric defense. *I hope you're telling them "hello,"* the Doctor sent.

Whatever she managed to do must have been effective, for one bioship went on its way while the other pulled up alongside him, opening an orifice/hatch in invitation. "It's accepted you, Doctor. I think it's offering you a lift."

Should I go in?

"Yes. There are no other sentients aboard, so you should hurry before it decides to go on its way."

The Doctor entered just before the orifice irised shut. Inside, the bioship/animal resembled the one described in Chakotay's reports from that first 8472 contact, except for the lack of gravity and the presence of the pervasive fluid throughout its interior. The Doctor drifted backward as it accelerated, so he grabbed for a handhold on what looked like a set of interior vertebrae. Once its motion stabilized, he looked around. *No windows. How do I see where I'm going?*

"Try touching an outer wall and getting a sound picture."

He did the best he could, but it only gave a vague sense. Kes broadened her perceptions, taking in his full surroundings. "See that opening in the wall with the luminescent tubes running through it? I think it's a neural interface. Try grasping it."

He did so, with no result. *I feel silly. I'm a hologram—I don't have any nerves.*

"Be patient." Reaching her mind toward the interface, she linked with its perceptions and fed them to the Doctor. Now they both had a full sensory experience of the journey as the bioship perceived it, primarily with sound, scent, and electrical impulse, with vision as a secondary component. It had monochromatic color perception, since all the light in this universe was yellow-green.

But the creature's other senses gave her a richer perception of fluidic space, and she committed it to her eidetic memory for later analysis, hoping it would provide some physical insight allowing a less destructive defense to be devised. From this perspective, it was a richer, more complex environment, its fluid divided into distinct currents and convection cells like an ocean's, though Kes was unsure what could drive such currents without gravity. Perhaps thermal differentials, with some parts of fluidic space being hotter and more energetic than others. There were no stars here; the energy that warmed this universe was the residue of its Big Bang, a cosmic background radiation a hundred times hotter than that of Kes's universe, since fluidic space had expanded so much less, attenuating the heat of its birth to a far lesser degree. But some parts must be warmer than others, as the activity of life generated and transferred heat.

This is extraordinary, the Doctor said. *The different convection cells seem to host different types of organisms. There seems to be a correlation between the shape and size of the convection cells and the organisms they host. And the currents between them appear to be delivering nutrients, removing waste. It's almost like the organs and blood vessels of a body, but divided by flow patterns and density differentials rather than walls of tissue.*

Soon it became evident that the bioship was heading for a particular convection cell, moving sideways in the current flow so as to pass across the interface and be shunted into the cell. Inside the cell was a dense concentration of large structures; Kes had to remind herself that they were alive, for they were immense, the size that living things could reach only in weightless conditions. But she sensed acoustically that they were hollow, and inhabited.

"Doctor, it's a city! I'm sensing hundreds of thousands of Species 8472, and other creatures of various types."

I'm not sure if I'd call it a city or a biome. It's almost like a school of immense fish. Indeed, the whole agglomeration of creatures moved in a stately gavotte, independent entities cooperating as a single unit. Smaller forms moved among the large ones, interacting, exchanging who knew what, and still smaller forms passed between them. The bioship spiraled in to become part of this unending dance, and opened its orifice once it was immersed.

"You should probably get out now, Doctor," Kes sent, "before the rush-hour crowd climbs aboard."

I was tired of being a straphanger anyway, he replied, letting go of the interface conduits and pulling himself along the wall until he reached the exit.

Through the Doctor's senses, Kes saw thousands of 8472 swimming through the motile city. Except they weren't the 8472 she was familiar with, the kind the Doctor was emulating. Instead of heavy tripedal legs, they bore three large, ribbed, triangular fins on their lower bodies. Their hands were much like the Doctor's, except webbed. The rear plates of their heads were swept back, better able to accommodate the tilting of their heads perpendicular to their bodies as they swam. *Now, that design makes sense for this environment!* the Doctor said. *So what am I, and why am I so different?*

"They feel the same telepathically," Kes said. "They're the same species, in mind, at least."

Could the tripeds we've encountered have been specially bred to function in our environment? Am I a soldier home from the war instead of just a nondescript Scourge on the street?

"It's possible. This could complicate things."

You're telling me. Uh-oh . . . I've got company. Some 8472—or 8472 and a half—are swimming this way.

"Just act natural."

I'm an artificial intelligence holographically disguised as a three-legged alien and swimming in a parallel universe made of lime gelatin! How do you define "natural"?

"Calm, Doctor. Remember, you're in no danger."

The rest of me isn't. But this little part of me would like to return to the whole intact! If you were a finger, would you be sanguine about getting amputated?

"I'm trying to communicate with them. Just try to play along."

She sent recognition and query to the swimmers. They responded without words, but in the tone of security guards demanding identification. "They want you to stay where you are."

With this anatomy, that's the easy part!

One swimmer had a smaller organism attached to it like a lamprey. It pulled it off and extended it toward the Doctor. "Don't let it touch you!" Kes called. His holographic skin might not have whatever chemical or thermal properties the organic device would test for. Better an unidentified fugitive than a confirmed Coalition spy.

The Doctor pulled back and began dog-paddling away at his best speed, such as it was. He headed for the nearest crowd of finned 8472. *If I can get lost in the crowd, I can change to look like one of them.*

"It's worth a try."

But something big suddenly swam into his path, a flat, translucent creature like a cross between a manta and a jellyfish. The Doctor looked around wildly for another way out, but the creature began to fold itself around him, reaching out tendrils to grasp him. "Open the rift!" Kes called to her crew, praying he was still in transporter range.

But then she felt the shock that went through his mobile emitter as the tendrils touched him. "Doctor!" she called. But his presence was no longer in her mind.

Something else was, however. It was the 8472, probing back along the telepathic signal she was sending, trying to get a taste of what was on the other end.

Kes shut them out with her mental shields and sighed, ordering her crew to activate the emitter's self-destruct system. "No contact," her tactical officer reported. "I can't confirm self-destruct."

"Shut down the deflector array," Kes ordered, resigned. There was no choice but to abandon the mission and hope the destruct command had gone through. Kes tried to take comfort in the knowledge that the Doctor's core consciousness was still intact. But it was this facet of him she'd been linked with, this one who'd feared destruction. This one that she had to condemn to his fate. She would have to live with that.

But could the Coalition live with the consequences of his exposure?

12

With the capture of the Doctor's avatar, the hardliners began pushing for immediate construction of the subspace field generator to collapse fluidic space. Janeway and Kes, with help from Chakotay, did their best to talk the council out of it, but Kilana argued that time was too short to wait for a less apocalyptic solution. Her eloquence, and her carefully calculated appearance of vulnerability and fear, carried the day in favor of constructing the doomsday device.

Their urgency seemed to be borne out when a quantum singularity was detected on the outskirts of the Vostigye home system. Only one ship emerged, but the destructive power of even a single bioship was well known, and thus a fleet was sent to intercept, with *Voyager* as its flagship.

But instead of engaging them in battle, the vessel came to a stop as the fleet approached. "Stand ready," Janeway ordered the other captains. "There's no telling what they intend."

"Captain!" Surt reported from ops. "They're hailing us. *Voyager* specifically."

Janeway frowned, trading a look with Harry. "They've never tried communicating other than telepathically before," her first officer said.

"Maybe they wanted to be sure we heard their ultimatum." Janeway rose from her chair, steeling herself. "On-screen."

Her composure wavered when the visage of the Doctor appeared, standing in what looked like the interior of a bioship. Unlike the ones described in Kes's report, this one seemed to have a gaseous atmosphere and artificial gravity. *"Ah. There you are, Captain. I'm happy to report that there's no need to launch the rescue mission you were undoubtedly planning to undertake,"* he said.

It certainly seemed unlikely that Species 8472 could fake that supremely sarcastic tone. Still, Janeway had to be sure. "Bridge to sickbay."

"Sickbay here, Captain," came a voice identical to the one from the bioship. *"I know what you're going to ask, and you needn't worry. I'm receiving feedback from him already, and I can confirm that he really is me."* He paused. *"Oh, my. I've just synchronized memories with him, and he's got quite a little surprise for you."*

On the screen, the other Doctor rolled his eyes. *"Just like me to steal my own thunder. I was hoping to ease into this, but . . . Captain Janeway, there's someone here I'd like you to meet."*

The Doctor stepped aside and another figure came into view—a wizened figure she'd never expected to see again in her lifetime, certainly not on this side of the galaxy. The incongruity of his presence was so great that she could not even bring herself to say his name. "Harry . . . are you seeing it too?"

Harry was on his feet now as well, gaping. "Groundskeeper Boothby?"

"Don't let your mouth hang open like that, son," the gaunt, elderly man said. *"You'll let flies in. Congratulations on the promotion, by the way."* His eyes shifted to Janeway. *"And before you ask, Captain, I'm not the same Boothby you knew back at Starfleet Academy. But then, you're not exactly the same Kathryn Janeway I met a little while back. Though I'm sure you still like roses just as much."*

A chill ran through her. At the Academy, the real Boothby had often given her fresh roses for her quarters. "I'm afraid I don't understand."

"It's a long story. And an embarrassing one for my people, I'm afraid. That's right," he told her. *"I'm a member of what you call Species 8472."*

His gruff features took on an impish grin, so like the genuine article. *"Quite a trick, isn't it?"*

The story told by Boothby—there was nothing else to call him—was remarkable. Apparently, the immensely complex genome of Species 8472 enabled them to alter their bodies in almost any way with the right chemical and enzymatic therapy. The soldiers sent to battle in the Delta Quadrant had been altered to function in environments with air and gravity, mimicking the conditions aboard the Borg vessels that had invaded their space, and their ships had been modified to match. This was why the tripeds encountered in the past seemed so mismatched to their fluidic environment.

But their transformational capabilities had served another purpose as well. Boothby had been part of a project to infiltrate Starfleet Headquarters on Earth—apparently Species 8472's reach extended even that far—to conduct reconnaissance and evaluate the threat humanity posed to them. Essentially it had been similar to the Doctor's spy mission, but on a larger scale, with hundreds of tripeds undergoing transformation into Alpha Quadrant species. They had impersonated everything from cadets to admirals, but he, their leader, had chosen the form of the man who had tended the grounds of Headquarters and Academy alike for generations—a man at once inconspicuous and universally trusted, the ideal infiltrator. (It made Janeway wonder how many secrets the real Boothby must have accrued over the decades.)

The astonishing thing was that, according to the ersatz Boothby, this infiltration had been in response to an attack that *Voyager* had launched on Species 8472 in conjunction with the Borg—even though *Voyager* had never formed such an alliance.

"He's saying he comes from an alternate timeline?" Kyric Rosh asked Janeway as they entered *Voyager*'s observation lounge, where Harry, the Doctor, and the 8472 emissary waited. The councillor had come aboard to debrief the visitor, not willing to risk letting an 8472 into Kosnelye but willing to take a personal risk in the hopes that Boothby's professed mission of peace was genuine.

"Actually I'm from another universe," the disguised emissary told him in Boothby's gravelly voice. "But last time I visited your universe—let's say I saw a different side of things. Where I come from, we only have the one timeline, but yours seem to multiply like tribbles. And that's the root of the problem."

Rosh shook his head. "I'm afraid I'm a little confused on the difference between a universe and a timeline."

"Harry, would you care to explain?" Janeway asked. She would've tried it herself, but the theory had too much in common with temporal physics, and she could do without the headache.

"Yes, Captain. Councillor Rosh." Harry rose. "Well, a parallel universe is just another place—a physical realm that's somewhere else in higher-dimensional space, with its own separate laws of physics, its own separate stars and planets—or not, as the case may be," he said, nodding to Boothby, "its own distinct inhabitants and history. But an alternate *timeline* is just another quantum facet of our own universe. It's physically the same place, but with a different history."

Rosh was still confused, and Harry tried to clarify. "It's like . . . are you familiar with the Schroedinger's Cat paradox?"

"I believe the Vostigye equivalent is Kamornen's Box," Janeway interposed.

"Ah, yes. The animal that's both alive and dead."

"Essentially," Harry said. "Quantum physics says a single particle can be in multiple different states at once. A radioactive atom, say, can be both decayed and undecayed. But set up a switch so that the decay releases a poison capsule, put it in a box with a cat—and is the cat alive or dead? Or is there a way it can be both at once? The paradox is whether a classical object like a cat can behave like a quantum particle.

"The thing Schroedinger overlooked, and Kamornen understood, is that the cat is made up of individual particles too, so it's a quantum object just the same. Each of its particles reacts to *both* states of the radioactive atom, and is in two simultaneous states as a result.

"But for a while, the question was: how do all the different states of those different particles add up to the reality we see? One theory was that they all averaged out to a single large-scale, classical state, similar to the way the individual motions of the atoms in the air around us average out to a single temperature and pressure. Supposedly, that's what makes a multiple quantum state seem to collapse into one when you measure it, the cat to be either alive or dead when you open the box—the particle's state doesn't really collapse, but the measuring device or the cat averages out to just one state, so it looks like the particle is in either one state or the other.

"But the other theory was that the different states aligned and reinforced each other in what's called a coherent superposition, so that the whole macroscopic system—the atom, the poison, the cat, the scientist, and everything that interacted with them— ended up in two distinct states at once, each isolated from the other, effectively splitting the universe into two different realities: both made up of the same particles, but experiencing different histories from that point on. When you measure a particle, it still looks like it collapsed into one state, because you can only see the state that aligns with the timeline you're in. One copy of you sees a live cat, the other sees a dead cat.

"Now, the problem with the second idea," Harry went on, "was that it's hard to get so many particles' quantum states to align like that. You can create a coherent superposition made of a large ensemble of particles, but just the general jostling it receives from the particles around it can cause that coherence to break up and collapse into a single average state. Like a sand castle in a sandstorm—you can build the sand into two or more different towers, but when the storm hits, they'll collapse and blend together again. Now try doing it with a whole universe's worth of particles."

Rosh frowned. "But we know alternate timelines do exist."

"That's right. We now know that when a coherent superposition forms, the two macroscopic states shift into slightly different subspace phases, giving them enough stability to survive as separate realities. That's also how two temporal copies of the same person can interact as though they were physically separate beings—essentially the subspace phase shift splits their bodies' quantum waveforms in two."

Rosh held up his hands. "This is all intriguing, but what does it have to do with Mister, uh, Boothby's presence?"

"Like Boothby said, fluidic space doesn't have alternate timelines," Harry went on. "We believe it's because their universe is so much denser than ours. Any particle existing in a multiple quantum state just interacts with too many other particles right from the start. The 'sandstorm' is so heavy that you can't build the sand castle in the first place, and so the subspace phase shift never happens. Our universe is constantly splitting into alternate quantum states, alternate histories, but in Boothby's universe, it all averages out to a single classical state."

"So there we were," Boothby said, "minding our own business, when a big ugly cube showed up and started talking about assimilating us. Naturally, we fought off the infection. And when more of them came through, we decided to take the fight out to them. Imagine our surprise when some of our troops came back—and then came back again."

"They were duplicated," Janeway clarified. "While they were in our universe, something happened that created a new timeline, splitting them into duplicate selves. But their home universe didn't undergo the same split. So both sets of duplicates returned to the same reality, shifted just enough in phase that they couldn't collapse together anymore."

"Remarkable," Rosh said.

"That wasn't the word we used for it," Boothby said. "If we normally used words, that is." He cleared his throat; no matter what, the alien remained in his Boothby character. According to what he'd told Janeway, the infiltrators had practiced their human personas so long and hard that they had become second nature to them. "The thing you have to understand is that our universe is a carefully balanced whole. We're not like you, with all these big empty voids keeping you insulated. What's bad for one part is bad for everybody. That's why we have to keep our universe pure, to fight so hard against contamination. It's the same reason your body has to kill off infections. Maybe you've got nothing personal against the germs, maybe they're entitled to live off in a pond somewhere, but once they get inside you and start to multiply, it's kill or be killed."

"And that's your species's function?" Rosh challenged. "To kill?"

Boothby threw him a sour look. "We're the brains of the outfit. Our job's to take care of the place. Tend the flowers, water the trees . . . trim the weeds. I guess you could say we're the groundskeepers." He smirked. "Got to be easier to say than 'Species 8472.'

"But we Groundskeepers are part of the whole, too. And it's all about the balance. We all have our own jobs to do, and we all get our fair share of the pie. A nice, neat, orderly system." He fidgeted. "Or it was, until some of us started coming back beside ourselves. Now there are too many of us. And the more your universe keeps splitting off new timelines, the worse it gets on our side. There are three, six, sometimes dozens of each individual wrestling over the same job, the same place in society, the same share of food and resources. All with the same perfectly good claim to it, since they used to be the same individual."

He fell quiet, as though he could say no more. Janeway was surprised it had been this easy for him; the first time, he could barely get the words out, and the Doctor had related most of the tale. Apparently this situation was a profound embarrassment to them. They prided themselves on their strength, their fitness to defend their realm, and the weakness of being divided into conflicting selves was intolerable. "The weak will perish"—that was the telepathic message Kes had gotten from them at first contact. It had been as much a justification as a threat—they saw this universe as the source of their own weakness, and they needed to prove their strength by conquering it or else die to pave the way for a stronger copy of themselves.

Boothby and his fellow "Groundskeepers" had not told any of this to the alternate *Voyager* crew they had encountered, finding it too shameful. The only reason he was confessing it now was because the Doctor had discovered it when he visited fluidic space. Apparently, the Groundskeepers who had approached him had suspected him of being not a spy, but another duplicate soldier returning from a branching universe, another cell in a growing cancer. They had been surprised by what they had actually found, though they had quickly adapted and neutralized his self-destruct mechanism before he could trigger it. But apparently Boothby had come to some kind of peace accord with the other *Voyager,* and he had intervened on the Doctor's behalf.

The Doctor, his secret-agent self now fully reintegrated into his neural matrix, picked up the story. "Essentially it's resulted in a civil war over there. Although it's not brother against brother, it's self against self. Duplicate selves are fighting, even killing each other over the right to claim their place in the social order. Only the strongest copy gets to survive. And the leaders are endorsing this . . . extroverted suicide because they think it's the only way to resolve the crisis. Except the number of duplicates keeps multiplying."

"Then it seems the solution is simple," Rosh said. "Keep out of our universe."

"It's not that easy," Boothby said. "We still have to fight off the Borg. And remember, we're fighting Borg from more than one timeline. Every time your universe splits, the invasion gets worse on our end. We have to take the fight to your universe, no matter the cost."

"What about your attacks on the Voth? On us?" Rosh demanded.

"Keep your shorts on, son, I'm getting there. Now, as I was saying. Things might not be quite so bad for us if not for you clever people on *Voyager*. In one of the timelines, you not only made an alliance with the Borg against us, you gave them the nanoprobe weapon you developed. They started hitting us damn hard after that, and we had to fight like nobody's business just to survive. Eventually," he said solemnly, "we had to set off a string of Omega molecules in that timeline and the few new ones that had branched off of it. Blew up half the Borg, stranded the rest at sublight. Wasn't much fun for the rest of the people in this part of the quadrant, I'd imagine."

Janeway stared in horror, while the others just looked confused. "What's an Omega molecule?" Harry asked.

"That's a question for another time," Janeway said, her tone commanding him to drop it now. Delta Coalition or no, she still intended to return to Starfleet one day and thus remained bound by her Starfleet oaths—including the one commanding strict secrecy about the most destructive force ever discovered.

"Now, there was another group of timelines," Boothby said, "where *Voyager* used their nanoprobe weapon against us once, to force us into retreat, but didn't give it to the Borg afterward. We left that branch of your universe alone for a while, since it was leaving us alone and we were busy with the fight elsewhere. Once we wiped the Borg out in the other timeline, we turned our attention back to Starfleet. After all, it had been a Starfleet crew, your counterparts, that created the nanoprobe weapon. We needed to find out if they were planning to invade us next. But they'd kicked our butts, so we decided to take the sneaky approach. And that's how I became the handsome devil you see before you now."

"But how does this explain your attacks in our timeline?" Rosh asked.

"The Borg here were nearly as bad as in the first one, once they got their own version of a nanoprobe weapon. As for the Voth, well, we figured we couldn't take any chances."

"But you've made peace with *Voyager* in that other timeline," Janeway interposed. Boothby hadn't quite gotten around to explaining this part before. "So why are your forces attacking the Coalition so aggressively now?"

"It wasn't my decision, Captain. I've been trying to convince the leadership to back down, but they've been through hell this last year, and we're not a forgiving people to begin with. Besides, there are a lot of timelines. I can only tend one plot at a time. I managed to convince them to lay off the timeline where I made peace with your other self, Captain, since there's no immediate threat from there." He gave a heavy sigh. "But even that is temporary.

"Borg aside, Voth and Federation aside, the very existence of your universe is seen as a threat to the stability of ours. The hardliners don't believe coexistence between us is even possible. The weak must perish, and a universe that can't make up its mind about its own history is mighty weak in their eyes. So they want to destroy your galaxy. One timeline at a time."

Silence filled the room. "Can they even do that?" Harry finally asked.

"Our universe has a lot more energy to spare than yours," Boothby said. "Your galaxy's just about the size of our universe, so destroying it should be enough. It'll take time, of course; Omega molecules don't grow on trees, so it'll be a few months before they have any more to spare. So for now, they're going about it the old-fashioned way, one planet and colony at a time. And they're starting in your block of timelines, since we've already got so much of our fleet here from the war with the Borg.

"You'll be the first to go—but the hardliners won't rest until they've wiped out your galaxy in every timeline they can reach."

13

"It's been months since I asked myself if we made the right decision," Janeway said. "If we would've been better off if we'd made that deal with the Borg. Now, I'm not so sure."

Chakotay didn't pause in massaging her soapy back—his own quiet way of offering comfort. Although his dwelling was modest for a government official, he'd made sure to have a sizable bathtub installed for her benefit. But Janeway was too busy studying the flexible (and waterproof) display sheet in her hand. To prove his claims, Boothby had provided information from the other timelines the Groundskeepers had visited, information that included copies of *Voyager*'s logs. The timelines fell into three major "sheafs," as he had described, and Janeway found it simpler to think in terms of only three timelines.

She knew that, right now, her focus should be on the threat of galactic destruction, on assisting Boothby's efforts to find a diplomatic route to avert the crisis. But it was impossible not to be preoccupied with the knowledge of her own life in other histories— alternative paths that had actually happened, that were happening right now in other facets of reality. She knew that everyone else who had been entrusted with this information must be similarly affected. Perhaps it wasn't so self-centered; getting a feel for what it was like to confront one's alternate lives could help her understand the plight of the Groundskeepers and see a way to a solution.

She recognized one of the alternate histories as the one Kes had described jumping backward through nearly two years ago. The

Borg-Groundskeeper war had only just started escalating then, so it was the earliest divergence the Groundskeepers had experienced. In that history, Kes had lived out her life aboard *Voyager,* and so had Tom Paris, who had become her husband. But Janeway herself had not lived to see it, dying with B'Elanna Torres in an attack by a race called the Krenim.

But before then, they had needed to get past the Borg. "True," Chakotay said, not looking up from her back. "We made an alliance with the Borg and gave them the nanoprobe weapon once they'd escorted us through the heart of their space. Whereupon they immediately double-crossed us and would've assimilated us if a Groundskeeper attack hadn't let us slip away." After which, apparently, they had salvaged a transwarp coil from a Borg wreck, allowing them to jump several thousand light-years closer to home and away from the Borg threat. That had undoubtedly saved them from the Groundskeepers' later Omega-particle attack.

"But as a consequence," Janeway said, "the Groundskeepers devastated this part of the quadrant to stop the Borg. And we endured a 'year of hell' at the hands of the Krenim."

"And we lost you."

"But we still had Tom. And Tuvok, and Carey and Vorik . . ."

"And lost others. How can we say one life is worth more than another? All I know is, I'm glad you're with me in this life."

"They destroyed trillions of lives in that history. Because of events I set in motion."

"That was their choice. You're not to blame—whichever you we're talking about." Chakotay reached over her shoulder and tapped the display sheet to bring up records of the other sheaf of timelines. "Meanwhile, in this version of history, we made our deal, but the Groundskeepers attacked us before we could finish the weapon, and the Borg double-crossed us and used *Voyager* to invade fluidic space. The Borg didn't get the weapon, but they remained a major threat once the Groundskeepers were driven out. And we lost Kes to some kind of accelerated evolution."

"But most of us lived, Chakotay. We stayed together as a family."

Chakotay came alongside her, met her gaze solemnly. "As a family, Kathryn? You and I were still just colleagues. Annika was buried beneath her Borg persona and never fell in love with Harry. Neelix had to live without Kes. Lyndsay Ballard was killed, along with Clemens, Pratt, and others. And the Delta Coalition never existed."

She matched his gaze. "So you're saying you were right to talk me out of the Borg alliance."

"You tell me. It could've gone either way. In fact, it did. All these histories are real. Every one is better for some people and worse for others."

"So what are you saying? That none of our choices matter?"

"No," he told her gently. "That our choices are all we have. We can't know, we can't control, how the random factors of the universe will shape the consequences of our choices. The same choice can lead to a universe where the Borg are a major threat and most of the crew is still alive, or one where this whole region of space has been blasted back to the impulse age and Kathryn Janeway is dead. So we can't let our fear of the consequences keep us from making choices. All we can do is try to be true to our own hearts."

Smiling at his words of comfort, Janeway pulled him to her. As always, it was bittersweet. She loved the life she had with him, but she still felt an obligation to get her ship home, to report to Starfleet, to reunite her crew with their families one day. She believed she could persuade Chakotay to come with her when that time came—but she didn't know if she should, when he had built such an important role for himself here, made so many friends and connections among the Vostigye and their allies. How could she choose when the time came? She couldn't abandon her home forever, but how could she ask him to abandon his?

★ ★ ★

Annika shuddered as she reviewed the alternate history files that Harry had shown her. "I can't process this. I've been trying so hard to cope with the Borg memories and thoughts in my head . . . and this, this other me *likes* being a Borg! She calls herself Seven of Nine!"

Harry tilted his head, studying the log image on the display sheet. "I like her fashion sense."

Annika glared, but Harry grinned back, letting her know he was just teasing to break the tension. He knew how much she looked forward to the day when she no longer needed to wear her dermal sheath under her clothes. Apparently this "Seven of Nine" had considered modesty and comfort irrelevant and had worn the body-hugging garment with nothing over it. Annika blushed every time she looked at the picture.

"Her clothes are irrelevant," Annika said, then caught herself and blushed. "I mean, what about her thoughts? Her feelings? Does she remember anything about Unimatrix Zero? About me, my whole life?"

"You couldn't remember her, either."

"There was no 'her.' Just a meat puppet for the Collective."

"Apparently there was more to her than you think. I don't want to push you, but you might want to think about taking a closer look at your Borg memories. Maybe there's something worthwhile there after all."

Annika pouted, then changed the subject. "What I can't get over is how we ended up on the same ship in two different realities." In the third one, the "Year of Hell" timeline, the Borg had also chosen "Seven of Nine" as a liaison with Janeway on the Borg cube she had visited, but that Seven had never been forced to beam aboard *Voyager* and so had never been severed from the Collective. She had probably died in the Groundskeepers' Omega attack, if not sooner. "What are the odds?" She grinned at Harry. "Do you think we were destined to be together?"

"It's a nice thought, but I don't think we're 'together' in that other history." In fact, the Harry of the "Seven of Nine" timeline seemed to be in a total rut—still a lowly ensign, still unattached, still languishing in Tom Paris's shadow. Not that he blamed Tom for that, of course. He would give a great deal to be in a timeline where his best friend was still alive. But he wouldn't give up Annika even for that.

He contemplated the paradox. "Maybe it's not such a coincidence. The logs from those other *Voyager*s say you were—Seven was—stored in an enclosed chamber in the heart of the cube. And she—you—seemed different from other Borg, with more personality and autonomy. Maybe there was something special about you, your function in the hive. That could explain why you were chosen as a liaison in those timelines, and that's what led to you ending up on *Voyager* in one of them. As for here, maybe being in the heart of the cube is what let you and the others survive when it was crippled. And we both ended up with the Vostigye because they're the ones who do the most to help out refugees. So it's not such a coincidence."

She smiled. "But it was your ship that found me, Harry. I like to think that's destiny. And don't try to reason me out of it," she said, putting a hand over his lips. "I want it to be destiny. I want it to be magic. Because Seven of Nine would *hate* that."

Harry nodded. "Okay by me." And she kissed him, and he realized that she had been magical to him all along.

B'Elanna flung the display sheet at the Doctor. It passed harmlessly through the hologram and shorted out against the force field across her cell door. "Why did you show me this?" she demanded.

"I thought you might like to know things could be worse. You could be dead."

She turned away from him. "What's so bad about that? At least Tom would be alive."

He came around to face her again. "Have you been taking your medications? Clinical depression is a chronic condition, and I'm seeing some rather overt symptoms."

"You think my pain is just a chemical imbalance? I lost everything that mattered to me. I killed innocent people. I almost killed my own friends. What makes you think I deserve to feel better?"

"Oh, just my own Hippocratical reasons," he gibed. His eyes roved over her, and she knew he was scanning her. These Vostigye mobile emitters had medical tricorders built in, and although the Doctor still used the face and voice of Lewis Zimmerman as a holographic interface for his humanoid patients, he no longer felt the need to mimic humanity to the point of wielding a conventional tricorder and scanner, one machine reading another machine in a triumph of conceit over efficiency. "Yes, your serotonin levels are disturbingly low. You've been a naughty girl."

She stared. "I'm in prison. What do you expect?"

"I expect B'Elanna Torres to be intelligent enough to listen to her doctor's orders," he told her, morphing one finger into a hypospray and applying it to her neck, the drug being shunted from the pharmasynth unit in his emitter. "There. Your neurotransmitters should stabilize soon. Then you'll only have to deal with your genuine guilt instead of the neurochemical exaggeration thereof. If you're going to punish yourself, at least you should do it with your wits about you."

Her eyes thanked him for not trying to cheer her up. "So. These other histories. You're still just a hologram aboard *Voyager*."

"So it seems. And in one, I've spent most of the past year off-line." He shook his head. "I can't imagine going back to only having one body, one locus of perception. It was so limiting."

"And I'm still chief engineer in one of them."

"And Mister Paris is still helmsman. You two are apparently quite the item there."

"But in the one where I died, he bounced right back and married Kes. The little slut. I always knew he had a thing for her."

"I'm sure it was after a respectable period of mourning."

"But in the other one, he didn't get together with me until Kes left. Was I just leftovers to him?"

The Doctor studied her. "Your neurotransmitters are still settling down. Your memories seem a bit compromised. As I recall, you two were flirting shamelessly with each other for months before we encountered the Groundskeepers. People were taking bets on when you'd finally stop deceiving yourselves and get on with it."

B'Elanna sank down onto the bench. "They were right. I should've admitted my feelings when I had the chance. Maybe it could've made a difference. Kept me out of this cell."

"Or it could've gotten you killed. Causality's funny that way." He put a hand on her shoulder. "My advice is not to dwell on it. There are countless realities out there, besides the ones the Groundskeepers have been able to access. They apparently can only access timelines that have branched off from ones they were already visiting at the time. There are bound to be realities out there in which we've all been destroyed, or were never born at all. You'll just cause yourself needless anxiety by dwelling on alternate possibilities."

That's easy for you to say, Doctor, she thought as he left the cell. *But what else can I do when this reality is intolerable?*

"Am I going to lose you?" Neelix asked, his tone bordering on panic. He stared at Kes as though he expected her to begin shimmering out of corporeality at any second.

She placed her hand on his. "Neelix, don't worry. There's no cause for concern yet."

"Yet. It took a few days for your symptoms to show up over there."

"They weren't symptoms. They were part of a metamorphosis."

"Either way, I lost you. Or he lost you. Or he lost her. Oh, now I know why temporal physics gives the captain a headache!"

Kes smiled. It all seemed quite simple and obvious to her now, but she could sense that he was in no mood for a detailed explanation. "I haven't interacted as much with the Groundskeepers as I did in that timeline. So my powers haven't been amplified nearly as much."

"But that Boothby—"

"Is in human form. His telepathy is dormant. As long as I don't have direct telepathic contact with the Groundskeepers or visit fluidic space, I should be fine."

"But you were connected with the Doctor in fluidic space."

"And I have felt a bit more energized since then. Things are coming a bit more easily to me. But that's all."

Neelix frowned. "You know, I hadn't thought about it . . . but in that first timeline, you never had any power surge at all, did you? Even though you had about as much contact with the Groundskeepers as you did here."

Kes nodded. "I believe that's because in that timeline, I hadn't yet been exposed to the temporal energies that affected me later in life. When I came back to this timeline, and the other one that branched off from it, I must have still carried a residue of those energies even after the Doctor purged them. I think that made me more receptive to the psionic energy of fluidic space." That, she believed, explained the difference in the way the Borg alliance had ended in the other two timelines. In the original history, which the crew was calling the "Krenim" or "Year of Hell" timeline, the alliance had proceeded as planned and the Borg had been given the nanoprobe weapon, with ultimately devastating consequences for the quadrant. In the other, the so-called "Borg" timeline, the temporal energy in Kes had made her more attuned to the Groundskeepers, so they had sensed the plan in her mind and sent ships to destroy *Voyager*. Whereupon the Borg cube had sacrificed itself to save *Voyager* and the nanoprobe data it bore, which had led to Seven of Nine and the other drones taking *Voyager* into fluidic space, which had triggered Kes's metamorphosis into . . . something more, something that she could not quite identify even with all her enhanced abilities and knowledge.

Something that had been forced to leave her friends, to leave Neelix, for their own protection. The thought that she might undergo such a metamorphosis herself was disturbing, however intellectually intrigued she might be by the prospect. She was happy with the life she had, and there were too many people who depended on her, professionally and personally.

Most of all Neelix. Leaving him now would devastate him, and she couldn't do that to him. Or to herself. Learning of the other timelines had just made her more committed to marrying him. At least he was alive in both the other main histories. In the original one, he'd suffered a similar crisis with his donated lung, but the Doctor had developed an effective replacement by that time; while in the other, he had actually died in an alien attack but had been revived by a Borg nanoprobe therapy that had apparently reversed the aging of his lung. But in both those histories, he had lost her, either to circumstances or to another man, and it seemed he hadn't found anyone else. He deserved better than that. She was so eager to marry him and let the *elogium* take its course, but the crisis with the Groundskeepers had forced them to defer those plans.

"Well," Neelix said, "I'm not sure whether to be glad that happened to you or not. On the one hand, it made you the extraordinary woman you are today. But you were always extraordinary. And it could take you away from me forever."

"Ohh, Neelix." She stroked his cheek. "Not forever. If my other self became what I suspect . . . I may not have been with you in body, but I promise you, I would always be with you in spirit. I'd find a way to watch over you."

She kissed him, and then she was with him in body for a good long time. Truth be told, she wouldn't want to lose that any more than he would.

Well, she would just have to avoid fluidic space at all costs. It was as simple as that.

14

"The field collapser is ready," Kilana reported to the figure on the viewscreen. "However, the arrival of the emissary from fluidic space has altered the council's plans. They are now assembling a *diplomatic* mission to try to make peace with these so-called Groundskeepers."

Minister Odala frowned. *"Fools. Do they not see that there is no compromise where survival is at stake? The Scourge will not compromise, and neither must we."*

"I agree completely, Minister. The Voth are truly a wise people." Odala smiled beneficently, and Kilana bowed her head—as much to hide her own disgust as to pretend reverence. These Voth considered themselves superior beings, but they were just another breed of lowly solids, untouched by the transforming power of the Founders. Indeed, they were perhaps the most solid of all solids, utterly rigid in their way of thinking and brutal in their enforcement of it. They represented everything the Dominion existed to stamp out.

Kilana quashed the fierce yearning for home that threatened to overwhelm her. She could not lose control now, not when dealing with the prickly Voth elder. "I assure you, I am doing everything in my power to persuade the council to deploy the weapon."

"Persuasion will not be enough. The Coalition council is too much under the influence of these humans. Their duplicity will be the downfall of us all. We must make certain the weapon is deployed. You must obtain it for yourself."

Kilana hesitated. "It would not be easy. The weapon is heavily guarded; I would probably lose several Jem'Hadar."

"*So? Is that not what they are for?*"

Technically, that was correct. But Kilana had to admit that she had grown fond of her little band of Jem'Hadar over their years together in this benighted backwater of the galaxy. True, it had hardly been reciprocal. Jem'Hadar held Vorta in little esteem, obeying them only because they were the voice of the gods. Out here, sixty thousand light-years from the Dominion, Kilana no longer had the direct backing of the Founders, and maintaining her troops' loyalty had been difficult. She had been bred by the gods as a diplomat, a seductress, a gentle persuader who disarmed her opposites with her vulnerable charm and delicate beauty. And such skills had served her well in dealing with races like the Rectilians and Gh'rrrvn. More importantly, they had let her cajole a Haakonian biochemist into devising a means of synthesizing the ketracel-white enzyme that the Jem'Hadar needed to survive. But her control over their white supply earned as much resentment as obedience from the Jem'Hadar, and in order to keep them in line—and to survive against the likes of the Krowtonan Guard and the Vidiians—she had needed to learn how to be tough, cold, and ruthless.

She must have been fairly successful at it, for her Jem'Hadar had not killed her and had kept anyone else from doing so. Still, she felt that inbred timidity and softness every day. She had always thought it just a façade to confound the enemies of the Dominion. But the will of the Founders had shaped her entire being, and they had put it in her heart as well, as her experiences here had forced her to discover. For all her learned toughness, her skill at survival in these wilds, she would give anything to return home to the Founders' embrace.

Sensing her hesitation, Odala leaned forward. "*You need not fear, Kilana. Once you have done this for us, you will know the benevolence of the Voth.*"

"You—you will send me home?" she asked, unable to keep the quaver from her voice.

"Nothing would please me more."

Kilana had no doubt of that; Odala would like nothing more than to rid her backyard of all species who posed any threat to Voth domination, or their pathetic pretense thereof. But that didn't matter. What mattered was their transwarp ships that could return her to the Founders' embrace in mere weeks. At last, to be with her gods again! To know their guidance, feel their divine certainty, and never have to worry about making her own choices, making mistakes!

She didn't know how other species could tolerate it—how they could have faith in their imaginary gods when they never knew them except as an abstract presence. It was all just a matter of guesswork to them; no wonder they were so torn by religious strife and existential turmoil. Kilana had lived that way for only a few years, and she would give anything to end it.

She smiled, able to tolerate politeness toward this bloated wretch because of what was in it for her—and because such pretense was what her gods had made her for. "Thank you, Minister Odala. I will obtain the weapon for you, and then we can all be secure in our homes. And the Dominion will be grateful for your cooperation; I'm certain we will wish to establish diplomatic relations with your people."

"We shall see," Odala said, clearly dismissing the very idea. Kilana didn't push; at this point, all that mattered was getting that ride home.

But what would she find when she got there? Undoubtedly, the Founders would have replaced her with another clone, just as she had replaced the original Kilana upon her death. That Kilana would have all her memories up to her last upload before her abduction, and would have continued in her life, her role in the Dominion. In a sense, Kilana 3 had more of a claim to being the real Kilana than she, Kilana 2, did. Would she find herself in the same spot as the members of the Scourge upon their temporal duplication? Would she be required to fight her counterpart in some way to prove who was worthier? If so, she was certain the hard edge she had gained in the Delta Quadrant would bring her victory. But the Founders would probably not see it that way. It was Kilana 3 who had been serving their will, keeping current with their policies and the politics of the quadrant. The Founders might consider Kilana 2 an obsolete copy, corrupted by her years in the wild. Perhaps they would kill both her and her successor and integrate their memories into Kilana 4. Perhaps they would simply discard her as an aberration.

She would have to prove her worth to them, then. Bringing them Voth transwarp technology would surely earn their favor.

No. Even then, they would show her no gratitude; she had simply been an agent of their will. Either they would find some new role in which she could serve, or they would destroy her. Either way, she would never return to her old life.

But either way, she would be back in the Founders' embrace, serving their holy purpose. She would know again, at long last, what her place in the universe was.

And if she had to destroy another universe to achieve that, what better proof of her devotion?

It was more than a theft; it was a massacre. The Jem'Hadar, using their innate shrouding ability to make themselves invisible, had not only killed the guards outside Kosnelye's military research facility, but had slaughtered the science team working on the field collapser itself, perhaps to reduce the chances of anyone devising a countermeasure in time. Chakotay was stunned when he heard; Rena White, whom he'd served with on *Voyager,* had been one of the casualties. At least she'd made a good showing of herself, using a plasma torch to take out one of the Jem'Hadar before she died. A number of Kes's scientific colleagues had perished in the attack as well.

"This is a disaster," Boothby shouted when Chakotay and Rosh informed him of the news, while Janeway watched from the monitor in Rosh's office. "What kind of circus are you people running here? First you invent a device that could crush my universe like a tin can—and thanks for not telling me about that until now, by the way—and then you don't even bother to put decent defenses around the thing!"

"The facility was shielded," Chakotay told him. "But we've found evidence that Kilana's ship's transporter was using Voth enhancements that can penetrate our best shields. We believe the Voth assisted Kilana in the theft."

"And I assure you," Rosh said, "we had no plans of deploying this weapon while there was any hope of a peaceful resolution. And we have been working nonstop to find a way to make it less destructive, to function as a deterrent only."

"But you went ahead and built it anyway. And then you let it get stolen."

"And the longer we stand here arguing about it," Kathryn pointed out, *"the less chance we have of stopping the Voth and Kilana before they deploy your weapon. As far as we know, Kilana failed to obtain the data on how to create a dimensional rift."* One of Kes's colleagues had given his life to ensure that information was deleted from the research facility's computers. *"She'll need Voth resources to achieve that. We've picked up the ion trail of Kilana's ship, heading toward Voth space, and* Voyager *is preparing to pursue them even now. Meanwhile, I've ordered Commander Kim to work with Doctor Kes and her research teams on devising a countermeasure to the weapon."*

"Somehow, I'm not filled with confidence."

"You can help us too, Boothby," Chakotay said. "Come with me to the Voth city ship. If they see you, talk to you, understand that there are factions in fluidic space trying to make peace, maybe we can persuade them to hold off their attack."

"Do you really think there's a chance of that?"

"Did you think there was any chance of peace with humans before you tried it?"

Boothby glared. "You're as smooth a talker in this timeline as the other one, son." He sighed. "But maybe that's just the kind of blarney we need. Let's go meet your relatives." Chakotay was unsurprised; the Groundskeeper's anger was no doubt rooted in frustration at being unable to take action to protect his home, as his every instinct demanded. At least this way he could feel useful.

"I need not stress the urgency of this to any of you," Rosh told them. "I was elected to protect my nation, but I would fail in that mandate if I allowed it to sacrifice its defining principles by destroying an entire civilization simply to preserve its own existence. Saving fluidic space is as urgent to us as protecting our own Coalition. For in a sense, they are the same thing. Go with the blessing of the Ancestors, all of you—and may They give you all the speed and wisdom you require."

"Politicians," Boothby grumbled as he left the office with Chakotay. "They never shut up, do they?"

Harry Kim had gotten to where he was today by never assuming a goal was unattainable. His optimism had served him well, for when he was given an assignment, he would waste no time lamenting the obstacles in his path but would just hunker down and figure out a way to get it done. True, he hadn't always had similar optimism when it came to women, but seeing the most beautiful woman in the quadrant in his bed every night had cured him of that. And Kathryn had hinted that one of the new long-range explorer ships the Coalition had commissioned using a mix of Starfleet, Carnelian, and other technologies might be his to command within a year. All in all, he had no reason to take a pessimistic view of life.

But it was hard not to believe that his captain and friend had given him an insurmountable goal this time. The Coalition's best

scientists had been working for weeks to devise a way to neutral-
ize the field collapser's effects, with no results. Now most of them
were dead, and Harry's makeshift team was expected to solve the
problem within hours. One didn't have to be a cynic to find that
an improbable goal.

The surprising thing was that even Kes seemed stymied. Harry
was convinced the wise Ocampa had an even deeper insight into
the fundamental workings of reality than she liked to admit.
But she was struggling with this as much as any of them. "The
problem," she'd told Harry, "is that it's so simple. All it takes is
one subspace field of the right kind activated one time, and from
there it's a chain reaction. Just by reducing the strength of the
dark energy in one area, you create an energy flow into it, just as
wind blows into a low-pressure region. And that energy feeds and
sustains the field, causing it to expand. It's based in such fundamental, straightforward physics that it's hard to cancel it without
rewriting the laws of the whole universe."

"Could you do that?" Harry had asked, sincerely curious.

Kes had grinned, blushing. "Not by myself, Harry! But it
doesn't matter—altering something as basic as the way energy
flows would make life impossible there anyway."

They had kept trying to think of some alternative, but Harry
had become increasingly convinced there was something they
were missing. He just couldn't put his finger on it. As brilliant
as Kes had become, Harry missed the good old days on *Voyager,*
when the crew had brainstormed its way through one insurmountable problem after another.

It gave him pause when he remembered a key element in that
brain trust: B'Elanna Torres. Time after time, her intuitive engineering genius and lateral thinking had spawned solutions no one
else could find.

The problem was, she was the last person Harry Kim wanted
to see. But that didn't matter when a universe was at stake. So he
wasted no time in beaming to the prison habitat.

"I never expected to see you again," B'Elanna told him when the guard let him into her cell. "You're looking good. Command agrees with you."

"And prison looks pretty right on you."

She lowered her head. "I won't argue. So did you finally come to gloat?"

"I wouldn't be here unless there were something really important at stake." He explained the situation.

When he was done, she looked at him in astonishment. "And you need my help? Oh, that's rich! With all your great success, all your accolades, the paragons of the Delta Coalition need help from a petty criminal and terrorist. You really must be desperate."

"Dammit, B'Elanna, are you ever going to stop reflexively fighting everything that moves? That's what got you into this in the first place! Why is it so hard for you to learn to accept things as they are and try to make the best of them?

"Look how much progress we've made over the past year and a half—not just the people from *Voyager,* but the whole region. We worked within the system. We found ways to make things better. And we didn't have to kick down the whole structure to make it better. You could've been part of that too, B'Elanna, if only you weren't so confrontational."

"You think I don't know that, Harry? You think I *like* being at war all the time—with the universe, with myself? That I wouldn't change myself if I could? But look around," she said. "It's too late for me. I crossed a line I can't uncross. All I can do now is pay the price for it."

"Fine. But don't let a whole universe pay the price because you're too busy wallowing in self-pity."

"You think you can win me over with guilt? Add it to the pile, I've got plenty already."

"I think that somewhere inside you, there's a decent person still trying to get out from under all that rage. You turned yourself in, remember. I would've thought you'd want to help save people if you could."

She scoffed. "From in here? With no computers, no sensors, no engineering team? You've got the best minds in the Coalition together on this and you can't figure out how to turn your little doomsday weapon off. And don't think I haven't noticed the irony that you built that thing after calling the Casciron terrorists for wanting to keep their stingers."

"Can we debate that later? Look, we've tried everything. Every permutation of subspace field theory known to man, Vostigye, Carnelian, you name it. And we just can't find a way to kill this field once it's formed."

B'Elanna stared. "Then maybe you shouldn't try," she said after a moment.

"What?"

"You said it yourself—don't fight it. Work with it to change it for the better."

Harry began to nod. "Since we can't prevent the field from forming . . . we stop trying and concentrate on changing the effect it has."

"Exactly."

"Change it how?"

B'Elanna was pacing the cell now, eyes darting as the idea came together in her mind. "Instead of changing the cosmological constant of fluidic space . . . we change its permeability. Increase the field density differential between our universe and theirs."

Harry saw what she was going for. "That would make it impossible for anyone to cross between the universes! It would solve everything! No more war, no more temporal duplication to endanger fluidic space."

"Well, they'd still have to deal with the duplicates they have. And any 8472s—sorry, 'Groundskeepers'—still on our side would be stuck here. Other than that, it would work."

"But how do we make it work? I see where you're going, but

how do we build a device that will make the field collapser do that? And from a distance?"

B'Elanna waved her hands in the air, tried to explain, then gave up and sighed. "Have you got five hours for me to explain it to your science team?"

"We may not have that long to build it."

"Then I have to build it myself." She glowered at his skepticism. "Come on, Harry. Turned myself in, remember? You don't think this is a ploy to escape?"

"I don't. The prison officials may not be so sure."

"Well, convince them!"

"I'm not sure they'd believe me, either." He furrowed his brow. "But I may know someone who can convince them."

She frowned at his hesitation. "So what's the problem?"

Harry sighed. "He's someone you almost killed."

15

The news of B'Elanna's plan could not have reached Chakotay at a better time. The Groundskeeper emissary had perhaps gotten into his Boothby character a little too well, and his plain-spoken, irascible manner had been infuriating Minister Odala. Or perhaps it was simply his people's innate pride, a match for the arrogance of the Voth. Although the dinosaurian Ministry of Elders certainly bore their share of the blame; Boothby was at least trying to negotiate in good faith, while they were convinced of their rightness and saw no incentive to back down. Chakotay couldn't really blame Boothby for his frustration.

So it was a relief when Janeway had contacted Chakotay with news of a third option that could break the impasse. He presented B'Elanna's plan to the Elders and Boothby as a solution that could satisfy both sides. "It would create an impassable wall between the universes. Both sides would be safe from any threat posed by the other. And all it would take is a few hours to modify the device you've already obtained," he told Odala. "It would cost you nothing."

"How can we trust in your sincerity, Legislator Chakotay, when you have given us no cause for it before?" Odala challenged.

"Why would the Coalition seek to deceive you in this? Our survival is at stake too. We want to end the threat posed by an invasion from fluidic space. And now we have a way to do that without getting the blood of a whole universe on our hands."

Odala merely stared until Chakotay felt compelled to break the

silence, to do something drastic enough to make a difference before it was too late. "All right. You want me to come clean? I will.
I gave Professor Gegen the data on Earth that has spread throughout your populace. I confess to that, and if you insist, I'll step
down from my post and turn myself over to your justice system.
I'll do whatever it takes if you'll just give this plan a chance." He
took a step closer. "Please, Minister. Whatever I may have done to
offend you, the Delta Coalition is not to blame for it. And neither
are Boothby's people. Give this plan a chance to work. Give the
fragile bonds of trust that your people have built with the Coalition a chance to prove their value. At least long enough to see if
the plan works. If it fails, you still have the device." He threw an
apologetic look to Boothby, who merely glowered.

"But if you did use the device," Chakotay went on, "I think
the Voth would regret it. Because you would have destroyed a
kindred spirit. The Groundskeepers are not so different from
you. They're a people who take great pride in their place in
the cosmos, a place they've held since time immemorial. And
they're willing to do whatever it takes to preserve their ancient
way of life, to defend the identity that defines who and what
they are."

Boothby nodded. "Well put, son. We've earned our place
through strength, discipline, and hard work, and we won't give
that up easily."

"And yet," Chakotay went on, addressing the council, "this being, this man, chose to take a chance. Even though he had every
reason to keep his guard up, to choose the cautious path and destroy any threat, he chose instead to extend a hand and strive for
peace. He dared to stand before his mortal enemies, to risk his
identity and place in his universe, to try to prove to both sides that
they didn't have to be enemies anymore.

"If that courage exists within his species, then I have to believe
it exists in the Voth as well. If the Groundskeepers, the Scourge
of the Delta Quadrant, can find the courage to take a chance on

peace, then surely the Voth, the guardians of the quadrant, can do no less."

He was coming to understand something about the Voth: what they needed above all was to save face. He had defined the situation so that they would look like cowards if they refused to cooperate.

Indeed, after some discussion with the other Elders, Odala spoke. "As the guardians of this quadrant, it is incumbent upon us to extend our benevolence to those who plead for it. We are willing to postpone the destruction of fluidic space and allow other options to be explored." Chakotay and Boothby sighed in relief, but Odala was not finished. *"If,"* she went on, "the fluidic emissary known as Boothby kneels before us and vows his obedience to the Voth Council."

"What?!" Boothby cried. "I'll do nothing of the kind!"

"If you wish to demonstrate your sincere nonhostility toward this quadrant, then you must declare your eternal loyalty to its ancient and rightful guardians. Surely this is no great burden if we are truly alike."

"We're nothing alike, you overstuffed iguana! We Groundskeepers play a vital role in our universe! You just close yourselves up in these city ships and pretend the rest of the universe gives a damn about you."

"Boothby!" Chakotay hissed.

"Stay out of this, son! No Groundskeeper will ever bow down to weaklings like this, I don't care how fancy you dress 'em up."

"If I may have a few moments to confer with my colleague," Chakotay said to the council, hustling Boothby out into the hall. He wasn't as frail as he looked, so it took an effort.

"Are you out of your mind?" he hissed when they were alone. "You know better than anyone what's at stake here. Are you willing to let your universe die just to salve your ego?"

"Just let them try! If your galaxy breeds thugs like that, maybe it's better off destroyed."

"That's not what you were saying before. If you were the sort who swallowed the Groundskeeper party line like that, you never would've come to us seeking peace. What's so horrible about submitting to this? It would just be a symbolic gesture. I think that's all it takes to get through to the Voth. They're willing to bend, so long as you allow them to make it *look* like they're firmly in control." He realized, in retrospect, that maybe things would have gone more smoothly with the Voth the last time if he hadn't been so stubborn. The penalty they had imposed for his recalcitrance was purely a token gesture to let them save face while still bending to the new reality. Perhaps if he'd played along with their need for ego-stroking then, they would have been more open to negotiation in return.

"You don't understand," Boothby said. "I can't submit to them . . . even symbolically. It would be like confessing . . ."

Chakotay frowned. "Confessing what?"

Boothby sagged, looking even more tired and elderly than before. "You're wrong about me, son. I'm not here because I'm some brave, heroic peacemaker. I'm here because . . . well, because there's nowhere else for me to be."

Realization came to Chakotay. "You're one of the temporal duplicates."

"That's right. I came marching home from the war one day, full of rip-snorting tales of how my squadron blew up a Borg cube . . . only to find another me already back home, regaling the folks at the corner bar about how he'd blown up a whole Borg armada. From then on, there was no place for me back home—not unless I proved myself the stronger. I went on that spy mission, changed myself into this skinny scarecrow, to prove my worth . . . but they assigned me to the mission in the first place so they could get me out of the way. I think they were hoping I'd get myself killed. When I got back, though, there were more of me to compete with. I'm not exactly the kind to fight it out with myself to the death, but there was no place for all of us in the order of things. And after spending months as a human and coming back talking about peace, I fit in even worse than I did before. So when your Doctor showed up, I came back with him as much to get out of the way as to try to patch things up with your universe."

"I'm sorry," Chakotay said after a moment. "I didn't realize. I can't imagine what it must have been like for you." He clasped Boothby's shoulder. "But I'm even more impressed with you than I was before. With so much stacked against you, it's remarkable that you were able to persuade them to consider peace talks at all. That accomplishment proves your strength more than any victory in battle. Surely you're strong enough to do this one thing too."

"You still don't get it! If I go in there and kowtow before those fossils, if I even pretend to lower myself before weaklings like that . . . I'd be humiliating myself in a way my people would never forgive. It wouldn't matter if I saved my universe by doing it; that's just my job. And there are more copies of me to take over that job, ones who wouldn't have that taint on them for the rest of their lives.

"If I do this, Chakotay . . . I'll be throwing away my last hope of getting my life back. I'll be an outcast forever."

Chakotay studied him for a time. "I do understand, Boothby. I know how it feels to be an outcast. As an Indian, as a contrary among my own people, as a Maquis rebel, as a refugee in the Delta Quadrant. All my life, I've been an outsider one way or another. But that hasn't made me weak. It's just meant I've had to find my strength within—and find others who could benefit from that strength and give me theirs in return.

"And I've found that here, first on *Voyager,* then in the Coalition. We've taken in countless other exiles, helped them find a new identity, a new sense of purpose. We can do the same for you. Being an outcast doesn't have to be a permanent condition."

"The Voth were exiles once," Boothby replied. "But they've

completely forgotten what they once were. Lost touch with their whole history."

"Only because they saw being an outsider as a source of shame. I've always found it to be a source of strength—a unique perspective that I can offer, a heritage I can take pride in even when I've become part of a new community. Yes, a home is a thing worth fighting for, striving for—but you can lose your home without losing who you are."

Boothby fell into quiet introspection for a time. "I guess if I don't do this, I won't be the only one losing my home. If giving those gnat-eating blobs of fat a cheap thrill at my expense is what it takes to preserve my universe . . . then at least I'll still be doing my job as a Groundskeeper."

Chakotay smiled. "You're the finest Groundskeeper I know, Boothby. No matter which Boothby you are."

The Groundskeeper sighed. "Well, let's get back in there so I can humiliate myself. You should've brought your holo-imager so you could get pictures."

"No! Not when we're so close!" Kilana cried. Everything had been falling into place. The Voth ship had rendezvoused with her vessel as planned, and the rift into fluidic space had been opened almost effortlessly with their technology. *Voyager* had arrived and attempted to block their entry into the rift, but it was no more than a token gesture against a Voth battleship. It had wielded every defense the Coalition had devised, barely managing to shake off the Voth's displacement waves and power dampers, but it was taking a heavy pounding from more conventional weapons and would no doubt be crippled or destroyed before long. It was inconceivable that anything could stop them now.

"The orders come directly from the Ministry of Elders," Sanctioner Haluk told her. "We are to stand down until further notice."

"But why?"

Haluk stared as though she were an idiot. "Because the Ministry has ordered it."

Kilana stared back, recognizing that this rigid, cold-blooded fool would be immune to any charm and reason she could bring to bear. "First," she told her lead Jem'Hadar. "Now."

It was over quickly. The Voth had formidable technology and inbuilt paralyzing stingers, but they were slow-moving herbivores, no match for any Jem'Hadar they had allowed to get close. On her orders, the Jem'Hadar restrained themselves from killing the Voth, merely incapacitating them. This ship had transwarp drive, but it was designed for swift response against threats or defiance within Voth territory, and thus was capable only of quick jumps over limited distances. Its drive would burn out before she could get a fifth of the way home. Even having taken their ship, she was still dependent on their indulgence if she wished to see the Dominion again. And so it was necessary to leave the Voth crew alive lest she alienate them irreversibly.

"Thank you," Kilana told her First once the Voth were all confined. "Now take us into the rift. Go through *Voyager* if you have to." She wished it weren't necessary. If the Voth had sent this ship on her mission in the first place, she would have already completed it. With their typical egocentrism, though, they had insisted that she come to them, considering it demeaning to come out to meet her. *Hidebound idiots!*

Yet she was so close to fulfilling the bargain now. Home was just around the corner. All she had to do was this one simple thing, and she would know the will of the Founders again.

But the Voth have changed their minds. Will they reward me for this now?

She shook off her doubts. The deal was clear: an escort home in exchange for destroying fluidic space. Whatever their reasons for hesitation, she was sure they would be grateful when she presented them with a fait accompli. And if she didn't do this, what reason would they have to take her back to the Dominion? Kilana simply did not see anything else she could do at this point. This was her only way home.

Neelix watched *Moskelarnan*'s viewscreen in alarm as the Voth battleship muscled *Voyager* aside and pushed its way through the rift. "What happened? Didn't they get the recall order?" Chakotay had just contacted them to confirm that the council had sent the message.

Kes gently touched his arm to calm him. "Kes to *Voyager*. Are you in need of assistance?"

"Janeway here. We're intact enough to follow them in, but we need that counterweapon."

Neelix followed Kes's gaze over to the engineering station, where B'Elanna was carrying on a running dialogue with Harry Kim's team over on *Voyager,* instructing them step-by-step on the construction of the device that would generate a counterfield to modify the field collapser's effects. The ex-engineer looked up and reported, "It'll take another twenty minutes at least if I have to do it over the comm. But if you beam me over once we're in range—"

"We can't wait that long. I'm taking Voyager *into fluidic space. We'll try to delay them as long as possible. You'll have to follow us in."*

"Acknowledged," Kes said. "We'll see you soon."

"Oh, and B'Elanna—good to hear your voice."

Torres blinked. "Thank you, Captain. Same here."

Neelix looked at Kes in alarm. "Follow them—into fluidic space? Kes, you can't! You know what happened to you in the other timeline when you went there!"

"Neelix, there's no time."

"You're right, we can't sit around here arguing. We have to get you to a shuttle or a—an escape pod. You don't have to go in there. The crew can handle it."

"They're my crew," she said sharply, chastening Neelix. He reminded himself that she was no fragile child anymore, if she had ever been. But then she softened her tone. "My place is with them. Besides, I may be needed to communicate with the Groundskeepers, tell them what we're doing."

Her bravery filled him equally with admiration and dread. "But . . . I don't want to lose you again. I—I've already got names picked out for the babies. And—and . . ."

She stroked his cheek. "You know what's at stake, my love. You know I have to do this."

Neelix struggled to be brave, as brave as she was. He couldn't dishonor this selfless, loving act of hers. "You're right," he said. "You have to do what you have to do. But I'll be with you every step of the way. A-as long as I can."

"I know you will," she said, clasping his hand.

But then she had to focus on the business of generating a new singularity so they could follow *Voyager* through. Neelix gave her room to do that, and found himself wandering close to the engineering station.

"I wanted to thank you," B'Elanna said, breaking the silence she'd maintained since *Voyager* had entered the rift, cutting off communication. "For vouching for me with the prison."

He cleared his throat. "I didn't do it for you. A lot of lives are at stake. You can help them. And I'm only here to make sure you get back to prison where you belong once you're done."

"I understand. I just wanted you to know . . . I appreciate the second chance. And . . . I'm sorry for what I almost did to you."

"There's no 'almost' about it. You killed me. Kes brought me back." B'Elanna lowered her head in shame, and Neelix couldn't help softening a bit. "But . . . Kes has forgiven you, so I should be willing to try to do the same. Just don't expect us to become friends again any time soon."

She gave him an odd look. "Were we ever friends?"

"I thought so," he said in surprise, making her abashed again. "At least, I wanted us to be. You never made it easy, though."

"No," she admitted. "I never did."

★ ★ ★

"The *Moskelarnan* has just entered fluidic space," Surt reported. Janeway nodded, acknowledging the report, but she had other matters occupying her. "Kilana," she called over the open comm channel, "please listen to me. You don't have to use the weapon. We can modify the device to close the border between the universes. It will end the war."

The Vorta appeared on the screen. *"Why should I listen to your Federation lies?"*

"I'm not speaking for the Federation, Kilana. I'm speaking for the Coalition that you and I are both a part of."

"I am a loyal servant of the Dominion! Everything else is just a means toward my return. You promised me the Coalition was researching ways to do that, but you've given me nothing! Just empty promises. This will finally give me a way home."

A way home. The yearning echoed in Janeway's mind. But her yearning had been tempered by loss and experience. "What makes you think the Voth will give you anything? They've just been using you to serve their ends. And you aren't even doing that anymore. What can you possibly gain by this?"

"What do I have to lose? You can't understand what it's been like for me. All these years away from my gods, with no place in the cosmos. I have nothing here!"

"You have the Coalition, Kilana. We can give you a new home."

The Vorta shook her head. *"You are gracious, Captain. But there is only one home for me. And this is the only path I can see that brings me closer to it. And I cannot let you stand in my way."*

The screen went dark, and *Voyager* trembled. "They're firing, Captain!" Surt reported. "On us and *Moskelarnan!*"

"Jenkins, evasive!" The pilot dodged the Voth ship's weapons as well as she could, but the ship was sluggish in fluidic space, and the fluid transmitted the shock of even near misses. Conversely, the fluid itself attenuated some of the weapons' force. Ayala used it deftly, firing phasers to heat pockets of the fluid and refract the oncoming beams. "Very good, Lieutenant," Janeway told him. But she realized it wasn't enough. Nothing Ayala fired at the Voth ship could penetrate its hide, and there was nothing to stop Kilana from activating the field collapser. "Bridge to Kim. Harry, we need that counterweapon now!"

"We can't build it fast enough, Captain. The only way to speed it up is if B'Elanna beams here to do it herself."

The ship shuddered again, hard this time, and Jenkins threw her captain a look of apology for letting that one get through. "Not an option, Harry. We need our shields."

"Doctor to bridge. I believe I—or rather, we—can help with that."

B'Elanna looked uneasily at the device that *Moskelarnan*'s copy of the Doctor was proposing to attach to her head. "What does this thing do, exactly?"

"It will allow you tap into the data channels I use to communicate with my other selves. Specifically, my counterpart on *Voyager.*"

"And have him relay instructions? Doctor, that'll slow things down even more!"

The Doctor sighed. This incarnation of him looked like a Vostigye but still acted like the Doctor she remembered. "Since time is of the essence, let me just show you." Still wary, she nodded and let him proceed. *What have I got to lose?* she thought as the vessel shook under a weapon impact.

After a moment of disorientation, she opened her eyes to find herself in a place she'd never expected to set foot in again: *Voyager*'s engine room. It had been heavily rebuilt with Vostigye and other technology, and the warp core was a different design. But its basic structure was instantly familiar, as was the sight of Harry Kim standing next to her, steadying her with a hand on her arm. Most of the other people here were unfamiliar, though.

And so was she, for that matter. She felt very strange. She

looked down at herself, seeing her own hands and body—but in a Starfleet uniform. "How did I get here?"

"You didn't," Harry said. "Look on your sleeve." She looked down to see the Doctor's mobile emitter there.

"I'm a hologram?" she asked, realizing that Harry hadn't been steadying her, but holding the emitter in place as she—or this holographic body—materialized. That explained the uniform—the hologram must be based on old image files in *Voyager*'s computer.

But then an explosion rocked the ship, and B'Elanna shook off her disorientation. "Okay, I'm a hologram. Let's get to work."

The interface was remarkable. She knew she was really back on *Moskelarnan,* and was even aware of her body there when she concentrated on it. But at the same time, she had a second body that she occupied as fully as the first, and she could localize her consciousness in either one. *Is this what it's like for the Doctor?* she wondered.

Minus several thousand, yes, said his voice in her head, startling her. *Don't be so surprised, Ms. Torres. This is my neural network you're piggybacking on, after all. I always wanted to give you a piece of my mind.*

So how do I shut you up? she fired back. *I've got work to do.*

The Doctor left her to it, and she and Harry got to work along with the rest of the team. All the frustration she'd felt trying to give instructions over the comm fell away when she was able to do the work with her own hands, or a reasonable facsimile thereof. Now the work went swiftly and smoothly, the pieces falling naturally into the places where they belonged. But she soon realized there was more to it than that. It felt right to be back here, in the engine room, solving a problem alongside Harry Kim and a crack team of engineers. This was the place where she belonged.

But this is the last time I'll ever be here. And I'm not even really here.

She shook it off. She'd made her bed. And she had a job to do.

★ ★ ★

"Oh, no," Kes gasped.

Neelix turned to her. "What's wrong now?"

"Kes to Janeway. She's activating the weapon!" Even as she spoke, she saw *Moskelarnan*'s sensor officer turning to report, sensed the information in his mind. But she had felt the change in the texture of local spacetime the moment it had begun. She was perceiving things with a clarity she'd never known. She was able to sense every particle that made up the fluid around her, fluid whose psionic energy was pouring into her, supercharging her mind. She could even sense the underlying strings themselves and the harmony they created. She could feel her own strings playing an ever livelier symphony, building up toward a crescendo. She could feel her body straining against the limits of its physical form, starting to let go of a molecular cohesion it no longer felt the need for. But she held herself together, focusing on her responsibilities.

"It's too soon," Janeway said, first in her mind, then over the comm at far slower speed. *"The counterweapon isn't ready."*

Kes felt Kathryn's despair, the fear that she would fail in her mission to protect the people of this universe. It was that compassion that had saved Kes so many times in the past, that had saved the Ocampa people and set *Voyager*'s crew on the path to where they were today. She would not let it fail this time, not if she could help it.

And right now, Kes was able to help far more than she ever could before.

Opening herself, she let the energy of this space fill her. She clasped it to herself, focused it, sent it back to act upon the space that generated it. In that space was a blemish, a growing tumor of negative energy that would engulf this entire universe if allowed to expand. Reaching out, Kes's mind encompassed that zone of corruption and shored up the surrounding space against it, resisting its expansion. It fought back, not out of conscious will but out of inevitable simplicity; holding back the influx of energy was like holding back an ocean from draining into a sinkhole. She had to spread her consciousness around the entire subspace field and hold back the energy in every direction at once, a whole universe's worth of energy crushing down on her. The effort drained her, but she opened herself, let more psionic power pour into her. And not merely from the fluid—she sensed the minds of its inhabitants reaching to her as well, sensing her need and her intent and giving her their support.

Through it all, she heard Neelix calling to her. "Kes . . . I think it's starting!" She saw herself through his eyes, starting to shimmer, her body threatening to dissipate like a cloud of smoke. She struggled to hold it together. This brain and body were the focal point for her efforts; if she transformed now, she would lose that focus and this universe would die.

She reached out and took Neelix's hand, though she hardly had enough cohesion to hold on to it. *I love you, Neelix,* she sent to him. *You're my anchor.*

Hold on, Kes. Hold on.

"Harry," Janeway called. "Whatever Kes is doing to hold back the field, it seems to be weakening. We're reading expansion again."

"Almost there, Captain! Just another minute."

Another burst of Voth weapons fire struck the ship, making sparks fly and lights flicker. "Warp engines are down!" Surt cried. Janeway caught herself looking up warily at the ceiling beam above her. *I won't let this happen. I won't lose more of my crew!*

"Kilana!" she called. "You've done what you came to do, now stand down! Return to normal space! Let us study the drive on that ship. We can figure out how to build a bigger one, one that will get you all the way home!"

There was no reply. "Please, Kilana, listen to me. I know what you're going through. I know how it feels to believe that getting home is worth any price. But if you let yourself become obsessed with that goal, you can miss the fact that the path you're taking is the wrong one. You can lose yourself in a way far worse than just being far from home.

"Kilana . . . there are more important things than going back to where you've been."

The only answer was another explosion, knocking Janeway to the deck. "Shields down to fifteen percent," Ayala said.

"Captain, we've got it!" Harry called.

"Activate now!" She gave the command without hesitation, but with sincere regret. When she looked at Kilana, she saw herself—the Janeway she had been two years ago, the Janeway she still was in another reality, still so fixated on getting back to a place that she'd lost all other purpose. *There but for the grace of time go I.*

Engineering reported the activation of the counterfield, which expanded through fluidic space to interact with the collapser field, the two field frequencies interacting and altering each other like two colors of light blending into a third. Except that this should be a permanent change, self-sustaining like the collapser effect itself would have been. *"The cosmological constant is returning to normal!"* Moskelarnan's first officer reported. *"And the quantum field density is increasing."* There was a pause. *"Captain, Kes has . . . She's no longer . . . The field is expanding again. We have to stay ahead of it or we'll never get home."*

Is Kes all right? Is she still even there? Janeway wanted to ask. But there was no time. "Our engines are down! You'll have to tow us."

A pause. *"Our tractors are destroyed."*

That simple phrase damned them. With no warp drive, they could never outrun the field fast enough, and it would take too long to create a rift. And *Moskelarnan* was too small to beam *Voyager*'s entire crew aboard. They would be trapped in this universe forever when it overtook them. It was a choice Janeway had made before, stranding her crew for the survival of another species. But this stranding would be irreversible, perhaps not even survivable.

"Go on without us," she told *Moskelarnan,* her voice heavy. There was no sense in them all being stranded here.

But then Surt called, "Incoming hail! It's *Ryemaren!* They must have opened a new rift!"

A russet-furred Vostigye face appeared on the viewer. *"Mister Kim,"* said Morikei Voenis. *"See where your ambition has gotten you?"*

"Good to see you too, Captain," Harry replied. "We could use a tow, if you don't mind."

She sighed. *"You refugees. Always asking for handouts."* She smiled. *"But this time, I'd say you've earned it. Thank you—all of you. Now let's go home."*

"Follow them!" Kilana cried as *Voyager* and the Vostigye ships retreated into warp to escape the expanding field. "We must capture that device so we can undo what they did!"

But the Jem'Hadar pilot looked futilely to his First. "I cannot engage warp. The local subspace field is in too much flux."

"Is there any way to use the collapser to reverse the effect?"

"As far as I can tell," the Second said, "it is *creating* the effect. Something has . . . changed."

"Well, shut it down! *Now!*" Unsure how to deactivate the device, and under orders to act with haste, the Second fired his weapon and destroyed the field collapser.

"No effect," the Third reported. "The field continues to expand."

Kilana quashed her panic, knowing what would happen if she appeared weak to the Jem'Hadar. "Open a rift. Take us back to normal space." Maybe there was a way to increase the range of this ship and get back to the Dominion on her own.

But the Jem'Hadar's efforts proved futile. "The rift . . . it will not form! The singularity is being created," the Second said, "but it is closed. There is no passage."

"Well, *fix it!*"

They jumped to comply. But they were fighters, not scientists. Nothing they did could make a difference. And the field was expanding too fast for them to escape at impulse.

Kilana was trapped. Not just in a different quadrant from her gods . . . but in a different universe. She was more alone than she had ever been.

Then a proximity alert sounded. "We are not alone," the pilot reported.

Kilana looked at the viewscreen and whimpered as the bioships closed in.

16

Chakotay watched from the city ship's pilot house as a singularity opened and *Moskelarnan, Ryemaren,* and finally *Voyager* came through. "It's good to see you back," he told Janeway once she checked in. "But what about Kes?" he added, since the science ship's first officer had been the one to speak. "Did she . . . change?"

"Well . . . yes and no. I'll explain later. Right now, I need to speak to Boothby."

"I'm here, Captain," the Groundskeeper said. "And itching to know what state you left my universe in."

"Intact, but changing. Our plan worked—the subspace field is expanding, but it will only block passage between our universes. Your people should be in no further danger."

Boothby let out a heavy breath and blinked several times. "I don't know how to thank you," he said. "Spoken language has its charms, but it can be pretty limited."

"It was our pleasure. I'm just sorry we couldn't reach a real peace—or help your people with their other problems."

"I understand." He cleared his throat and turned to Chakotay. "Listen, son. I appreciate all you said about making a place for me in the Coalition. But I'm still a Groundskeeper. And outcast or no, my place is on the other side of that hole in space out there. Nothing personal, but there are a lot of other Groundskeepers over there in the same fix as me. Maybe I can . . . bring back some of the lessons I learned here, help them figure out a new role they can play in the order of things. A lot of people have been lost in the war, after all; maybe we can adapt to their roles, maybe even create some new ones. Find new homes, like you all have done. Though it won't be easy to get them to listen to me."

Chakotay smiled. "I believe you can do it. You haven't let your universe down yet."

Boothby looked back at the viewscreen. "Umm, Captain, any chance I could take your field-fiddling contraption back with me? Seems to me I can use it as a bargaining chip. Maybe they won't kill me or ignore me if I can offer them control of their own borders."

"Sounds like an excellent idea," Janeway replied. *"With the . . . the Torres Generator,"* she said with a smile, *"you should be able to adjust the boundary conditions of fluidic space however you like. Maybe you won't have to stay cut off from us forever. But you'll have control of whether and how you interact with us. No more fear of invasion or temporal doubling."*

"Good fences make good neighbors," Boothby acknowledged— but then he gave an impish smirk. "As long as they have gates in them."

Chakotay shook his hand. "I'm glad that other Chakotay wasn't the only one who got to know you. I think the real Boothby would be proud to have you as his double."

"Well, that may be—but I can't wait to get out of this skinny body and put on my swim fins again. This walking business is hard on the knees."

Janeway looked around *Voyager*'s sickbay, amazed at the faces who looked back at her. Chakotay, Harry, Annika, the Doctor, B'Elanna, Neelix, and Kes, all together with her once again. She'd never expected it to happen again. Indeed, she was still rather surprised that Kes was there at all. "So you're not going to turn into a ball of light any time soon?" Harry was asking the Ocampa.

Kes smiled, and that alone brought more light to the room. She did seem bigger somehow, more luminous, though physically she was the same as ever. "I think I could if I wanted to," she said. "But I'm not ready to try that just yet."

"So what was different here than in the other timeline?" Janeway asked.

"Time, basically," the Doctor said. "Our Kes has had over a year and a half to adjust to her first dose of power enhancement before getting her second, whereas the other got the full dose all at once and was apparently overwhelmed by it. It's analogous to the way a muscle that's been exercised and conditioned can more easily lift a weight that would cause a less conditioned muscle to give way from fatigue."

"So you have as much power as that other you," Annika said, "but more control over it?" She looked envious and curious, as if hoping that Kes could help her gain more control over the Borg presence that still haunted her.

Kes tilted her golden-tressed head. "Not more control, so much as different," she said, and to Janeway it seemed she was speaking from certainty, as though she were in communication with her other self. "I came at it by a different route. I could leave this body if I wanted, but only when I wanted—and I'm confident I could re-create it again."

"If you can re-create it," Neelix asked, his voice hushed, "does that mean you could also . . ."

"Halt its aging? Or reverse it?" She beamed, and for a moment she was a younger Kes again, a slender waif with close-shorn hair baring her elegantly scalloped ears. Then she changed back to her familiar tumble of curls and the subtly more rounded face and fig-ure of the woman she was today. "Don't worry, Neelix. I won't ever leave you again. Not permanently, anyway." She grinned. "There's so much more I can explore now than I ever could before. I only wish I knew how to communicate most of it to you all."

"Just don't let it go to your head," B'Elanna said. "Power has a way of corrupting, you know."

Neelix glared at her. "I don't think you remember who you're talking about."

"No, Neelix, she has a point. It's easy to lose your way with power like this. That's why I'm so glad I'm still with you—all of you," Kes said, taking in B'Elanna. "You're my family. You remind me of who I am."

Janeway took her hand, as proud of Kes as she would be of a daughter. "I think if anyone can be trusted with this kind of power, it's you, Kes."

The Ocampa—if that was still what she was—studied Janeway. "I could probably find a way to take you all back to the Alpha Quadrant, if you'd like. Not right away, but I'm sure I could figure something out. After all, the Coalition is safe now."

Janeway looked around at her current and former crew, and saw a similar sentiment in all their eyes. "I still miss my family back on Earth," she said. "I miss the old familiar Starfleet, the old familiar stars. I wouldn't mind seeing them again someday. But if I did . . . it would only be for a visit.

"I thought I'd lost something I'd never have again—all of you, working together as a team, as a family. But it was all of us, playing our own separate roles in pursuit of a common goal, who made this victory possible. We didn't lose our family—it just evolved.

"And now that I see that . . . I'm finally able to admit something I never could before.

"That what we've built here in the Delta Quadrant is too precious to abandon. That we've all come farther by staying in one place than we could have by chasing a distant star. That where we are now—and who we're with—matters more than where we came from."

She took Chakotay's hand in one of hers, Kes's in the other, and took in the rest with her gaze. "That I *am* home."

Epilogue

February 2376

Starfleet Headquarters, San Francisco

Earth

"Admiral Paris." Janeway beamed as she shook her old mentor's hand. "It's a privilege to be here."

Owen Paris returned the handshake and the smile, though the latter was subdued. He'd had a few months to adjust to the news of his son's death, sad news that Kes had brought on her first journey to the Federation along with the happy news of *Voyager*'s survival and its crew's accomplishments and discoveries. But the loss had still diminished him, as it had Tuvok's family, Carey's wife and son, and all the others who had had to face the loss of their loved ones a second time. Janeway hoped they could take comfort in the knowledge that those loved ones still lived and thrived in other realities—or at least had done so as of the last contact with the Groundskeepers. There had been no word from them since Boothby's return to fluidic space. Apparently they were still busy cleaning up their affairs, and might be for a long time to come.

"It's a privilege to greet you," Paris told her. "Except, of course, that you're not really here."

"Transgalactic holoconferencing," Janeway replied. "The next best thing to being there." Recently, *Voyager* had succeeded in tracking down a relay station in the galaxy-spanning communications network that the Hirogen used to stay in contact with one another. Mister Malken had managed to persuade his fellow Hirogen to permit the use of their network, and from there it was simply a matter of adapting the holographic telepresence system the Doctor had rigged for B'Elanna. Now, it was possible to travel any place that was in range of the network and that had holotechnology available, all without leaving the Coalition. And now that Starfleet had built a relay station to bridge the Hirogen network and the UFP communications grid, it meant the entire Federation was just a holosuite away.

Which was good, because Janeway wasn't in any condition for a long journey right now—at least, not until five months from now, when her and Chakotay's daughter would be born. She looked down at the holographic representation of her swelling abdomen, looking forward to the moment when the diplomatic obligations were over and her mother and sister could come in to meet her, and to feel the kicking—by proxy—of the newest member of their family (and hopefully the first of many to be born in the Delta Quadrant), little Shannon Sekaya Janeway.

She looked forward to introducing them to the baby's father as well, but Chakotay was busy with affairs of state. The Voth had been satisfied with a formal statement of apology for his act of dissidence rather than a resignation, perhaps because knowledge of the Voth's origins on Earth had spread too widely through their populace for the regime to keep denying the reality. Especially since it would now be easy for any Voth scholar or student to pay holographic visits to the old neighborhood.

The admiral followed her gaze and smiled. "You've achieved some remarkable things on your end of the galaxy. On both the personal and the interstellar scale. I only wish the news we had for you was happier."

It had been a shock to learn, upon Kes's return, that the Federation had been immersed in a years-long war with the Dominion. "The important thing is that you won the war," she said. "My only regret about being where I am now, though, is that we couldn't be there to help."

"Your friend Kes helped us a great deal," Paris reminded her.

"Who knows how much damage the Breen would have done if she hadn't been here to repel their attack? And who knows how the war might have gone if her display of power hadn't scared the Breen into abandoning their alliance?"

After saving San Francisco, Kes had been tempted to intervene further, but she was still feeling out the extent of her powers and hadn't wanted to risk draining herself and becoming stranded, leaving little Thomas, Tuvok, and Alixia without their mother. At four months old, the half-Ocampa, half-Talaxian triplets were nearly half-grown, but still not ready to function without her guidance, especially as their telepathic powers began to manifest. Kes had also made the painful choice to apply her own Prime Directive to the situation, recognizing that she did not have the right to make the Federation's and the Dominion's decisions for them. Though Janeway keenly felt her sense of guilt, she now had more faith than ever that Kes could be trusted with the remarkable powers she had gained.

Still, Kes had made a difference. The Breen's withdrawal had deprived the Dominion of a powerful ally and embarrassed them before their Cardassian subjects, giving a much-needed boost to a fledgling rebellion within Cardassia. The Dominion had been forced to retreat and retrench in the face of a combined assault from the Federation, Klingons, and Romulans—an alliance that astonished Janeway, who'd thought it had been difficult enough to get Vostigye, Nyrians, and Tarkan working together. A Starfleet doctor had soon discovered that the Founders of the Dominion were suffering from a deadly disease, no doubt a factor in their desperation to win the war at any cost. The Federation, negotiating from a position of strength, had offered them a cure in exchange for their retreat from the Alpha Quadrant. And so the war had ended, probably sooner and less bloodily than it would have if Kes had not acted when she had. Though of course every war had its aftermath: Cardassia was now in the throes of civil war, while Klingon chancellor Gowron's absorption with the military occupation of Cardassia had left him vulnerable to a coup by a rebel named Morjod, leaving the Klingon Empire in similar chaos. And there was no guarantee the Dominion would stay on their side of the wormhole; indeed, many in Starfleet feared their resentment at being indebted to "solids" for their survival (and their suspicions, no doubt unfounded, that the Federation had infected them in the first place) might compel them to attempt a later conquest in order to save face. Janeway hoped the Coalition's experience in negotiating with the Voth could help avert a second Dominion War.

"And the rest of you made a big difference yourselves," Paris went on. "If your Groundskeepers had invaded us, there's no way we could've survived a war on two fronts. The whole galaxy owes you a debt.

"And more importantly," he went on, "you supported and advanced the Federation's ideals at a time when we in the Alpha Quadrant had to concentrate on survival alone. In so doing, you've built something very special and given us all renewed hope for the future of the Federation."

"Well, I think that's my cue," Neelix (or his hologram) said, stepping forward. Next to Paris, the Federation's ambassador stepped forward as well, ready to accept transmission of the document his counterpart held. Ambassador Neelix cleared his throat and began to speak.

"On behalf of the member worlds and habitats of the Delta Coalition, and in the spirit of galaxywide cooperation and friendship . . . I hereby present our petition for membership in the United Federation of Planets."

Blinking away tears at his words, Janeway looked down and laid a hand on her belly. *Welcome home,* she told her daughter. *Welcome home.*

Seeds of Dissent

James Swallow

For Pete and Nicola, who both understand that the best reality is the one you make for yourself.

1

Defiance moved through the darkness, a predator on the hunt, visible light bending and reshaping around her hull. The ship was a wraith, a ghostly knife slipping unseen toward its target, ready for the kill.

The command deck was running with battle lighting, a deep red that gave every console a patina of crimson, like spilled blood. From his control bench on the command dais, the warship's captain glanced down at his tanned, strong hands and studied them. *Clean,* he mused, *hard-worked and resilient, but clean.* There was no trace of the blood he had shed with those hands, no scarring, no disfigurement; but then, it was the nature of his kind. He, and all his kindred, were embodiments of the quest to become perfect. Flaws, even of the smallest sort, were things to be overcome, not to be dwelt upon.

He looked away, peering briefly into a viewing pod on an armature. The display showed a map of the Bajor Sector, the lines of demarcation and jurisdiction for the territories of each of the local commanders, and the minefields that ringed the Cardassian Control Zone. A glowing glyph signifying *Defiance*'s position placed them at the umbra of the Ajir system. The device sensed his scrutiny, and without waiting for his orders, it presented him with a data-digest on Ajir; it was an unremarkable, uninhabited collection of rocks around a nondescript sun. At first glance, there seemed to be little of interest there to a ship of the line.

The rest of the tactical map remained static. Their target did not present itself, even though he knew for certain that it was out there. He threw a look across the chamber. "We will not return to home base without a victory," he said, addressing his crew. The commander's words were level and they were not spoken in censure; but anyone who had served aboard the *Defiance* for more than a few weeks knew that he seldom raised his voice, seldom railed at his crew or denigrated their rare failures. He had no need to. His cool disappointment, and the inevitable punishment details that would follow, were enough to keep them focused on their duties. "If that means we stay out here until we are on quarter-rations, then so be it," he went on. "We will not give them up."

In the red shadows, a woman cleared her throat with studied care. "Princeps, if I may have permission to speak?" He gave her a curt nod and she continued, absently tracing the line of a copper torc around her throat. She was shorter than the rest of the command crew, but her height was not all that differentiated the woman from them; whereas the others wore uniforms of ornate cut, her clothing was simplistic, just an oversuit with a nondescript tunic. She seemed awkward and out of place. "The datasets we received before we set sail were several days old. It is quite possible that the rebels have already left this region, or perhaps gone to ground. I would respectfully suggest that—"

The tactical officer, a stocky man with a severe military haircut, turned in his chair to glare at her. "What gives you the right to question my work?" he demanded. "You should remember your place!" The officer looked up at his commander. "Lord, with all due respect, perhaps you might keep your helot silent unless she has something of use to add to the day."

"Optio," said the commander, putting a hard emphasis on the other man's rank, "she is here because she has a duty to perform, just like you. Do not sully yourself by turning your anger on her. Just find me my target." When the tactician didn't reply straightaway, the commander's lips thinned and he leaned forward. "Optio!"

The officer held up a hand. "A moment, sir." Something shimmered on the officer's console and he turned his head, the flicker of a cold smile there and then gone on the other man's lips. "My apologies. It looks like we have no issue after all, Princeps." He tapped a key and the command deck's primary screen altered to show a three-dimensional strategic plot. "We have them."

There, visible through a slight haze of stretched starlight, was a spindly ship with downswept wings, resembling a bird as it took to the air. It moved cautiously at a low warp velocity, clearly attempting to avoid detection.

The commander saw the woman shrink a little, chagrined. He ignored her reaction and brought his palms together beneath his chin. "Good. We will close to engagement range. What is the status of our cloak?"

At the console to his right, the commander's adjutant broke his silence. "Unchanged, Princeps," said the ebon-skinned youth. "The rebels have no idea we are here."

"We are certain it is them?" murmured the woman, but no one answered her.

"Tactician," the commander said, drawing himself up. "Bring the nadion pulse antenna to bear on their drive chamber. I want them disabled on the first pass."

"At your command, aye."

He gestured with a wave of his hand. "Commit."

The blast seemed to come from nowhere. There was barely a motion of perturbed radiation from the concealing sphere generated by the *Defiance*'s cloaking device before an emerald rod of light connected the unseen warship with the rebel transport. The nadion pulse, tuned to filter through conventional deflector shields, bathed the other vessel's aft quarter in a wash of hard energy.

Organic forms inside the strike zone perished instantly, bodies overloaded in a concentrated blast that destroyed neurons and electrochemical impulses. The same field effect blew out dozens of duotronic conduits and smothered the churning matter/anti-matter reaction in the ship's warp core like a hand snuffing out a candle.

Automatic safety protocols snapped into place, and with a sudden, punishing deceleration, the rebel vessel crashed out of warp and into the unforgiving reality of normal space. Listing, spilling streams of crystallized breathing gas from vents in the hull, the smaller ship was immediately caught by Ajir's gravity and began a slow drift into the system.

Defiance, her first strike a complete success, followed suit and dropped below lightspeed. The cloak disengaged, allowing the lethal shape of the warship to be revealed. She came in on a fast, showy arc, her hull shedding energy in a glowing halo, her gun ports open and phaser maws drawn; it was a calculated display designed to unman any surviving rebels still reeling from the surprise attack.

There were codes of engagement that demanded protocol be followed, that the warship's identity be declared and the usual offer made, even though the likelihood of acceptance was near to nil. Still, rules were rules. Across a subspace waveband, the commander's voice issued out to the rebels.

"Attention. I am Princeps Julian Bashir, of the Earthfleet Starship De-fiance, a duly appointed naval officer and empowered agent of Quadrant Command. You will immediately disarm yourselves and surrender your vessel without resistance. All citizen and bondsman privileges have been revoked. As of this moment, you have no rights."

Julian chose the short sword and clipped the scabbard to the molecular adhesion pads on the back of his torso armor, securing his assault phaser in a holster at his right hip. He went without a helmet, instead fixing a communicator monocle-headset over his eye; it was not good battle practice, as O'Brien often reminded him, but the tactician was inclined to be rule-bound, and Bashir knew that there was something to be said about letting an enemy see your face. A man of the rank of princeps should not go about concealed behind the blank mask of blast armor; his face should be known—known and respected.

He joined O'Brien and the rest of the boarding party at the teleport pad. The other officer gave him a curt nod and signaled the controller. A silent blaze of seething red enveloped them; *Defiance*'s interior re-formed into the dank, smoke-choked corridor of the rebel transport, and they were aboard.

Julian turned to give O'Brien his orders, and something moved at the corner of his eye. With a guttural cry, a figure threw itself off an overhead gantry and fell at him. Bashir registered the keen silver shape of a naked dagger in his attacker's hand, the accelerated neural pathways of his mind processing the threat in a fraction of a second, reflex turning him to defend against it. He pivoted on his heel and his hands shot out to block the attack; one snared the forearm that held the knife, the other clamped about a throat of soft flesh, cutting off his assailant's war cry in mid-voice. Julian let the man's momentum do the work for him, distantly registering the nasal ridges that identified his target as a Bajoran, spinning him about. He felt bones in the attacker's wrist snap like twigs under his viselike grip, and heard the man gasp for air through a strangled throat. Bashir let go, and the Bajoran tumbled headlong into a stanchion, striking his head with a dull cracking noise. Julian turned away, his enemy dismissed, knowing that the man would never rise again.

O'Brien and the rest of the men in the optio's cohort were quickly dispatching other rebels foolish enough to try and engage them in hand-to-hand combat. Bashir watched the tactician slay a Cardassian with a single downward slash of his *bat'leth*. The gray-faced alien wailed and dropped to the deck, slumping into a pool of himself. Bashir's second-in-command had taken the curved weapon from the body of a Klingon he had killed in single combat many years ago, in a duel on the surface of Ixion. Julian considered the weapon to be crude and inelegant, but it was certainly quite lethal and it had its uses—rather like the Klingons themselves.

The kills were fast and efficient, just as the princeps expected. He gave a grim nod of approval. "Any sign of Kira?"

"Negative," said the optio, and his face soured. "It is possible she may not be on board."

"We shall see," he began. "Leave it with me. Take men and move to the engine core. You will not allow them to scuttle the ship."

"Aye, lord." The tactical officer barked out orders in the clipped snarls of battle language and ran aft, with black-armored troopers at his heels.

Bashir paused, surveying the chamber. The craft seemed old but well-maintained, and he frowned at the thought. The rebels were supposed to be poorly equipped, lacking in support and matériel; but even a cursory look at this ship revealed otherwise. For all the assurances that the Bajoran government was giving Quadrant Command, someone among them was still helping the rebels prosecute their guerrilla war. *Sisko will not be pleased,* he mused, filing away his impressions for later dictation into the mission report his commander would demand.

"Lord?" Tiber, the squad leader, beckoned him over to where an olive-skinned Bajoran male lay panting on the deck. The man's face was darkening with a bruise where a blow to the head had put him down. "This one is still alive."

Bashir bent at the knee and put his face close to the rebel's, examining the contusion. "That is unsightly. You may have a concussion. You should probably have a doctor look at it." He reached out and took the front of the Bajoran's tunic in his fist, and without any effort, he lifted him off the deck until his boots dangled in the air. The princeps studied him coldly. "Understand me," he began, "you are going to die here unless you answer my questions."

The Bajoran made a gasping noise.

"Where is Kira Nerys?"

"She's not . . . here," he managed. "Gone . . ."

Bashir looked into the Bajoran's eyes, his gaze hard and steady. "You are lying to me." It was a skill he had honed throughout the years, a talent that many said ran strong in the men of his blood-line; there was nothing preternatural about it, nothing beyond the physical, but to those who had never seen it before, one might have thought Bashir possessed some measure of psychic ability, like a Vulcan or a Betazoid. It was nothing so distastefully alien as that, though. Julian Bashir had simply mastered the ability to read a face, to see it like the page of a book. He could see the difference between a falsehood and a truth, and he had never encountered a time when he had been wrong. It was a useful tool.

The Bajoran seemed to know it; he swallowed hard and blinked.

"I will ask you once more," Bashir told him, "and if you lie to me again, I will choke the life from you."

The injured man nodded weakly.

O'Brien reported in that the nadion pulse had done its work; not a single rebel was found alive on the drive decks, and with the application of a few carefully aimed phaser bolts, the warp core's control conduits were severed from the rest of the ship's systems, ensuring that power would never be restored. Lights flickered as the craft switched over to emergency battery stores, and almost immediately the temperature began to fall. Faint vapor puffed from Bashir's mouth with each breath, but the chill was a distant, unimportant distraction. It would take some time before the vessel's interior reached subzero temperatures low enough to affect the *Defiance* boarding party; but the same could not be said for the rebels. For a moment, he considered simply waiting them out. The Cardassians among them would succumb first, of course. Being from a hot and arid environ-ment, the gray-skinned aliens loathed the chill of space; and after them, the Bajorans would follow their allies into the grip of hypothermia.

But why delay the inevitable? There was too much risk of a premature fatality, and there was one particular rebel aboard this ship whose death had already been ordained, to take place in surroundings much more public than these.

Predictably, he found his target in the escape pod gallery, attempting to bleed power from a disruptor pistol into the stalled ejection mechanism. He was slightly disappointed that she chose to flee over a confrontation, but then again her kind were of a lower order. It was wrong to expect them to show human courage.

There were others with her, and they leapt to the woman's defense. The narrow gantry had little room to fight along it, but the short sword made easy work in the circumstances. Those he didn't kill, Bashir sent spinning away with open cuts that steamed in the icy air.

The woman, Kira, abandoned her stillborn escape plan and struck him across the head with the butt of the spent disruptor, at last in the desperation of the moment exhibiting some sort of strength of character—not that it did her any good. In return, Bashir hammered her away with the brass eagle-head pommel of his sword and spun the still-bloody blade about to rest its tip on her throat.

"Nerys!" One of the wounded Cardassians cried out in stark terror, stumbling to his feet.

Bashir drew his pistol with a sweep of his free hand, aimed at the alien, and hesitated with his finger on the trigger. The lined brow of the male seemed familiar, and in an instant he had drawn an identity up from the depths of his eidetic memory. "Skrain Dukat," he said carefully. "Now this is an interesting happenstance. Lord-Commander Sisko will be pleased. Two birds with one stone."

The woman spat something in gutter Bajoran, her eyes burning with raw hatred. Beneath all the dirt and fury, she might have been attractive under other circumstances.

Troopers emerged from behind the Cardassian and forced him to his knees at Kira's side. Bashir drew back the sword slightly and Dukat pulled the woman to him, ignoring the thin runnels of blood darkening his arm from the deep wound on his shoulder.

"I'm sorry, Skrain," she managed, her breathing labored, her bitter face turning to him.

"It's all right, my love," replied Dukat, cradling her gently, his eyes wet. "We're still together."

Bashir sheathed his sword. "Touching," he offered, and glanced at O'Brien as he arrived. "Take all the survivors back to *Defiance* for interrogation and processing."

"Aye, lord. Shall I put these two in stasis tanks?"

Julian smiled thinly. "We are not barbarians, Optio. Give the lovers adjoining cells in the brig."

Dax was waiting for the princeps in his quarters when he returned to the warship. Bashir threw her a sideways glance as he discarded his weapons and unlimbered his armor.

She approached him cautiously, gracefully. With a hand, she reached out and traced the line of his chin. Ezri had changed clothes since he had seen her last on the command deck, substituting her nondescript helot uniform for something more flattering, a gossamer thing made of Tholian silk. Only the copper bondsman's torc about her neck remained. She came closer.

Julian did not look at her. "I knew you would be here," he said quietly. "You like the scent of combat on me."

Dax's hand fell away. "If you want me to leave, Princeps, you have only to give the order." She looked at the deck. "It has been a while. . . . I thought, perhaps, as the mission had gone well, you might wish to—"

She wasn't allowed to finish. Bashir pulled her roughly to

him and kissed her. She gasped and surrendered to him, as she always did.

That was what he wanted, and she was very good at understanding his wishes. Living a dozen lifetimes could do that for a woman. O'Brien and the other Earth-born aboard the ship might sometimes look askance at him for taking the diminutive Trill science helot as his concubine, but Julian cared nothing for what they might say behind his back. He was princeps; aboard *Defiance* there was only his word, and it was law.

With a jerk of his wrist, he ripped away the shift-dress she wore. Ezri was naked beneath it—naked except for the torc. He reached into his pocket and removed his dominae key, aiming the small slab of plastic at the woman. Dax tensed through reflex; a single motion of his finger would activate the neural servo circuit inside the torc and send a brutal charge through her nerves, if he wished it. But instead, he touched a different switch and the necklet gave a soft click, parting to fall softly to the bed. Ezri carefully placed it on the nightstand and waited for him to come to her.

Bashir took his time and let himself get lost in the animal intimacy of the sex. When Dax was spent and he was thirsty, he left her among the snarl of bedsheets and went to the fabricator for water.

In the dimness of the blood-warm chamber, he stood at the window and watched the static vista of the starscape, his hand splayed over the transparent port. Distant suns shone between the gaps in his fingers, and for a moment he imagined reaching out into the cold void, closing his grip and holding a thousand worlds in his fist. A smile tugged at his lips. Was it any wonder he had such idle thoughts of empire, given the imperial bloodline that ran through him?

His attention shifted, finding the darkened shape of the Bajoran transport ship drifting off the starboard beam. Now and then, the actinic flash of a laser cutter blinked on the surface of the rebel craft's hull. *Defiance*'s Andorian engineer Rel sh'Zenne was over there with a salvage detail and a forensics squad, gutting the vessel for data and clues that might aid Quadrant Command in stamping out the dissidents. The blue-skinned subaltern had been part of Bashir's crew for several years; like the rest of her species, sh'Zenne had a favored status within Earthfleet. Not quite the standing of a human, of course, but with far more respect than a common bonded servile. The sons and daughters of Andoria had a complementary position to the people of Earth, as a gesture of respect dating back hundreds of years to the time when they had made themselves the first true allies of mankind in space. Bashir found much to admire about their clannish culture, their sense of destiny, their understanding of their place in the universe.

Julian felt Ezri behind him. She rested her head against his shoulder. "How long until the rebel ship has been completely scoured?"

"A few more hours," he noted. "I will have O'Brien destroy it when sh'Zenne's work is done."

He sensed Dax's moment of displeasure at the mention of the tactical officer's name. She knew better than to voice her dislike of the optio in his presence, even here where they were alone; to do so would mean he would be compelled to discipline her, and that might ruin the mood. "I assume that Lord-Commander Sisko is very pleased with your performance here today," she said, steering the conversation in another direction. He heard the soft click of the torc as she replaced it around her neck. Their liaison was over, and she understood she was to return to her bonded status once again.

Bashir sipped the water again. "Sisko has not yet been informed. I will wait until I have everything I can gather from Kira's ship before I delight him with the news." He couldn't keep a mocking tone from his words. Julian considered his commanding officer for a moment, recalling their last conversation aboard Station D9 just before *Defiance* pulled out of Bajor orbit.

★ ★ ★

"Princeps Locken is making you look bad, Julian." Sisko had said it with the usual deep, level diction. The man was a slumbering volcano, quietly rumbling away, but ready to thunder into a violent rage at a moment's notice. He had seen it happen more than once, and it was a dangerous thing to behold.

Not for the first time, Bashir idly considered calling the other man to the arena for a duel, just to teach Sisko a lesson, mind, not to kill him. Just to instill a little respect. But such behavior would be seen as dishonorable and likely earn him censure. He wondered how far he would get in a real fight with Sisko; but then, the shape-shifter was never more than a few steps away from D9's commander, the alien's curiously featureless face watching him impassively from across the lord-commander's chambers. Julian had heard the stories about Sisko's bodyguard, but they were webs of conflicting narrative that surely couldn't all be true. All he was sure of was that the alien could kill in a heartbeat; he had witnessed it on one occasion, when a Bajoran assassin had attempted to stab Sisko during some planetside festival. One moment the odd, unfinished man had been standing at the lord-commander's side; the next, he had become a coil of amber fluid arcing across the room, matter shifting solid to liquid to solid, enveloping the foolish killer and crushing him to a pulp. Bashir had never heard the creature speak, and wondered if it was actually capable.

"Quadrant Command demands results, Julian. Locken has many victories to his credit, while you continue to bring me nothing of real value. Ferengi refugees running the blockade are hardly the best of adversaries."

"My kinsman Ethan is only lucky," Julian retorted, frowning. "I am thorough. I will give Quadrant Command what they want. Never doubt that."

"I don't, Bashir," and he said it with a rare smile, "and that's why you're still at this posting and not flying make-weight missions along the rim of the Klingon Protectorate." Then the smile went away again. "But do try to do something worthy of your noble bloodline. The swifter, the better."

"What will happen to them?" Ezri's question broke his reverie. "The Bajoran, Kira, and her lover, the Cardassian?"

"Dukat," he offered. "They are enemies of the state. They will be treated as such."

"Executed?"

"Eventually." He couldn't escape a sudden twinge of disgust. Bashir, like every warrior in the Bajor Sector, knew of Sisko's reputation for cruelty toward Earth's enemies. It was something he found distasteful. After all, when a foe was beaten, when defeat was acknowledged, it was ignoble for a victor to go on punishing the vanquished. In war, sometimes it was required for a warrior to be ruthless—that was a universal truth of battle; but there was a line a man should not cross, where the delivery of a punishment moved from the necessary to the sadistic. He imagined that the deaths of Kira Nerys and Skrain Dukat would come with neither swiftness nor principle. Even though they were aliens, they deserved a clean finish. *To give them less diminishes us all.*

Dax gave voice to his thoughts, and he allowed her to do so. "They will be tortured, I would imagine. One might say that was a shameful fate for two people who only did what they thought to be right. Who fought for what they believed in."

"They opposed us," Bashir replied. "They brought their fate upon themselves." He was dismayed at how unconvinced he sounded.

She hesitated, and he knew she was trying to frame a response that would not anger him. "If you were defeated in battle by your enemies, what would you ask of them?"

He answered without thinking. "Little. Only a moment to pay respect to my bloodline and a quick death."

"Kira and Dukat will not have that."

Bashir turned and looked directly at her, realizing that he

had allowed the helot to speak too freely. "I may find the lord-commander's methods somewhat coarse, that is true, but I do not question them. Nor do I allow them to be questioned aboard my ship."

Ezri backed away a step, toward the shadows of the room. "Forgive me, Princeps. I spoke out of turn."

"You did," he agreed. "If it happens again you will be punished." Bashir sighed, wanting to let the matter drop, but unable to leave it alone. "I have no sympathy with Kira's rebels," he went on. "The religious militants she called to her banner are throwbacks, fearful and willfully primitive. They rejected Earth's offers of stewardship, our gifts of genetic enhancement. Her small cadre of terrorists have ruined it for all the good, forward-looking Bajorans who willingly accept our rule."

"As you say, lord."

He nodded to himself. "And the Cardassians . . ." He made a negative noise. "Hardly worth a blade's edge, at the end of the day. Dukat's people are like desperate, panicked animals, lashing out at everything. The Cardassians do not have the intelligence to accept the inevitability of their own extinction. We would have a greater peace if they just drew back to their worlds and died quietly." Animated by his irritation, Julian crossed the room and began to dress.

"But still they fight you," Dax said quietly, slipping back into her duty uniform.

"Of course they do," Bashir retorted. "As I said, they are cornered animals. But not a serious threat." When Ezri didn't respond, he went on. "There are no credible enemies for mankind, little that could even come close to menacing the dominions of Earth across the Alpha Quadrant." Julian swept his hand around, as if he were taking in the galaxy ranged out all about them. "The Klingons? They are a spent force, rightfully respectful of our martial prowess. Cardassia and their satellites are slowly starving to death. The Tzenkethi, the Breen, the Tholians, all have had their faces bloodied by us and backed down into their own territories! The Romulans are a pathetic echo—they let themselves be drawn into a struggle with those cyborgs from the Delta Quadrant . . . And what does that leave?" He gave a dry chuckle. "None of the apathetic vassal-worlds in Human Space have the will or the courage to defy Earth. Vulcan? Tellar? Betazed?" He shot her a hard look. "Trill? Are any of them a match for us?" Bashir snorted in derision, and Ezri backed farther away, gathering up her clothes, sensing the shift in his mood. "Some may cry about lost freedoms, but the truth is, the galaxy is better for humanity's place in it. Only we are fit to rule. I ask you, what shame is there in knowing one's place?"

"You are correct, Princeps," she said, but even as the words left her mouth he knew she was ready to say more.

"Tell me what you are thinking," he told her. "Tell me, and do not even consider insulting my intelligence by pretending otherwise."

It was a long moment before she answered him. "You are correct," Dax repeated, "but as strong as Earth is, it cannot be eternal. Every empire crumbles eventually. The Tkon, the Shedai, the Promellians, and the Menthar . . . All gone. All dust now. Perhaps because they made the same choices that Earth does now."

Julian felt a surge of anger in the balling of his fists, and he held on to it for an instant, unsure of where it had come from: Ezri's words, or his own silent misgivings.

"You are dismissed," he told her, at length. "Go to your duties."

Dax bowed slightly and left without uttering another word.

He went, as he always did, to the one place aboard the *Defiance* where he could be sure of some clarity. Bashir entered the counsel chamber and walked the short steps to the platform in the center of the room. The black-and-yellow grid across the walls glowed as the holo-diodes inside came alive.

On the platform, there was a lectern with a sensor pad in the shape of a hand. Julian placed his fingers against the outline and a warm tingle touched his skin. The sensors inside the device probed through the flesh, taking the measure of him, looking deep into Bashir's cellular structure. They found his DNA, patterned it, confirming his lineage and his right to be where he stood. Satisfied, the room's walls became smoky and indistinct, gradually re-forming into a perfect simulacrum of a view familiar to every Earth-born child.

The Great Palace on the slopes of Mount Kilimanjaro. As always, it was a perfect day, a pure sky of teal blue against the white and gold of the palace's columns and domes. Water mumbled through the ornamental ponds, and the olfactory simulators presented him with the scent of flower blossom. Although none of it was real, it was still enough to calm Julian, to guide him back to his focus.

And then, with steady and purposeful footsteps across the gray marble, Bashir's counsel came walking toward him. Here was the one man who had never failed to bring him perspicuity, the single person whose guidance had always left him enlightened. By reflex, the captain of the *Defiance* dropped to one knee and bowed his head.

"Julian Bashir," said the familiar voice, "brother and kinsman. Stand up, my friend, stand up and tell me, what do you seek?"

"Guidance, sir," he began, rising to his feet once more. "Answers."

"The quest of any rational man." There was a smile in the words that put Bashir instantly at ease.

He looked up and met the steady, cool gaze of Khan Noonien Singh, the Eternal Master, the Supreme Lord of Earth and all her dominions.

2

The sensor return glittered on Dax's console, and she checked the data twice before daring to clear her throat. O'Brien, in de facto command of the ship while Julian was elsewhere, had spared her a cold glance as she entered the command chamber to take her station, casting an eye over her uniform in search of some minor infraction he might use to single her out; but she had been careful. Ezri was always careful. A handful of lives, all but one of them spent in service as a bonded helot to the Khanate of Earth, had taught her to be conscientious in all things. *Never give them a reason,* she told herself, *not even the illusion of one.* Of course, men like Miles O'Brien would never accept that a joined Trill was worthy of anything approaching their respect. The innate sense of ultimate superiority bred bone-deep into the Children of Khan would not allow it. She was alien, abhuman, forever marked as unworthy. It was a status she did her best to live down to.

On the main screens, a cloudy fireball collapsed in on itself; it was all that remained of Kira Nerys's vessel. Once it had been wrung dry of any intelligence it could provide, O'Brien had given the order to obliterate it. Now, the optio was stalking toward her. "That noise you made. Was that an attempt to attract my attention, or are you suffering some sort of illness?" He curled his lip at the idea of being physically unwell.

"Your pardon, lord," she began, "but the sensors have detected an object on the far side of the Ajir system." Dax turned her screen so the tactician could see the data plot.

"A ship?" he wondered aloud.

Across the command chamber, Julian's young adjutant got to his feet. Tall and dark, in his duty battle gear Jacob Sisko resembled his father in his intense gaze. "I will take a summons to the princeps," he began.

O'Brien shook his head. "There is no need to jump the gun, lad. The princeps is in counsel, and he will not want you disturbing him unless it is for a damned good reason." He leaned in toward Dax's station. "Intensive scan," he ordered, "show me what it is."

"Definitely not a ghost image, lord," she told him. "I read refined hull metals, although somewhat cruder than those of the *Defiance*. Low-level energy readings, faint traces of what may be life signs. No ion trail or apparent motive power in use. It is adrift."

"A derelict, then," offered Jacob.

The tactician's lips thinned. "Or perhaps some sort of trap, laid by that Bajoran harpy and her spoonhead friends."

"We should inform the princeps," insisted the adjutant.

O'Brien scowled and finally nodded. "Do it, then. Where is sh'Zenne?"

Dax looked at her panel. "She is in main engineering, Optio."

"Get her up here. Run a deep analysis on the data you have so far. Get me something more tangible to present to the commander. The princeps will want more information than just 'a derelict,' understand?" He glowered at her.

"Aye, lord."

He stalked away. "Get to work, helot. And Khan help you if it turns out to be a Pakled barge or some other waste of time."

The counsel was a standard fitting on every ship of the line in service to Earthfleet and the Khanate. In the years before holodecks, it had begun as an expert system, a limited artificial intelligence programmed with all the knowledge of Noonien Singh, an advanced suite of software that could mimic his personality almost exactly. As human technology advanced, so the counsel became more accurate, until now it was a true representation of the First Lord of Mankind. The device was a way for the liege lord to have his wisdom, his incredible wealth of knowledge, available to every commander who served his legacy.

Julian had never known a time when the Great Khan was alive, having been born centuries after Noonien Singh had died at the age of 213; but the counsel made that fact irrelevant. To Bashir, Khan was as real and as vital as any other member of the ship's crew. He was not some dusty representation of a historical figure, like the other holo-characters in *Defiance*'s database. The counsel called upon ten times the processing power of a typical simulation in order to perfectly emulate Noonien Singh in every detail.

Some starship commanders tailored the aspect of their counsel to their personal tastes. He knew that Ethan Locken, Princeps of the *Prometheus,* chose his Khan to appear as he had toward the end of his life, as the great elder statesman of Earth's empire; William Riker of the *Excalibur* favored Khan as he was during the Romulan campaign of the twenty-second century, as a general and warlord. In accord with a moment of vivid personal memory, Bashir elected to have his counsel mirror the first image that the young Julian had ever seen of Khan Noonien Singh: strong and vital, only a few years his superior, from his time of ascendance during the Eugenics Wars, his dark black hair held back in a queue like ancient Japan's samurai, the tawny aquiline jaw firm and steady, dressed in a simple red tunic and trousers with the gold chevron insignia of a princeps senior on his chest.

With an easy smile playing on his lips, Khan reached out and placed his hand on Bashir's shoulder in a brotherly manner. "Julian, my friend, tell me what troubles you."

"The situation with the rebels," he began, frowning. "I have some concerns."

There was the tiniest of pauses, as if Khan were considering something. Then his face broke into a grin. "You did well to capture them. You should be pleased!" Julian had no need to explain the *Defiance*'s mission or its current circumstances; the counsel holo-program could call upon full and unfettered access to all the ship's logs and databases if it required them, all the better to provide a ship's commander with the best advice possible in a given situation.

"I am," he admitted, "but . . . I find myself returning to the fate of our prisoners, time and again."

Khan's smile faded and his expression became one of paternal concern. "I know you, Julian. I know that you are noble and strong of heart, but there are some days when the bloody business of war cuts close." He lowered his voice. "Do you think you are alone in that? Do you believe there was never a day when I too felt a moment of weariness? When I questioned the fight? Doubts are what make us men. They are the flaws that we overcome on the road to perfection. We need them to know that we are alive, just as we need the sting of a wound to remind us of the threat of death."

Bashir smiled. He always found himself slightly awed when the Khan spoke in this manner, as if they were merely two men who shared the same battlefield, a pair of warriors of equal rank ranged against a hostile universe. Not for the first time, he wondered what it must have been like to fight alongside the real Noonien Singh, to charge with him across the battle zones of Eastern Europe, the Altairan tundra, or the ironfields of Beta Rigel. He had stood in all those places, followed in Khan's footsteps to the rubble of the temple atop Mount Seleya where the Vulcans had surrendered, to the Tower of Kaur on Mars, and elsewhere, seeking to touch some of the history of the man. He closed his eyes for a moment and dwelled on the thought. *To fight with the First Khan at your lead . . . It would have been glorious.*

"We are human," Khan continued, "and that makes us warriors by definition. It is our way to do what we do best, Julian.

We offer the universe order. And we do that not by cowering in the dark, but by making the stars turn according to our will." He tapped Bashir lightly on the chest. "It would be easy to lose what we are along the road to our destiny, to have our hearts grow cold in our breasts. That we do not, shows that the sons and daughters of Earth are fit to rule." He nodded. "Compassion, Julian, is not a weakness for a warrior, *if* it is employed in moderation. After all, there were many times when Caesar or Alexander decided 'I will not kill today,' yes?" Khan smiled slightly.

Bashir found himself echoing Dax's words. "But these rebels . . . They only fought for what they believed in. As we do. They had courage, if misguided."

His counsel leaned away, studying him. "Only a fool does not respect his enemies. But it is an unwise commander who allows that respect . . . that *compassion* . . . to turn to sympathy. Remember, kinsman. Moderation."

Julian nodded. "You're right, of course. As always." He felt uplifted. It refreshed him to be in the counsel's presence. He never saw the shadow of deception on the Khan's face, not even the casual, tiny untruths that the members of his crew employed, that he pretended not to see for civility's sake.

Khan soberly returned his nod. "My friend, it is a hard truth that sometimes deeds we think distasteful must be undertaken in order to preserve the integrity of Earth and the Khanate. Ask yourself this: what coin do the lives of a few ragged zealots carry when balanced against the security of a thousand worlds?"

"None, my Khan."

"Just so—" The counsel hesitated in mid-speech, as if he sensed something only he could see. His eyes narrowed.

"What is it?" Julian asked.

"A message," Khan said, with mild irritation. "Your adjutant, the youth Jacob. He has arrived with a summons to the command deck. He awaits you outside my chamber."

"Urgent?"

"The boy seems to think so."

Bashir bowed. "Then, my lord, I will take my leave of you." He straightened. "You bring me clarity as always."

"I am always here, Julian," he replied, and walked away toward the palace. The hologram hazed and vanished, and Bashir was alone on the grid once more. He smothered the moment of dismay at being called back, and strode to the hatch.

He found Jacob with a datapad in his hand. At they walked along the corridors of the *Defiance,* Sisko passed him the device and quickly explained what Dax had discovered.

"Whatever drive system propelled the ship is not operating anymore," said the young man. "Helot Dax opined that the vessel was captured by the Ajir star's gravity well and drawn in."

Bashir examined the images on the pad. He raised an eyebrow as he scanned the text from sh'Zenne's initial report on the craft. "Is this meant to be some sort of joke?"

Jacob's serious expression did not waver. "Far from it, Princeps. I double-checked the Andorian's findings, as usual. She appears to be correct. The vessel does indeed match a known design of Terran origin. From the pre-Khanate era."

Bashir found it difficult to accept at first glance. "A slower-than-light colony ship, a craft more than three and a half centuries old, here, hundreds of light-years across the quadrant from its planet of origin." Even as he said the words, he felt a tingle of excitement in the depths of his chest. *If sh'Zenne is not mistaken, then this craft would have been launched at the same time Khan Noonien Singh was battling to liberate the Earth from the corrupt warlords who dominated it.*

The thought of venturing aboard such a ship fascinated him. It would be like stepping back in time . . .

"It is unprecedented," Jacob continued, "but it is not beyond the realms of possibility. Without motive power, the ship could have drifted for decades outside the well-traveled space lanes of the Alpha Quadrant. It may even have been dragged here by some form of spatial phenomenon, perhaps a wormhole or a graviton ellipse."

The guard at the command deck saluted Bashir and opened the hatch to allow him entry. O'Brien turned as he entered, catching the tail end of Sisko's explanation.

"Here it is, lord." The tactician nodded at the main screens.

Bashir looked at the image, comparing the reality with the computer-generated mock-up drawn from *Defiance*'s records of the early twenty-first century. The vessel reminded him of the design of an ancient submersible warship: a long, cylindrical hull with a broad dorsal fin. A cluster of what had to be modular fuel tanks marred the otherwise bullet-smooth, aerodynamic lines of the craft.

Jacob's thoughts mirrored his commander's. "A streamlined body design," he noted, "designed for atmospheric egress and landing."

The princeps glanced at sh'Zenne. "Any more data?"

She shook her head. "Not yet, lord. I am still running a search protocol through our historical database, but information from that period is . . . patchy."

He nodded. During the Romulan Wars of the 2100s, attacks on Earth had cost the nascent Khanate much, and among the casualties had been libraries of contemporary history. It had only been because of Noonien Singh's diligence and interest in his ancestors that any records of Earth's ancient cultures had survived the bombardments.

O'Brien grimly folded his arms across his chest. "I think we should destroy it," he said flatly.

Bashir nodded at a tertiary screen, where the wreckage of the rebel Bajoran ship still drifted. "Did that not provide enough target practice for you?"

"A derelict appearing from nowhere, just as we capture Kira Nerys and her militants?" O'Brien sniffed. "It is too coincidental. I do not trust coincidences."

The commander's eyes narrowed. "You must learn to understand, Optio," he said lightly, "not every happenstance is a trap. Not everything about the universe is directed toward you." He wandered to Dax's console. "Is the vessel's structure intact? Can we take it in tow with our tractor beam?"

The Trill nodded. "Aye, lord. I believe the derelict's hull is capable of weathering faster-than-light velocities, if we can extend our warp field out to enclose it."

"That can be done," offered the Andorian. "But it would severely impact *Defiance*'s flight performance. We would be forced to remain at a relatively low warp speed, no more than factor two at best."

"Make preparations," Bashir ordered. "We shall see if this is indeed some strange form of elaborate snare." He gave O'Brien an arch look. "Inform Doctor Amoros to assemble a medical detail and prepare a boarding party. Light weapons and armor." The optio nodded and spoke into his communicator headset.

Jacob looked up from his console, running a visual scan over the old ship's fuselage. "Sir? I have something." As *Defiance* closed on the derelict, powerful spotlights on the warship's hull stabbed out to cast hard disks of white across the gray metal, revealing the lesions of thousands of micrometeor impacts. Up close, the disfigurements of decades of space travel were clear to see.

There were pale shadows on the plating. For a moment, Bashir thought he was seeing carbon scoring, but the lines were too regular, too evenly spaced. There were letters on the side of the ship, radiation-faded into ghostly glyphs. "Enhance that," he said, and Jacob did as he was ordered.

The scanner's image patching software extrapolated the available data and brought the symbols to life. The first was a colored disk with what appeared to be a globe of Earth upon it; the second, two strings of letters. "D-Y-one-zero-two," Sisko read aloud. "An alphanumeric code. A designation, perhaps?"

"I am not sure," Bashir admitted. The mystery of the ancient ship tugged at him, and his earlier concerns fell away. With each passing moment, the desire to venture aboard the old hulk grew stronger.

Dax's console gave a chime. "I have a correlation, lord. The code DY-102 is a vessel identification, apparently one of several craft constructed during the early 2000s. Registered as part of a Terran pan-national extra-solar exploratory organization, rendered obsolete during the age of the Great Ascension." She looked up and met Bashir's gaze. "The ship is called the *Botany Bay*."

As soon as the lights came on, Bashir reached up and took off his helmet. A wash of cold air, heavy with dust, struck his lungs. At his side, Doctor Constantin Amoros shot him a severe look, gripping his hand computer. At length, Amoros's head bobbed. "Atmosphere is breathable," he allowed. "We may unhood." Bashir's boarding party followed suit.

"If I may say, that was a foolish gesture," Amoros said from the side of his mouth. "There might have been toxins in the atmosphere."

"I am in no mood for hesitance," Bashir responded airily. "Boldness, Constantin. It is a commander's prerogative."

The doctor's hard look rolled off the princeps. Both men were quite alike in stature and aspect, enough that some might even have thought them to be brothers; but in manner they were at different ends of the spectrum. Amoros was dour and humorless, his cold demeanor rarely cracking, and then only when he was presented with a scientific challenge. Their physical similarity stemmed from their shared bloodline. Both men were of Joaquin stock, able to trace their lineages back through the decades to the family of the First Khan's trusted warrior adjutant; in a way, they were cousins more than brothers, but thanks to the foresight of Noonien Singh, in these times all humans could consider themselves to be blood kinsmen.

The Andorian stood up from the portable fusion generator she had connected to the derelict's power train. "Systems are coming online all through the main decks," she reported. "Several outages across the length of the ship, but that is only to be expected."

"Life signs?" Bashir directed the question at Amoros.

The doctor was quiet for a moment. "From a distance, this vessel would seem dead," he began, in the lecturing tone he often adopted. "That may explain why it has traveled so far and never fallen foul of an aggressor."

"Then there *are* crew aboard?" Squad Leader Tiber ventured the question on everyone's mind.

Amoros nodded, consulting his portable scanner. "Below us, two decks down, inside a gravity carousel. A conglomeration of organic traces and life signs." A slight smile tugged at the corner of the man's lips, but it was gone before anyone else could see it. "Humanoid, without doubt. But very reduced . . . I would say near to death, but the readings are too uniform."

Bashir ran a gloved hand over a console; a rime of oxygen frost glittered across the panel. "The crew have not seen fit to come greet us. We will go to them." He beckoned Amoros to go with him and, with a jut of his chin, summoned Dax as well.

Ezri's first impression was of a mausoleum. She had a quick, blink-fast flash of memory from the life of Lela Dax, of a cemetery asteroid where the dead of a dozen worlds had been interred in shallow alcoves along an endless winding corridor. In similar fashion, the crew bay of the old Earth ship was a technological rendering of the same structure. Horizontal compartments with slit-windows ranged up along the walls of the chamber, and white vapor pooled around her boots as she moved in, two steps behind Bashir, Amoros, and the troopers. Through the frosted-over glass she could clearly make out the shapes of human beings, all of them in silent repose. Next to each chamber, a series of monitoring devices blinked and cooed quietly, displaying vastly slowed

respiration and heart function. There were dozens of them, and
visible through an observation window, another two chambers
beyond this one. She made a quick estimate: a hundred people,
give or take.

"Sleepers," said Amoros. "These people are in cryogenic suspension, Princeps. It was a common practice in the era before
faster-than-light travel was invented. All of them are in a deep
somnolent state, like an induced coma."

Tiber seemed unconvinced, panning his phaser rifle back and
forth across the room, as if daring an unseen assailant to leap out
and attack them. Ezri gave him a wide berth as she crossed to a
data terminal set into one of the walls. Her hand computer made
short work of establishing a basic interface.

Something had drawn Bashir's attention. "Asleep, you say?"
He bent to study one of the monitors, on the compartment closest to the hatchway. "I think this one may beg to differ."

The levels on the monitor were slowly rising, and even as Dax
watched, she saw a twitch of movement from inside the compartment. "Is it safe to wake them, lord?" she asked.

Amoros answered the question. "We cannot be certain. After
so long, there could be damage . . . An uncontrolled revival . . ."

"Stop it, then," Bashir ordered. "We do not want to kill any of
them."

"I think it may be too late," Dax ventured. "Princeps, it may be
that we triggered this by venturing aboard the ship."

"The Trill is correct," said Amoros, scanning the compartment
with a sensor wand. "He is already too far along." The doctor
reached for the medical kit in his backpack.

"He?" She heard the spike of interest in Bashir's voice.

The compartment hissed, and on hinges over three centuries
old, the ice-covered door came open. Pallid and shaking, a figure
in an orange ship suit half-fell from the cramped, freezing tube
to the metal deck. Bashir was there in an instant, holding the
man up.

For a moment, Ezri wondered if the man was a Trill or a Bajoran. Certainly, he couldn't be an Earther. He was too small to be one of them, without the height or the broad chests of the Children of Khan. His muscles lacked the definition of an Earth-born physique. Even the youth Jacob was taller than this one.

Amoros applied a hypospray to the man's neck, and his eyes fluttered open. He blinked and swallowed, unable to speak. His mouth emitted dry, gasping noises.

"Do not try to talk," Bashir told him. "Do not be afraid. We are not here as your enemies. We are from Earth. We found your ship adrift."

The man nodded, and the effort seemed to drain everything from him.

Bashir shot the doctor a look. "He is barely alive. Take him back to the *Defiance*'s sickbay."

The doctor shook his head. "I beg to differ, Princeps. I am not sure his body would survive the shock of teleportation. I will have to work on him here."

"Then do it." Bashir laid the man down on his pallet and stepped back. Ezri heard him take in a sharp breath. "Who are these people?" he said quietly.

Dax stepped away from the other console, leaving her hand computer to sift through the ship's systems, and studied the monitor. There was a discolored panel beneath it, with an image of the man, although without the matted beard that now grew about his face. She saw a name and rank, and read it out aloud. "Mission commander, *S.S. Botany Bay,* Captain Christopher, Shaun G."

"Captain . . ." Bashir nodded at that. "Of course. It is sensible that the ship's systems would awaken the vessel's most senior officer first, in the event of an emergency."

Tiber grunted. *"Captain?"* he echoed. "That cannot be right, lord. I mean, look at him." He pointed at Christopher with the muzzle of his gun. "He has to be a helot, a humanoid from a

servant-world. And one of them would never be granted rank."
The trooper glanced at Dax and sniffed.

All at once, a cold rush of understanding washed over Ezri, and
in that moment she saw that Bashir had felt it too.

The princeps assembled them in the *Defiance*'s briefing room, the
senior officers taking their seats on the benches on the upper tier,
while the helot ranks stood on the lowered level in front of them.
Bashir came to the commander's lectern and began without any
preamble; his words were being broadcast throughout the warship.

"At this time, every piece of data we have recovered points to
the same conclusion. The derelict we detected, this *Botany Bay,* is
indeed exactly what it appears to be."

On his bench, O'Brien folded his arms, but said nothing.

Bashir continued, his strong, clear voice carrying across the
room as images blinked into life on translucent holo-panels hovering above them. "Carbon-dating of hull metals and compara-
tive radiation patterning confirms the age of the ship. Log records
recovered from the vessel's main computer core were partially
corrupted through age, but Helot Dax is working to reconstruct
some of the missing elements. According to their logs, this ship,"
he said, as an image of the *Botany Bay* formed before them, "lifted
off from a military facility called Groom Lake, on Earth's North
American continent, in November of the year 2010, Terran calendar."

The princeps paused to let the revelation sink in among the
Defiance crew; a ripple of surprise passed through the room, and
he let it subside before he continued.

"There is a crew of ninety-two humans on board in a state of
artificially induced suspended animation. Doctor Amoros is currently working to stabilize a handful of the crew so that we might
revive the rest of them successfully at a later time." He glanced
across the room. "Doctor Douglas, will you elucidate, please?"

A woman with dark, shoulder-length hair stood up; Sarina Douglas was currently *Defiance*'s senior medical officer while Constantin was with the boarding party. "Lord," she said, with a nod. "We have determined that five members of the *Botany Bay*'s crew perished due to system malfunctions during their remarkable odyssey. Quite amazing, when one considers the comparatively crude nature of their technology. A large percentage of the remainder are in a delicate condition, enough that they would require a lengthy and careful reanimation process to bring them around. As the princeps stated, Doctor Amoros has brought a group of the strongest individuals to a waking state."

Tiber gave a derisive snort.

"You have something to add, Squad Leader?" Bashir shot him a look. "Speak, if you wish. I give my officers freedom to make their opinions known."

"Just an observation, if it pleases the princeps," said the trooper. "Those . . . *people* on that ship are hardly what I would consider strong by any proper measure of the word. They are just . . ."

"Basics," said Douglas. This time the pause for the revelation was a little longer, and several of the officers showed signs of annoyance or disbelief.

"Sarina is correct," Bashir continued. "The sleepers are, to a man, all pure-strain Earth-born humans, but they are from a time before our Great Ascension. Remnants from an era when mankind had not yet embraced the gifts of genetic augmentation to improve itself."

O'Brien leaned forward. "Princeps, I think a better word to describe them might be *throwbacks.*" Tiber grunted in agreement with the tactical officer. O'Brien gestured at a holo-image of a sleeper captured from one of Amoros's medical scans. "These are primitives, sir. Unenhanced, weak relics of a past that humanity has left in the dust."

"They are our ancestors, after a fashion," offered Douglas.

The optio didn't even look at her. "Our species shares an ancestry with apes, too, but I would not want to unlock a cage full of them. Those sleepers are a lesser subspecies of our race, something we bred out of our bloodlines for good reason!" O'Brien fixed his attention on Bashir. "Lord, why are we even wasting time with this distraction? Our mission at Ajir was to intercept and capture the rebel Kira, and that we have done. This . . . distraction . . ." He waved his hand dismissively. "This is not something for a ship of the Khan to be loitering over. Give it to the Vulcans. Or better yet, let me dispose of that distasteful old hulk and be done with it!"

Dax gingerly raised her hand, and Bashir nodded to her. "Dax, you wish to add something to this discussion?"

"Does a Trill maggot's opinion carry more weight than mine?" O'Brien grumbled.

The princeps gave him an acid glare, and the optio fell silent, realizing that he had spoken out of turn. Bashir glanced at Dax and nodded again. "Speak."

"Respectfully, I would suggest that the *Botany Bay* and her crew will be of great historical interest to Quadrant Command and the Khanate. May I remind you that His Excellency Tiberius Sejanus Singh, grandson of Noonien Singh and Earth's Khan Imperator, has himself spoken of his interest in archaeology? Many of your planet's libraries and knowledge bases prior to the rise of the First Khan were lost during the chaos when the Romulan Wars swept across your solar system. Between them, ninety-two humans from the twenty-first century could do much to fill those voids." She swallowed and went on, talking quickly in case one of the Terran officers tried to speak over her. "What I have recovered from the crew records indicates that the ship is manned by an eclectic mixture of experts from several disciplines. Scientists, engineers, all of them with superior skill sets . . ." Dax paused, taking a breath. "Superior by 2010 human standards, of course."

Bashir was silent for a long moment, musing. Dax's invocation of the name of the current Khan of Earth had silenced any further dissent. "We cannot ignore the historical importance of this find," he said finally. "As culturally dislocated and inferior as this *Botany Bay* is, it remains a part of Earth's past. We will return with it to Station D9, deliver the rebels, and bring our primary mission to a close, as the optio noted."

"That will take us weeks," said O'Brien. "With that wreck under tow, we cannot even reach cruising speed."

The Andorian raised her hand in request and Bashir acknowledged her. "If I may make a suggestion, Princeps, there is a way that we might reduce our travel time."

"Go on."

"I have confirmed Helot Dax's estimation of the sleeper ship's condition. I believe I could install a structural integrity field generator and rig a temporary warp sled from the nacelles of our shuttlecraft."

"You can make the *Botany Bay* warp-capable?"

"Aye, lord. Warp five, six even. The infrastructure is essentially no different from that of a conventional starship. In the broad strokes, the technology has changed little in the past three hundred years."

"A better solution," Bashir allowed. "Very well. Get it done." He gave the room one final sweep of his gaze, and found no one ready to question him. "My orders have been given. Return to your duties."

Julian found Jacob waiting for him after the chamber had emptied. The young man was watching him intently. "I know that look," said the commander. "You said nothing in the briefing, but now you come to me with a concern you were unwilling to voice in front of the others."

"The optio seems determined to ignore the value of this discovery. I do not understand why."

Bashir smiled without humor. "Miles O'Brien maps his life by what he considers to be hostile, Jacob. If it is not something he can kill, it makes him uncomfortable."

"You make him sound almost Klingon."

"His bloodline is McPherson-Austin. He has their wit and temper. Battle is the only thing that focuses his mind." The princeps studied Jacob for a moment; as with the elder Sisko, the young man had the hard eyes of those who carried the pure strain of the Amin lineage in their DNA. Jacob's father also shared the same predilection for ruthlessness that the original Elijah Amin was said to have shown, when the Somalian warlord was Khan Noonien Singh's contemporary.

"Bloodline only sets the mold for a man. It does not predetermine his character."

"Some would dispute that," Bashir said carefully, considering the youth, searching his face for a measure of his honesty.

Jacob took a breath. "I know that many aboard the *Defiance* think I am my father's eyes and ears," he began.

"I have never said those words," Bashir replied, but the young man kept talking.

"The reality is, he had me assigned to this vessel not so I might keep an eye on you, lord, but so that *he* could watch over *me.*" Jacob's face softened a little. "My father . . . is not a generous man. Control is very important to him."

"Why are you telling me this?"

"Because I know that when you arrive in Bajor orbit with the *Botany Bay* following on behind, he will take it from you and make certain it is his name that Khan Tiberius Sejanus Singh hears, not yours. He will make this prize his own."

Julian was very still. "A loyal son would want that, would he not? Glory for his father?"

Jacob's eyes flashed. "The only glory I wish for is the glory of the Khanate and Earth . . ." He hesitated. "And if some fraction of that might come to you, Princeps, then it would also touch your crew."

A slow smile crossed Bashir's face. The boy was telling the

complete truth. There was no artifice about him. "Tell me, Jacob. What do you want from your service?"

"A command of my own, one day," he admitted. "But only one that I earn myself, not one granted to me through my father's influence."

"If Lord-Commander Sisko learned of this conversation, he would not be pleased, you realize that?"

Jacob nodded. "I see no need for him to be told, Princeps, do you? All I have done is what a good adjutant must do: give his commander all the information there is at hand."

"Indeed," Bashir replied. "And so you have." He turned to leave.

"If I may ask, sir, what will you do?"

Julian didn't look back as he walked away. "I am going to meet these people from the past, and see how unlike we truly are."

3

Bashir had to bend down to step through the hatchway into the *Botany Bay*'s gymnasium/recreation room. Several heads turned to study him as he entered, and on their faces he saw a mixture of anxiety, fear, and distrust. Each of the awakened sleepers wore the same kind of single-piece ship suits, largely characterless except for nameplates over the right breast and a pair of insignia patches on the shoulders. One symbol showed the sleeper ship in flight against a starry background; the others differed in color and pattern. After a moment, Julian recognized the sigils as national pennants from the countries of old Earth.

Dax was already there with Amoros, seeing to the welfare of a dark-skinned man lying on a temporary gurney. The princeps nodded to them, gesturing for them to continue.

One of the sleepers drew himself up, and Bashir recognized the man from the cryo-chamber. *The captain.* He still seemed tense and haggard, but his deathly pallor was gone. Like all of them, the man was a head shorter than any of the *Defiance*'s human crew. Julian evaluated him as he took a step forward: the man moved with the awkwardness of someone recovering his balance, but still he had the watchful air of a career soldier about him. For a moment, Bashir thought of how he would kill this man, if the need arose. If matters turned to that, it would not be difficult. He had no doubt that any one of his crew could end the life of a Basic with a single, well-aimed blow. *I wonder: is he now asking himself a similar question about me?*

"I'm Captain Shaun Christopher, commander of the *Botany Bay*. I take it we've got you to thank for our wake-up call?" There was open challenge in the man's words.

Bashir gave a nod in return. "I am Princeps Julian Bashir of the *Starship Defiance*. You have already met some of my crew . . ." He gestured toward Amoros and Ezri.

"Star-ship?" An auburn-haired woman sounded out the word, making it a question. "And you say you're from Earth, is that right?" The name *O'Donnel* was visible on her uniform.

"We are," Bashir allowed. "Although some of my crew are from other worlds. Dax here, for example."

O'Donnel studied the elfin Trill and gestured at her own neck. "Those dots on your flesh . . . That's natural? Not a tattoo?"

"She is not human," Bashir answered for the helot. "She is from a world called Trill."

Christopher gave the woman a sideways look. "Let's take this one step at a time, Shannon." He glanced up at Julian. "Shannon O'Donnel's my senior engineer," he explained. "These are my other core staff; Hachirota Tomino, copilot. Rudy Laker, environmental ops, and Rain Robinson, navigator. The guy on the gurney is Reggie Warren."

Tomino gave a curt nod but said nothing, cradling a squeeze-bulb of water in his hands; the man wore a set of corrective lenses over his eyes, and Bashir found himself wondering why someone with less than perfect optical acuity had even been considered for the crew of an interstellar vessel. The rail-thin Laker had a dour expression, and he too did not venture any words.

But Robinson looked up, pushing back an unkempt line of dark hair from her face, and her eyes widened as she ran her gaze over Julian. "Whoa. They sure breed you fellas big out here, huh?"

A tic of amusement tugged at Bashir's lips. Robinson was the only one of them who looked at him without fear. There was a spark of intelligence in her eyes he found interesting. She was appealing, in an everyday sort of way.

Christopher's cautious manner remained unchanged. "As you can imagine, we've got a lot of questions," he continued, "and frankly, your people haven't been very forthcoming."

"Caution is a matter of course in space, Captain, would you not agree? You must understand, we did not expect to encounter your ship in this region."

Robinson spoke before Christopher could answer. "And where exactly is *this region?* Your men haven't let us take a star fix or anything."

The captain nodded. "That's as good a place to start as any, uh, Princeps." Bashir's rank seemed awkward coming from his mouth. "How about it?"

Julian hesitated, unsure how much he should reveal at once. "You have covered a very great distance. Over one hundred light-years."

"A hundred?" repeated Shannon. "Then . . . Eta Cassiopeiae, where we were aiming for . . . We didn't get there . . ."

"Your journey was extended by quite a measure."

Christopher stepped closer to Bashir, his eyes narrowing. "We've seen the equipment you brought aboard our ship, your gear . . ." He jabbed a finger at the pistol and hand computer hanging from Bashir's armor, and then at the medical kit in Amoros's hands. "What kind of technology is that? I've never seen anything like it."

"They are tools," Julian mood-shifted; he was starting to take issue with the man's tone, his lack of respect.

"Let's start over." Christopher folded his arms. "I have a different question. Tell me what year it is."

Bashir began to turn toward Amoros. "Perhaps, if—"

"Did you mishear me?" Christopher demanded. "It's not a tough one. What's the date?"

Julian gave him a cold stare, his expression hardening. "By your system of calculation, it is June eighteenth, in the year 2376."

O'Donnel's hand flew to her mouth in shock, and Bashir was

slightly pleased by the sudden, stunned expression on Christopher's face. The statement had blown the wind from the captain's sails.

Only Robinson spoke, in an awed gasp. "Three hundred sixty-six years. Holy shit." An amazed grin flashed across her face. "Wow. I'm *old*."

"That can't be right," insisted Tomino. "*Botany Bay* only had enough longevity for the flight to Eta Cas."

"It seems your vessel was better constructed than you thought," Dax offered, and Bashir nodded, giving her permission to go on. "It is remarkable that a craft like yours has survived for so long."

"Everything we knew is gone . . ." O'Donnel said softly, her voice heavy with quiet shock. "All of it, just dust . . ." She clutched her hands together to stop them from trembling.

"We left Earth behind," Christopher told her. "Remember, Shannon, we left all that . . ."

Laker nodded. "He's right. This doesn't change anything."

"It doesn't?" The woman shot her captain a severe look. "Dammit, Shaun! You didn't say a thing about being on ice until the twenty-fourth century! You told us we'd wake up in orbit around a new planet, somewhere we could make a fresh start!"

"There *is* a thriving colony in the Eta Cassiopeiae system," said Amoros, packing away his medical gear. "It is called Terra Nova."

Warren sat up. "Maybe we should head back there . . ."

The doctor paused, musing. "You would not fit in."

O'Donnel glared at the deck. "Isn't that why we left home in the first place?"

Bashir saw the spark of silent communication that flashed between Tomino and Christopher at the other woman's terse statement. *She spoke out of turn. They are concealing something from us.*

"We examined your ship's logs," said Dax. "There was some data loss. The circumstances of your departure from Earth were unreadable . . ."

"We . . ." Christopher hesitated for a moment, and then let his shoulders sag. He placed a hand on his head and rubbed the bridge of his nose. "I'm sorry. Could we discuss this at another time? I'm growing . . . fatigued."

"Yeah," added Tomino. "Me too."

Robinson caught a sharp glance from her commander and nodded slowly. "Oh, right. Yeah. Tired."

Amoros opened his mouth, a disagreement forming on his lips, but Bashir spoke first. "Of course. Forgive me, this ordeal must be quite trying for you. We will let you rest."

"I appreciate that," Christopher replied.

Bashir nodded, his smile never touching his eyes. "And of course, I will leave a contingent of my men on board to assist you."

"That's not necessary."

He turned away, weighing the man's blatant lie in his thoughts. "Oh, I insist, Captain Christopher."

Rel spun the Vulcan *lirpa* around in a sharp arc and brought it down at Bashir's head; the princeps blocked it with the short sword and shoved her back. Her bare feet skipped across the combat room's pliant flooring and she sucked in a breath, her chest heaving. He nodded, wiping a line of sweat from his brow. "Go on," he told her. "What else have you learned?"

The Andorian engineer stalked around him, watching for an opening, delivering her report as she shifted on the balls of her feet, the *lirpa* sliding through her fingers. "Deep search through the . . . *Defiance*'s engineering database . . . was fruitless," she panted. "Aside from the most cursory of mentions, *Botany Bay* . . . does not exist. The records talk only of such craft in a . . . conjectural sense. As if they were designed . . . but never actually constructed."

"The vessel drifting alongside us would seem to put the lie to that statement," he told her, and attacked, stabbing with the sword. Her parry was a poor one, and the blade edge nicked the azure skin of her arm, just below the shoulder. She didn't cry out; Bashir liked that about sh'Zenne. Even though she was just a subaltern helot, even though she was an engineer, the woman still fought like a warrior. The Andorians were a hard people, and in their way they had taught humanity much about the challenges of life in the galaxy at large. In the end, they had lost their war against the Khanate, of course, but they did not let it make them slaves, not in the way that the Vulcans or the Trill had. Andorians were hunting wolves; they were the raptors on Earth's glove. They had a place of special honor.

He liked sparring with the alien; she did not think like a human, and that made her difficult to predict. The sparring kept Bashir sharp, even if it did make him seem eccentric to the other officers in Quadrant Command. *Defiance* had more alien crew in senior roles than any other ship in the fleet. Some men told Bashir he would regret his generosity toward the nonhumans, but he ignored them. His jaw hardened and he pressed the attack. He felt a closer kinship to the blue-skin than those Basics on the sleeper ship. Julian thought of Christopher's arrogance, his outright lies, and hit out hard in anger.

Rel went down and lost the Vulcan weapon, a moment of panic in her eyes. Bashir saw it and reeled himself back before he did sh'Zenne some real damage. "How is it that a human vessel can vanish completely from our records? Were those files lost in the war?"

The Andorian shook her head and swallowed hard. "No, Princeps, as far as I can determine. It is simply . . . not there. Quadrant Command's database has no information on any manned extrasolar space launches from Earth in the year 2010, no mention of any starships called *Botany Bay* . . ." She got back to her feet.

"That is because it is a phantom," said a new voice.

Bashir turned to see O'Brien striding across the room, his regulation short sword sheathed at his waist. Like the princeps, the optio was dressed in a light sparring tunic and trousers. "If it is a mirage," snapped Julian, "then it is a very convincing one."

"Aye, lord, it is." O'Brien approached and sh'Zenne backed away, sensing that her presence was no longer required. Miles drew his sword and saluted his commander.

The princeps had been sparring for a few hours, and he would have been well within his remit to reject the casual challenge; but to do so would be seen as weakness, and he was not one to display that, not even for an instant. Julian mirrored the gesture before dropping into a ready stance. "Must I hear you speak of secret conspiracies again?" he asked. "That thread of conversation is drawing thin."

O'Brien attacked, hitting hard and fast. "You must, lord," he snapped, between sweeping slashes of his blade. "I would be worthless to you if I did not voice my suspicions."

Bashir blocked each blow easily. "You suspect everything."

"That is what makes me such a good tactical officer. 'All war is deception,' lord."

"Sun Tzu," said Bashir, recognizing the quote. Their swords met and the horns of the blade-guards locked for a long second. "You still think the sleeper ship is some sort of intricate honey-trap?"

"Why not?" O'Brien put his weight behind the weapon, trying to turn it free. "It is not—*ugh*—beyond possibility. The Bajorans doctor a rabble of non-Terrans to appear as Basics, leave this derelict for you to find. Your interest in the past and in . . . in *unusual* thinking is well known, sir. It is the perfect lure for you."

"Ha!" Bashir abruptly reversed his grip, robbing his opponent of his balance, and slammed into the optio with his pommel, punching him away. "Anyone who believes that proves only how little they know me!"

O'Brien shook off the strike and steadied himself. "If you say so, Princeps." He moved back toward him, raking the sword through the air. "Then at least, will you hear my advice and place the Basics under isolation? Leave the dormant ones as they are and hold those awake in the cells."

"They have done nothing wrong," Bashir countered. "They pose no threat to us."

All at once the optio dropped his guard and stepped back off the mat, abruptly ending the bout as if his commander's recalcitrance had tired him out. "Sir," he said with a sigh, "what do you think will happen here? These Basics, if they truly are our commonplace ancestors lost for centuries, they have no place in the Khanate. Do you think they will be granted citizen status because of some distant kinship to us, if they really are Earth-born? They are fragile little things, weak as any helot, inferior to us in every way. What can they ever be except a . . . a curiosity?"

"And we should cull them because of that, is that what you believe?"

O'Brien looked at his commander from hooded eyes. "Ultimately, what I believe matters nothing. *You* are princeps, and at this moment, their fate is in *your* hands." He sheathed his blade. "Unless, of course, you abrogated responsibility of the *Botany Bay* and turned charge of it over to Lord-Commander Sisko. Then the ship and its contents would be a millstone for his neck and not yours."

Julian thought about Jacob's words to him after the briefing and said nothing. O'Brien wasn't a fool; he saw that if Bashir had made up his mind to preserve Christopher and the other sleepers, then distancing himself from any potential blowback over their discovery was his only alternative. A cold thought crystallized in Bashir's mind. *How many of my crew think the same way as Miles does? Am I diminishing myself in their eyes by doing this?* He recalled Tiber's unguarded comments and his lips thinned.

Without warning, with his still-bared blade, the princeps struck out at the optio and O'Brien was caught off guard. Before the tactical officer could react, Julian had taken the short sword's keen edge right to the other man's throat. "A bout is only over when I say it is," he hissed, "just as my orders remain inviolate until I see fit to countermand them. Clear?"

O'Brien barely moved, a thin thread of blood forming where the blade rested against the flesh of his neck. "Clear, lord," he replied huskily.

Dax halted at the entrance to the security tier and waited for the last of the sensor inspections to come to a conclusion. Finally, the lights in the scanner tunnel went blue, and she stepped through into the brig's anteroom to find herself confronted by an imposing female trooper. Lean and tall, she had olive skin and a dark plait of hair coiled over her shoulder. Ezri didn't know the woman's name, but she recognized the Terran's bloodline archetype immediately; she was of Tiejun extraction. They were usually aggressive and taken to argumentative behavior.

Dax bowed slightly; not as deeply as she would to a line officer, but enough to show her obeisance to a pure-strain human. "I am here to conduct an interview with the prisoner, Kira Nerys." She offered the trooper a datapad bearing the authorization of the princeps.

"Why?" demanded the woman. "Tiber has already 'interviewed' her."

Ezri hid her distaste at the thought of what Squad Leader Tiber's tender mercies would have entailed for the Bajoran freedom fighter. "This is a noninvasive interrogation. I am here to confirm points of data from engineer sh'Zenne's study of their vessel."

The trooper grimaced and tossed the pad back to her, stalking away toward one of the force field–barricaded cells without waiting to see if Dax was following. Ezri glanced through the haze of yellow-orange energy shrouding the doorways that she passed, spotting Cardassians and Bajorans beyond them in various states of disarray. By turns they looked pitiable, angry, or broken.

"In here," said the Tiejun woman. She pressed her palm to a

control pad, and the field over one cell guttered out. "Use your communicator when you want to leave."

Dax bowed again and entered Kira's cell; she was barely inside when the barrier sprang into place once again. The trooper walked away, throwing her an arch look as she returned to her post.

Inside the compartment, the atmosphere was heavy with sweat and desperation. The air had a flattened sensation to it, where a noise-deadening security sphere enclosed the cell. The sound-proofing was adjustable, so that interrogators could conduct their work toward grisly extremes if required, without ever alerting the other prisoners; similarly, the sphere could be turned down to allow other inmates to hear the screams of pain, if it was thought that could soften the resolve of others. The Khanate's security staff often found it to be a very strong motivator.

Kira Nerys sat on a spartan bunk molded to the far wall, her back pressed into the corner of the cell, hands flat against a plastifoam mattress. There were contusions on her face and neck, bruising around the skin visible on her wrists. The Bajoran's eyes were hard, though, not those of a dispirited woman but someone tempered and annealed by the attacks upon her. *Hardened, like sharpened steel,* Dax imagined.

"I'll give you nothing, slave," said the Bajoran, her voice hollow and weary. "Don't waste your time."

The Trill produced a hand computer from her pocket and scanned the room. The device chimed softly and she nodded to herself. "We are not being monitored. I took care of it."

The words had barely left Ezri's mouth when Kira exploded into motion and rocketed off the bed, punching the helot hard in the sternum. Dax stumbled, breath gusting out of her lungs, and she fell against the wall.

"Nerys . . ." She coughed out the name and looked up, seeing Kira standing over her, her fists in tight balls, her whole body vibrating with barely caged fury.

"You stupid lapdog bitch!" growled the prisoner. "We trusted you! You were supposed to protect us!" She seemed to become aware of herself, and the tension in her faded a little. The Bajoran sank back onto the bed.

Dax dragged herself off the floor, tasting the tang of blood in her mouth. "I did the best I could . . ."

"Your best?" Kira's voice was a razor. "Your best got a dozen of my men murdered, my ship captured—"

"Do not blame me for your failure!" Ezri snapped back at her fiercely. "O'Brien found you, despite all my attempts to divert the *Defiance* away from this system! He picked up your ship because you spent too long waiting at Ajir! Why did you divert from the plan? You should have been long gone."

"I . . ." Kira's face creased with emotion, and she shot a glance out at the force field, to the cell across the corridor where her lover was being held. "Skrain. I waited for Skrain . . ."

"And that is how O'Brien tracked you. The ion trail pooled and the energy return tripped *Defiance*'s sensors." Dax shook her head. "You should have gone on without him."

The other woman's shoulders drooped. "I thought it was worth the risk."

Ezri mirrored her actions. "You were wrong." She reached out and placed a hand on the Bajoran's arm.

It was evening in Africa, and the Great Palace was lit by a stream of orange-purple light reflected off the clouds from the setting sun. There was a cool breeze in the air, and Bashir tasted the scent of an oncoming rainstorm. He stood with his hands on the carved stone of the balustrade, looking out over the wide expanse of the savannah.

Khan joined him, adopting a similar stance. "Julian. I confess, I did not expect to see you here again so soon."

"Forgive me, lord, but this is one of the few places where . . . I can find a moment to hear myself think."

Noonien Singh chuckled softly. "The demands upon a leader

are sometimes his greatest test, my brother. The key is to know what truly requires your attention and turn the full force of your will to it in the most opportune moment."

For a moment, the princeps was distracted, barely even registering the counsel's ready advice. He nodded absently.

The Khan sensed it immediately. "Bashir!" he snapped, and Julian was jerked out of his reverie by the hard edge in the voice. "Are you so overwhelmed that you ignore even me?"

The princeps colored and shook his head. "No, my Khan. I am sorry. It is just . . . in recent days, events are causing me to consider things that I have previously left alone."

"What sort of things?" demanded the hologram.

"Questions of loyalty. And the matter of the ship we discovered in Ajir's halo zone."

"The ship," repeated Khan, pausing as the counsel tapped into the *Defiance*'s database for more background.

Bashir nodded. "A relic from the past. A craft called the *Botany Bay.*"

And then the program did something that Julian had never seen happen before, not in all his time as an officer of the Khanate. Noonien Singh's image froze in place, every gesture and tiny realistic motion of him suddenly suspended, turning him into a perfectly carved statue.

The princeps was confused, and hesitantly reached out a hand to touch the counsel, then thought better of it. *Some sort of system malfunction?* It hardly seemed possible. The moment the name of the old derelict had left his lips, something had been triggered deep in the heart of the holographic matrix.

In another heartbeat the moment passed and the counsel jerked back to life, but now the Khan's expression had altered, turning hard and serious. "Julian, listen to me carefully. Until direct orders arrive from my grandson himself, you are to isolate that vessel and everyone on board it. The *Botany Bay* is to be contained at all costs. Do you understand me?"

Bashir gave a slow nod. "I understand, my lord." Bashir had never heard of a counsel giving a ranking princeps an order before, although there were always rumors about the holo-programs and the length of their reach. He recalled the elder Sisko once hinting darkly of a ship whose command crew had been killed and whose counsel had activated automatically and assumed the role of captaincy for itself.

"Do it now," said Khan, and before Julian could say any more, the palace balcony melted away, reshaping itself back into the bare walls of the holo-chamber.

Immediately, Bashir's communicator headset chimed and he tapped it with a finger. "This is the princeps."

"Adjutant, lord," Jacob's voice was tight and urgent in his earpiece. *"An encrypted subspace transmission was just sent directly from the counsel chamber to Quadrant Command on Earth. . . . Is there a problem? Something we should be aware of?"*

Julian felt unsteady, giddy, as if the world had suddenly started to move around him, out of his control. "No," he said distantly.

"Very well, sir." He heard the doubts in his aide's tone. *"In the meantime, engineering corps informs the command deck that we are ready to move to warp velocities on your order. The prize crew is standing by to board the derelict and take it under power. Shall we proceed?"*

"Not yet." Bashir's answer seemed to be coming from a different person. He felt disconnected, his thoughts turning again to Shaun Christopher and his people. To the woman, Robinson. The counsel's abrupt reaction absorbed him. It seemed almost . . . unreal. He had to know why the hologram had reacted that way. What did the sudden response to the name *Botany Bay* mean?

All at once, Bashir wanted nothing less than to grasp the secrets of the sleepers, and to know more about Rain Robinson in particular.

★ ★ ★

Dax's eyes flicked to the hand computer; the sensor returns still read in the null end of the spectrum. "What did you tell Squad Leader Tiber?"

"Not much. A few choice suggestions about the kind of farm animals his mother might have had sexual intercourse with." She chuckled stiffly, over a jolt of pain from her broken ribs. "These ubers get very irate when you make fun of their breeding. It's easy to push their buttons if you know how."

Ubers. It was actually a term from an old Terran language, Dax recalled, a name that had somehow slipped into pejorative use by all those who stood against the Khan and his arrogant kindred. Just to say the word aloud in the halls of this ship would see Bashir turn the dominae key on her for a disciplinary reprimand. "You should be careful, Nerys. Tiber hates nonhumans with a passion. He would rip you open just to amuse himself, if the chance was offered to him."

"It won't be, though. At least, not yet," the Bajoran replied. "I'm Kira Nerys, remember? Enemy of the Khan, dissident and terrorist. My death's going to be nice and public. I'll bet they're already planning it. Up against the ruins of the *bantaca* spire in Ashalla, a firing squad or a beheading, maybe." She sniffed. "Perhaps it will do some good. All my blood on the stones, color-corrected and broadcast wideband across every planet of the Khanate. Perhaps it will make some people *think.*"

"Nerys, I will do my best to find a way to get you out of here, Dukat and the others as well—"

Kira kept speaking as if she hadn't heard Dax. "But that's not likely, is it? All those worlds out there, they cling to Khan's hems like abused children. All of them, beaten and downtrodden so many times that they've come to think of it as a gesture of love, like some kind of *honor.*" She spat the word. "Nothing but apathy and slave-state minds. Too scared to resist. Too weak."

Dax sighed. "Servitude is all they know. Most of them have never lived in true freedom."

"You have." Kira prodded Ezri in the chest, where her symbiont lay. *"Dax* has. You know how it feels. And you know the humans have no right to take that from us."

"No," said the Trill. "No, they do not. But they do not care about what is right. They care about their destiny. They believe in it, to the exclusion of all else. 'One day, a Khan will rule the galaxy.'" She quoted the human axiom with rote diction.

"Not while I'm still breathing," grated Kira. "We could break their grip if only we had the numbers!" She shook her head. "Khan Noonien Singh's greatest crime was convincing billions that they were *inferior.* If we could rally those people, make them see . . ." The woman ran out of energy and her voice trailed off. "I hate that man with every fire of my *pagh.* Khan was dead before I was born and still I hate him. There's nowhere in the quadrant that bastard's shadow doesn't fall. But it's too late now. Too late for me." She sniffed, attempting to recover some of her poise. "When's my execution, then? I'm surprised we're not down there now. Or is Sisko going to keep me for himself?"

Dax shook her head. "Kira, we still haven't left the Ajir system."

"What? Why are we still here?"

In low and urgent tones, Ezri began to explain about the derelict, and of what the *Botany Bay* might represent.

4

"Shaun," said O'Donnel, gripping his shoulder tightly. "We need to talk. Right this second."

Instinctively, Christopher glanced up from his work at the environmental control console and looked to see where the troopers from the *Defiance* were standing. Two of them were across the cryo-chamber at the main hatch, like black-clad sentinels either side of the steel door. He hadn't seen them speak, not once since they had come on board. The thickset men looked like thugs with a molecule-thin layer of respectability sprayed on over the top. Shaun couldn't help but wonder what kind of space vessel—scratch that, *starship*—would need men like that in her crew.

"Hachi," he said, turning to Tomino. "Shannon and me are gonna take a look at the regulators. Keep an eye on the gauges here, will you? Sing out if the needles start to twitch." He tapped the panel and gave the man a nod.

"Gotcha." Tomino's look in return showed he understood exactly what was going on.

Shannon moved to the snarl of cryo-tank ducting between the first and second sleeper bays and ducked down into a narrow maintenance crawlway, making a play of using her penlight to examine the tubes. Shaun crouched and joined her, examining a perfectly serviceable joint for a fault he knew wasn't there. Among the hissing, grumbling pipes it would be difficult for anyone to hear them talking, and the captain had the certain sense that everything they did was being scrutinized by Bashir's crew.

"Where's that doctor of theirs?" he said quietly.

She pointed at the floor. "On H Deck with Reggie and Rudy, checking the tube seals. He said he wanted to make sure we weren't going to lose any more."

Shaun nodded. Along with himself, Rain, Shannon, and Hachi, Warren and Laker had been woken up by the DY-102's auto-revival sequence before Amoros had been able to deactivate it. At first, Christopher had thought the *Defiance* crew might be responsible for the deaths of the five whose pods were found dark and lifeless, but soon he realized that the ones they had lost had been through systems malfunctions, through normal wear and tear along the course of the ship's voyage.

One death for every seventy or so years we traveled through the dark, he mused. *Was it worth that price?*

Brown. Tyler. McShane. Summerfield. Jones. He'd known them all. Everyone on *Botany Bay* was like family—that was what a crisis did to you: it made people forge those kind of bonds—but for now they couldn't afford to mourn. Not until they knew what the hell was going on.

Shaun sighed. He wished Jack were here. He could have used his old mentor's guidance right about now; but Jackson Roykirk had stayed behind, given up his seat. He was centuries away from them now, gone behind a veil of time and space that left Christopher feeling more alone than he had ever thought possible. He realized Shannon was waiting for him to speak. "What about Rain?" he asked.

"She went over there." O'Donnel jerked a thumb at the hull. "To the *Defiance*."

"What?" He glanced over his shoulder, to see if his reflexive snarl had caught the attention of the guards. "You let her suit up and walk over to another ship? Is our atmosphere gear even still viable?"

"Didn't exactly have much choice," she snapped back at him, nodding in the direction of the big men. "And she wanted to go."

"Yeah, of course she did." Shaun shook his head. "Dammit, that girl treats everything like it's some kinda game. What if Bashir decides he doesn't want to let her come back?"

Shannon frowned. "Likely, judging from the way he was looking at her. But that's not the thing. She didn't use a suit, Shaun. None of them did. They didn't EVA over from their boat."

"What are you talking about?" He knew for certain they hadn't docked with the other ship.

"I don't know what it was they used, but Bashir just talked into that headset of his and the pair of them . . . *disintegrated.* Right in front of me." She shook her head. "That blond bruiser, Tiber? He laughed when he saw the look on my face. Said they were teleported back to the ship."

"That's impossible," he retorted, but O'Donnel's hard gaze said otherwise. "Holy Hannah. What's that thing that Professor Clarke said?"

"Any technology sufficiently advanced will be indistinguishable from magic."

"Ray guns. Aliens. Matter transporters. What else?" He shot a look at the guards. "Mind readers?"

"I'll admit, that Bashir looks like he can see right through me . . ." Shannon shook her head grimly. "But I'd say not. If they knew what we were thinking, we'd be dead."

Something in her words brought him up short. "Why would they do that?" He leaned closer. "Shan? What aren't you telling me?"

Rain blinked and did a double take as the doors slid back into the walls to reveal a striking desert landscape of towering rust-red buttes and canyons. "Whoa." She stepped through, under an arch of pale metal, and walked slowly forward. The doorway appeared to have deposited her on the flat top of one of the mesas, the level crown of the mountain the size of a basketball court. With the bowl of a sharp blue sky above, it was almost like riding among the clouds.

"I could do that for you, if you wish it," Bashir said, pouring a glass of wine.

Rain colored slightly, realizing that she'd been thinking aloud. "Really?"

"Oh yes." The *Defiance*'s commander stood by a small table covered in cutlery and glassware that seemed to have been transplanted from some upscale restaurant. "This is a synthetic environment, completely malleable, completely adjustable. I can program it to reflect the real or the unreal." He looked up. "Computer? Nighttime."

Instantly the blue sky became a black curtain dappled with stars. Candles solidified on the table, issuing a warm glow. "That's pretty cool," Rain said, attempting to hold in her instinct to gawk. "Do you get ESPN on this thing?"

He gave her a curious smile. "I do not understand."

"Never mind." She approached the table, expecting him to seat her—she'd dated guys who did the 'gentleman' thing before and she knew the drill—but Bashir didn't. He took his own chair and nodded at hers, as if he expected her to automatically know her place.

Rain sat, keeping her face neutral. "I've gotta say, I'm surprised you asked me, uh, over."

"Indeed?"

"Yeah. I was worried the age thing might make it a problem getting dates. Not many guys go for women in their late three-hundreds." The glib comment tripped off her tongue, but to be honest, she was nervous in the extreme. The humor was a defense mechanism.

Bashir chuckled and placed the glass of wine in front of her before pouring one for himself. "You are here, Ms. Robinson, because you are the only person from the *Botany Bay* who did not look at me with outright suspicion and fear. Has that changed?"

"That . . . teleport thing of yours was a bit of a shock," she admitted, not wanting to say that the stark transition had almost made her throw up. "But I'm not quaking in my boots, if that's what you're asking." She sipped the wine; it was a heavy red with a thick, caramel aftertaste to it. "I'm a scientist," she continued. "The unknown is my business. I guess right now, that's you."

"And your companions? Captain Christopher and the others? Do they feel that way as well?"

"Doubt it," she replied. "Don't get me wrong, Shaun's a stand-up guy, and he knows his stuff. But he's *military,* you know? A bit stiff."

Bashir raised an eyebrow. "What does that make me, then?"

"You're different," Rain admitted, unsure where her words were leading her. "You've got more of an aristocrat thing going on. It's cute."

He helped himself to food from a cluster of silver servers and Rain followed suit, careful to pick things that seemed familiar. "Captain Christopher and his crew have been very guarded about the origins of your voyage," Bashir continued. "Why is that?"

Rain shrugged the question off. "Like I said. *Military.* Shaun, Reggie, Rudy, they're all ex–air force or navy, all NASA monkeys. Astronauts," she added, seeing a flash of confusion on the man's face. "You know the kind."

"I do," he admitted. "But you are not like them. You are a . . . civilian."

Bashir leaned forward, and Rain was struck by just how much bigger he was than her. Not just taller or broader, but denser. It was odd; it seemed like the *Defiance* was run by a crew of linebackers. She nodded at his statement and went to the wine again, barely wetting her lips with it. *Careful, girl,* she told herself. *He's charming, but you know next to nothing about him.* "How about your ship?" she asked. "You have civilian staff on board?"

"In a manner of speaking. There is a contingent of helots on board to assist with the minor duties."

"Helots? I don't know what that means."

Bashir paused. "I suppose you could call them auxiliaries. Servants, that sort of thing."

"Right." Rain sounded out the word, uncertain of how to take his explanation. Maybe she had been closer to the truth than she realized when she called him an aristocrat. Maybe the Earth of this era had some kind of feudal government system. Bashir could be a lord or a baron. Robinson didn't want to dwell on what deeper meaning that might have.

"I have been giving a lot of thought to you," he went on, nodding to himself. "I want to know more about you, about your time. To be honest with you, I am going against protocol just having this conversation . . ." He gestured with his wineglass. "But I have read as much as I can about twenty-first-century history. Ever since I was a child, I have been fascinated by that era. And now, to actually meet someone who lived there . . ." Bashir broke into a boyish, incongruous grin. "I have so many questions."

"You and me both," Rain admitted.

The *Defiance*'s commander nodded. "Yes, of course. I can only guess at how you must feel at this moment. Dislocated, adrift in time." He put down his glass. "I want to help you."

"How are you going to do that?"

His grin widened. "You have lost centuries, Rain, but I can give them back to you. I can show you what happened while you slept." Bashir got to his feet and spoke to the air again. "Computer? Run program Bashir Iota One. Historical database tie-in."

Rain flinched as the mesa melted away and re-formed, the sky lightening, the rusty stone morphing into gray skyscrapers and city streets. "This is New York," she gasped, recognizing the location. They were sitting in Grand Army Plaza, looking out across the corner of Fifth Avenue and Central Park South. It seemed so real, she could barely grasp the idea that this was all an elaborate simulation.

"These events took place two years after you left Earth," he

told her. "The holo-program was constructed from surviving ar-
chive footage."

The buildings were as she remembered them: striking and
bold, but still a shadow of their former glory, with many windows
boarded up and dark. There were no gunships overhead though,
not like there had been the last time she had visited the city. And
no smell of smoke in the air, no trace of the grim texture of a
metropolis on the edge of war. Where were the checkpoints and
the police patrols? There were no food lines choked with tired
people, none of the street-screens showing endless cycles of footage from CNN's embedded crews on the Eurasian and Mexican
fronts.

But there were cheering crowds lining both sides of the street.
Many of the people waved pennants that seemed blurry and indistinct. *Not American flags,* she thought.

"Here he comes," said Julian. "Look!"

Rain got to her feet and stared in the direction Bashir was
pointing. Rolling steadily up the avenue from Midtown came a
line of heavy armored vehicles in urban camouflage, troop carri-
ers, self-propelled guns, and main battle tanks. Each of them bore
a symbol across its hull, a crescent moon crossed over a circular
sun picked out in yellow.

Ice formed a hard ball in her stomach, and Robinson heard her
blood rumbling in her ears. She reached out a hand to grab the
table for support; Bashir didn't notice. He was too engaged by the
sights around them.

No, her mind echoed the denial, *no, no no no no . . .*

She couldn't look away. She wanted to, but it was impossible
to turn her head. The big tanks parted to roll past them, going
onward in the direction of Harlem, and the rolling murmur of
the excited crowd surged like a tide as one armored personnel
carrier, bristling with communications antennae, grumbled up
the middle of the avenue. Standing proudly atop the roof of the
vehicle was a man in a bright red tunic and trousers, his dark face

turned imperiously to the people, greeting them with waves and fatherly nods. In one of his hands he held the Stars and Stripes, cradling it in a gentle, respectful fashion.

"Dear god." The words fell from her lips. "He won." She couldn't take it in. As an astronomer, Rain had seen stars millions of light-years distant, galaxies and supernovae, cosmic sights on a massive scale, and held them all in her thoughts; but this sight was beyond her. The enormity of it was just too much.

Unable to take her eyes off Noonien Singh's face, she was dimly aware of Bashir nodding at her side. "This is the beginning of his victory march to Washington, D.C., where he accepted the surrender of the president on the White House lawn," he told her. "The Khan chose to land in New York, because that was where those who had come to America in the past had landed when they sought a new future . . . But instead, *he* brought a new future to America."

Khan's vehicle passed them, and the man in red spared them a glance and a smile.

Bashir returned it. "He freed the American people from a cruel and callous government, and in doing so he laid the last stone of his foundation for a better world." He looked down at Rain and smiled sadly. "If you had not left, you could have seen this with your own eyes." He looked away, shaking his head. "But I understand the choice you made. Two years before this . . . it must have seemed as if the world was shrouded in a darkness that it would never escape."

"Yes," she managed, forcing out the word through a wall of shock. *There was darkness,* Rain recalled, the memory chilling her, *and Khan Noonien Singh was the one who brought it down on us.*

Shannon spoke slowly and carefully, her voice carrying no further than Shaun's ears. "I tried to get some more information out of Amoros. He's not easy to have a conversation with, but he opened up when I worked the idiot angle a little." Her lip curled. "These folks seem to respond well to that, thinking they're the smartest guys in the room."

Christopher nodded absently. Bashir's people wore their arrogance plainly, it was true. "Go on."

"He told me they're bolting an engine sled to the spaceframe. FTL drives capable of pushing us to, get this, hundreds of times light velocity."

"That's imposs—" He halted. "Okay, I keep forgetting. Three and a half centuries of technological advancement, right. Plenty of time for them to learn how to twist the laws of physics into a pretzel." Shaun sniffed. "Nice of Bashir to ask before he let his goons start messing with our ride."

"Forget that, the engines thing is just for starters. It gets worse," Shannon insisted, her eyes hard.

"It usually does."

"Amoros told me that *Defiance* isn't just a starship, it's a *warship*. They're out here protecting Earth's interests. Showing the flag."

"A hundred light-years away from Sol?" The concept of such a distance pulled at Christopher's reason. "Who the hell are they protecting Earth from all the way out here?"

"I asked him the very same question. *'The enemies of the Khan,'* he said."

"Khan?" The air in the cryo-chamber was bitter, but the chill that ran through Shaun Christopher's body at the sound of that name was far deeper, far colder. He grabbed her and pulled her close. "No," he insisted, "that has to be wrong! Three hundred sixty-two years, Shannon! He can't still be alive! Not even *him,* he can't be alive!"

"He isn't," she replied, with some slight relish in her voice. "But what he left behind is. We thought he'd kill himself, that those augmented freaks would rip each other to bits . . ." O'Donnel shook her head. "Seems we were wrong."

Shaun sagged against the pipe work, the cold leaching the heat from his skin. "Noonien Singh," he said to the air, "you son of a bitch. You couldn't let us get away, could you? After everything we gave up, everyone who died . . . You still couldn't let us go."

Bashir showed Rain moments from across the next ten decades, skipping over the years in blinks of holographic pixels. She saw gaudy renditions of Khan leading from the front against the warlords of China; Khan liberating orphans in Yugoslavia; Khan dissolving the United Nations amid a storm of cheers; Khan setting foot on Mars and Europa; Khan breaking the light barrier aboard the experimental starship *Morningstar;* Khan and Khan and Khan . . .

She sat on the chair, her hands in a tight ball as Bashir talked her through each scene. He was absorbed in the display, unaware of her silent disgust at it all.

The images were so sanitized, so blatantly false that she wanted to scream. Each holograph made Noonien Singh appear as a benevolent leader, a warrior-king who showed both nobility and compassion in addition to his battle prowess. The Khan was cast like a colossus, striding the Earth and freeing it from a series of oppressors. The people in every program were always happy and joyful in Khan's presence, as if he illuminated them just by being there.

It sickened her, the great monstrous falseness of it. Where, she wondered, were the scenes of the "containment facilities" where Khan sent his enemies and those his ethnic profilers felt unsuitable to remain in the gene pool? Where was footage from the cities and civilian targets obliterated during the bloody advances across Europe? There was nothing about the terror attacks, the secret murders, the biological experimentation, the conspiracies and pacts of a dictator with his claws about the world.

And Bashir was part of it. He could see the glimmer in the commander's eyes, the need to believe the brilliant, stunning perfection of the lie.

The next image was of a more somber scene. Rain hesitated,

and realized what she was looking at: a state funeral, but one of such huge scope it dwarfed that of an ancient pharaoh. She saw Noonien Singh's face upon a towering, black-bordered banner standing tall beside the white minarets of the Taj Mahal. *His funeral,* she realized.

"He died in 2172, having lived for more than two hundred years," Bashir told her, sensing the question before she voiced it.

Not soon enough. Rain wanted to say it out loud, but she couldn't, afraid of the response she might invoke.

Out of sight of the troopers, they quietly slipped into the companionway that ran the length of G Deck. O'Donnel's voice was low and intense. "You realize what this means? We're on borrowed time here, Shaun."

He nodded, thinking it through. Most of the *Botany Bay*'s sleepers had been on The List. They'd been on borrowed time since the very beginning.

Noonien Singh had made it very clear, chasing some of them, men like Jack Roykirk, all the way to the Atlantic after Khan's tanks had rolled over the concrete wall around Paris, after he had rained nuclear fire down on London. The List was a document that Singh's lieutenant Joaquin Weiss had compiled, of all the best thinkers and scientific minds, the greatest intellects that Earth had to offer. While Khan's soldiers marched across the world, his agents ranged even farther, kidnapping, coercing, or simply buying off every genius he could find. Khan didn't just want the world; he wanted the *future,* and the minds who would shape it. Those that went with him became little more than slaves to Khan's war machine. Those that defied him were marked for death.

It was Wilson Evergreen who brought them together in Nevada. He gathered as many as he could from the ones who escaped Khan's net, engineers like Roykirk, Nobel-winning theoretical physicists like Andrei Novakovich, genius cosmologists like Geoff Mandel, and more.

Wilson was a strange, studied man with his odd turns of phrase and piercing gaze. A multi-billionaire before Khan had plunged the world into war, Evergreen owned Groom Lake, buying up the former USAF base from the crumbling, cash-poor American government. He had rockets, he had men and machinery. He offered them a way out. An escape clause.

Shaun Christopher had thrown in with him because he had nothing left. Dorothy and the girls were gone, their lives snuffed out by a Khanate-backed terror cell in just one of a thousand bombings, assassinations, and sabotages designed to soften up America for the inevitable invasion. It had worked in Russia, in China, and in Australia. It would work in America too. It was just a matter of time.

A hard dart of memory cut into Christopher's thoughts.

The night before the launch, out on the pad. In the distance, the moonlight gleaming off *Botany Bay*'s sister ships, *Savannah* and *Mayflower,* where they rested on the alpha and delta pads. In defiance of safety regulations, he'd come across Evergreen smoking a thin cigar beneath the engine bells of the silent DY-102.

"Those things will be the death of you, Doc."

Wilson gave him a grin in return. "If I'm lucky."

"Why aren't you coming with us? You never did say. God knows, you've put more of yourself into this project than anyone else on Earth."

"Someone has to remain, Shaun. Someone has to see how it plays out."

"Khan's going to destroy this planet. I know the kind of man he is. He'll burn it to ashes if he can't rule it all."

Evergreen gave him a hooded look and said something that made his blood run cold. "What makes you think he won't win?"

The next day they broke orbit; contact with mission control was lost a few hours later when a suicide bomber detonated herself inside the command bunker. *Savannah* and *Mayflower* never made it off the ground. From then on, they'd been on their own.

"Sooner or later, someone is going to realize who we are, and what the *Botany Bay* represents."

Christopher gave a slow nod, thinking of the cargo they carried down on I Deck.

"When they do," she continued, "they'll kill us all."

Shaun shot her a look. "We don't know that. We don't know what the situation is, Shannon."

"Really?" She glared at him, her hands on her hips. "Think of it this way. Suppose in 2010 we found a schooner off the coast of New England, full of guys from 1781 who had proof positive that Benedict Arnold had actually founded America, and that George Washington was a killer and a traitor? What would happen to them?" Shannon took a shaky breath. "We've woken up in the middle of Khan Noonien Singh's bloody legacy, and that makes every one of us a threat to the lie of his empire."

Christopher pushed past her. "This is . . . It's like a nightmare. Tell me we're still in the cryo-pods, still dreaming."

"Nobody dreams during cryo-sleep. This is the real thing, Shaun." When he didn't respond, she stepped toward him. "Shaun?"

He held a finger to his lips and pointed. In the shadows, in the lee of a wiring conduit, a figure was barely visible. "Who's there?" he demanded, after a moment.

The petite, elfin girl from the *Defiance* stepped into the light, the one with the strange dappling on her skin. "Dax," said Shannon. "You're their science officer."

"That's right."

Shaun's jaw hardened, as suddenly the possibility of being forced to do something dangerous pressed itself to the front of his thoughts. "How long have you been standing there?"

" 'We're on borrowed time,' " Dax repeated. She kept her hands flat at her sides, trying to appear nonthreatening. "Long enough, Captain Christopher."

"Then we have a problem," Shannon said darkly.

Dax shook her head. "No. In fact, what we have here is an opportunity."

5

"I have kept things hidden," Dax told them. "There is nothing in the *Botany Bay*'s logs I cannot read. Any file corruption there was easily correctable." For the moment, she didn't mention that what information the Khanate's files did have on the DY-102 bore a high-level security encryption. "The data I released to the crew was what I wanted them to see."

Christopher and O'Donnel exchanged a loaded look. "And why would you do something like that?" asked the captain. "I don't imagine your boss would be understanding with you if he found out about it. These people don't seem like the type."

Dax fingered the torc around her neck. "Do you know what I am? Do you know what this collar represents?"

"I have a feeling you're going to tell me."

Her eyes flashed. "I'm a helot, Captain Christopher. A bonded woman."

"A *slave?*" O'Donnel's lip curled in disgust at the word.

Ezri nodded. "This collar marks me. At a single command, the princeps could use it to strangle the life from me without ever laying a hand on my neck." She sighed. "You are not blind. I know you have noticed the differences. Bashir and Amoros, they are pure-strain humans, but as the princeps was so clear to point out, I'm a Trill. An alien."

Christopher folded his arms. "Yeah, about that. You look human enough to me, the speckles notwithstanding."

She glared at him. "I am the humanoid host for a centuries-old vermicular symbiont that lives inside my chest cavity. Is that alien enough for you?"

"I'll take your word for it," he replied, sensing the seriousness in her tone.

"They *are* different from us," said O'Donnel, thinking. "She's right about Bashir and the others. Those men and women, they're a magnitude above us. Physically and mentally, I'd guess. Stronger and faster."

Christopher nodded grimly. "And three hundred years of natural evolution wouldn't advance them that much, would it?"

"There is nothing natural about the Children of Khan," said Dax. The name brought the two humans up short, as if it were a curse. "Every thread of DNA inside them has been enhanced, altered, re-formed."

"He got what he wanted," said the captain, in a voice laden with regret and cold fury. "He remade humanity in his own image. Damn him."

"What does that make us, then?" demanded the woman. "Are we going to become slaves as well?" She grimaced. "To hell with that."

The captain shook his head. "No. Remember what you said? We're the men in the eighteenth-century schooner, right? They'll stick us in a cage, poke us with sticks. Show us off to their kids as a sad reminder of what humanity used to look like." He snorted. "If we're lucky."

The woman stepped closer to Dax, her eyes hard. "You told us there's an opportunity. What did you mean by that?"

Ezri nodded. "I know from your flight log that you lifted off ahead of schedule. You were forced to."

"Khan's agents attacked the launch site," said Christopher. "We were ready to go, so we lit the motors and set the clock running." His expression darkened. "His men massacred hundreds of good people at Groom Lake. People who were my colleagues and my friends. Civilians and scientists, not soldiers."

"There are references in the logs to a 'cargo,'" Dax continued. O'Donnel stiffened at the mention of it, and Ezri knew that her instincts were on track. "Something you had to protect."

"The sleepers," said Christopher, looking away.

Dax shook her head. "We both know there is more aboard this ship than your sleeping crewmates, Captain." She blew out a breath. "We do not have time for any more veiled comments or half-truths."

"Why should I tell you a damn thing?" Christopher replied. "If what you're saying is right, I ought to be going for the weapons locker right now."

"Why?" Steel entered her voice. "Because I am like you. Because I have lost friends and comrades resisting Khan's dynasty over the centuries, but unlike you I could not sleep through all the madness and the bloodshed. I had to watch Noonien Singh's augments cut a path of murder and conquest across the stars. I was there for it all. I saw them subjugate whole races and wipe out worlds that did not conform to their ideals of genetic superiority. I watched his kind grind freedom into dust, feed innocent people fear and insidious lies until they bowed their heads and willingly put on their own chains. I saw them build his bright, shining lie, stone by stone." She sucked in a tight breath. "I have resisted Khan and his kindred since the day their ships blackened the sky over Trill. And I have done it from the inside, year after year, used and abused by them with this cursed collar marking me forever."

The *Botany Bay*'s captain was silent for a moment. "If what you're telling me is right, if the Khanate's reach extends out this far, then what could we possibly do to oppose it? Less than a hundred people, and each one of Bashir's crewmen as tough as any five of us?"

"That's if we could even get the others awake," O'Donnel said bitterly. "Right now, six flight crew is all we've got."

"Five, with Rain still over on the *Defiance*," he corrected.

Dax gave Christopher a level look. "I think you can help us, Captain, because I think I know what your cargo is, and I want you to show it to me."

O'Donnel shot him a glare. "Shaun, we can't trust her—"

He rounded on the other woman. "Look around, we can't trust anyone!" His jaw hardened. "We ran, Shannon! We ran from Earth because we thought we couldn't win against Khan. Well, guess what? We were right! And that son of a bitch followed us out here. He got here first."

"So we fight?" O'Donnel snapped back. "With what?"

"With the only weapon that we have."

"As a senior warrior-captain, I am entitled to the full benefits of citizenship in the Khanate," Bashir was saying, helping himself to another glass of wine. "One of the First Khan's greatest gifts to mankind was the creation of a system of governance and society that is both firm and fair. He used the model of the Roman Empire as a basis." The hologram room had taken them to Geneva, on the roof of a sculptured cylinder of glass and steel the *Defiance*'s commander had called the Senatorial Assembly.

The vista of the snowcapped Swiss mountains in the distance all around them was postcard-perfect, but Robinson wasn't seeing it. Rain's hands knitted; she had to put them together for fear she might pick up something and hurl it in a fit of undirected anger. "Roman?" she repeated. "Did he include all the stuff about slavery and conquest?"

Bashir let out a short, humorless snort. "Perhaps I am moving too quickly for you—"

She glared at him. "Don't patronize me. If all this is supposed to impress a girl, it's not working."

The princeps put down the glass. "I apologize," he said tightly. "I thought you would appreciate a better understanding of the realities of the situation. Perhaps I expected too much."

"What is too much is all this!" Rain gestured around, her temper finally showing itself. "This . . . this propaganda! What, do you think that I'm some dumb-ass hick just because I'm from a different century? You think I'm gonna be impressed because you show me some high-tech dog-and-pony show? News flash, pal. I was *there* when all this stuff happened, and this fairy story isn't how it went down!"

He advanced toward her, a strange look on his face caught half-way between anger and dismay. She got quickly to her feet, aware that she might have said too much, forgetting exactly where she was. But Rain was too far down the road now to back up. She couldn't even if she wanted to; her distaste at the whole display was just too much to hide.

"These are representations of the established historic records," Bashir told her. "This is fact."

Rain stabbed a finger down at the plaza below, where a radiant Khan accepted the adulation of a massive crowd. "That," she snapped, "is bullshit."

"You dare?" She saw his fist clench, and for a second Rain thought he was going to strike her. Suddenly, she realized the depths of the mistake that she had made.

"You're not trying to play me." She shook her head, sounding out the thought. "You actually *believe* this garbage, don't you? You people really think that's how it happened."

"I would know if it was a lie." He ground out the words like pieces of broken glass. "I would know."

The words flowed out of her, unbidden. "That scene in New York? That never happened!"

"How can you be certain of that?" he demanded. "You were not there! You had already fled!"

"I know because I know the people who lived there. I know because *I* lived in that city!" she shot back, her ire rising, old hurts thundering back to the fore. "Me and a million other refugees from California, Kansas, Ohio . . . forced to live in tent towns all along the Eastern Seaboard after Khan's sleeper cells detonated suitcase nukes in a half-dozen cities!" Rain stepped up to Bashir, looking up into his cool, blue eyes. "It was his fault! Khan! He made it happen. Los Angeles, Denver, Atlanta, San Diego, Seattle, and all the others, wiped off the map! He hit the country like a hammer, shattered it into factions and infighting . . ."

"It was a conspiracy inside the U.S. government that was responsible for those atrocities. Khan saved your country. He saved the world from itself."

"He didn't save the world, he stole it!" She prodded him in the chest. "New York would not have welcomed Khan! America hated him! The world hated him! He was a dictator, steeped in blood—"

"Be silent." The words were so quiet she almost missed them.

"He built his empire on suffering! Do you want to know what he did in Canada, Eastern Europe, India? The death camps, the enforced termination of pregnancies? The sterilization programs, the ethnic cleansing? The bombings and the mass graves?"

"I told you to be *silent!*" Bashir's words became an angry shout, and he reached out to grab her. Rain tried to dodge, and he caught the sleeve of her ship suit, ripping it open as she pulled away.

"You're standing inside this lie, and it's so huge you can't even see it!" Sharp tears spiked her eyes; Rain was remembering all the people the Eugenics War had taken from her. "Turn it off! Turn it off!" she shouted up at the perfect sky. "Computer! Shut the damn thing off!"

But the crowd below went right on cheering. "It will only respond to me." Bashir's gaze was as hard as iron as he spoke the words aloud. "Computer. End program."

The images shimmered and died, and they were there in an empty room with walls of glowing yellow grids. Robinson was shaking, her breath coming in gasps. She knew she should stop now, before she said any more, but the words kept coming. It was as if they had been bottled up for so long inside her that they could no longer be contained; and there was the smallest glimmer of doubt in Bashir's eyes that made her keep on, hammering at the armor of his indoctrination.

"You think Khan's a liberator and a hero, but he was a murderer," she told him. "All he cared about was creating a master race of augmented humans just like him." Rain stifled a shuddering sob. "I look at you, O'Brien, Amoros, and the others, and I know that he succeeded. And the victors always get to write the history books, don't they?"

"You are lying to me," he said, and for the first time she heard hesitation and true uncertainty in Bashir's voice.

With Christopher taking the lead, it was easy enough for them to avoid Tiber's troopers where they stood guard, by working their way down through a series of maintenance ducts to I Deck, the very lowest level of the *Botany Bay*. O'Donnel knew the vessel like the back of her hand; the woman had been part of the team that came up with the original DY-series design. Dax had scrutinized the plans of the sleeper ship; on the blueprints, the tier of the vessel lying against the DY-102's keel was labeled as algae tankage and hydroponic gardens. She knew there was more, however. The modifications stood out to her trained eye. The volume of bulkheads and interior spaces on I Deck was slightly less than it should have been.

O'Donnel was at her shoulder as the three of them moved down the corridor, the lighting dim on its standby setting. Ezri sensed the engineer's eyes boring into her back. It would take a lot more to win Shannon's trust than just some impassioned words, she realized, but for now there were more important things to concern herself with.

Christopher halted by an atmospheric processing panel. "Here we are," he said. Dax hesitated. At first glance, nothing seemed out of the ordinary, but slowly she became aware that the cable trunking in this section bypassed the control module completely. The panel wasn't connected to anything except a tertiary power supply.

"Shaun, are you sure about this?" O'Donnel asked pointedly.

The captain nodded. "I guess I am." He adjusted two control dials at the same time, and the panel gave off a deep thudding noise. *Magnetic locks,* Dax realized.

With effort, Christopher pushed the dummy panel and it slid away on concealed runners to reveal a hidden compartment, hardly bigger than the 'fresher cubicle in Ezri's cabin.

Inside was a steel rack of dark bricks made from dense, non-reflective plastic, each one held in a vibration-damping armature, each one connected by cables to a stand-alone computer console. The air inside the chamber was cool and dry, and smelled faintly of ozone. "This is it," said the captain. "This is the truth."

Julian advanced toward Rain. The woman trembled, but she held her ground. On one level, he felt a fleeting glimmer of respect for that. Others would have backed away, turned, and run, but Robinson showed courage. She was afraid, but she still faced him.

Her eyes. Bashir was drawn to them, just as he had been the first time he had seen her aboard *Botany Bay.* He searched her gaze, the motion of the muscles of her face, trying to find any tic, any sense of a lie. Julian's teeth set on edge as he found nothing, and in annoyance his hand shot out and grabbed her chin, holding her in place.

"You're hurting me!" she grated, struggling against his grip. "Let go!"

He brought himself down to her level, their faces less than an inch apart. "You are lying," he growled. "Admit it! Tell me you are lying!"

"I . . . will not . . ." She bit out the retort.

"You are lying!" he bellowed, an edge of wild desperation entering his tone. He wanted it to be a lie, he wanted to know that Rain was some sort of spy just as the optio had suspected, but the truth was there, written across the girl's face like words on a page. He knew for certain that Rain Robinson believed everything she

had told him. She believed that the First Khan was a tyrant and a killer, and she blamed Noonien Singh for ruining her world. Everything she said flew in the face of the Khanate's historical record, of the imperial mandates and doctrine that had been a part of Julian's life since he first left his gene-crèche.

But what disturbed him even more than that was the sense of real uncertainty inside him. He thought of Ezri, of their conversation about the prisoners, and the words of the holographic counsel. Doubts coiled in his thoughts, and he released the woman, stepping away.

Rain staggered backward and gave a strangled cough. "You're just like *him*," she spat, "all that silky manner, all the playacting at being a civilized man, but underneath you're nothing but a thug. A bully."

"I am a son of the Khan," he replied, but the words seemed shaky. "A proud legacy, the pinnacle of mankind's prowess, the ultimate in genetic enhancement!" Bashir pointed at her. "Far superior to the rudimentary, mundane strain of humanity that you represent!"

She massaged her bruised neck. "You may be stronger and faster and smarter, but you're not *better*, not by a long shot." Color returned to her cheeks. "While Khan was busy tinkering with you in his test tubes, he lost something along the way! He cut out whatever it is that makes you human!"

"You're a Basic, a woman out of time! How could you possibly understand what I am?" Bashir threw his hands wide. "You lived your life in the cradle of a single planet! You don't know what it is like out here in the dark, every species we come across challenging us for territory and resources, every world a new hazard. We must be strong and ruthless to endure!"

"That's Khan Noonien Singh talking," she snapped back. "Those are the words of a man with nothing but arrogance! Someone who had to control, to kill! A man who lived for war instead of peace!"

He sneered at her. "And what kind of galaxy would you have us live in, then? What would humanity be if we were not augmented, if we were forced to evolve at nature's slow pace? Answer me that!" Bashir looked down at his hands, at the slender, powerful fingers that could have crushed Robinson's windpipe in a heartbeat. "What would *I* be if I were not princeps?" Julian glared at Rain. "If we were all still like you, mankind would be extinct, or at the very best struggling to survive in a hostile universe. But the path laid down for us by the Khan has made us masters of all that we survey!"

The woman seemed so very small, so very fragile, as she looked up at him with those stark, honest eyes. "But at what cost?" she asked him.

Bashir opened his mouth to speak, but found that he could not answer her.

"How much is in here?" asked the alien.

"All of it." Shannon answered the question before Shaun could reply. "Each core contains terabytes of super-compressed information. It's everything we could assemble before we left. Hours of high-definition video, digital audio recordings, still photos, millions of pages of text."

"We hid this bulkhead and retrofitted the compartment into the spaceframe during the final phases of the ship's construction." Christopher gave a solemn nod. "Barely a dozen people knew it was here. We were afraid we'd been infiltrated, you see? If any of Khan's agents had learned about this, they'd have hit us before the ships were even finished." He sighed. "Even so, it was only us who got away, in the end." The *Botany Bay*'s captain tapped one of the dark blocks. "A complete history of the Eugenics Wars, from stolen copies of the first research of Project Chrysalis, right through to the fall of Europe and the razing of Japan. An accounting of the war crimes of Khan Noonien Singh and his kindred, gathered for all to see. Every execution, every death list, every casualty count, every atrocity. The stark and brutal truth. We call them the Black Files."

Dax glanced at her and produced the small handheld device O'Donnel had seen her use before. The thing appeared to be some kind of cross between a personal data assistant and a sensor package. "I have an interface program already prepared," she told them. "With your permission, I want to copy everything you have." She showed Christopher a thin, translucent stick of plastic.

"A memory stick?" he asked.

"An isolinear chip," she corrected. "I can get it all on here."

"Then go ahead," Shaun said, nodding.

Dax set up the hand computer and Shannon watched her. After a moment, the elfin girl turned and looked her in the eye. "You have something to say to me?"

"A lot of people died for the data inside those modules," she began, unsure of where her words would take her. "I want you to know that. To know how much it cost us to gather and hoard it . . . and then to take it and run." O'Donnel felt weary. "We didn't know what we would find on Eta Cassiopeiae. We truly believed that Singh and the others would rip the world apart, that humanity on Earth wouldn't live beyond the twenty-first century. We wanted to make sure that if we survived to start again somewhere else, then our descendants would know the reason why we fled."

The alien nodded gently. "I understand. Believe me, I know exactly how precious this information is . . ." She hesitated, sighing. "In fact, it is you who do not realize the importance now. Before, the things in these files could touch the fate of Earth only, a single world. Now, hundreds of years later, what is contained inside them has the power to tip the balance across a quarter of the galaxy."

"What do you mean?" said Shannon.

"There is a resistance out here," Dax told her. "People from dozens of planets, some of us fighters, others contacts or spies, like me. We have been trying to strike back at the Khanate for decades, but the pockets of opposition are isolated and scattered. The ubers . . . the humans are very good at keeping us cordoned off from one another."

Christopher nodded. "Divide and conquer. They prevent you from joining up, stop you sharing intel and resources. That's textbook tyranny. It's easier to deal with a dozen tiny factions than one single powerful enemy."

"There are people out there who would help us if only they thought they stood a chance. If they could be convinced they had a reason." Dax tapped a control on her device. "And thanks to you, now we have the means. Indisputable proof of Khan Noonien Singh's bloody past and living witnesses who were there. This will open up the whole rotten heart of the Khanate for everyone to see." She nodded to herself. "With this, we can tear down the myth of the benevolent liberator and show him as the despot he always was."

On the monitor screen, Shannon saw a blur of images flicker past as the data was copied at a lightning-fast rate, pictures barely registering in her brain in blinks of color and shade: a building on fire, a DNA helix, a horde of refugees . . . "What are you going to do with it?"

"The resistance has deep-cover operatives on a world called Bynaus, people who can get me access to the interstellar subspace communications network." Dax's portable computer chimed, indicating that the data transfer was complete, and she picked it up. "I am going to set this information free. It will sow the seeds of dissent on every world of the Khanate, trigger insurrections and open rebellion."

Shannon felt a cold smile tug at the corner of her mouth. Her fiancé, Hank Janeway, had been on board the *Savannah*. His death was still raw and painful; from O'Donnel's standpoint, he had only been gone for a matter of weeks, and even that had not been enough to satisfy Khan. She fought to keep the grief locked down tight, but the dictator was reaching out from the grave to attack them again. The thought that she could strike back at Noonien Singh filled her with grim purpose. Shannon nodded to Dax. "How do we help you make that happen?"

Bashir finally broke eye contact with Rain and turned away, glaring at the walls of the holodeck. "I am finished with you," he said in a low voice. "You are dismissed."

"Dismissed?" she repeated. "I'm not one of your crew or your— what did you call them? Helots? You can't order me around! I'm a United States citizen!"

"That nation-state hasn't existed since 2102," he told her. "You have no rights, no country, nothing unless I grant it to you . . ." Bashir waved her away. "Now get out. Leave me."

"Where am I going to go—" she began, but he rounded on her and roared.

"Get out!"

Fear flashed in her eyes, and she backed away toward the arch, the doors automatically opening. She stumbled into the grip of a waiting trooper, who threw the princeps a questioning look.

"Take her away," he ordered, and the doors slid shut on Rain's panic.

Alone in the silence, Bashir stood and tried to make sense of the churning maelstrom of emotion in his thoughts. Julian could not easily dismiss the look of horror and accusation he had seen on Rain's face, the unshakable certainty that the woman had no doubts about her hatred of the Khan. The things she had said . . . They tore at the very fabric of Bashir's reason. They ate like acid into the core of everything he held to be true. For a moment, he thought of the old mythologies of Earth, of the backward religious beliefs that had been rife before the Great Ascension had done away with such factionalism. *Was this how it felt to have one's faith challenged?*

The sudden, terrible thought that Julian Bashir might be found wanting filled him with a powerful sense of dread. He tried to wave the moment away, striking distractedly at the air as if he were dealing with a nagging insect.

In the next moment his communicator chimed from the pocket where he had placed it. "Computer, communications tie-in," he said aloud. "Relay."

There was an answering beep from the air, and Jacob Sisko's voice sounded across the empty holodeck. *"Princeps, my apologies for interrupting you . . ."*

"What is it?" His reply was terse and clipped. "I left orders that I was not to be disturbed!"

Jacob hesitated before answering, a certain sign of something amiss. *"Lord, we have received a priority omega subspace message."*

"Omega?" It was the highest security classification a starship commander could ever expect to hear, reserved for declarations of war, emergencies on a galactic scale, or for the word of the Khan himself. The last time Bashir had heard that code, it had been to warn of a Borg incursion in the Tarod system.

"The signal originates from the Great Palace on Earth," continued the adjutant. *"It bears the personal cipher of his excellency Khan Tiberius Sejanus Singh. He awaits your immediate answer, sir."*

6

"What do you think you are doing with me?" Rain demanded, trying to put up a false front of stern displeasure; but the tremor in her voice was as clear as day. The trooper in black shoved her forward, pressing his hand to the small of her back. Robinson stumbled and lost her balance, the deck plates of the *Defiance* turning and coming up to meet her.

Strong hands gripped her arms and suspended her in mid-fall. The jarring motion made her wince in pain as she was pulled back upright.

"Clumsy. I never thought Basics would be so uncoordinated. You should watch where you are walking. You could end up hurting yourself."

O'Brien. Rain remembered hearing his name in passing. The big, thickset man had the look of a heavy, as if he'd be better suited to wearing a black tux and dark glasses at the door to some rich-bitch nightclub on the Strip. . . . *But the Strip doesn't exist anymore, Rain,* she told herself, *Sunset and Melrose, Griffith Park and Dodger Stadium, all of L.A. ashed by the nukes . . . And this creep's great-grandpa was probably one of the people who made it happen.*

She shook off his grip and he released her. "Get your paws off me, you ape."

O'Brien's face creased in anger and he cocked back his fist, ready to backhand her. When she flinched, he smirked and relaxed. "You are a lot closer to the primates than we are, girl. Do not forget that."

"Monkey see, monkey do," Rain couldn't stop herself tossing in one more jibe, but O'Brien let it go.

He gestured to the trooper escorting her. "Orders from the princeps?"

"He told me to 'take her away,' sir," repeated the other man.

"Did he?" O'Brien leered at Robinson. "Well, then. You had better do as our commander demands. Come with me. We will find a nice cell to keep this Basic trash out of the way."

"Hey," Rain broke in, "you can't do that, I haven't done anything wrong—"

He ignored her. "I do not want to dirty my hands on this throwback anymore. If she resists in any way, break one of her limbs. The arms first. But leave the legs, so she can still walk."

Dax schooled her face to show the usual blank obeisance that was expected of her, so that when the tingle of the matter transporter faded away, she greeted the hatchet-faced woman at the control console in precisely the way a helot should; head bowed, eyes averted. "Thank you, technician," she said, but the human woman wasn't paying her any attention.

She stepped off the pad and exited the chamber, throwing the operator a quick look over her shoulder. The woman had already forgotten about the Trill, and was working through a diagnostic series. Transporter staff duty was one of the few "menial" shipboard tasks that was never given to a helot to perform, except in the most dire of emergencies. It was a matter of trust. Nonhumans were not deemed dependable enough to be in charge of a device that could scatter a person's molecules to the solar winds; it was one of the myriad ways that the ubers used to remind others of their inferior status.

Dax clutched the hand computer to her chest, thinking of the precious data hidden inside it. The innocuous device had the capacity to be more lethal than a bomb; it was a weapon of incredible destructive potential, if only she could use it correctly.

She halted, glancing around the transporter chamber's anteroom. She had expected to find Rain Robinson here, waiting to be returned to her vessel. The fact that the woman was nowhere in sight instantly sent a warning chill across Ezri's skin. The helot went to the translucent data panel in the wall and tapped it. "Interrogative," she said, "location query."

"Recognize Ezri Dax, helot ordinal." The synthetic female voice was stern and abrupt. *"Your access is restricted. This activation of ship's systems will be noted."*

She nodded absently. *Defiance*'s main computer, like many systems aboard the ship, was off-limits to nonhumans except by prior approval. But as with much of the web of rules and permissions in operation within the Khanate, Dax had long ago found ways to get around them. "Override, Dax Kappa Twelve."

The panel emitted a peculiar squawk as an illegal pass code program Ezri had secreted inside the mainframe activated. *"Ready,"* said the voice, in a more polite tone.

"Where is the woman called Rain Robinson? Is she still aboard the ship?"

"Confirmed," came the answer. *"Uncategorized humanoid female designation 'Rain Robinson' is aboard the* Defiance. *Current location, security tier, section six. Subject is undergoing processing."*

Dax's brow furrowed. *Section six; the cells.* She had been there only hours earlier, to speak privately with Kira Nerys. The term *processing* meant just one thing. Rain was now a prisoner of the Khanate, and there was little doubt in Ezri's mind that the rest of her crewmates aboard the *Botany Bay* would soon share the same fate.

"Attention," said the computer. *"There is an alert awaiting your notice."*

She leaned closer to the panel. "Tell me," Ezri demanded. Along with a backdoor subroutine into the warship's security protocols, Dax had also set certain criteria to run in an invisible scan program. If any one of a number of key events, orders, or conditions was highlighted, it could be quietly and covertly brought to her attention. Similar techniques had allowed her to stay one step ahead of her masters for decades.

"Communications reports that a priority omega subspace message is being received by Princeps Bashir."

"Who is sending the message?"

"The Khan."

There, alone in the anteroom, she allowed herself a rare moment of openness and swore a gutter oath. Things were proceeding far faster than she had wanted; it would be necessary to accelerate her plans.

Dax deactivated the panel and walked into the corridor, returning to her passive, submissive mien. Inwardly, however, she wore a very different aspect. The choice had been made for her by the arrival of the *Botany Bay;* she had known it from the moment she read the files on the sleeper ship. A deep-cover mission that had spanned lifetimes was about to end, all because of one lost vessel and its cargo of deadly, blinding truth.

"Security tier," she said to the controls as she entered the turbolift. "Section six."

The elevator began to move, and her hand drifted toward the torc around her neck; then Dax's expression soured and she pulled a fat plastic disk from a pocket in her tunic. With a twist of her fingers, it opened to reveal a compact holdout phaser. Ezri thumbed the selector to a lethal setting and hid the tiny gun in the palm of her hand.

Julian took the summons in the counsel chamber, as he was ordered to. The mere fact that he had been commanded to hear the communication there, rather than on the bridge or relayed to the holodeck, spoke volumes. The counsel chamber was one of the most secure areas aboard any starship, shielded from emissions and armored with defenses both physical and ephemeral. It was the most isolated, most private place on *Defiance.*

The chamber's systems synchronized with the ship's subspace communications array, locking data-protecting firewalls in place, and a figure shimmered into existence. There was none of the extraneous environmental detail of Bashir's holographic counsel, no rendition of the palace in Africa, no simulated skies. This was a live transmission inside the chamber's bare walls, being bounced from Earth through one secure relay station to another. To do such a thing, to send a real-time signal, required a tremendous energy cost. But the Khanate's ruler doubtless cared little for that, so long as his will was done.

Julian went down on one knee and bowed his head as Tiberius Sejanus Singh, grandson of Noonien Singh and the Third Khan of Earth, hazed and became reality before him.

"Look up at me." The command came hard and blunt from the man's lips, and Bashir did as he was told.

The Khan was by no means the mirror of his imperial grandfather, but he was still an impressive sight. In his fifty-fifth year, Tiberius Sejanus had a wide mane of gunmetal hair that hung out from his head, reaching to his shoulders. Hard green eyes bored out from a prematurely lined face like firm leather, and a thick blade of facial hair accentuated the stark lines of his expression. Earth's master wore a fleet prefect's dress uniform and carried a curved scimitar at his belt. The man appeared attired for some kind of formal state event, and the severe aspect of his expression was that of a parent called from other duties to find a child in need of discipline.

"Bashir," he said, taking the name and stretching it. "You are known to me, Princeps. Of the Joaquin, aren't you?"

Julian nodded. "I am, lord. It honors my ship that you would seek to speak with me—"

The Khan silenced him with a gesture. Julian had never stood in the presence of Tiberius Sejanus Singh, only seen him in images and heard his voice in official diktats. His presence, even attenuated through the medium of the holographic communication, was far different from the simulated Khan that Bashir spoke with in his times of doubt. This man had a bellicose swagger about him, lacking the lean and hungry aspect of his grandfather, the whipcord strength and searching gaze. He lacked, for want of a better word, the charisma of the First Khan. Tiberius Sejanus exhibited none of the raw, magnetic aura of his great ancestor.

"Stand up," he was told. "Get off your knees, Princeps. It's unbecoming for a warrior-captain of my fleet to behave like a common helot."

Bashir rose, and realized that the hologram was at a slightly greater scale than it needed to be. *Magnified, to intimidate me,* he realized. *Like a cat, arching its back.* "What is your bidding, lord?"

Tiberius Sejanus's face creased in a grimace. "You've created a small crisis, Bashir. You and your discovery."

"The sleeper ship."

He got a languid nod in return. "It beggars belief," said the Khan, "that a craft from my grandfather's time could venture out to the Bajor Sector and still be found intact after such a journey."

"The void of space preserves everything, sir. The miracle is that there are still any people alive on board the *Botany Bay.*"

"Just so." The man's hand strayed to the hilt of his sword and rested there. "But for the moment, I want this 'miracle' to be kept from the galaxy at large. For reasons of security, you understand? This matter must remain contained."

Bashir nodded warily, uncertain as to where the conversation was heading.

"It's been made clear to me that you have yet to inform your sector commander of this find." Clearly, the counsel holoprogram had transmitted more back to Earth than just an alert. Julian began to speak, but the Khan cut him off once more. "I'm not interested in your explanation, or in any maneuvering you may be doing against Benjamin Sisko. Just continue on as you have been. Maintain radio silence."

Julian was affronted by the accusation that he would use this incident to score points over Lord-Commander Sisko—he was a line officer and such things were beneath him—but he swallowed it down. "As you command. But my mission, the Bajoran and Cardassian dissidents. I am required to return to Station D9 as soon as possible."

"And so you will. I have this hour sent orders to the *Starship Illustrious* to make maximum warp speed to rendezvous with you, before you arrive at D9. They will relieve you of your burden."

Illustrious was Picard's command, a dreadnought-class battleship and one of the most powerful vessels in Earthfleet. In less guarded moments, the ship—and its cold-blooded commander—went by another name. *The Khan's Dagger.* Princeps Jean-Luc Picard was widely known to be the personal agent of Khan Tiberius Sejanus Singh, with a reputation for rigidity and combat prowess that few in the fleet could match. If the *Illustrious* was coming to meet them, then the Khan was certainly intent on ensuring that the *Botany Bay* remained a secret . . . perhaps even indefinitely. He had no doubt that he and his crew would be given some cover story. Sisko would never be told what happened in the Ajir system, and Bashir was not so foolish as to dare cross a man like Picard. He knew the stories: The Khan had given Picard the dangerous Sector 221-G to patrol when several other Earth ships had been destroyed there by a local coalition of warrior cultures. In a matter of months, through sheer applied brutality, Picard had forced the rebellious peoples of Thallon, Xenex, and Danter to surrender unconditionally.

Bashir remembered O'Brien's comments on the sparring floor, about the abrogation of responsibility. Now the choice was being taken from him. "Lord, if I may ask you. What will be done with these . . . people?"

The Khan gave him a measuring stare, the slightest flicker of subspace interference making the image turn grainy for a moment. "With all the sons and daughters of Earth living as pinnacles of genetic augmentation, there is something to be said for the usefulness of having a handful of our flawed, somewhat inferior ancestors."

The way the man said the words, it conjured images in Julian's thoughts of experimentation and dissection. He saw Rain's face in his mind's eye and felt a curious flutter of emotion in his chest, a sudden sense of wrongness. *Death camps and mass graves, she had said.* He suppressed a shudder.

"It's not a matter for you to concern yourself with," continued the Khan. "You will isolate the Basics from the rest of your crew and contain them aboard their craft until Picard arrives. Contact is to be kept to an absolute minimum, Bashir. Is that quite clear?"

"Why?" The question slipped out before he could stop it. "If it pleases the Khan, these sleepers pose no threat to us. Is there a danger aboard the *Botany Bay* I am not aware of?"

Across the light-years, Tiberius Sejanus narrowed his eyes and glared at Bashir for daring to show such impertinence. "There are many things you are not aware of, *Princeps.*" He put a hard emphasis on Julian's rank. "And that is as it should be."

But still he could not stop himself from asking the question. "The crew of that vessel are living links to the greatest era in our history," he said, the words coming of their own accord, "and they can help us rediscover the missing years of Earth's past. Is that not a glorious discovery, my lord? Surely every citizen in the Khanate should hear what they have to tell us?"

When the Third Khan spoke again, it was with iron in his words. "It is said that the noble Joaquin never once questioned the orders of my grandfather, no matter what they were. Tell me, Bashir. Would you shame your ancestor's bloodline by daring to behave differently?"

Julian's answer never came; the sound of the alert sirens cut off any reply before it had the opportunity to form.

★ ★ ★

Rain had seen jails before. Once, when she and a hundred other refugees were crossing Idaho in an old San Dimas school bus, a group of rangers pulled them off the highway a few dozen miles outside of Glenns Ferry. They took them all into an old military stockade and told them they were out-of-staters, potential terrorists, guilty of illegal border violations, that they had no rights. She remembered the terror, the fear over losing control of her life. Rain thought she would die in those dingy cells, lost and forgotten. She had been imprisoned not because of something she had done, but because of who she was. Some army general had taken control of the state during the chaos of the attacks and decided he didn't like the migrants heading east across his land, with the lethal fallout clouds churning at their backs. Rain and the others, they were guilty of running, guilty of wanting to live; but to the Idaho men they were guilty of being different, and that had been enough.

That old fear uncoiled in her chest, awakening as the trooper shoved her again, marching her into the *Defiance*'s detention level. She saw a corridor of open-faced cells, most of them ringed with a halo of bright light. There was a buzzing in the air, like the noise of an electric motor.

O'Brien was talking to a towering oriental woman. "Status?"

"One of the Cardassians killed himself."

"How?" The tactical officer didn't seem overly concerned, as if he was asking only for the sake of protocol.

"Forced himself into the screen," she said, equally bored with the report. "The shock caused heart failure."

O'Brien shrugged. "Space the corpse, then. We do not need it cluttering up the ship." He turned to leer at Rain. "You are in luck, Basic. A nice new room has just become available." He shot a glance at the trooper. "Put her in."

The coldly familiar desperation tightened around her chest. "You have to let me go back to my ship!" she cried. "You can't hold me here!"

"Oh, we can do whatever we want," O'Brien replied. "We are the superior." He prodded her in the temple with a finger. "Maybe all that sleep made you hard of thinking? Or is your limited mind having trouble grasping the concept?"

"No—" A protest died in her throat as the trooper grabbed Rain by the scruff of her neck and dragged her forward, off her feet.

He pushed her down the corridor, past the glowing doorways. Robinson caught a glimpse of a man slumped against the wall of one of the cells. He gave her a dejected glower. He seemed almost human, except for a strange set of bony ridges across the bridge of his nose.

"Keep moving." The trooper pushed again, and this time Rain stumbled and fell, landing flat in front of another doorway. "Get up!"

She was doing as she was told when a pallid face reared out from the depths of the cell. Rain yelped in fright at the apparition: corpse-gray skin tight across a skull formed from cords of bone, deep-set and accusing eyes glaring at her from dark pits. It looked like a mutilated body, like some horror-flick zombie reanimated and fueled by fury. "Uber scum!" shouted the gray-face. "Let us out of here!"

The trooper slammed his fist toward the open doorway, and Rain jumped as it struck an invisible wall of force, sending crackles of orange sparks flying. "Be silent, you Cardassian weakling!"

"Drop this barrier and we'll see who's the weak one!" The gray-face—*the Cardassian?*—reeled back but didn't retreat, baring its teeth in a jeering grimace. Belatedly, Rain realized it was a female.

"Ocett," said another voice, and Rain turned to see a second Cardassian—this one unmistakably a male—at the barrier of the cell opposite. "Don't give them a reason."

"That's right," snarled the trooper, "do as Dukat tells you, alien."

Ocett spat into the hissing force field and stepped back, her eyes blazing. Rain looked again at the male Cardassian, and he gave her a rueful nod. The small gesture of solidarity, of compassion, was the most human thing she had seen since she had come aboard the *Defiance*.

Robinson was moved on once again, until she stood at the mouth of an open cell. "Please," she begged, some part of her hating the pleading word as it left her lips. But suddenly the guard's attention was distracted.

At the far end of the corridor, the girl with the strange freckles had appeared. She had a gun in her hand.

O'Brien's head snapped up as Dax stepped through the sensor tunnel without waiting for the scan cycle to complete. "What are you doing here, helot? You should be on the command deck at your station." A sneer formed on his lips. "Or perhaps providing the princeps with your services?"

The Tiejun woman didn't join him in his sport. She was absorbed by something on the security console in front of her. The panel sounded a sour tone. "The scanners detected a weapon," she began, her hand already pulling her own phaser from its holster at her hip.

The microgun in Dax's hand discharged with a shriek of noise, and a white pulse of light slammed into the guard's chest, blowing her back against the bulkhead. Her body tumbled away into an untidy heap.

O'Brien came at her; like all of the ubers, he was *quick*. Dax let her size work to her advantage and dodged away, feeling the wind of a haymaker punch as it barely missed her face. The blow would have broken her jaw if it had connected.

But she wasn't fast enough to avoid the follow-up. The optio's other hand cut down and clipped her wrist, knocking the small gun from her fingers, sending it clattering across the deck plates. Pain lanced up her arm and Dax extended into her turn, pirouetting away as O'Brien made a clumsy lunge toward her.

"I never trusted you," he barked, and drew his *bat'leth* from the sheath on his back.

Rain's guard hesitated for a moment as the phaser went off, and she saw the opportunity. Without thinking, she did the same thing she had done whenever a guy had tried to get his own way with her; she brought her knee up hard into his crotch. The impact made the big man grunt, but Rain got a blinding spike of pain down her leg, as if she had hit a brick wall.

He slapped her to the floor like he was swatting an insect. "Armor, idiot," he told her, in a disgusted voice. The guard unhooked a wicked-looking combat knife and left Rain there, walking purposefully toward the unfolding fight at the other end of the corridor with the blade gripped tight in his fingers. He didn't look back at her. She didn't even rate consideration as a threat.

The pain and the guard's condescension got Rain back to her feet, driven by the energy of her anger. Her fear was still there, cold and hard in her chest, but it gave way to something else. A desperation, a need to fight that she had never known back in the dingy cells in Idaho. There, three and a half centuries ago, she had been just another refugee from California. Here and now, she realized she was something different.

A survivor.

Ignoring the pain in her leg, Rain threw herself forward with a grunt of effort.

The prongs of the battle-worn Klingon weapon sliced through the air, and Dax moved like quicksilver, balletic and smooth, almost dancing. O'Brien wasn't aware of it, of course, but she had watched him fight on many occasions since her assignment to the *Defiance*. She understood his techniques, perhaps even better than the optio himself did. O'Brien's fighting style was all about speed and impact, about doing the most damage to his opponent as quickly as he could. He wasn't one for the long bout.

Dax ducked and dodged, seeing his ire grow by the moment as

each attack missed its mark by a tiny span. She was drawing him out, waiting for him to lose his temper and make a mistake.

She didn't have to wait long. "Hold still, you Trill bitch! I'll cut that bloody maggot from your gut and feed it to you!"

The microgun could have killed him if only she still had it. O'Brien had dealt with that quickly, stamping the disk into powder beneath his boot.

"You'll need to do better than this, if that's what you want, Miles." Between panting breaths, Ezri threw him a cocky smile, calculated to irritate. "But then you're a poor crossbreed, aren't you?" She made a mocking sad face. "McPherson and Austin . . . Never the best of the augment bloodlines, either of them. Did your parents really think a mingling would produce something *superior?*"

The optio snarled and brought the *bat'leth* down in an arc of sharpened steel, ripping through the security console in a flash of sparking cables. Belatedly, an alert siren began to sound.

The blow had almost taken Dax's head off, but she played it as if it meant nothing. "But then purity is overrated, don't you think?"

O'Brien's teeth bared in a growl. "How long have you been a traitor to the Khan?" he demanded. "Tell me, so I can carve it on your face before I put that pretty little head of yours in a box."

"How long?" she repeated. "Seven lifetimes' worth, before this." Ezri placed her hand on her chest, backing into the mouth of the cell corridor. "Tobin, Emony, Audrid, Torias, Joran, Curzon, Jadzia . . . All of us defied you in our own ways, and we made sure you arrogant fools never knew it." Suddenly, Ezri felt impossibly old, her bones heavy with the weight of years, the mercy and the warmth of her young soul bled out by Dax's centuries of suffering, of oppression. "Come and kill me if you can, augment. I outlived your mongrel Khan. I will outlive you."

That was enough. O'Brien flew at her, leading with the blade, sweeping it through the air in rolling loops. Dax defied logic and threw herself at him, diving inside his guard and snatching at the middle of the *bat'leth*. The cutting edge bit into her hands, but she used the pain as a spur, and struck out with all her might at the optio's right knee.

Twelve years earlier, on a punitive mission to wipe out a Cardassian colony on Setlik III, Miles O'Brien had been stabbed in that knee by an enemy combatant. The wound had healed, but secondary infection had set in and the joint had never truly been the same. Dax knew this because Jadzia had known it, because Jadzia had been a nondescript medical helot aboard the battleship *Phoenix*, where O'Brien had been assigned at the time.

The line of the old wound sent a bolt of agony into the optio's body and his leg gave out, suddenly robbing him of his balance. Executing a perfect *Mok'bara* pivot—something that Curzon had been taught in his youth—Ezri let the man stumble and fall.

O'Brien collided with the force field across the door of a sealed cell and screamed as the energy field tore into every nerve in his body. He writhed, the *bat'leth* slipping from his fingers, orange sparks crawling across him. Dax retreated, clutching her cut palms.

After a long moment, the human fell away from the glowing partition and collapsed, wisps of thin white smoke issuing out from gaps in his armored suit.

Dax glanced up and met the gaze of a Bajoran man on the other side of the barrier. "They're not so superior after all, are they?" he asked her.

Rain ran and hit the guard full in the back with all her momentum. His feet slipped and he tried to throw her off, but it was too late.

Gravity snared them both, and the guard went down with Robinson atop him, the man's armor-clad form hitting the floor with a bone-shaking shock.

Rain fell off him and struck the deck plates. The guard made a strangled choking noise and was still. A puddle of red began to spread from underneath him.

From behind the shimmering barrier of light, the Cardassian man watched her. "Fell on his blade," he said grimly. "It has a monomolecular edge. Slices through polycarbide plate like a knife through *mapa* bread."

She nodded jerkily, the rage she had felt suddenly spent. The coppery smell of the blood touched her nostrils and she gagged.

Rain heard someone cry out, but the sound seemed foggy and indistinct. She found it difficult to look away from the dead man.

7

Ezri worked quickly, the lowing siren urging her on like the ticks of a clock in the back of her thoughts. First, she opened the panels hiding the main cable trunking that served the detention level's secure doors, and tore out everything that could make them work. Her timing was impeccable; no sooner had she done it than the sound of angry thuds from the other side became audible. *Squad Leader Tiber and his men,* she guessed. It wouldn't take long before they went to the nearby armory for a beam cutter. *Time is against us.*

Using the dermal key implanted in the meat of the Tiejun woman's thumb, Dax deactivated the lockdown and opened all the containment cells at once. A handful of Bajorans and Cardassians stumbled out into the corridor, their body language betraying a mixture of elation, anger, and despair. She saw Kira give the corpse of a fallen guard a swift, brutal kick; and nearby there was Rain, bent over. Dukat was crouching by her side, talking in soft tones.

She went on with her work, reaching into the guts of the control console bifurcated by the wild blow of O'Brien's *bat'leth.* The thug's error had an unexpected benefit; part of the command circuitry he'd smashed controlled the anesthezine nozzles in the ceiling. Unless Tiber found a way to patch the system—which was possible, she had to admit—at least for the moment they were free to move around without fear of being gassed into unconsciousness.

Taking up the Klingon blade, Dax systematically beheaded every sensor cluster in the room. One of Dukat's people, the woman Ocett, stalked toward her as she finished, giving O'Brien's supine form an arch look.

"Huh. Couldn't you have saved one for us?" She eyed the diminutive Trill. "I saw what you did. Impressive, for a woman of your body mass."

"I have had a lot of time to practice," Erzi returned.

"Can we save the back-slapping for later?" Kira bit out, approaching them. She had the dead guard's phaser pistol in her hand, adjusting the energy setting. "Not that I don't appreciate what you've done, but it's an empty gesture if we don't get out of here."

Dax bristled at the Bajoran woman's tone. "You *appreciate* it? Do you have any idea of what I have just done, Nerys? Centuries of work building an airtight deep-cover persona, burned just like that." She snapped her fingers. "Just to get you and your ragged band out of holding."

Kira shook her head. "Don't pretend you did this for us." She looked back down the corridor to where Rain and Dukat were standing. "You're here for her."

Another Bajoran, an older man with a scarred cheek, gestured around. "We need to get back to the *Meru,* light out of here."

"Your ship?" said Dax. "It is wreckage now. They stripped it and blew it apart."

"For fire's sake!" he spat. "Then how the *kosst* are we going to get away?"

"Don't panic, Mace," Ocett said to him. "We'll take this vessel instead."

The man made a scornful face. "A bunch of beaten rebels against a full crew of ubers? I know you Cardassians have a death wish, but you can forget about dragging the rest of us along for the ride. I'll go to the Prophets in my own good time, thanks."

Kira's eyes never left Ezri's. "Dax has a plan. She always does."

"That is right," admitted the Trill, as Robinson walked unsteadily toward them, helped by Dukat. "Rain here is going to give us a lift."

"What?" said the human. She was pale and shaky. Dax found herself wondering just how the other guard had been dealt with. *Did she kill him? She doesn't seem capable of something like that.*

"I take it back." The look on Kira's face was a mix of shock and fury. "Are you making a joke? You're proposing we flee aboard a ship that's almost as old as your symbiont? An unarmed sublight barge with no phasers or shields? Why don't we just open our throats now and be done with it?"

"*Botany Bay* has been fitted with a warp-sled," Ezri corrected firmly, "with a navigational deflector and integrity field generators. It is now FTL-capable."

"And that makes it a match for the *Defiance,* does it?" growled Mace. "I'm starting to wish you had left us in the cells!"

"Focus," said Dukat, his voice cutting through the tension. "If Dax says that she has an escape route for us, then she does. I trust her."

"Even after she got us captured?" snapped the Bajoran man.

"Our capture wasn't her fault." Dukat stepped closer to Kira, and in a strangely tender moment amid all the stress, he kissed her gently. "It was mine," he finished, looking at the deck.

"Skrain's right," said Ocett. "We've got to concentrate. What's our next move?"

Dax had them remove another set of panels from the bulkhead at the far end of the corridor. "There is a maintenance crawlway in here. I set a worm program running to release the hatch bolts. We can access the Gomez tubes and move down-ship, straight to the engineering tiers."

"Better hurry," added Kira, shooting a look toward the main hatch behind them. Fists of bright white sparks were flaring from the edges of the heavy door. "They're cutting their way in."

"How are we going to get to the other ship?" asked Mace.

"Are you gonna use that beamer thing?" Rain looked queasy as she asked the question.

"Teleport," said Dax, "yes. But there are a few things we need to take care of before we leave." She placed a hand on Rain's shoulder. "I need you to keep yourself together for me. Can you do that?"

Robinson's eyes flicked in the direction of the dead man.

"Rain, you only did what you had to, to survive." Dukat spoke in a careful, soothing tone. "Now you have to help us do the same."

She nodded slowly. "Okay."

"What is going on?" demanded the Third Khan. "Bashir! Answer me!"

Julian tapped his communication headset, ignoring the order. "Command deck, Princeps. Status report!"

"Security alert on the detention tier," said Jacob. *"Sir, there appears to have been weapons fire. Monitors are down and the hatchway is sealed. Squad Leader Tiber is attempting to gain entry."*

Tiberius Sejanus Singh's eyes widened with annoyance at the adjutant's words, but Bashir focused on the moment, not on the fury of a man half a galaxy away. "Gas the cells," he ordered.

"Unable to comply, lord. The system has been disengaged."

Julian's face twisted. "Who did this? Show me the playback from the monitor feeds!"

"As you wish."

A pane of phantom glass appeared in midair, wavering to become a distorted fish-eye screen displaying the anteroom of the security chamber. Bashir felt his stomach twist and knot as the images played out. He let out a gasp as Dax murdered the duty officer. *Ezri? It wasn't possible . . .*

"Off," he snapped. *"Off!"* The screen obediently vanished.

"It appears one of your helots is a turncoat and a terrorist." Ice formed on the Khan's pronouncement. "This matter will be dealt with, and you will have a full accounting by the time the *Illustrious* arrives, if you wish to see Earth again!" Before the princeps could respond, the hologram guttered out and vanished.

Julian stood there for a long moment, his mind churning with hard, razor-edged questions. He absently fingered the dominae key in his pocket, wondering at his own mistakes.

Shaun knew their time was up when Amoros arrived on F Deck with Warren and Laker a few steps behind. The expression on the doctor's face was like something carved from granite—hard and uncompromising. They'd found Tomino on the way and given him the nod, telling him to quietly make his way to the bridge, while Christopher and O'Donnel had been trying to work toward the weapons locker. Amoros's appearance put an end to that.

The doctor strode across to the armored guardsmen and spoke urgently to them in low tones. Rudy threw him a look that asked *What's the problem?* and in return, Shaun shook his head slightly. At Laker's side, Reggie Warren stiffened. The guy was ex-USAF, like Christopher, and both men shared the same kind of situational awareness that applied in face-to-face confrontations as much as it did in aerial dogfights. Warrern moved as though he knew something was going to kick off.

Amoros turned and looked Shaun right in the eye. "There is a medical emergency aboard the *Defiance* that requires my immediate presence," he said, and Christopher smelled the lie in there. "I am returning to the vessel immediately." Amoros inclined his head toward the guards. "These men will remain here."

"What about the cryo-systems?" O'Donnel feigned interest in one of the consoles. "Are we waking up anyone else or not?"

The doctor gave Shannon a severe look. "That would be illadvised. This ship has been through an ordeal. It would not be a good idea to tax its systems further." She opened her mouth to say something else, but Amoros tapped his headset. "*Defiance*, transfer," he said, and with a flash of energy, the man dematerialized.

"Holy cow," said Laker, his eyes wide. "Did you see that?"

Christopher ignored him, trying not to wonder what else the matter transport device could do. He was watching one of the troopers. The big man's head was cocked slightly; he was listening to a radio signal over his headset.

"The situation has changed," the man said abruptly. He addressed Shaun. "Assemble your crew on the recreation deck."

"What's going on?" Christopher asked.

"Do it now," the guard told him, and his hand dropped to his pistol. "That is an order."

Warren stepped out, putting himself between the captain and the two guards. "Who the hell do you think you are, buddy? You think you can come in here and throw your damn weight around? I'm getting pretty sick of your attitude." He advanced a step.

Shaun saw Laker's eyes flick to the doorway behind the two men and then away again. *Someone behind them. Hachi?* Who else could it be? He realized that Reggie must have spotted Tomino too, and guessed the way the situation aboard *Botany Bay* was going; his sudden burst of argument was a distraction. Christopher smiled inwardly. Warren caught on quick; that was one of the things he liked about the guy.

"Why don't you boys just step off?" Warren was saying, putting a little swagger into his step.

But the trooper's tolerance snapped and his hand came up, as fast as a striking cobra, with the blunt shape of his weapon there in his fist. "You speak to me that way once more, Basic, and I will put you down."

"Basic?" Laker echoed. "What the heck does that mean?"

"It is what you are," sneered the other man, the taller of the two. "Weak. Useless. Primitive."

"Back on the block, I kicked a guy's ass for less than that—" Warren retorted, and at the same moment Christopher saw a flash of motion. Hachirota plunged into the room, swinging an emergency fire extinguisher with all of his might.

He connected with the taller guard, but the man shook off an impact that would have put down a normal person as if it had been a love tap. His armed companion didn't hesitate; a line of orange-red lightning stabbed out and struck Reggie Warren point-blank in the sternum, the shock of the blast knocking him down.

Everything happened at once. He heard Rudy cry out Reggie's name in astonishment. He was dimly aware of Shannon diving over the console to come to Hachirota's aid. Shaun went in on automatic pilot, swinging hard to plant a punch in the gunman's throat. He got a reaction, but not the one he had hoped for.

The pistol came down toward him and the butt struck his shoulder; a hair to the right and his clavicle would have snapped beneath the impact. His previous words about the odds of their opposition against Bashir's men resonated in his skull; *each one of them as tough as five of us.* Or maybe it was just the sound of his teeth rattling as the trooper cuffed him brutally across the head.

Christopher felt the air rush out of his lungs in a gust of breath as the man slammed him bodily into a control panel. Dials and switches broke against his back. His feet had left the ground somewhere along the way. He threw chopping blows at the trooper's exposed neck, but he couldn't tell if he was doing any good.

His opponent was still holding on to the ray gun. *Why doesn't he just shoot me?* The question pressed itself to the front of his brain, and the answer followed quickly, as he saw the feral grin on the trooper's lips. *Because he's enjoying this, that's why.*

Dax knew the route without needing to think about it. Navigating the interior of the *Defiance*'s maintenance tubes was a skill she had perfected within weeks of being assigned aboard the ship; part of her mission remit had been to plant listening devices and gather intelligence about this class of Khanate starships, and in the process she'd learned the layout by rote. The escapees—Ezri and Rain, Dukat and Kira and the others—were a ragged bunch.

Dax was already aware that some were flagging, still suffering the effects of harsh interrogations at the hands of the ubers.

She kicked out a vent, and one by one they dropped into an auxiliary cargo store two tiers down from the detention level. The sound of the alert sirens was clear through the hatch.

"We need more weapons." Ocett pawed through the containers around them, searching for something she could use to do damage. The only pistols they had were in Dukat's and Kira's hands.

Dax went to the door controls and set to work on them. She had already surrendered O'Brien's *bat'leth* to the scarred Bajoran, Mace. He stood across from her, his ear pressed to the duranium hatch.

"What happens now?" asked Rain, kneading her hands.

"We are on the central engineering deck," explained Ezri. "We will need to break into two groups and hobble the ship before we go any further."

"How can we do that?" asked one of the other Cardassians.

"The warp core," said Dukat, catching on. "If we can disable it . . . the *Defiance* would be unable to go to lightspeed."

Dax nodded. "Exactly. The hard part is going to be getting to it."

Mace held up his hand in warning, his ear pressed to the duranium hatch. "Someone's coming!"

"Hide!" snapped Kira, and the group went for what little cover there was behind cargo drums and support pillars. Dax dropped down low, beneath eye level, as Mace pulled the Klingon blade to his chest and tucked into the lee of the hatchway.

The door retracted, and Ezri caught the last part of a conversation.

"Just get it done," said an angry voice, retreating down the corridor outside. *Sisko,* thought Dax, *Bashir's adjutant.* "The Trill did something to the internal sensors. They take priority." The threat of punishment hung silently on the words.

"Yes, lord," came the brusque reply, as a blue-skinned figure entered the compartment.

The hatch was barely closed behind Rel sh'Zenne when Mace came out of the shadows, sweeping the *bat'leth* at the Andorian's throat.

"No!" Dax shouted, and the Bajoran pulled his blow to a halt.

Fixed in place, the engineer turned her head to glare at Ezri, her antennae stiffening in surprise. "You," she said. "You are a dead woman." She didn't say it as a threat; she said it more as a pronouncement, as something she already knew was a fact.

"I beg to differ, Rel," Ezri returned.

"You know her?" asked Kira, emerging with phaser at the ready.

"I would like to think so." Dax pushed Mace's blade away.

"Oh. Wow." Rain blinked. "She's . . . blue."

"Tiber has men sweeping the ship from bow to stern," said sh'Zenne. "He has offered a personal bounty to any trooper who captures you." She hesitated. "Is it true? Did you really kill the optio?"

"He did not give me a choice."

After a moment, the Andorian nodded. "Good. Arrogant bastard. He had it coming."

Dax took a chance. "Help us."

"I am helping you right now by not screaming for security," said Rel.

Ocett gave a derisive snort. "*Huh.* Typical Andorian. Good little dogs for the ubers, the lot of them."

The engineer glared at Kira, the antennae on her head flattening against her skull in annoyance. "Tell your woman to keep her mouth shut, unless she wants me to knock the teeth out of it."

"You're worse than the humans," Kira said. "At least they can't help being conceited—they've bred it into themselves. But you? Your species willingly bent the knee to Noonien Singh, and for what? So you could live out your lives as second-class citizens, doing all the dirty jobs the ubers think are beneath them?"

"You know nothing about what they did to Andor," said sh'Zenne, her voice as hard as ice. She looked at the Trill. "This is the company you are keeping, Dax?" Rel shook her head. "What is wrong with you? Have you gone mad?" She pointed at Ezri's chest. "Has that thing inside you finally gone senile?"

A dry smile of amusement crossed Dax's face. "It is . . . complicated."

"In all the time I have known you, you have never raised your head," said Rel. "Not like me, talking out of turn and getting slapped down for it." The Andorian touched the copper torc around her throat, a mirror of the one worn by Ezri. "Why this, why now, for *them?*" She gave Kira, Rain, and the others a cursory nod. "Explain it to me."

"We're wasting our time with her," Mace said, hefting the *bat'leth*. "Let me deal with the blue-skin and we'll be on our way."

"*No.*" Dax's retort had steel in it. "You want the truth? I will give it to you." She sighed. "I am with the resistance. Dax . . . the Dax symbiont has been there since the very beginning. I have been fighting the Khanate for nearly three hundred years."

"I don't understand," Robinson said quietly.

Dukat spoke out of the side of his mouth. "She's the host for a symbiotic intelligence. Ezri is the body. Dax is the memory."

"Oh, right. I get it," Rain replied, in a way that made it obvious she didn't.

"But you are Bashir's helot," Rel went on. "His concubine."

"I am a spy. But now that is done with. Now I am a dissident, the same as them." She nodded at Kira and the others. "And we need your help. *All* of us."

Sh'Zenne seemed suddenly tired, and Dax saw the hesitation in her eyes. "What can you do? Of course there have been times when I wanted to defy Bashir and the others. . . . I thought about disengaging the safeties and letting this ship rip itself to bits. . . . But I have family on Andor, and they would be made to suffer.

Destroying one ship will make no difference, Ezri. The humans are too strong. We cannot win against them."

"This is bigger than you know, Rel," Dax told her. "Rain's people have something that is going to tip the balance. Something that will show the galaxy what the Children of Khan really are."

"We do," said Robinson, her voice piping up. "We have the truth about Khan Noonien Singh. And we're gonna tell *everyone.*"

Dax held out her hand. "Help us," she repeated.

On some level, Hachi was marveling at the number of dents the fire extinguisher was collecting and the fact that the tall trooper *just wouldn't fall down.* He was holding Shannon by a fistful of the pilot's flight suit and choking the air from her lungs. Tomino blinked; it looked like she was turning white, but he could barely see straight. Hachi's face was already a mess of bruises, his spectacles still clinging to his face, one lens a broken spider web of glass.

He blotted everything else out of his mind: Warren lying there on the deck with Rudy at his side, Shaun being pummeled to within an inch of his life across the room. Tomino put that all aside and channeled every ounce of his strength into a spinning blow that placed the blunt nozzle end of the extinguisher right into the base of the trooper's skull.

Hachirota was rewarded with a dull cracking sound, and the tall man abruptly went slack, like a discarded puppet. He fell forward, crushing the coughing O'Donnel against a console. Tomino moved without thinking, ripping the strange pistol from the trooper's holster.

The gun was bulky but lightweight, and it sat easily in his hand. He tried not to think about what he had just done—and then he did it again.

The trigger pull was slight, and there was no recoil. Just a shrill keening sound, a flash of amber, and the man trying to beat Shaun Christopher to death collapsed with a strangled cry.

Tomino stared at the pistol and felt sick. He tried to release his grip, but it refused to move. It was as if the thing had welded itself to him, as if his use of the weapon had made him part of it.

Slender fingers with raw, bloody knuckles came and pried his hand open. He looked up at Shannon and she nodded at him, her breath coming in gasps through a bruised throat. "Easy, Hachi. I got this." She took the gun away from him, and he settled heavily to the deck plates, his eyes hazing.

"Sorry," he said to the air.

Shaun took the gun from Shannon and rubbed his chest, probing gently for broken ribs. "What do we do now, Captain?" she asked him, taking the other trooper's pistol for herself. He glanced at her. O'Donnel only ever used his rank when the situation was a bad one. He had to admit, this was the worst.

"Reggie?" he asked.

Rudy looked up at him and shook his head, the man's big eyes shimmering. "Warren's dead."

Christopher took the grim news with a wooden nod. "Put him in medical. We'll see to him later."

"Later?" Laker was blinking furiously. "Is there even gonna be a later?"

"*Rudy,*" Shannon said firmly. "Do what the captain says. Hachi, help him."

"Right," said Tomino, moving like he had woken from a daze. In a moment, it was just the two of them there in the room with the men who had tried to kill them. "We're not leaving without Rain," Shaun said, with finality. "We've lost too many people already. We get her back, and then we go."

"Where?"

"I'll figure that out when we get there."

Sh'Zenne entered the *Defiance*'s main engineering chamber at a quick pace, her antennae erect and her dark eyes hooded. The

first person she encountered was Glov, one of the Tellarite ser-
viles. "You," she barked. "Assemble the crew and get them out of
there. I'm sealing off the compartment."

Glov gave her a porcine blink. "What? Why? The systems are
functioning within normal parameters—"

"Why do your kind have to argue about everything?" she
snapped back at him. "An order is an order. Do it now!"

The Tellarite heard the tone in her voice, the sharp edge that
told him this was one of *those* commands, a directive that he had
better obey if he wanted to go another five minutes without a
beating. He scrambled away, and Rel's gaze swept the room.
Every technician and operative down in the engine core was a
nonhuman helot. Mostly hardworking Tellarites like Glov, along
with a Vulcan, a Son'a, and a team of morose Ferengi; the Earthers didn't stray down here too often, as if they thought the running of the warp core was beneath them. Sh'Zenne suspected that
the truth was far more pragmatic—she had heard rumors that
prolonged exposure to the churning energies of a matter/antimat-
ter reaction was detrimental to their augmented genetic makeup.
Whatever the reason, the engine room was belowdecks territory,
and helot country.

All of which made her tense when she spotted the trooper in
black duty armor standing with a weapon at the ready by the main
systems console. Rel recognized the characteristic blond hair and
arching cheekbones of an Ericsson bloodline.

"Subaltern!" said the trooper, approaching her. "What is going
on here?" The woman gestured to Glov as he scuttled about the
perimeter of the room.

"A lockdown," said sh'Zenne, walking straight past her to the
warp core monitor display. "The escapees from the detention
decks are suspected to be heading toward this level. The princeps
wants us to secure the engine core in case they try to sabotage the
ship." She started calling up control menus on the screen.

"I was not informed," snapped the trooper, reaching up to tap her headset communicator rig. "Do nothing until I have confirmation."

Rel turned and glared at the woman, her face turning a dark cerulean. "With respect, I am the chief engineer," she retorted, "and this must be done now!"

"You are an alien," came the trooper's reply, slow and careful as if she were talking to a retarded child, "and I am a human. You are subordinate to me." She looked away. "That is all that you need to know."

"I suppose it is," began the Andorian, as raggedly dressed figures dropped from the shadows of the maintenance catwalks in the ceiling.

To her credit, the Ericsson woman was quick. *"Alert!"* she snapped, bringing up her weapon. "Security breach in—"

The trooper's words were cut off as sh'Zenne struck the human across the temple with the hyperspanner she had concealed down her sleeve. The blow knocked the communicator headset off her and sent the woman staggering.

"Who did you say was in charge?" spat the Andorian. In her darker, most secret moments, Rel had often wondered what it might be like to kill one of the humans. When the princeps called upon her to spar with him, she sometimes imagined the consequences of taking the fight to the furthest conclusion; but she had always stepped back, always halted. Bashir would have seen the thought in her eyes; but this one? This one lacked the skill and insight of the princeps.

Glov and the others hesitated at the doors to the corridor, unsure of what to do in the face of the subaltern's act of open defiance. The Cardassian woman, Ocett, brandished a stolen pistol at them. "What are you waiting for?" she snarled. "Get out, before I put a stun bolt up your backsides!"

"Filthy . . . blueskin . . ." moaned the trooper. "You're all . . . worthless."

A sudden flash of anger, white-hot and murderous, lanced

through her. Rel lashed out again, and this time the blow put the human out for good.

"You looked like you enjoyed that." The Bajoran who carried the optio's old *bat'leth* came closer.

She shot him a leaden look, but he was right. It *had* felt good; and suddenly, she wanted to do it again. Rel wanted to cause them pain, every human, every uber on the ship. Her fingers went to her collar. Although it was still around her neck, she felt as if she had just torn it away, ripped it apart along with a lifetime of servitude.

"Help me with this," she told the Bajoran. She pointed at an identical console on the far side of the room. "You see that?" He nodded, cautiously eyeing the thrumming column of blue-white energy contained inside the warp core. "Get over there, and follow the sequence I set in motion. Do it now."

He nodded and sprinted across the chamber. From behind her, sh'Zenne heard the Cardassian call out. "They're all out. What now?"

"Seal the blast door," she told her. "Green panel, by the injector matrix monitor."

"I see it." Ocett stabbed at the controls with her long-fingered hands. Alarm chimes, singing out at a different tone from the security alert already in progress, began a warble as the door dropped from the ceiling, cutting off main engineering from the rest of the vessel. The heavy duraplast gate was designed to deploy in the event of a plasma leak or energy surge; it would be enough to keep out any more of Tiber's troopers until their sabotage was done.

Rel found it strangely easy to do; some small, curious part of her wondered how she would survive the crime she was enacting, but for the most part her mind concentrated wholly on the deed. It was as if she had been waiting her whole life for this moment.

"There," said Dax, as the sound of the alert siren reached them. "Rel has done it."

"Now what?" demanded Kira.

"Now we steal the key to our escape." The Trill started off down the corridor at a run. "This way, quickly!"

Nerys came after her, with Dukat and Rain at their heels. The human girl lagged back, panting.

"Let me help you," said the Cardassian, and Skrain took her arm.

She blinked at him. "Sorry. Sorry. Just . . . got no energy. I think it's the wine and the cryo-sleep lag. My legs feel like lead and I want to puke."

"You're doing fine," said Dukat. "I don't think I would be as brave as you if the circumstances were reversed." He smiled at her, showing flat, white teeth. "I can only imagine what you must be feeling."

"Oh, it's cool," Rain said, her voice breathy, "aliens and spaceships, people shooting at me. Walk in the park." She swallowed hard. "Ugh."

"Quiet!" Kira threw the word over her shoulder. The four of them drew back into an alcove. A few meters ahead, the corridor branched to the right and ended in a security door. "That's it?"

Dax nodded. "In there."

"Cool," repeated Rain, wondering just what it was they were risking their lives to find. "But how do we get past those two bruisers outside?"

A pair of armored troopers, each of them holding a fully charged phaser rifle, stood at parade-ground attention either side of the hatchway.

Dax had done well. As sh'Zenne ran through the protocols, she found dozens of places where security encryptions and data blocks were missing. Normally, what the Andorian was about to do would have required multiple authorizations from senior human crew members, but the Trill had been as good as her word. Rel felt a small tug of irritation; the sad, docile little helot was nothing of the kind. She had fooled all of them, sh'Zenne included, worming dozens of viral programs into the computers Rel worked with every day, with such subtlety and finesse that the engineer had never known it. In a way, she had to admire Ezri for her daring, but by the same token she cursed her own negligence for failing to see any signs of the interference.

Three hundred years of hiding in plain sight, though, Rel thought. *With that much practice, is it any wonder we never suspected her?*

"Ejection circuit bypass is complete," called Ocett, her reedy voice carrying over the hard rhythmic growl of the warp core reaction. "Ready on this end."

"Good." Rel looked up, through the transparent observation window and into the area beyond, where the core bisected the room like a glowing rod of light. There was no sign of the Bajoran at the tertiary console where she had told him to stand.

Sh'Zenne started, throwing her gaze around, looking up at the overhead catwalks, down to the maintenance pits. The man was gone. She swore an epithet under her breath and stabbed at her panel, setting the programmed sequence running, and dashed out across the decking.

Activation lights were blinking fiercely, demanding her attention. The damned fool hadn't done anything! Rel's blue fingers danced over the surface of the console, tapping out the command string. The heel of her hand touched the panel, and she felt wetness. The Andorian turned her palm over and there was red liquid on it. It smelled of copper.

Small perturbations in the air touched her antennae, motions generated by subtle pressures other than the deep subsonic rumble of the core. She ducked and pivoted in time to avoid the stabbing blow of a ship-issue short sword.

Another trooper! A man this time, a Dhasal clanner by the look of him. The human compensated for the miss and tried to cut her, but Rel slid away from his reach. Too late she realized that he was pushing her into a corner, cutting off her escape routes. Her boot skidded slightly on another wet patch, and the copper smell touched her nostrils again. A heaped shape protruded from behind the cover of one of the plasma conduits: the Bajoran man, dead from a slit throat, lying discarded with the careworn *bat'leth* on the deck by his corpse.

How had she missed the human? *Of course there would be a second trooper!* But Rel had been too caught up in her new and daring rebellion to think that far ahead. Masked by the pulsing beat of the warp core, any death cry the Bajoran might have made would never have reached her. She thought about calling out to Ocett, but sh'Zenne knew this would be over before the Cardassian could reach her.

No. There is only one way this can end now.

The trooper shook his head grimly. "I would have expected this from one of the others, but an Andorian?" He gestured with the still-wet blade. "Didn't we train you people better than that?"

"Apparently not," she said, and threw herself toward the console.

★ ★ ★

As they raced down the corridor past him, Bashir grabbed one of the men by his arm and dragged him closer. "Report!" he barked.

"Princeps!" gasped the trooper. "The . . . the internal sensors are still down, lord. Some sort of sabotage program in the mainframe. Adjutant Sisko is attempting to fix it as we speak."

"Where are the dissidents?" he demanded. "Where . . . where is Dax?"

"Still at large. Squad Leader Tiber has locked off the bridge and the shuttlebay," continued the man. "We're sweeping down the ship, level by level."

"Belay that," Bashir growled. "Double the guard on the armory and main—"

Tiber's gruff, urgent tones interrupted him, crackling over the ship's internal communications net. *"All details, alert! Engine room does not answer security! Get a team down there, now!"*

"Too late," spat the commander, shoving the trooper away. "Too late!"

Dax walked slowly around the corner with her hands raised. Immediately, the two troopers guarding the hatch brought up their guns and took aim. Targeting lasers danced on her chest, wavering over her heart. "I am unarmed," she began.

"Stay where you are," said the senior of the two. "Take another step and I will burn you down."

"You do not want to do that," Ezri told them. "I have activated the *Defiance*'s corbomite self-destruct mechanism. It will atomize this vessel in under six minutes, unless you do exactly what I say."

The other trooper brought his gun to his shoulder and sighted through the scope, the laser dot moving to a point on her forehead. "Impossible."

"You are bluffing," added the first. "The ship has no such system."

"Are you really willing to take that risk?" She closed the distance between them, resisting the urge to shoot a look back to the alcove, where Kira and the others were concealed.

"Yes," said the senior trooper. "Kill her."

Rel fell against the panel and struck the three keypads in the correct order, the consequences of the choice she had made suddenly slamming into her thoughts. She barely had an instant to articulate them before burning, white-hot pain turned her nerves into an inferno.

The blade of the short sword entered her back where her hexaribs connected to her spine, breaking hard bone and piercing the lower lobe of her left lung. Her mouth filled with a foamy cyan fluid that spilled from her lips, trickling across the console to mingle with the blood of the dead Bajoran. Sh'Zenne fell forward off the blade of the sword and spun away, her legs turning to water. She hit the deck and landed at the trooper's feet as he raised the blade for the killing blow. The throbbing light from the matter/antimatter pillar cast dull illumination over the Dhasal man. Rel thought she heard Ocett calling out, but then the wind came.

It shrieked and tore at everything around them, every small loose item in the engine chamber suddenly taking to the air and racing across the space. With hissing flashes of spent power, the warp core dropped through the deck, trailing sparking cables behind it. The trooper pivoted, shock frozen on his face, as the full understanding of what the Andorian had done came to him.

Hull plating on the ventral fuselage of the *Defiance* exploded away on emergency ejection charges, allowing the entirety of the warp core mechanism to detach and follow it out into the void. Normally, the expulsion of the core was a last-ditch option employed if a critical, unstoppable overload was in progress, but Dax had laid a path for sh'Zenne to exploit. With a few commands, she had disengaged the safety interlocks—including the emergency force field that should have sealed the ejection port closed after the core vented. The ship's systems were thrown for a loop as the main power was abruptly torn away, and lights and functions across every deck of the *Defiance* dimmed as one.

But for Rel sh'Zenne there was only the storm; the *razor-storm*. She remembered it with punishing clarity, the blinding fines of sleet that fell from the ice hurricanes off the Tavda Mountains, near the settlement where she had been born. Here in this human ship, it returned again and tore at her blue flesh, screaming and howling. She watched as the trooper tumbled backward and away, into the pull of the storm, over the lip of the gantry and gone. Rel felt the wind take her as well, pulling her off the deck, her numbed legs twisting beneath her. Her skull slammed against a stanchion and Rel felt her right antenna snap, lighting pinwheels of new, lancing pain.

The storm carried her into the empty cradle where the core had stood and she plunged downward, dragged into the black and bitter cold of space, dreaming of Andor.

Power ebbed and automatic mechanisms scrambled to switch *Defiance* over to backup generators and battery stores. The illumination panels in the corridor's ceiling blinked and went out, plunging Dax and the troopers into darkness. The Trill threw herself away from the probing red threads of the targeting beams, down to the floor in a tuck and roll, clearing the way for an open field of fire. Distracted by Dax, the troopers were exposed to beam fire from Skrain Dukat's stolen pistol.

Bright spears of energy flashed over Ezri's head, and the short, brutal engagement became a series of strobe-effect afterimages on her retinas. Each phaser bolt threw millisecond-fast flashes of light about the passageway, casting jumping shadows in hard, stark outlines. She heard a muffled scream and the wet tearing of cut flesh; the concussive energy transfer as a beam struck a living target; the clatter of a falling body.

It was all over in heartbeats, and like a rising curtain, the warship's power train reset itself and brought the illuminators in the corridor back to operational power. The first thing Dax saw was Kira Nerys pulling a knife from the body of the senior trooper's slumped corpse, the blade inserted in the thin gap between the plates of duraplast mesh. His companion lay next to him, an ugly, smoking crater in the center of his armor's chest plate.

"Oh god." Rain had kept back, as Dax had told her to, hiding in the lee of the alcove while Ezri and the resistance fighters took on the human troopers. But now she stood, her hand at her mouth, over the Cardassian. Dukat was against the floor, a streak of blood arrowing down at him where he had slid across the wall. The pale gray skin of his face was blackened where the nimbus of a high-power phaser bolt had slammed into him.

Kira dropped the knife and flew to Dukat's side. "Skrain! *Skrain!*"

He coughed and shuddered, trembling with agony. "Nerys. It's . . . still dark." Dax realized that the beam blast must have blinded him.

"Skrain . . ." Tears streamed from Kira's eyes, cutting tracks through the patina of dirt on her cheeks.

Dax found Rain looking at her, the question she couldn't utter in Robinson's expression. Ezri shook her head, ever so slightly.

The Trill watched the strong, vital woman she had seen in the holding cell disintegrate by degrees. Kira Nerys, warrior and freedom fighter, the most wanted terrorist of the Bajor Sector, fell to pieces in front of her, holding the Cardassian to her chest. Dukat coughed again and touched at her face, tracing the lines of her tears.

"Nerys, my love," he said huskily. "You mustn't . . . Don't dwell. Don't wait for me again." He shook his head. "You should go."

"No." The single word contained an ocean of heartache.

"Yes," he replied. "Yes. Take the . . . human girl. Go with Dax. You know what must . . . be done." Dukat's head bobbed, as if he were agreeing with something. His lips parted to say more, but only a faint gasp emerged.

The moment turned brittle and long, but it ended with Kira drawing a hand across her face, wiping away the last of her tears. She stood stiffly, letting the Cardassian's hand drop to the deck from where she had held it.

"This way," said Dax, opening the hatch and moving through it. "We don't have much time."

Rain followed Kira, unable to meet the churn of emotion tumbling in the Bajoran's eyes.

The compartment beyond the hatch was a hexagonal chamber surrounding a single piece of equipment. Set on a narrow dais, a spherical module made from a translucent white material pulsed quietly. A power nexus at either pole blinked with systems displays, and rods of monitor gear surrounded it in a cage of technology. The device had a slightly out-of-place look to it, as if it had its origins in the science of a different culture.

"Help me deactivate the interlocks," Dax ordered, keeping her voice level, giving Kira something to focus on. The Bajoran set to work without saying anything.

"What is that thing?" asked Robinson.

Dax didn't look up from the console. "We call it a cloaking device."

Squad Leader Tiber snapped into a salute as the princeps approached him. Bashir's expression was stormy; Tiber couldn't recall a time when he had seen such naked fury on his commander's face. He bowed his head automatically. "My lord, a number of the escapees have been terminated, but—"

"Spare me," Bashir snarled. "I want answers, now!" He stabbed a finger at the heavy drop-hatch across the entrance to the engine room.

"The chamber has been vented to space," Tiber reported. "The warp core was ejected."

"Dax!" He spat out the helot's name.

Tiber shook his head. "Uh, no, sir. It appears that Subaltern sh'Zenne was responsible. She locked off the compartment. Two of my troopers were in there with her, but they were lost—"

"Where is Dax?" Bashir demanded.

"Not there, lord. Scanners show others were inside in the compartment at the time of decompression, a Bajoran male and a Cardassian female—"

"*You are pathetic!*" Bashir exploded with fury, and Tiber recoiled as if he had been struck. "What kind of soldier are you, man? These inferiors are running rings around us! You are supposed to be their better!"

"The helot has seeded the ship's systems with a viral program!" Tiber tried to defend himself. "Her access to the *Defiance*'s controls allowed her to lay traps!"

Bashir prodded Tiber in the chest. "Is that an accusation, Squad Leader? Are you blaming me for your lack of vigilance?"

The senior trooper balanced on the edge of voicing the culpability he knew should be laid at his commander's feet. Not a single officer aboard the ship would disagree with him if he did, but still he could not bring himself to openly defy a sworn princeps of the Khanate.

No. That would be beyond a squad leader's remit. Instead, Tiber bowed his head and shook it. When Picard arrived aboard the *Illustrious,* there would be more than enough blame to be apportioned, and Bashir would have to answer for his indulgence toward the aliens.

"If Dax is not here, then where is she?"

"Transporter rooms, airlocks, and shuttlebays are all secure. She has not left this vessel," Tiber replied, keeping his voice flat.

Then the squad leader saw a flash of understanding in the eyes of the princeps. "Make sure you keep this area secure!" Bashir shouted, breaking into a run. "She may have sympathizers among the other helot crew!"

Tiber took a step after him. "Lord, where are you going?"

The princeps had his sword and gun drawn, and he ran on without giving him the grace of an answer. Tiber grimaced and went after his commander.

"Done," said Kira quietly.

A series of metallic claws around the upper and lower regulator modules sighed open, and the energy moving through the cloaking device stuttered and died. Warning lights immediately began to blink on the console dais.

Ezri gave Rain a nod. "It is inert now. Twist the mountings, it will detach."

Gingerly, the human woman cupped the spherical device between her palms and pulled. There was a snap of static discharge, and then Robinson had the unit clutched to her chest. "It's light," she said, surprise in her tone.

Dax nodded distractedly. "Most of the wave-functionality of the unit occurs in subspace. It's little more than a glorified antenna array."

Kira was looking at the gun in her hand. "They'll know we've done this. Bashir's men will be here in seconds." She glanced up. "I can destroy the module with a single shot."

"If I had wanted to destroy it, I would have done that the moment we entered the room," Dax replied. "We are taking it." A humorless smirk tugged briefly at the corner of her lip. *Just like Noonien Singh did, when he stole one for Earthfleet from the Romulan commander he seduced and murdered.* She beckoned the two women closer. "Come here. You need to be within the field radius if this is going to work." Ezri reached inside her tunic, feeling for a concealed skin-pocket. The surgical alteration had been done shortly before she was joined with the Dax symbiont, and the pouch of synthetic flesh was virtually undetectable except by the most invasive of medical examinations. She bit back a jolt of pain as her fingers probed for the seam and found it; within, her fingers closed around a small disk concealed there.

"What are you doing?" asked Rain, horrified.

Dax said nothing. The skin ripped slightly as she removed the object, and she gasped. Inert fluids coated the surface, and Ezri wiped them away with her thumb. "Closer," she said. "I need you to be close to me." The device sensed the warmth of her fingers and opened itself along its length, revealing a blinking activation stud.

"Beacon?" asked Kira in a dull voice.

Dax shook her head. "A prototype emergency transporter device, microminiaturized. A single-use unit. The power output is so extreme that it burns itself out after one pulse."

Rain blinked. "That thing's a teleporter? It's no bigger than a quarter!"

"The design was copied by a Vulcan agent from the Khanate's own testing laboratories. I have already preprogrammed the destination coordinates."

Nerys advanced on her. "A transporter? You had a transporter on you all along, and you waited until now to tell us?" She raised the gun. "We could have beamed out straight from the security tier!" Kira shot a pained look at the door and the bodies that lay on the other side of it.

"No," Dax said sadly. "We were too deep inside the ship. And the unit's field effect isn't designed for more than one or two signatures . . . Frankly, I am not even sure if it will manage all three of us."

"Then you stay!" Kira leveled the gun at Dax's head. "Stay here and perish, just like you let Skrain die!"

"She didn't kill him," said Rain.

"Shut up!" snarled the Bajoran. "Don't be fooled by her! Ezri, the youthful, quiet little woman . . . She's a sham, a mask for that callous old worm in her chest!" Kira blinked back fresh tears. "She never intended to get Ocett or Mace or the others out! Beneath all that, she's heartless! Dax doesn't care about any one of us . . . Just her damned mission!"

"Yes," said Ezri. "That is true. That is what I am, a liar and a fake. I have never tried to be anything else, Nerys. Because I know that my mission is more important than my life, your life . . . Skrain's life."

Kira gripped the gun tightly. "Don't say his name again!"

And then the Trill's face shifted, and the saddened aspect that she wore fell away; she let them see the real Dax, just for a brief moment. When she spoke again, every word was hard-edged and cold. "Do you want to stay here and join him? Do you want to waste his sacrifice, or do you want to come with me and make his killers pay tenfold for it?"

The Bajoran's gun dropped away. "Fire's sake, you are a hateful one. I thought I knew enmity, but you're steeped in it."

"That is what my mission requires of me." Dax twisted the microdevice, and it emitted a pulsing whine. "Get ready."

The three of them sharing looks of conflicting emotion, Rain and Kira and Ezri clustered together. Yellow-gold radiosity flared out from the transporter, and it expanded to envelop them in a haze of glittering color.

As the interior of the *Defiance* melted away around them, Dax was dimly aware of a figure bursting through the hatchway. She caught an accusing stare, but then the face was gone, lost in the fog of transit.

"Ezri!" Bashir bellowed her name and reached out to snatch at her, but the matter transport cycle was too far advanced, and all he took was a handful of empty air. His heart turned stony in his chest; he had looked her in the eye just as she dematerialized. And there . . . There he had seen it. The truth. The punishing reality.

It was like a knife blade being pushed with even, gentle pressure through the plates of his armor and into the meat and bone of his chest. The knowledge, cutting his heart, opening him. The princeps staggered to a halt, his hand curling into a fist.

"They stole the cloaking module," Tiber said angrily. "First they disable the ship, then they take away our defenses." He snorted. "I did not think a Trill capable of such base cunning."

"Then you are as much a fool as I am!" Bashir shouted, stunning the squad leader into silence.

He leaned forward against the empty support frame, his hands tensing on the metal bars. They bent beneath the pressure of his powerful grip as the tension in him grew worse. Julian wanted to rip the thing to pieces and smash everything he could see. A directionless rage welled up inside him.

Her eyes.

Ezri's gaze, that momentary spark of contact between them. It was enough to shatter his self-control. He could hardly stand to form the thought in his mind, and yet he could not deny it.

All this time he had been with her, worked with her, lay with her, and looked into her eyes over and over again, supremely confident that he *knew* the color of her loyalty, with ironclad certainty. She could not lie to him; no one could. It was Julian Bashir's unyielding sight, his ability to turn the light of his will upon those around him and never be wrong. *No one can hide a lie from me,* he told himself. *No one!*

No one but her, it would seem.

Nothing in Julian's life had prepared him for this moment. He stared down at his clean, hard-worked hands, as if they belonged to someone else. How was it possible, for a woman he had shared his bed with, a woman who—in his own way—he had actually *cared* for, to be able to deceive him?

More than anything, he wanted to believe that he had been mistaken somehow, that perhaps there was some other explanation for this chain of events. *It is some kind of duplicate of her, perhaps Sisko's shape-shifter taking on her form or some other kind of subterfuge . . .* Bashir's thoughts groped at any avenue of explanation, desperate to find a way to put aside what he knew was the certainty of the matter.

Her eyes.

As the transporter spirited her away, she had been unguarded and open in a way that he had never seen before, not in all the time she had served him.

"She lied to me," he whispered so quietly that Tiber could not hear his words. "She has lied to me from the very start." The depths of Bashir's failure rose up around him, the blood rushing in his ears. When Picard arrived, when the Khan learned the full measure of his error, Julian would not even be granted the honor of a soldier's death. He would be lucky if the commander of the *Illustrious* did not vent him to space like the corpse of a fallen helot.

He became aware of Tiber speaking into his headset, and he turned on the squad leader. "Who are you talking to?" he demanded.

"Adjutant Sisko," said the senior trooper. "With your permission, Princeps, I thought he might be able to track the teleporter's energy signature . . ."

Bashir drew himself up, forcing down the thunder of self-recriminations echoing in his mind. "No need." He bit out the words. "There's only one place she could have gone." Slamming his sword back into its scabbard, he pushed past Tiber and stalked away, his hands in tight, white-knuckled fists.

"What the hell is going on over there?" Shannon used the optical scopes to range along the hull of the *Defiance,* peering toward the reflective viewports of the warship, which was separated from the *Botany Bay* by only a few hundred meters. She could see most of the lower hull of the vessel, including the train of frozen gas that streamed out from the circular vent along the midline.

Shaun was at her shoulder. He had seen the panel blow off and tumble away into space; then both of them watched the glowing mechanism follow it out from the hull and drift off. At first, Christopher had thought the thing might have been some kind of weapon deployment, but then the bodies drifted out afterward, and they quickly understood that they were watching an accident unfold.

"Or maybe sabotage," offered Hachirota. Rudy stood by his side, silent and morose.

Shannon shot Shaun a look. "Dax?"

"She said she had a plan," the captain noted, but his tone belied his belief. O'Donnel knew him well enough to know that Shaun Christopher wasn't the kind of man who waited on others to get things done. It was one of the reasons Wilson Evergreen had picked him to captain the *Botany Bay*. He turned to Laker. "That drive sled they bolted to our hull . . . Any ideas on how it works?"

Rudy blanched. "I don't know. The power train looks relatively simple, but the engines . . . Ah, I feel like a caveman looking at a V8. I don't even know where to start."

"You're a nuclear physicist, Rudy," Shannon said sharply, "one of the smartest guys around. Help me figure it out."

But Laker shook his head. "I don't feel so smart anymore."

"Forget that!" Tomino cried, gripping a heavy spanner in his hand like a club. "We got company!"

The perturbation of the air oscillated around the cabin and Shannon turned from the scope to see a sparkling golden cloud emerge from thin air. *The teleport!* But this time the field effect was different, the cycle longer and more labored. O'Donnel wondered how safe the technology was. What error could a malfunction in matter displacement cause? What would a software glitch do to living tissue? The very idea made her stomach turn over.

"Rain!" Rudy called out the girl's name as the transport field melted away. She had a weird-looking device in her hand and her expression . . . Shannon saw the new distance in Robinson's gaze, and she wondered what kind of horrors Rain must have seen aboard the *Defiance.*

Dax was with her, along with another female. Like the speckle-patterned woman, she seemed human enough, except for a striated ridge on her nose. The new arrival caught O'Donnel staring at her and growled. "Seen enough?"

"Who's this?" demanded Shaun.

"Kira Nerys," Rain explained. "She's, uh, with us."

The woman glared at Dax. *"This* is your escape route? An ancient derelict crewed by time-lost humans."

"I grow weary of your attitude," Dax retorted, and Shannon heard a marked change in her words. "They need your help, Kira. Show them how to operate the impulse motor and the warp drives. Otherwise, we give up and wait for Bashir's men to repair my sabotage. The choice is yours."

Kira's lip curled and she surveyed the crew. "Which of you is the engineer here?"

"That's me," said O'Donnel.

Kira beckoned her forward. "Come on, then. For all our sakes, I hope you're a quick study."

"You brought us a popcorn maker?" Tomino asked Robinson, as the captain watched Kira and Shannon head downship.

"It's called a cloaking device," Rain replied.

"A what now?"

"It will make this vessel invisible to sensors," said Dax.

"Stealth technology," Christopher noted, examining the sphere. "Like electronic countermeasures?"

"Far more sophisticated," continued the Trill. "I would be happy to give you a complete description of the unit and its functions, but right now I need to power it up." She glanced at Tomino. "Your fusion reactors are still operable, yes?"

"Yeah, more or less."

"Then show me where they are."

Hachi gave Shaun a questioning look and he nodded. "Go ahead. Give her what she needs. Rudy? Help them."

"Gotcha, boss."

In a moment, Shaun was alone in the compartment with Rain, and he saw the twitch of emotion in her shoulders. "I, uh," she began, trying to find the words to articulate something she didn't want to voice.

Christopher went to her and put a supportive hand on her shoulder. "Rain, don't worry. You're back with us now. It's okay." He didn't know what had happened to her on the *Defiance,* but he knew Rain Robinson, and he knew her moods. The girl was like the younger sister he had never had, and his jaw set hard at the thought that Bashir might have hurt her in some way.

"It's not okay, Shaun," she told him. "It is so very, very far from being okay. If that ship is an example of what the rest of the galaxy is like, then we should have never woken up. It's a war. It's all built on lies and slavery. It's Khan's twisted dream come true." She shook her head. "He won, Shaun. After everything that happened, he won."

"No." He shook his head. "I thought that, but just now I realized something. Khan hasn't won, not while one of us is still breathing. He only wins if he silences us, and I'm not going to let that happen."

"He made the whole world like him," she said in a small, tight voice. "Killers." Rain was staring down at her hands, her eyes misting. "I don't want to be that."

"We'll make him pay." Shaun nodded to himself. "Lies can't survive in the light, Rain. And we're going to bring it."

9

Jacob Sisko found his commander on the mid-decks, amid the chaos of the howling alert sirens and damage control teams.

"My lord!" he called. "We are attempting to stabilize the *Defiance*'s systems, but the viral weapon program continues to move from subroutine to subroutine. It is affecting environmental control, gravity management, atmospheric processing . . ."

"I want it eradicated." Bashir gave the order with a flat, distracted tone.

The tall youth nodded. "I have deployed a counterprogram to sweep the mainframe layer by layer, but it will take time. We are discovering several dormant packets of sabotage protocols embedded in the primary computer core. The code resembles an Iconian machine language . . . I believe the viral program is based on the data-phage that destroyed the battlecruiser *Yamato* seven years ago."

"Varley's ship . . ." Bashir's lips thinned. "Dax served as a helot aboard that vessel."

Sisko nodded again. "Perhaps she retained some element of the alien code and weaponized it."

"Damn her!" Bashir struck out in blind fury and smashed a wall panel with his fist. Jacob saw a haze of conflicting emotion on his commander's face. He could only begin to guess what questions were torturing the princeps at this moment.

For an instant, Jacob thought of his father aboard Station D9, utterly unaware of what was taking place aboard *Defiance*. If the elder Sisko had been here now, what would he have said to his son? *He would tell me to distance myself from Bashir as quickly as possible. He would tell me to let the man make every mistake he could, to help him do so, even, so that when he falls he falls hard. The Khanate does not forgive failure easily, and Julian Bashir has failed his Khan.* Jacob's eyes narrowed. *Yes. He would tell me to throw my princeps to the wolves; but I am not my father.*

"She's out there," said Bashir, his voice hollow. "On the sleeper ship. It's the only place she could have gone."

"Sir," Jacob went on, "we have no motive power and our sensors have been blinded. However, weapons have limited functionality. There are photonic torpedoes loaded in the forward tubes. Blind-fired, I believe their seeker heads could still find and target the derelict."

"That would destroy it!"

Sisko frowned. "Lord, you . . . *we* unwittingly gave them the means to flee the Ajir system! They must be stopped!" *Or else,* he added silently, *your failure will be total and complete.*

Bashir seemed to sense what remained unspoken. "Dax . . . Dax must not escape. I must have her alive, do you understand?" There was a flicker of manic fury in his tone. "I have to look her in the eye! I have to be the one . . ."

"Sir, the *Botany Bay* is already moving off. It may only be a matter of minutes before they go to warp speed." He leaned closer. "Lord, please. Give the order."

But the princeps shook his head. "The teleporters," he snapped, pushing past Jacob toward a transporter chamber farther down the corridor. "Are they still functioning?"

"They are," Sisko replied, keeping up with him, "but only the matter displacement systems. Dax's program has crippled our scanners, including the transport lock. We cannot target her biosigns and retrieve her."

Bashir strode into the transporter room, to the command console, pushing the technician on duty out of the way. "That is not my intention." He ran through the activation cycle, turning the power to operating levels. With two swift steps, the princeps crossed the room and mounted the pads, throwing the crewman a hard nod. "You will send me over to the *Botany Bay*."

"Sir?" The technician was incredulous.

Jacob gaped in surprise. *He has taken leave of his senses!* "Princeps, did you not hear my report? The targeting sensors are down!"

"Then aim them manually."

He shook his head. "Without scanner lock, you could materialize inside a bulkhead or—"

"Or as close to the ship as you can place me," Bashir broke in. The commander stiffened, running through a series of swift *kata* exercises, drawing the air from his lungs, setting his body into a suitable, ready state. "The sleeper ship's dorsal conning tower has an airlock hatch on the port side. Transport me to that point. Do it now, Jacob. That is a direct order from your princeps."

Sisko swallowed hard and nodded to the technician to step away from the console. An order was an order, even if it was a nearly suicidal one, and Jacob could not allow a junior officer to take the responsibility of obeying it. He laid his slender fingers on the control sliders. "As you command, lord."

Sisko's hands traced over the panel; there was a silent flicker of red energy, and Julian Bashir vanished.

The alien woman's hands flashed across the console that Bashir's people had retrofitted to the *Botany Bay*'s engineering station, and O'Donnel did her best to keep up with her, but Laker was right. This technology, the kind of blue-sky knowledge that in her day had been science fiction, was at the very edge of Shannon's ability to understand.

In my day, she thought bleakly. *My day seems like it was only a few months ago, not hundreds of years. This damned voyage, it's taken everything from me. My world, my family, the man I loved . . .* Hank

Janeway's face rose up in her thoughts, and she pressed down a hard jag of pain.

"Hey," snapped the woman, giving her a severe glare. "I said, watch the power regulator feed! If the discharge is too fast from your reactors, it will blow the servo conduits!"

"Okay." Shannon bristled but said nothing more. She felt like a first-day student thrown in on the end-of-term test, struggling to grasp the basics of something that was barely within her experience, without even a second to process it all.

But the woman, Kira—she'd tersely told O'Donnel she was something called a Bajoran—wasn't done with her. "*Kosst,* I need you to focus! If you foul this up, we'll be stranded here for your uber friends, and I'm not going to let that happen!"

All the stress and irritation, all the anger and fear, flared hard in a surge of resentment. "Those people over there on that ship, they're not our friends. They're nothing like us!"

The Bajoran's face split in a sneer. "You're human. That's close enough." A sour tone sounded from the console and Kira grimaced, moving swiftly to where Shannon was working a control panel. She shoved her away. "No, wrong!" she snapped, changing the settings herself. "Maybe that's true." Kira threw the comment at her, as an afterthought. "Maybe you're not like them. They're just arrogant. You people are idiots."

The last of O'Donnel's tolerance snapped. "To hell with you! Let's put you on ice for three-and-a-half centuries, rip away everything that meant a damn, and then see how well you do!"

Kira rounded on her, eyes flashing, and Shannon saw the mirror of her own anger. "I *have* lost everything I care about," snarled the woman. "They *did* take it from me! He's dead and it's because of your kind!"

He? The word echoed in O'Donnel's thoughts. A hard knot of understanding pressed into her, a sudden sense of empathy for the woman.

The Bajoran blinked back tears. "Why couldn't you have killed

Khan Noonien Singh back then? None of this would have happened!"

"We tried," O'Donnel offered. "Believe me, the whole bloody world tried." Shannon's moment of fury melted away. "I am sorry," she told Kira. "And I know what you must be feeling. We all do." She gestured at the walls. "Everyone on board this ship lost people we loved to Khan. And now we've lost more than that. We've lost our world, our entire past."

The hard set to the Bajoran's jaw softened slightly, and she nodded. "Yes. Of course. I'm . . . sorry too."

"Forget it," said O'Donnel. "Let's just get this done."

His faith in Jacob's skills was not in error. As the teleporter deposited him in place, Bashir had a momentary glimpse of a stark wall of gray hull metal curving away from him, before the punishing impact of deep space struck away what little air remained in his body. A crippling chill crawled across every exposed inch of his flesh and he lashed out, his hand snaring an antenna rod protruding from *Botany Bay*'s fuselage.

In the black silence, Bashir's blood thundered in his ears and he felt the rimes of frost flash-forming on his body, as the wisps of air molecules caught in the transporter's aura instantly turned to ice. The soft tissues in his eyes prickled and stabbed like needles. His empty lungs were black, razor-sharp stones cutting him inside.

The killing cold coiled around him and began to squeeze the life from the princeps. He had little time; with dogged, agonizing motions, he moved over the hull toward the red ring of the airlock hatch, one handhold after another.

This would have been death for a normal humanoid, for a being of limited nature like the Basic girl Robinson or the *Defiance*'s helots. Unprotected and exposed to the icy kiss of the void, their flesh would swiftly blacken and die, their organs cease to function; but three hundred years of augmentation made an Earth-born like

Julian a very different breed. Enhanced stamina, increased physiological prowess. He was a better, stronger design of man.

Bashir resisted the pull of the dark and grasped the airlock handle with ice-flecked fingers, turning the mechanism to release the bolts holding it shut. A puff of displaced air fluttered past him, and the hatch rolled open. With an effort, Julian grabbed the frame of the airlock and pushed himself inside, one hand reaching out to slam the control pad that would initiate an emergency repressurization sequence.

Sound returned with the high shriek of air. Bashir reached up to touch his face and found blood frozen in lines from his nostrils and the corners of his eyes. He shook the ruby red fragments away, his body shaking with the cold.

Inside him, a very different kind of chill had taken hold.

Over Christopher's shoulder, Rain watched the power curve displays flex and bend in ways that the DY-102's designers had never considered. "Is that bad?"

"Beats me," Shaun replied, chewing his lip. "The remote systems control stuff that blue-skinned woman set up in here might as well be labeled in Sanskrit for all I can tell." He shook his head. "Shannon's either going to love this or else she'll throw a fit. And then the ship'll blow up."

The color drained from Robinson's face. "Please tell me you're kidding."

The captain glanced at her. "I hope so. I can't tell." He frowned. "One way or another, we'll find out soon enough."

Rain studied the laser ranging display. "*Defiance* hasn't come after us yet. If anything, it looks like they're drifting."

"Dax really did a number on them. Bashir's not going to take it well."

"Hopefully, we will not stay around long enough to find out." Dax came through the open hatch onto B Deck, with Hachirota trailing behind.

"Is it done?" Shaun asked.

Tomino gave him a sheepish look in return. "I guess so. She plugged the popcorn maker into the main bus and, well, it didn't make any popcorn, so I suppose that means it's working."

Dax peered at one of the temporary control panels, tapping at keys. "I have slaved the cloak controls to his console. As long as the field dispersal remains constant, we should be able to maintain invisibility."

"We're going to turn see-through?" Rain couldn't keep the incredulous tone from her words.

"Basically, yes." Dax ran through an activation sequence.

"Where's Rudy?" Shaun asked.

Hachirota jerked his thumb at the corridor. "We got a red light on the E Deck egress hatch. He went to go check."

Christopher nodded. "Good. We don't want to break the light barrier with a door open." He hesitated, a brief smile crossing his lips. "Damn. Never thought I'd be saying that."

Rain tapped the intercom. "Shannon? We're all set up here. How's things at your end?"

There was a momentary pause before O'Donnel replied. *"Kira says the power flux is . . . uh, nominal. We're good to go. I think."*

Shaun nodded to himself. "Moment of truth, then." He looked across the cramped bridge space to the Trill woman. "It's your show, Dax. Where do we go from here?"

"Nowhere." A new voice issued out of the intercom grille. *"Unless you want Mister Laker to die."*

"Julian." Dax said his name like a curse.

"Son of a bitch!" Hachi snapped, and he glared at Dax. "You told us those teleporter things were knocked out!"

"I blinded them," she retorted, her brow furrowing.

"Not well enough," said Shaun, feeling his gut twist. "Bashir?" He directed his words toward the intercom unit. "You're not going to stop us."

"He's probably killed Rudy already!" snapped Tomino.

There was a scraping sound from the speaker and Laker's voice issued out, thick with fear. *"Uh . . . no . . . I'm not dead. Not yet. He jumped me in the airlock. He has a gun."*

Shaun seized the moment. "How many of them are there?"

"Just him, but—" Laker was cut off by the sound of an impact.

"Captain Christopher," Bashir continued, *"listen to me. I do not want you or this ship or your people. Run, flee, do whatever you want, I do not care. A hundred Basics are meaningless against the millions of augmented humans in the galaxy, and one more Bajoran dissident will make no difference. I only want the woman. Ezri Dax. Only her."*

"He is lying," Dax retorted. "He will never let this ship leave."

"I want her now!" His voice was loaded with anger and menace. *"Bring me Dax, or this man dies! Answer! Or you can listen to me choke the life from him with my bare hands!"*

"Shaun, wait," said Rain, turning to him.

But Christopher already had the phaser pistol in his hand.

"You will never be able to escape without me," Dax told him. "You know that."

He gestured toward the hatchway. "I'm not losing any more of my people. Start walking."

Dax was the first out of the access well, with Christopher directly behind her. Reflexively, Bashir's grip tightened where he was holding on to Laker's neck, and the man moaned in pain. They moved into the open space of the recreation area, and to Julian's surprise he saw Rain following with them. She was clutching Dax's tricorder to her chest, as if it was something precious.

His gaze found Ezri, and the turmoil inside him grew stronger. She seemed like a different person, some other entity wearing the skin and bones of the woman he had shared his bed with. He did not recognize her. The cold and unflinching expression she wore belonged to some dark mirror of Dax, a strange and hateful duplicate.

"You betrayed me." The words fell from him in a rush. "You . . . *lied* to me."

Dax nodded, just once. "How does it feel, Julian? To know that the truth has been kept from you by someone? To know that you have been treated like a lesser?"

He shoved Laker forward, closing the distance between them. Christopher had a weapon in his hand, but Julian paid little attention to it. He had other, more important matters in mind. He had to understand, he had to know. How had she done it? What kind of trick had she used on him?

"Did the telepath screeners miss something?" he demanded. "Is that it? Do you have some Vulcan or Betazoid in you? Did we not corral enough of those blighted psionics? Is that how you did it?"

She shook her head. "No. No, Julian. Khan killed more than enough of them. And the Ullians, the Cairn, and the Talosians, and any of a dozen other species that dared to exhibit the telepathic ability you augments find so abhorrent."

He glowered at her. "I have never heard of any of those races."

"And what does that tell you?"

"The Khan would not commit genocide!" Julian snarled, affronted by the mere suggestion of such a thing. "He was above such deeds!"

Dax gave Christopher and Robinson a long, slow look. "Is that so?"

"More lies . . ." Bashir struggled to keep a leash on his fury. Part of him wanted to let it loose, to beat his answers out of her. With a sudden, savage motion, he threw Laker across the room and the man stumbled into Rain's arms.

Julian tore his dominae key from a pocket in the cuff of his jacket and brandished it toward Ezri's neck.

"Go on," she told him, holding up her hand to wave off Christopher. "Do it. Use the collar to choke me to death. And then you will never have to hear my lies again."

His thumb hovered over the activation stud. Around her neck, the copper collar glittered dully.

"But you will not do it," she continued. "Because my death is not enough, is it? You have to understand first." Dax glanced at the others. "That is why he wants to take me alive. Because Julian Bashir cannot be lied to, and the thought that someone *could* mislead him so completely consumes him."

"Yes." He could not help but admit it. "Yes, damn you."

Ezri spread her hands in a gesture of surrender. "I am a spy, Julian. A liar and a charlatan by duty and life, thanks to the reign of your Khanate. Your Khan made me what I am. A silent weapon, hidden in the rotten heart of your slave empire." She sighed, and in that moment, she seemed to age decades.

"No one lies to me," he said. "You are glass! I see every falsehood . . . How could you keep this from me? What did you do to my mind?"

"You're not the first guy to be lied to by a woman," Laker sneered, emboldened by his new freedom. "Get over yourself. It happens."

"But not to Julian Bashir." Dax shook her head. "You cannot judge the Children of Khan by the same rules you apply to your kind. The princeps here, he is of a different breed. He has singular talents."

"A human lie detector," offered Rain. "I've heard of folks who do that. People who can read the 'tells' on a face."

"Ethnopsychologists call them microexpressions," said the Trill. "The very smallest of fractional gestures counter to whatever a person is actually saying. The ability to recognize them is a skill many of the Khanate's senior interrogators possess, is that not right, Julian?"

"No one lies to me," he repeated quietly.

"I'm guessing poker games are a bust on your ship, then." Christopher adjusted his grip on the gun, and Bashir read him, read the conflict in the tightening of flesh around his eyes, the slight flush of color in his cheeks. The man was willing to kill him, if pushed to it.

Dax sighed. "I lied to you and you never knew it, because my face is my tool. It is all a matter of control. I have the ability to match your skill, point for point." As if to mock him, Ezri's aspect shifted; brief expressions of sadness, pleasure, hate, and love passed over her pale skin, one after another, as if they were nothing more than a series of still images projected upon a screen. She returned to the cold neutrality she had shown him before, as she escaped from the *Defiance.* "Did it never occur to you to think that someone like me might exist? Someone at the opposite of the emotional spectrum to you? The perfect fake?" Dax nodded. "That is why the rebellion chose me to infiltrate your crew, Princeps. What better place for me than to hide in plain sight?"

"She played you," said Christopher. "You and all of Khan's stooges."

His head shook of its own accord. "I showed you compassion, and this is what you offer me? Betrayal! I . . . I gave you . . ."

The ghost of a sneer touched her lips. "Please do not say *love,* Julian. Your kind do not understand the meaning of the word. All you did was beat me less than the other men did."

He looked away, resentment and hurt burning in his chest, and found Rain staring at him. The woman had pity and regret in her eyes.

"Everything I have done," Dax went on, "every lie I told you, every virus I seeded, every bit of data I stole for my people, all of it was toward a single goal. To break you, Julian Bashir, you and the rule of Earth. To undo everything your Khan brought about."

"We give the galaxy order!" He shouted the words. "You would have that swept away by chaos and anarchy?"

"She's not talking about chaos," said Rain. "She's talking about freedom."

"You do not know the meaning of the word!" he retorted.

"Oh, but I do," Dax insisted. "I remember . . . *Dax* remembers the time before Khan bled the stars white, the time that these people come from. When your 'master' was busy setting Earth afire, before he forced his empire on the rest of the Alpha Quadrant." Her voice became distant, and Ezri seemed to look inward. "Dax witnessed it all. The punitive killings and the bombings. The threats that drove the Trill to surrender rather than perish, as dozens of other worlds had, and the dozens more that followed."

Bashir shook his head. "No. Khan Noonien Singh brought Earth to unity, and then he took that dream to the stars. Every world under his aegis prospers! You are protected, cared for—"

"Imprisoned. Enslaved," Dax broke in. "Khan's legacy is a sham! A tyranny of genetics, imposed by a despot who practiced genocide on his own race, and perfected it against mine and a hundred others!"

"*That is not true!*" he thundered, his voice drawing a start of fear from Laker.

"It is," Robinson insisted, stepping closer to him. "I was there. I told you. I saw it."

"Rain, stay back!" said Christopher, but the woman shook her head.

"No, Shaun, this is the only way. I'm not like Ezri. I can't hide what I really believe. What I know to be true." She stood in front of Bashir, matching his level gaze. "You take a look at me, Julian. And you tell me if I am lying about the horrors committed in the name of Khan Noonien Singh."

"I . . ." He found that he could not look away from her. The things he had glimpsed in her eyes, back in the holodeck . . . He saw it again, but this time so raw and so close to the surface. Her emotions burned into him. Such hurt and agony was there, written deep across her expression. It was repugnant to see, the face of a woman as pretty as Rain marred by such dark memories. Whatever had happened to her, she had been marked by it. He saw it as clearly as if it were a scar across her cheek. Bashir glanced at Christopher and Laker and saw shadows of the same thing on each of them.

He tasted metal in his mouth, heard the rumbling of his blood in his ears. Suddenly, Julian was teetering on the edge of an abyss of understanding. *If they did not lie . . . If they did not lie to me, then the truth . . .*

In his mind's eye he saw his holographic counsel, smiling benignly and reaching out a hand to pat him on the shoulder. *Kinsman. He called me kinsman.* But that was not Khan; it was just a machine simulacrum, an approximation built to be the most perfect avatar. *Only an ideal of the man, not the real thing.* His gaze dropped back to Rain. *Not the crude, flawed matter of a human being.*

Julian thought of the Third Khan, the vain and posturing man dressed up in brocade and medals, the belligerent reality of the Khanate. "Is that what we are?" he asked himself. "Is that how the galaxy sees us?"

Rain took the tricorder off the strap over her shoulder and offered it to him. "I want to show you something," she said. "In that simulator room, the holodeck, you showed me your history. The past as it had been taught to you."

He nodded, taking the device from her. There was an isolinear data chip already loaded in the playback matrix, and by reflex his thumb found the display controls.

"I'm going to return the favor. I'm going to show you my history. The *real* history."

Bashir reached out to touch the hologram control and found his hand was trembling.

"I want results," said Jacob, scowling at the Tellarite, "not excuses." He backhanded the alien helot to the deck of the *Defiance*'s bridge with casual annoyance, almost as an afterthought. "All your efforts are to focus on restoring the sensor systems, do you understand?"

Glov nodded, eyes wet. "Y-yes, Adjutant. Forgive me, it is just that Squad Leader Tiber ordered me to concentrate on the weapons array—"

"Those orders are rescinded." Sisko moved to the command bench and hesitated, unwilling to take the position usually occupied by the princeps. "Get to work."

The Tellarite bowed and excused himself. Jacob's grimace deepened. With Bashir off the ship, O'Brien lying dead in the ship's morgue, and chaos on every deck, Tiber was already trying to diminish Sisko's position, doubtless already planning how he might have himself raised to the post of optio—or perhaps even princeps. The underhanded politicking of it dismayed the young man. It was the sort of thing he would have expected from his father.

Jacob dismissed the thought and glared at the tripartite viewscreen panel. The display was thick with interference, great washes of gray static flickering back and forth where Dax's sabotage had rendered the scanners all but sightless. He could just about pick out the vague bullet-shape of the *Botany Bay* growing ever smaller as the two ships drifted farther and farther apart. He thought of his commander and wondered again if he had done the right thing by sending him out there. Was Bashir even still alive? There was no way to tell. The Trill had covered every angle of attack, even knocking out the warship's subspace radio transmitter, stopping them from signaling for help—or in this case, attempting to learn if their princeps was dead.

It came as a surprise, then, when the Patil-clan woman at the communications panel shot him a look. "Adjutant . . . we are receiving a signal."

"From the sleeper ship?" His adrenaline surged. *Perhaps this situation could still be salvaged, if Bashir has recaptured the DY-102 . . .*

"Negative," said the vox officer. "It is on an Earthfleet waveband. We can read it, but we cannot respond."

"Let me hear it."

She hesitated. "The signal is directed to Princeps Bashir."

"And he is unavailable!" Jacob faced her. "Play it!"

"As you wish, Adjutant." She tapped a string of keys and a stern voice filled the bridge. Sisko knew the speaker's identity immediately; the man had been a rival of his father's for many years, and Jacob had seen him in the flesh during a graduation ceremony at Earthfleet Institute in Calcutta.

"Defiance, *this is Princeps Senior Picard of the dreadnought* Illustrious." The message was a recording, an order sent rather than an invitation to converse. *"I am two hours from the Ajir system. Bashir, prepare to stand down your command to me on arrival. In the Khan's name.* Illustrious *out."*

"In the Khan's name," Jacob repeated the phrase by force of habit, without conscious thought.

"Adjutant?" said the Patil woman. "How shall we proceed?"

Sisko looked down at the command bench, an abrupt understanding of the cost of that position forming in his mind. *This matter will not end well for any of us.*

"We wait," he told her.

The tricorder's display emitter sketched a holographic screen in the air before Julian, and in rapid clips of pictures and sound, imagery of a world turned to ashes unfolded before him.

Many of the things that he saw struck the breath from him. Moscow on fire, and Khanate troopers, Ling bloodline by the looks of them, executing civilians on the grass of Gorky Park; pregnant women being loaded into transport helicopters by the hundreds; endless lines of starving, hollow-eyed refugees lining a city street; military satellite footage of nuclear blooms over the California coastline.

He witnessed events that he had read about as a child, but shown from shattering perspectives that lay at polar opposites to the history he had been taught: A young Noonien Singh raging and furious on the steps of the United Nations building, surrounded by soldiers in blue helmets—*but they had welcomed him!*

Grainy video of a woman strapping explosives to her chest in front of a poster of the Khan's smiling face—*but the fanatics had been those fighting against him!* And then his ancestor, the great Joaquin, stepping forward at a nod from his master to execute an unarmed man with a single stroke of a sword—*but that was not his way!*

All these and hundreds more, assaulting him with hard reality. Every image burned into his mind, etching itself on Julian's consciousness. He felt unsteady, as if the deck were turning to mud beneath his feet.

Was it all fiction? He dared to ask the question of himself. *How much of the record of the rise of mankind is twisted like this?* In the holodeck, Rain had reminded him of that ancient adage, that the history books are always written by those who win the wars; but here he saw great swaths of events that simply did not exist in the Khanate's official past. Atrocities and slaughter that had been made to unhappen, edited out of Khan Noonien Singh's life.

And that is the falsehood I have been raised to believe in.

"Enough," he said, pushing the tricorder away. "Enough, I say. Take it away from me!"

The hologram faded, and Bashir found himself looking at Rain, the woman's sad face the only solid point among his reeling thoughts. "This is what really happened." She gestured with the tricorder. "All that, and more, all in here."

Dax looked at him with icy contempt. "You have been lied to your entire life, Julian. Raised on the teat of a totalitarian empire, the favored children of a dictator. Earth's rule of the galaxy is not one of strength and power, as you want to believe. It is built on a foundation of blood and deceit that stretches back for generations." She pointed at Rain. "I can hide the truth from you, but she cannot. Look at her, Julian, and tell me if you still think this is a lie."

After a long moment, he held up his hand, and in it was the dominae key. Reflexively, Ezri's fingers went to the copper torc at her neck.

Bashir never met her gaze. Instead, he tapped the key and the collar made a soft click. It parted from her pale neck and clattered to the deck.

Julian changed in front of her eyes. Rain felt her throat tighten; after everything, she actually felt sorry for him. Between them, she and Ezri had hollowed this man out with a few simple words. *We've broken him,* Rain told herself. *We've torn his whole world down.*

"I think you're done here," said Shaun.

Rain turned to look at the captain. "You're not going to kill him?"

Christopher swallowed hard, the phaser wavering in his hand. It was one thing to fight a man to the death, but to execute someone in cold blood—Shaun wasn't capable of such a thing. Or so she thought.

"Take him as our prisoner," Dax said gravely. "He has tactical value to the resistance."

"No," insisted Rain. "We're letting him go."

"We're doing what now?" Laker cried, massaging his throat. "Hey, he just tried to choke me! And now you want to let him walk away?"

"I am worth nothing," Bashir said in a dead voice. "You people . . . this ship . . ." He glanced around. "It is my disgrace. I will be cashiered for my failures."

Rain shook her head and turned to Laker. "Rudy, prep an EVA suit at the main lock."

"What for?"

Shaun nodded as he understood. "For him."

"You are making a mistake," began Dax, her tone hardening.

"My ship," retorted Christopher, "my choice to make."

Laker frowned and moved off to carry out his orders, and Robinson stepped closer to Bashir. "Take this," she said, ejecting the isolinear data chip from the tricorder.

His hand was cold as she pressed it into Bashir's palm and closed his fingers over it. He looked down at his fist and nodded slowly. "Yes. I will."

Rain found she did not know what else to tell him. "I'm . . . sorry." The words sounded weak and feeble. "But you had to know, Julian. You have to see it all and make up your own mind."

"He is a human," said Dax. "His only loyalty is to his own kind."

Rain rounded on her. "I'm a human as well," she snapped, "and all I care about is what's true." She looked back into Bashir's barren gaze. "Are we so different?" Robinson stepped away. "Take the files, Julian. Prove her wrong."

10

They detected the object the instant the *Defiance*'s short-range sensors came back online, and Jacob's first assumption was that the *Botany Bay* had ejected some kind of slow-moving drift munition into their flight path; but the scanners registered a life sign, and with growing concern the adjutant realized what he was looking at.

They brought the suited figure aboard, transporting it to the shuttlebay where Squad Leader Tiber and a team of armed troopers were waiting. A momentary grin split the Sisko youth's face when the figure removed the helmet to reveal the princeps beneath; but then he saw his commander's expression, and his smile faded away.

Bashir arrived on the bridge, still clad in the *Botany Bay* environmental suit, with an incredulous Tiber at his side. Jacob saluted and automatically stepped away from the commander's bench. Bashir looked in his direction, at his station, and seemed not to see it. The princeps looked around the *Defiance*'s bridge as if it were something foreign to him.

"Lord?" ventured Jacob. "Are you all right? The sleeper ship . . . What happened over there?"

Bashir ignored the questions and wandered past the command dais toward the tripanel screen. The static was fading away at long last, and the portside display was a tactical plot. The red glyph of the *Botany Bay* was tracking away from them as it moved closer and closer to lightspeed.

"Drives are still offline," Jacob offered. "But we have weapons and targeting systems, Princeps. I was in the process of calculating a firing solution when we located you." He walked to the firing command panel. "With your permission?"

"They will be out of range in a few moments," insisted Tiber. "Sir, we must act now!"

Bashir wasn't looking at the screens anymore. He was staring down at his gloved hands. "No," he said distantly. "Hold fire."

Jacob blinked in surprise. "Lord? But—"

"You will do as I command," he added. "Let them go. The damage . . . has already been done."

The tactical glyph flickered and faded. From the engineering console, the Tellarite helot made a hissing sound. "Target has cloaked. Firing solution has been lost."

"Why?" demanded Tiber. "My lord, why did you allow them to escape? We had them in our sights, we could have obliterated that Khan-forsaken hulk and every one of those throwbacks in a single shot!" He grabbed Bashir's shoulder roughly and yanked him around, all thought of protocol cast aside. "*Why?* Now you have doomed us all to fall to the Khan's displeasure!"

The princeps shrugged him off and walked away, toward the hatchway. "There is no escape from the truth," he said.

Jacob dared to shout after him as Bashir left the command tier. "Princeps!" he called. "What happened over there? What did you see?"

A shimmering blue glow hazed briefly through the decks of the sleeper ship, and the energy traces on the console screen settled into a slow, resonant wave.

"Is . . . that it?" Hachirota asked, his fingers knitting together.

A crooked smile crossed Kira's lips. "That's it. The cloaking device is at full power. We're ghosts." She shook her head. "How about that? I thought this wreck would have come apart first."

"There's still time," Laker bleated. All around them, the *Botany*

Bay's hull had settled into a rhythm of creaking and shuddering as the warp-sled propelled them toward the light barrier.

"She'll hold," said Christopher, placing a hand on the wall. "She got us this far. She'll take us all the way."

"Your confidence has little bearing on reality," Dax told him. "Would you like to know the probability of our successfully making a warp transition?"

"No," said the captain. "We've beaten the odds at every turn. If I were that kind of man, I might wonder if fate's keeping an eye on us." He looked across at his crew, his gaze settling on Robinson.

"Maybe so," offered Rain. "I've had enough of running for one lifetime." She threw a nod to Shannon and Kira, who returned it. "This is where it ends."

Dax's attention turned to the display as the figures approached warp insertion velocity. "No," she told her, "this is where it begins."

A phantom bathed in starlight, *Botany Bay* surged beyond lightspeed, a loosed arrow shot into the night sky.

"My lord." Jacob's voice had an edge of panic in it. *"The* Illustrious *is closing to boarding range. Princeps Picard is demanding you acknowledge his signal! Sir? Sir—"*

Bashir silenced the intercom and let the counsel chamber's hatch seal shut behind him. He stepped up and placed his hand on the lectern, and the walls shimmered, becoming the palace grounds once more. Julian paid them no mind. In his right hand he held an isolinear chip; with his left he worked a panel on the lectern and flipped it open, revealing a snarl of data circuits inside.

"Julian?" said a voice. He didn't look up as the figure in crimson approached. "Kinsman, speak to me. What troubles you?"

"More . . . more than you could ever know," he replied.

Khan Noonien Singh stopped in front of him and folded his

arms, his eyes narrowing. "You will look at me when you address your Khan," said the hologram. "And you will moderate your tone!"

Bashir glared at the simulation. "You are a ghost," he said coldly. "A phantom parody of a man."

"How dare you speak to me with disrespect! I am your counsel! I am the essence of Khan Noonien Singh, master of mankind!"

Julian shook his head and reached into the guts of the console. "You are a *lie*." Before the hologram could respond, he pulled a handful of optical cables from their sockets, and the image of Khan shimmered and vanished. Blue-white light bled from the severed wires, flashing in a staccato pattern across Bashir's hands.

"My hands . . ." He turned the isolinear chip over in his fingers. "How much blood is upon them?"

The princeps inserted the chip into a socket, and the white vista of the palace melted away. Around him grew walls made of images, towering planes of sight and sound from decades dead and gone. The riot of noise and color assaulted his senses, and he opened himself to it, unflinching, never turning away, accepting every moment of a bloody past denied too long.

In the isolation of his private sanctum, he drowned himself in the black and terrible truth.

Acknowledgments/Authors' Notes

A LESS PERFECT UNION

Thanks first to Marco Palmieri, for giving me the opportunity to take part in this project and for letting me get away with a *lot* more than I expected to.

Thanks also to the many *Star Trek* scriptwriters over the decades, whose works I took as inspiration and/or shamelessly pilfered and twisted for this story. Though there are too many to list in this space, special mention is due Manny Coto, Andre Bormanis, Garfield Reeves-Stevens and Judith Reeves-Stevens, who were responsible for the penultimate, two-part episode of *Star Trek: Enterprise,* as well as Gene Roddenberry, who wrote the original pilot episode, "The Cage" (not to mention creating the whole shebang in the first place).

Sandra McDonald and John G. Hemry, both SF authors and former U.S. Navy officers, were kind enough to answer my questions about shipboard disciplinary procedures. Credit to them for what rings true; blame to me for what rings false. Many other questions were answered thanks to the efforts of the folks behind Memory Alpha (www.memory-alpha.org), Memory Beta (www.startrek.wikia.com), and Paramount Home Video. (Is TV on DVD not the greatest thing *ever?*)

And finally, thanks to my parents. If not for them . . . well, that would be another "what if" story, wouldn't it?

PLACES OF EXILE

This tale is built largely on concepts established in the third season and early fourth season of *Star Trek: Voyager.* Portions of

Chapter 1 are adapted from "Scorpion" by Brannon Braga and Joe Menosky, which introduced Species 8472. Braga and Menosky also created the Voth, including Odala (Concetta Tomei) and Haluk (Marshall Teague), in "Distant Origin," as well as Zahir (David Lee Smith), the Mikhal, and the Tarkan in "Darkling," and Unimatrix Zero in the two-part episode of the same name (from a story by Mike Sussman). By himself, Joe Menosky depicted Kes's transformation in "The Gift" and introduced the Potato People, er, Hierarchy, in "Tinker, Tenor, Doctor, Spy." Kenneth Biller depicted Kes's original future and its version of the Year of Hell in "Before and After," and introduced Danara Pel (Susan Diol) in "Lifesigns" and the Borg Collective in "Unity."

The Vostigye were briefly mentioned but never seen in "Real Life" by Jeri Taylor. The Ocampa reproductive cycle was established in "Elogium" by Biller and Taylor. "Boothby" (Ray Walston) and the 8472 infiltration plot are from "In the Flesh" by Nick Sagan. The Nezu and Etanians are from "Rise" by Braga, and the Nyrians and various minor species are from "Displaced" by Lisa Klink, who also introduced the Hirogen in "Message in a Bottle." The Swarm and the Doctor's memory loss are from "The Swarm" by Sussman.

Lyndsay Ballard (Kim Rhodes) is from "Ashes to Ashes" by Robert Doherty and Ronald Wilkerson. Ensign Jenkins (Mackenzie Westmore) is from "Warhead" by Michael Taylor and Biller. Mister Ayala (Tarik Ergin) was a bit player seen throughout the series. The Kilana seen here is the predecessor to the Kilana (Kaitlin Hopkins) seen in *Deep Space Nine:* "The Ship" by Hans Beimler.

Thanks to Marco Palmieri for his determination to get this alternate-timelines project published, and for giving me the chance to participate in it. Thanks to Bernd Schneider's Ex Astris Scientia website for pointing out the need for frequent twin or triplet births in the Ocampa reproductive cycle. And thanks to the cast and writers of *Voyager* for showing us so many possibilities that fired our imaginations but never got followed up on.

SEEDS OF DISSENT

Arguably one of the most famous archetypes of alternate history stories is the "Hitler Wins" scenario, and with *Seeds of Dissent*, I approached that concept through the lens of *Star Trek*, casting the most famous *Trek* dictator in the key role—and so, my thanks to Gene L. Coon, Cary Wilber, Jack B. Sowards, Harve Bennett, and Greg Cox for their stories of Khan, from which this tale grows. Respect is also due to Robert Silverberg, Larry Niven, Michael Moorcock, Fritz Lieber, Philip K. Dick, and many more writers for the inspiration that came from all the alt-history fiction I've enjoyed over the years; and a special bow goes to Marco Palmieri, for letting me go the distance.

About the Authors

WILLIAM LEISNER's first professionally published story was an alternate *Star Trek* universe tale, "Gods, Fate, and Fractals," which appeared in *Star Trek: Strange New Worlds II.* He placed two more stories in that annual contest, followed by a *Star Trek: Starfleet Corps of Engineers* novella, *Out of the Cocoon.* He also contributed the short story "Ambition" to *Constellations,* the *Star Trek* 40th Anniversary anthology, and the novella *The Insolence of Office* to *Slings and Arrows,* the *Star Trek: The Next Generation* 20th Anniversary eBook miniseries. In another timeline, he's an Academy Award–winning writer/director, residing in Los Angeles with his supermodel wife; in this timeline, he works an office job in Minneapolis and enjoys looking at supermodel websites.

CHRISTOPHER L. BENNETT is the author of the critically acclaimed novels *Star Trek: Ex Machina, Star Trek Titan: Orion's Hounds,* and *Star Trek: The Next Generation—The Buried Age,* as well as the eBooks *Star Trek: S. C. E. #29—Aftermath* (now available in a trade paperback of the same name) and *Star Trek: Mere Anarchy, Book Four: The Darkness Drops Again.* His *Next Generation* novel *Greater Than the Sum* debuts in August 2008. He is the only author to have stories in all four *Star Trek* anniversary anthologies: ". . . Loved I Not Honor More" in *Star Trek: Deep Space Nine—Prophecy and Change;* "Brief Candle" in *Star Trek: Voyager—Distant Shores;* "As Others See Us" in *Star Trek: Constellations;* and "Friends with the Sparrows" in *Star Trek: The Next Generation—The Sky's the Limit.* In addition to *Places of Exile,* he has also contributed an alternate-reality tale to the upcoming *Star Trek Mirror Universe: Shards and Shadows* anthology. He has branched out beyond *Star Trek* with *X-Men: Watchers on the Walls* and *Spider-Man: Drowned in Thunder*. He has recently learned to drive, and extends his heartfelt apologies to the Earth's atmosphere. More information, original fiction, and cat pictures can be found at http://home.fuse.net/ChristopherLBennett/

JAMES SWALLOW is proud to be the only British writer to have worked on a *Star Trek* television series, creating the original story concepts for the *Star Trek: Voyager* episodes "One" and "Memorial"; his other associations with the *Star Trek* saga include *Day of the Vipers,* the first volume in the *Terok Nor* trilogy, the short stories "Closure," "Ordinary Days," and "The Black Flag" for the anthologies *Distant Shores, The Sky's the Limit,* and *Shards and Shadows,* scripting the video game *Star Trek: Invasion,* and writing over 400 articles in thirteen different *Star Trek* magazines around the world.

Beyond the final frontier, as well as a non-fiction book (*Dark Eye: The Films of David Fincher*), James also wrote the *Sundowners* series of original steampunk westerns, *Jade Dragon, The Butterfly Effect,* and fiction in the worlds of *Doctor Who* (*Peacemaker, Dalek Empire, Destination Prague, Snapshots, The Quality of Leadership*), *Warhammer 40,000* (*Red Fury, The Flight of the Eisenstein, Faith & Fire, Deus Encarmine,* and *Deus Sanguinius*), *Stargate* (*Halcyon* and *Relativity*), and *2000AD* (*Eclipse, Whiteout,* and *Blood Relative*). His other credits include scripts for video games and audio dramas, including *Battlestar Galactica, Blake's 7,* and *Space 1889.*

James Swallow lives in London, and is currently at work on his next book.

ENJOY THIS SNEAK PREVIEW OF
TOKYOPOP's LATEST...

STAR TREK THE MANGA: UCHU

AVAILABLE IN STORES AND ONLINE NOW!

ART OF WAR

STORY BY WIL WHEATON
PENCILS AND INKS BY EJ SU
TONES BY CHOW HON LAM
AND MARA AUM

FOR MORE INFORMTION PLEASE VISIT
WWW.TOKYOPOP.COM

Sneak Preview of TOKYOPOP's Star Trek the manga: Uchu

Sneak Preview of TOKYOPOP's Star Trek the manga: Uchu

Sneak Preview of TOKYOPOP's Star Trek the manga: Uchu